Praise for Bentley Little

The Association

"With this haunting tale, Little proves he hasn't lost his terrifying touch. The novel's graphic and fantastic finale . . . will stick with readers for a long time. Little's deftly drawn characters inhabit a suspicious world laced with just enough sex, violence, and Big Brother rhetoric to make this an incredibly credible tale." —*Publishers Weekly*

The Walking

"Wonderful, fast-paced, rock-'em, jolt-'em, shock-'em, contemporary terror fiction with believable characters and an unusually clever plot. Highly entertaining." —Dean Koontz

"Bentley Little's *The Walking* is the horror event of the year. If you like spooky stories, you must read this book." —Stephen King

"*The Walking* is a waking nightmare. A spellbinding tale of witchcraft and vengeance. Bentley Little conjures a dark landscape peopled by all-too-human characters on the brink of the abyss. Scary and intense." —Michael Prescott, author of *Last Breath*

"The overwhelming sense of doom with which Bentley Little imbues his . . . novel is so palpable it seems to rise from the book like mist. Flowing seamlessly between time and place, the Bram Stoker Award–winning author's ability to transfix his audience . . . is superb . . . terrifying. [*The Walking*] has the potential to be a major sleeper." —*Publishers Weekly* (starred review)

continued . . .

The Ignored

"This is Bentley Little's best book yet. Frightening, thought-provoking, and impossible to put down."   —Stephen King

"With his artfully plain prose and Quixote-like narrative, Little dissects the deep and disturbing fear of anonymity all Americans feel. . . . What Little has created is nothing less than a nightmarishly brilliant tour de force of modern life in America."   —*Publishers Weekly* (starred review)

"*The Ignored* is a singular achievement by a writer who makes the leap from the ranks of the merely talented to true distinction with this book. This one may become a classic." —*Dark Echo*

"Inventive. Chilling."   —*Science Fiction Chronicle*

"A spooky novel with an original premise."   —SF Site

"Little is so wonderful that he can make the act of ordering a coke at McDonald's take on a sinister dimension. This philosophical soul searcher is provocative." —*Fangoria* magazine

"*The Ignored* is not average at all."   —*Locus*

THE
COLLECTION

Bentley Little

A SIGNET BOOK

SIGNET
Published by New American Library, a division of
Penguin Putnam Inc., 375 Hudson Street,
New York, New York 10014, U.S.A.
Penguin Books Ltd, 80 Strand,
London WC2R 0RL, England
Penguin Books Australia Ltd, Ringwood,
Victoria, Australia
Penguin Books Canada Ltd, 10 Alcorn Avenue,
Toronto, Ontario, Canada M4V 3B2
Penguin Books (N.Z.) Ltd, 182–190 Wairau Road,
Auckland 10, New Zealand

Penguin Books Ltd, Registered Offices:
Harmondsworth, Middlesex, England

First published by Signet, an imprint of New American Library,
a division of Penguin Putnam Inc.

ISBN 0-7394-2761-X

−2003−

For the editors, small press and large, who accepted my stories for their magazines and anthologies. I wouldn't be here without you.

Contents

The Sanctuary

Religious fanatics have always seemed scary to me, and when I hear them espousing some wacky eschatological theory or promoting their perverse interpretations of the Bible, I always wonder what their home lives are like. What kind of furniture do they have? What kind of food do they eat? How do they treat their neighbors and their pets?

"The Sanctuary" is my version of what life would be like for a child growing up in such a household.

—⚏—

The drapes were all closed, Cal noticed as he came home after school, and he knew even before walking up the porch steps that something terrible had happened. The drapes hadn't been closed in the daytime since . . . since Father had had to pay.

He shifted the schoolbooks under his arms, licking his dry lips before opening the front door. Inside, the living room was dark, the heavy brown drapes effectively keeping out all but the most diffused light. He almost didn't see his mother curled up in a corner of the couch. "Mother?" he said nervously.

She didn't answer, and he walked over to where she was

sitting, placing his books on the coffee table. This close, he could see the wetness of tears on her cheeks. "Mother?"

She leaped up and grabbed him by his shoulders, holding him close, pressing him against her bulk. He could smell on her housedress an unfamiliar odor he did not like. "Oh, Cal," she sobbed. "I didn't mean to do it! I didn't mean to!"

Cal suddenly noticed that the house was silent. There were no noises coming from the back of the house, and he had a funny feeling in the pit of his stomach. "Where's Chrissie?" he asked.

Her hands clutched tighter, hugging him. "I couldn't help myself," she wailed. Tears were rolling down her puffy cheeks. "I had to kill him."

"Kill who?" Cal asked, fighting back his fear. "Who did you kill?"

"I was walking home from the store, and I saw this man walking his dog, and The Rage came over me. I couldn't help myself."

"What happened?"

"I—I told him my car wouldn't start, and I had him come into the garage with me to see if he could figure out what was wrong. Then I closed the door, and I used the ax. I—I couldn't help myself. I didn't think I'd do it again, I didn't want to do it again, but The Rage came over me." She ran a hand through Cal's hair, and her voice was suddenly free of emotion. "I sinned," she said. "But it was not my fault."

"Where's Chrissie?" Cal demanded.

"Chrissie had to die for my sins."

Cal pulled away from his mother and ran down the hallway, through the back bedroom, to The Sanctuary. There, next to Father's cross, was the crucified form of his sister. She was naked, spread-eagled, her hands and feet nailed to the wood, her head hanging down limply.

"Chrissie?" he said.

She did not move, did not reply, but when he hesitantly touched her foot the skin was still warm.

Behind him, he heard the door to The Sanctuary close. The only light in the windowless room came from the candles flickering in front of the altar. As Cal stared at the unmoving form of his sister, at the small streams of blood which flowed from her impaled hands and feet, his mother's strong hands grasped his shoulders. "She will be resurrected," his mother said, and when he turned he saw the tears in her eyes. "She will be resurrected and will sit at the throne of God and we will pray to her and worship her as we do your father."

She dropped to her knees beside him and gestured for him to join her. He saw faint red traces in the lines which crisscrossed her palm. Her life line, he noticed, was totally obscured with a thin smear of blood. "Pray," she begged. She folded her hands in a gesture of supplication.

Cal knelt down before his father's cross and folded his hands in prayer.

"Dear Jim," his mother began. "Hallowed be your name. We thank you for protecting and providing for this, your household. Lead us not into temptation but deliver us from evil. We beseech thee, O Jim, to keep us safe from harm. You are great, you are good, and we thank you for our food. Amen."

Cal knew his mother's prayers were not exactly right. He remembered some of what he had learned in Sunday school, when they used to go to church, and he could tell that her entreaties were a little off. But he said nothing. If he did speak up, she would only scourge him until he repented of his blasphemy and then make him kneel for hours praying to his father, so he kept his mouth shut.

His mother was muttering next to him, reciting a private prayer, and though he knew he was expected to do the same, he glanced around The Sanctuary instead. Below Chrissie's hands and feet were the sacred bowls used to catch her martyred blood. They would drink it later for Communion, and Cal grimaced at the thought. Already he could taste the sickening salty herbal flavor of the blood, and it made him want to vomit. In the corner of the room, bathed in a swath of shadow not penetrated by the candlelight, he could see the outline of the bloody ax leaning against the wall. On the floor in front of the ax was the hammer she had used to crucify Chrissie, and next to the hammer were scattered extra nails.

His mother stood. "You may leave," she said. "I want to be alone right now."

He nodded silently and left The Sanctuary. He wanted to cry, but could not; instead he sat at the kitchen table and stared into space blankly. Bocephus scratched on the door, and he let the dog inside, feeding him on the kitchen floor. The shadows lengthened, the sun set, and still his mother did not come out. He made himself a sandwich, drank some milk, and after watching a sitcom on TV, went into his bedroom. He was tired but found himself unable to fall asleep. He turned on the small black-and-white television on the dresser. He needed company.

Sometime later, he heard his mother's footsteps and the rustle of her clothes as she emerged from The Sanctuary and went directly to her bedroom. Through the thin wall, he heard her praying, her hoarse voice rising and falling in rhythmic oratorical cadences.

Bocephus came into his room and jumped on the bed, tail wagging, tongue hanging happily out. Cal pulled the dog close and buried his face in the clean golden fur, hugging the pet to him. Hot tears spilled from his eyes and he wiped them on the dog's soft hair. "Chrissie," he said. "Chrissie."

The house was silent. Sometime after he had fallen asleep, his mother had come in and turned off the TV, and now it was so quiet that he could hear his mother's deep, even breathing in the next room, punctuated by an occasional snore. He stared up into the blackness, thinking about his mother, about The Rage, about Chrissie, and about what he should do. He stared up into the blackness—

and heard Chrissie's soft whisper.

"*Cal.*"

A wash of goose bumps arose on his skin as a wave of coldness swept over him. He closed his eyes, pulling the blanket up over his head. His heart was hammering in his chest. He was imagining it. He had to be.

"*Cal.*"

The whisper was clear, only slightly louder than his mother's sleep-breathing.

"*Cal.*"

He wanted to scream, but his mouth was suddenly dry. He plugged his ears with his fingers and shut his eyes tightly, but though he could not hear Chrissie's whisper, his mind filled the sound in for him and he knew that if he lifted the fingers from his ears he would hear the voice again.

"*Cal.*"

What did she want? He thought of Chrissie's crucified body, nails driven through hands and feet, her head hanging down limply, an expression of lonely terror frozen on her face, and suddenly he was no longer afraid. Or not *as* afraid. He was still a little scared, but the fear was tempered with sadness and sympathy. She was his sister; she had been killed to pay for their mother's sins, and now she was alone, all alone in The Sanctuary with Father.

She had always been afraid of The Sanctuary.

She had always been afraid of Father.

He unplugged his ears and pulled the blanket from his head.

"*Cal.*"

The whisper was not malevolently beckoning to him as he had originally thought. It sounded more like a plea, a plea for help. He slipped out of bed, careful not to make any noise. He walked slowly down the hall, past his mother's room, through the back bedroom to The Sanctuary.

He looked around the darkened room. Only one candle was still flickering, and like the others it was almost worn down. He could see, however, that the pewter bowls at the foot of the cross were full again, and the man Mother had murdered was now shards of bone, blackened and unrecognizable. A faint haze of smoke still hung over the room.

"*Cal,*" Chrissie whispered.

He looked up.

"*Kill her,*" Chrissie said. "*Kill the bitch.*"

He went to school the next day as if nothing had happened, but reading and spelling went in one ear and out the other, and he could concentrate neither on history nor on math. His mind was on his mother. Part of him knew that he should tell someone what had happened, but part of him did not want to tell. Besides, who would he talk to? Miss Price did not particularly like him and he wouldn't feel comfortable telling her what had happened, and he would feel even more awkward talking to the principal, whom he had only seen a few times striding across the playground toward his office. He should go to the police, he knew. That was who would really want to know. But then they would take his mother away, and they would take Father and Chrissie away, and he would be all alone.

Besides, he was afraid of what his father might do. Father's wrath was great, and he had the power of God on his side. And what could policemen do against the power of God?

At lunch, on the playground, Cal stood alone, sometimes wanting to tell someone about his mother, sometimes not.

He did not even consider Chrissie's option.

He walked home slowly after school, taking his time, thinking. His mother would be praying in The Sanctuary— that was what she had done the last time The Rage came over her and Father had had to pay—and he didn't want to join her. He still wasn't sure what he wanted. His muscles were tense, he had a bad headache, and he felt trapped.

He walked down the street toward his house and stopped in surprise. His mother was not in The Sanctuary. Instead, she stood on the front lawn, hose in hand, watering the green lawn and the bed of flowers which grew beneath the kitchen window. The street was filled with the noise of out-of-school kids playing games in their yards, riding up and down the sidewalks on bikes and Big Wheels. Farther up the street, Mr. Johnson was mowing his lawn, the gas-powered engine a constant buzz underneath the more random noises of the kids.

Cal walked slowly forward, watching his mother. She glanced over at him and smiled, and then a change came over her face. Her eyes widened as if in fear, and the corners of her mouth flattened out. Her entire body took on a rigid robotic stance.

The Rage, he thought, panicking.

And then she dropped the hose and was running down the

sidewalk. He ran after her, but she was already talking to a boy he didn't know, a kid from some other street. The boy nodded, then pushed his bike alongside as both of them headed back up the sidewalk. Cal stood lamely in front of them, not knowing what to do.

His mother shot him an unreadable look as she passed, a look filled simultaneously with tortured agony and malicious glee.

"Mother!" he cried, running behind her.

She turned, smiling, and slapped him hard across the face.

As he fell to the ground, he saw his mother lead the boy into the garage.

He jumped to his feet and followed them through the small garage door. The boy was standing in the middle of the room, looking around, confused. "Where is it?" he asked.

Cal heard the boy's chin hit the cement as his mother pushed him to the floor.

"No!" Cal yelled.

The boy was too stunned to cry, and he merely looked up in blank confusion as the shovel slammed into his back. He flopped around on the concrete floor like a fish, blood streaming from the long slice where the shovel dug into his back.

Cal staggered out of the garage, but he could hear the sickening, squelching sound of the shovel chopping into flesh with short quick bites.

And then his mother ran out, her hands bloody, a look of abject terror on her face.

Cal cringed, but she dashed past him, rushing around the side of the garage. He saw her take from the side yard two long eight-by-fours. She dragged the boards to the back of the house, and he heard the slow regular sound of wood being sawed. He stood there unmoving. The sawing stopped a few minutes later, and he heard the irregular whipcrack of hammer against nail.

She was constructing a cross.

He wanted to leave, to run, but something held him back. He stood, then sat alone in the front of the house listening to the sound of the hammer, as around him neighborhood life went on as normal. He was still sitting there when he heard the back door slam and saw through the front windows of the house his mother carrying the cross down the hall to The Sanctuary.

It hit him then, what was going to happen to him, and he quickly jumped to his feet. He was not going to let her have him. He would run if necessary, fight if he had to.

Bocephus barked once, loudly, a short harsh yelp that was immediately cut off.

Then there was silence.

"Bocephus!" Cal yelled. He ran into the house, down the hall.

The dog was already splayed on the cross, all four legs stretched in a pose of crucifixion, long nails protruding from his paws.

His mother dropped the hammer, and fell to her knees. There were tears rolling down her cheeks, but she was not sobbing. She began to pray. "Bless this house, bless our feet, good food, good meat, good God, let's eat. Blessed are the meek. Blessed are the peacemakers. In the name of the Father, the Daughter, and the Holy Dog, Amen." She genuflected first toward Father, then toward Chrissie, then toward Bocephus.

Cal remained standing. She was gone, far gone, crazy, and he realized now that the only option open to him was to contact the authorities and turn her in. His insides felt stiff and sore and he had a pounding headache. Father might think his decision blasphemous, but Chrissie probably would not, and she sat at God's side as well.

His mother left The Sanctuary and returned a few moments later, dragging the boy's mutilated body. She threw it into the pit and set it afire. Though the fan was on, The Sanctuary was filled with a black foul-smelling smoke, and Cal staggered into the bedroom, taking huge gulps of the fresh air. In his head he could hear the maddening *drip drip drip* of the blood into the altar bowl.

Maybe he should kill her.

"*Cal.*"

Chrissie's voice, still little more than a whisper, sounded clear and smooth through the smoke and din. He wanted to go back into The Sanctuary and talk to her but could not bring himself to do it.

"*No,*" Chrissie whispered, and she said the word again. "*Nooooo.*"

No? What did that mean?

But he knew what it meant. Chrissie had changed her mind. Maybe she had talked to Father, maybe she had talked to God, but she no longer wanted him to kill their mother, and she obviously did not want him to turn their mother in.

But what could he do?

"*No,*" Chrissie whispered.

He ran out of the house and dropped onto the grass of the lawn outside, the cool wet grass which felt so fresh and new beneath his hot cheek.

Todd MacVicar from down the street rolled by on his Big Wheel. "What's the matter with you?" he asked. His voice was filled with disgust.

And Cal felt The Rage come over him. He knew it was

happening, and he didn't want it to happen, but an unbridled hatred of Todd filled him from within, and he knew that nothing would abate this anger and hate save the boy's death. Thoughts of Todd's head, bloodied and smashed on the sidewalk, brought to his voice the coolness he needed. "Come here," he said. "I want to show you something in the garage."

He hoped his mother had not disposed of the shovel.

Cal stood in the center of The Sanctuary. He was crying, filled with a sadness and remorse he hadn't known he could experience. Behind him, Todd MacVicar's body burned in the pit, and he thought the smoke smelled clean, pure.

He looked down at his mother.

"You have no choice," she sobbed. "I must pay. I must die for your sins." She stretched a trembling hand against the crossbeam, palm outward. Her fingers twitched nervously.

Cal pressed the point of the nail against the lined skin, drawing back the hammer.

The voices in his head offered encouragement:

"*You have no choice.*" His father.

"*You must.*" Chrissie.

He swung the hammer hard and flinched as his mother screamed, the nail impaling her palm to the wood. Warm red blood streamed downward.

This was crazy, he thought. This was wrong. This wasn't what he was supposed to do. But as he looked up, he thought he saw approval in Chrissie's running, clouded eyes, in his father's dry, empty sockets.

He swung the hammer again.

And again.

By the time he finished the last foot and propped the

cross up next to Bocephus, he was already feeling better, purified, cleansed, as if he was an innocent newborn, free from all guilt.

He sank gratefully to his knees.

"Our Mother," he said, "who art in heaven . . ."

The Woods Be Dark

"The Woods Be Dark" was written in the mid-1980s for a creative writing class. At the time, I was under the spell of William Faulkner and turning out a slew of interconnected Southern Gothic stories all set in the same rural county. I lived in California, had never been anywhere near the South, didn't even *know* anyone from the South—but, arrogant and self-important jerk that I was, I didn't let that stop me.

—⁓—

Momma let the dishes set after supper instead of washing them and came out on the porch with us. She kicked Junior off of the rocker and took it for herself, just sitting there rocking and staring out at Old Man Crawford's trawler out there on the lake. It was one of them humid July nights and the dragonflies and the bloodsuckers was all hanging around the porchlight looking for a good arm to land on. Petey was up with a magazine, running around trying to kill all the bugs he could.

Momma was out on the porch with us because Robert hadn't come home before dark like he'd promised and she was waiting up for him. She pretended it wasn't no big deal. She sat there and talked to us, laughing and joking and telling stories about when she was our age, but I could tell from the expression on her face that she was thinking about Daddy.

I was standing off by the side of the railing, away from the door, by myself, trying to loosen my dress from where it'd caught on a nail. I was listening to Momma tell about the time the brakes went out on her at Cook's Trail and she had to swerve into the river to keep from smashing into a tree when I heard a low kind of rustling sound coming from the path on the side of the house. I scooted next to Momma on the rocker. "What is it, Beth?" she asked.

I didn't say nothing. Then I heard the sound again, only this time all of them heard it. Momma stood up. Her face was white. She walked to the railing where I'd been standing and looked off toward the path. We stood around her, holding on to parts of her skirt.

Petey saw it first. "It's Robert!" he called. He pointed off to where the path met the woods.

Sure enough, Robert was coming out of the woods across the clearing carrying a whole lineful of fish. I heard Momma's breath start to relax when she saw it was Robert, but then she pulled it all in like someone'd hit her. Robert was kind of staggering across the clearing, weaving like he was drunk or something.

But we all knew he wasn't drunk.

"Get the shotgun," Momma said quietly.

I ran into the house and grabbed the gun out of Daddy's closet. I ran back out and gave it to Momma. She loaded it up and pointed it at Robert without no hesitation.

We could see him pretty clear now. He was halfway across the clearing and the lights from the house sort of lit up his face. He was still staggering around and walking like he was drunk and he was still carrying his line of fish. His face looked real white, like Daddy's face, and he didn't seem to even see us standing there on the porch. Petey was calling out to him—Petey was too young, he didn't really know what was going on—and Junior was holding him back.

Robert stopped about ten yards away from the house and waved. His wave was real slow, real strange. "Hey, Momma!" he said, and his voice was strange, too. "Look what I got."

Momma kept the gun trained on him. "Don't you come any closer," she said.

He shook his head. "Momma . . ."

"If I'm still your momma you'll wait there for me 'til dawn. If you're still there come morning you'll be welcome back. But until then you just stop and wait right there."

He took a step forward. "Aw, Momma—"

The gunshot blew his head clean off. His face just exploded in on itself and little pieces of blood and bone and eye went flying every which way. Petey started screaming and the rest of us watched while Robert fell onto the meadow grass. His hand was still holding onto the fish line. Momma reloaded the gun and aimed it at the center of his body just in case, but he didn't move. His body just lay there, the mash of skin that used to be his head bleeding into the grass.

We stayed on the porch all night. Petey, Junior, and Sissy fell asleep a little while later and I fell asleep about halfway through the night, but Momma stayed awake the whole time.

After the sun came up, we all went out in the clearing to look.

There was nothing there. His body was gone.

Momma spent that morning explaining things to Petey.

We waited on the porch again that night, eating supper early and standing out there before it started to get dark. Sure enough, he started staggering up the path about the same time he had last night. There was nothing we could do this time, so we just stood there huddled together and watched.

"Robert Paul's come home," he said, and his voice sounded like it was coming from the bottom of a well. "Robert Paul's come home again." We could see his grin even from this far away.

When he got to the spot where Momma'd shot him, he stopped.

And his head exploded.

He fell onto the ground just like before, and in the morning he was gone.

We went out to the spot. The grass was trampled and brown and looked like it'd been burned. "That's all," Momma said, kicking the spot with her shoe. "It's over now."

But I knew it wasn't. I could tell. I could feel it in my bones. I knew that we'd have to do the same thing we did for Daddy. And I was scared.

Scared bad.

That was one of them weird days when everything was backwards and all the directions was wrong. Our house was suddenly facing south when it'd always faced west, and I stayed close to home. I knew that if I lost sight of the house I wouldn't never get back to it.

It was overcast the whole day, and in the kitchen things broke for no reason. Momma'd walk out to the living room for a minute to talk to one of us kids and when she'd go back into the kitchen all the silverware would be poured out on the floor or one of her good dishes would be smashed or something. She tried to ignore all this, but one time I caught her saying the Prayer to herself when she thought no one was looking.

I said the Prayer, too. I knew what was happening.

After supper we all just sat around and waited for night to fall. We didn't sit on the porch this time. We stayed inside. Sissy closed all the windows and drapes and Junior turned on all the lights.

I was almost asleep when something huge crashed against the north wall of the house. I jerked awake. It sounded like a cannon. Everyone else was wide awake too and Petey was crying. Momma held us all tight. "Stay here," she said. "Don't go near the windows." She didn't say nothing after that and I looked up at her. Her eyes was shut and it looked like she was praying to herself.

Something crashed hard against the wall again, making the whole house shake.

Outside, I could hear voices. It sounded like there was at least six or seven of them out there. Their words was all running together and I couldn't understand what they were saying. I plugged my ears and closed my eyes but I could still hear the voices talking inside my head.

And I could feel it when the thing crashed against the wall again.

I fell asleep plugging my ears.

I dreamed about Daddy.

We went to see Mrs. Caffrey the next day. All of us. We went into her little trailer out there by the edge of the lake and waited in the tiny waiting room out front. When she came out she was all dressed up. Momma told her what happened and Mrs. Caffrey prayed over her small bag of bones and threw a handful of sticks onto the table. When she was through she nodded. She held her head in her hands, closed her eyes, and sort of hummed to herself. When she looked up she was staring at me.

I tried to look away but I couldn't.

Mrs. Caffrey reached over and grabbed my arm and I could feel her sharp nails digging into my skin. "You must go to the bad place," she said. "You must go through the ritual." Her voice got real low. "But be careful. There are many dangers. The woods be dark."

She let go of me and I ran out of the trailer. I was crying bad. I knew this would happen and I didn't know if I could go through the ritual again.

Mrs. Caffrey came outside a few minutes later and put her arm around me. She opened up her Bible, closed her eyes, put her finger down, and made me read. "Walk while you have the light," I read, "lest the darkness overtake you."

She closed the Bible, smiled at me, and patted my head. "It'll be all right, child," she said. She went back inside to talk to Momma.

No one said nothing on the way home.

It was noon by the time we got back to the house and Momma said there wasn't enough time to do it today, I would have to wait 'til tomorrow.

I was glad.

They came back that night, pounding on the walls and talking in our heads. All us kids sat on the couch together, holding on to each other. Momma pretended like she didn't hear a thing, and she worked on a big sack for me to carry the next day.

I fell asleep listening to the pounding and the voices.

Momma woke me up before it was even light and told me I had to take a bath before I went out. "You must cleanse yourself," she said. I took my bath real quietly, but everyone

was up by the time I got out of the tub. It was already starting to get light out.

Momma gave me the sack and told me to be careful, and
I said goodbye to everyone just in case. I didn't spend too
long on goodbyes, though, because I couldn't afford to
waste no time. I had to get back before dark.

It was overcast again and the sky was covered with solid
gray clouds and I couldn't see the sun. I walked down the
path through the clearing, past the spot where Momma'd
shot Robert, into the woods. Momma packed me a flashlight
in my sack and I got it out. I needed it. The woods was dark,
real dark, darker even than when I went in for Daddy, and it
was completely silent. Usually you can hear the sounds of
the lake or someone's car or people talking out by the boat
launch, but I couldn't hear nothing. Even the birds was
quiet. My footsteps sounded real loud, and I had a headache
from my heart pounding and thumping the blood in my
head.

I was scared.

It took me about a half an hour to get to the shack. I could
feel it before I saw it and I looked in the other direction as I
ran past. I didn't want to see them open windows and that
black doorway. I didn't want to know what was inside. I
made that mistake the last time and I almost didn't get no
farther than that, so this time I just looked the other way and
ran by.

There was something inside the shack, though.

I could feel it.

And I thought I heard it when I ran by.

I slowed down when I was out of breath, a good ways
from the shack. It was hidden way back behind the trees
now, so I didn't have nothing to worry about. The shack was
about halfway to the bad place, I knew, maybe a little less,

but the second half of the trip was a lot tougher and took a lot longer. The path ended a little ways up ahead, I remembered, and I'd have to find the rest of the way myself.

No path led to the bad place.

Sure enough, the path just sort of petered out. It got smaller and smaller and harder to see and after a while I realized it had ended some ways back and I hadn't noticed.

I was on my own.

It was real dark here and it kept getting darker the deeper I went into the woods. I saw shadows of things moving through the trees out of the corners of my eyes, but I ignored them and pretended they wasn't there. I said the Prayer to myself.

I didn't really know where I was going but I knew I was headed in the right direction. Tons of moss was hanging from the tops of the trees and it kept brushing my face and my blouse as I went past. I climbed over old dead logs and through thickets of sticker bushes. I started getting hungry, and I pulled out one of the sandwiches Momma made for me. I didn't sit down and eat, though. I kept walking.

Finally, I came to the ruins and I knew I was getting close.

I remember Momma used to scare us when we was little by telling us that she'd take us out to the ruins and leave us there if we didn't behave, but I'm the only person I know that's actually seen them. They used to be part of an old stone fort during the war. A bunch of soldiers was stationed there to protect the county, but something happened to all the soldiers. All kinds of government people came down to check on the fort afterwards, but none of them could figure out what happened.

The people around here knew what happened, though.

They built the fort too close to the bad place.

Now the ruins was just old piles of stone block and pieces of wall with plants and ivy growing all over them. A few buildings were still left, but I got the same feeling from them that I got from the shack and I just ran by.

After the ruins, the trees started to grow weird and the directions got all lost again. I was going south, then all of a sudden I was going west and I hadn't even changed my course. The trees became all gnarly and twisted, and the moss started to grow into shapes, strange shapes that I knew what they were but I didn't want to admit it.

It got even darker.

And then I was there.

The bad place looked just like I remembered it. The leaves of the trees was all black and brown and they twisted together to make a roof over the clearing and completely block out the sky. It was always night there. On the sides, small trees grew in between the big trees and made a solid wall except for the entrance where I was coming in. The middle of the clearing was covered with bones and skulls and the teeth of rats, all lain out in little rows, like crops. Dead possum skeletons hung from frayed old ropes in the trees, and they was swinging but there wasn't no breeze.

Nothing grew in the center of the clearing. It was all dust. Even the plants was afraid to grow there.

In the very center was the open grave.

I swallowed hard and took Momma's Bible out of my sack. I was scared, even more scared than I'd been with Daddy, and all of a sudden I wanted to run, to run back home to Momma. The noises at night, the voices and pounding, didn't seem so bad now. Not compared to this. I could live with them.

But I couldn't run. I had to go through the ritual.

I walked slowly into the middle of the clearing toward

the open grave, holding tight to my Bible. The little white wood cross at the head of the grave was tilted and almost falling over. I kept my eyes on that and didn't look into the hole. Finally, I reached the grave and stood at its foot, trying to calm down. My heart was pounding a mile a minute and I couldn't hardly get no breath.

I stood like that for a few minutes, staring at the cross, trying to be brave. And then I looked into the hole.

Robert lay on the bottom. His skin was pure white and glowing and his face was smooth and perfect and I couldn't tell where Momma'd shot him. He was holding his hands up in the air toward me and they was moving a little, twirling in strange little circles.

Then his eyes jerked open and he smiled. His eyes was pure red and evil and I started to shake. "Robert Paul's come home," he said. "Robert Paul's come home again." It was all he said. It was all he could say.

His voice was just a whisper.

I reached around to my sack and took out the page with the Words written on it. The grave was deep, I was thinking. It was deeper than last time. The sides went down maybe ten feet to Robert at the bottom. I put the Words on the Bible. "Lord protect me in this ritual," I read. "Keep me safe from harm. See my motives not my actions. Keep me safe from harm. Give this tortured soul his rest. Keep me safe from harm. Guide me through this and preserve me. Keep me safe from harm. Amen."

I folded the paper and put the Words into the Bible.

At the bottom of the grave Robert was moving even more now. His head was rolling from side to side and his arms was still twirling in the air and he was grinning even worse. I could see all of his teeth. They was glowing.

I took a deep breath, said the Prayer, held the Bible to my chest, and jumped into the open grave.

I fell, fell and landed with a soft thud on Robert's body. His grin got bigger and his eyes got redder and I could see them right next to my face.

He started laughing and his voice changed.

He was no longer Robert.

And he took me.

I woke up by the ruins. My sack was gone and the Bible was gone and my clothes was all torn up and half hanging off me. I still felt kind of dopey or sleepy or whatever it was, but I knew I had to get out of the woods before dark. I didn't know what time it was so I just started running. I ran past the ruins and somehow found the path again.

Something was standing in the doorway of the shack when I ran by but I didn't look at it. I kept running.

It was broad daylight when I came out of the woods. The clouds had all burnt off and the sun was shining. Everything was okay. Momma was waiting for me and she ran up and hugged me as I came down the path. I could see she was crying. "You went through the ritual?" she asked.

I nodded and told her I did.

She led me back to the house where I slept for two full days.

Two weeks later my belly started growing.

It was just a little bit at first. But a month later it was obvious.

People didn't bother me none about it though. Folks around here understand about the bad place. A lot of women around here've got pregnant the same way when they was my age. No one talked to me about it or paid me no never mind.

Two months later I was ready to give birth.

Momma took me to Mrs. Caffrey's. She didn't tell none of the other kids about it, she just said that we was going into town for the day and for Junior to keep an eye on everyone else and not let them leave the house.

It was just like before. The thing was all slimy and pink and wormy. It made horrible squawking noises and tried to claw up Mrs. Caffrey as she held it.

It had Robert's face.

"Do you want to see it first?" Mrs. Caffrey asked me.

I shook my head. I could see it good enough as it was, and I didn't want to see no more of it. I sure didn't want to touch it.

"I'll take it outside then."

"No," I said. "Wait a minute. Let me do it."

Momma shook her head. "No. You're too weak."

"It's all right," Mrs. Caffrey said.

Momma helped me out of the bed, and Mrs. Caffrey took the baby outside. She put it on the ground by the trailer and it started squawking and twirling its arms in circles.

I searched the ground and picked up a boulder. I held it up as high as I could and the creature looked up at me and spat.

I smashed its head.

It lay there twitching for a minute, a small trickle of black blood flowing out from beneath the boulder, then it was still.

I watched as Mrs. Caffrey took the dead thing into her trailer. She cut it up and burned it and put the ashes into a stew. I ate a bite of the stew and said the Prayer.

Momma drove me home.

That night, Momma was inside washing the dishes and all us kids was out on the porch. Petey was trying to kill bugs, and Junior and Sissy was fighting on the rocker, and I was standing by the railing looking out at the woods when all of a sudden I heard a rustling sound coming from the meadow. I looked back quickly at the other kids but none of them'd heard it. I held my breath and looked closer, leaning over the rail to see better, saying the Prayer to myself. But it was just a scared little jackrabbit, and it stopped and stared at me and then ran across the path and disappeared into the bushes and meadow grass at the side of the house.

The Phonebook Man

For a while, I worked as a phonebook deliveryman. The job allowed me to walk into every business in the city from legal offices to liquor stores, strip clubs to mortuaries. One day while I was striding down the street, stacks of phonebooks under my arm, I started to think about what a supernatural being could do with such a position, particularly if he was irrationally and obsessively devoted to the cause of phonebook delivery. "The Phonebook Man" was born from that.

—⁂—

Nina was reading the morning paper and slowly sipping her coffee when she heard the knock at the door. She was barely awake, her eyes still not fully open, her senses still not fully alert, and she thought at first that she had made a mistake. Jim had gone to work sometime ago and Erin had long since left for school with Mrs. Bloomenstein, so it could not be either one of them trying to get back in, and she did not know anyone who would be over this early in the morning. But then the knock came again, and she stood up quickly, almost knocking over her coffee, and moved to answer the door.

She was about to open the dead bolt when she suddenly thought the better of it. After all, who knew what kind of crazies were out there these days? Instead, she stood on her tiptoes and tried to peek through the glass window situated near the top of the solid oak door. She could see only the crown of a brown-haired head. "Who is it?" she called.

"Phonebook man."

Phonebook man? She pulled back the dead bolt and opened the door a crack. Standing on the stoop was a nondescript young man in his early twenties with a load of phonebooks under each arm. He smiled at her as she opened the door. "Good morning, ma'am. I'm delivering your neighborhood phonebooks. How many would you like?"

Nina pulled her robe tighter around her chest to make sure nothing was showing and held out her other hand. "Just one will be fine."

"One it is." The man pulled a book from under his arm with a theatrical flourish and handed it to her.

"Thank you."

"You're welcome, ma'am." He turned and was about to leave when he stopped, as though he had just thought of something. "Ma'am?" he asked.

Nina stood in the doorway, still clutching her robe with one hand. "Yes?"

"I'm sorry to bother you." He looked sheepish. "But could I use your bathroom?"

She was acutely aware that she was alone in the house, that both Jim and Erin were gone, and she hesitated for a second. He noticed the hesitation and started to back away. "It's okay," he said. "Sorry to bother you. I understand."

Nina mentally kicked herself. What kind of person was she? "Of course you can use the bathroom." She stepped all the way inside the front alcove and held the door open. "It's down the hallway. Last door on the right."

The phonebook man walked past her, still carrying his

books, and hurried down the hall. Nina closed the door and returned to her paper and her coffee. She turned on the TV— the *Today* show—for some background noise.

Three articles later, she realized that the phonebook man had not left. Her heart gave a short trip-hammer of fear. She should have known better. She should never have let a stranger in the house. She put the paper down and stood up, moving toward the hall. She peeked around the corner. The bathroom door was closed. He was still in there.

And he was taking a shower.

She could hear, below the surface noise of the television, the familiar sound of the water pipes and the running shower. Her first instinct was anger—how dare he?—but that was replaced instantly by fear, and she crept back to the kitchen and took the phone off the hook, dialing 911.

The phone was dead.

She heard the shower shut off.

She hurried into the bedroom, grabbed a pair of jeans and a blouse, and ran back out. She put the clothes on in the kitchen as fast as she could.

He walked in just as she was buttoning the top button of her blouse.

His hair was black. He had a beard. He had gained at least sixty pounds.

Nina gasped. "Who are you?"

He held up the load of phonebooks under his arms and smiled. "Phonebook man." He looked around the kitchen admiringly. "Nice kitchen. What's for breakfast?"

"D-don't hurt me." She knew her voice was trembling obviously with her fear, but she could not help it. Her legs felt weak, as though they would not support her. "I'll d-do anything you want."

The phonebook man looked puzzled. "What are you talking about?"

She stared at him, trying to keep her voice steady. "You cut the phone lines. So I couldn't call anybody."

He chuckled. "You're crazy."

"I let you use the bathroom and you used it to take a shower and now your hair's different and you have a beard and you're . . . you're . . ." She shook her head in disbelief. "You're not the same person."

He looked at her, uncomprehending. "I'm the phonebook man." His eyes moved down her body as he noticed her changed apparel, and he smiled. "Nice clothes."

"What do you want from me?"

He looked surprised, caught off guard by her outburst, and he held up the phonebooks under his arms. "I'm here to deliver your local phonebooks."

"You delivered them! Now get the hell out of here!"

He nodded. "Okay, lady, okay. Sorry I was born." He started to walk out of the kitchen, then turned around. "But if I could just have a piece of toast. I didn't have anything to eat this morning—"

Nina ran past him and out the front door, leaving the screen swinging behind her. She couldn't take this anymore. She couldn't handle this, couldn't cope. She realized she was screaming by the time she reached the McFarlands' house next door, and she forced herself to quiet down. Breathing heavily, she pounded on the door and rang the bell.

A minute passed. No answer.

She realized that both of the McFarlands must have already gone to work, and she looked fearfully back toward her house. From the McFarlands' doorstep she could see into her own kitchen window.

The phonebook man was making himself some eggs.

She ran back down the sidewalk to the Adams' house, on the other side of hers. She pounded on the door and rang the bell, but again there was no answer. The Adams must have gone someplace.

Nina looked around the neighborhood. They had only moved in a couple of months ago, and hadn't met many of the neighbors. She didn't feel comfortable walking up to some stranger's door. Especially not with this wild tale.

But this was an emergency. . . .

The car!

The car. She didn't know why she hadn't thought of it earlier. There was an extra set of keys in the little magnetic box attached to the wheel well. She could get the keys and take off. Moving slowly, quietly, she pushed through the wall of bushes which separated the Adams' house from her own. Ducking low, she ran along the side of the house to the garage.

The phonebook man was sitting in the driver's seat of the car.

He smiled at her as she ran up. "We have to go to the store," he said. She could see his phonebooks piled on the seat next to him.

Anger broke through her fear and shock. *"That's my car! Get out of there!"*

He looked at her, confused. "If you don't want me to drive, that's all right. You can drive."

Nina sat down on the floor of the garage, her buttocks landing hard on the cement. Tears—tears of anger, hurt, frustration, fear—ran down her face. Snot flowed freely from her nose. She sobbed.

Vaguely, through her tears, through her cries, she heard the sound of a car door being slammed, of feet walking across cement. She felt a light hand on her shoulder. "Would you like a phonebook?"

She looked up. The phonebook man was bending over her, concern on his face. She shook her head, still crying, and wiped the tears from her cheeks. "Just go away," she said. "Please."

He nodded. "You sure you don't need another phonebook?"

She shook her head. "Just go."

He shifted the load of books under his arms, looked at her and started to say something, then thought the better of it and walked silently down the driveway toward the sidewalk. He walked up the street toward the McFarlands'.

The tears came again—tears of relief this time—and Nina felt her whole body relax, tension leaving her muscles. When the crying stopped of its own accord, she stood up and walked into the house through the side door. The kitchen was a mess. He had spilled milk and coffee all over the countertops and had left the eggs, shell and all, in the pan on the stove. Salt and sugar were everywhere.

She started to clean up.

She was washing out the sink when the phone rang. She jumped, startled. She recalled that the phone had been dead, and she approached it with something like dread, afraid to pick up the receiver. The rings continued—five, six, seven times—and slowly, hesitantly, she picked up the receiver.

"Phonebook man." The voice was low and insinuating.

She dropped the receiver, screaming.

It was then that she noticed the note. It was taped to the broom closet next to the refrigerator. The note was attached low to the door, below her line of vision, and it was scrawled in a childish hand.

"Gone to pick up Erin. Be back for lunch."

It was unsigned, but she knew who it was from. She ran to the bedroom, grabbed her keys, and sped out to the car. The car bumped over the curb on the way out into the street, but Nina didn't care. She threw the car into drive and took off toward the school.

She should have known better. She should have known he wouldn't leave her alone. The car sped through a yellow light at the intersection. She would pick up Erin and go straight to the police station. He was still around somewhere, between home and school; they should be able to catch him.

But where had he called from?

Someone else's house, probably. He was now torturing some other poor soul.

She swung the car into the school parking lot just as the kindergarten classes were letting out. Hordes of small children streamed out of the school doors. She left the keys in the car and dashed across the asphalt toward the kids. She scanned the stream of faces, looking for Erin (what was she wearing today? red?), and finally saw her, chatting happily to a friend.

She ran over and picked up her daughter, ecstatic with relief.

Erin dropped the phonebook she'd been holding.

Nina stared at her in disbelief. "Where did you get that?" she demanded.

"The phonebook man gave it to me." Erin looked at her innocently.

"Where is he now?"

Erin pointed up the street, where the children were starting to walk home. Nina could see nothing, only a sea of heads and colored shirts, bobbing, skipping, running, walking.

"He said for you to stop bugging him about the phone-books. He can only give you two." Erin pointed to the book on the ground. "That's your second one. He said he's not coming by anymore. That's it."

That's it.

Nina held her daughter tight and looked up the street, her eyes searching. She thought she saw, over the children's heads, a shock of brown hair above a clean-shaven non-descript face. But it disappeared almost immediately, and she could not find it again.

The children moved forward in a tide, walking in groups of two or three or more, talking, laughing, giggling.

Somewhere up ahead, the phonebook man walked alone.

Estoppel

"Estoppel" is a legal term that means "it is what it says it is." It applies primarily to pornography, allowing prosecutors to more easily prove in court that a magazine is "obscene" or "pornographic" if it is specifically advertised as such. I learned about estoppel in a Communications Law course, and since I was bored in class that day, I thought up this story instead of paying attention to the lecture.

Side note: There's a reference in here to the Chico Hamilton Quintet. Known to mainstream audiences primarily for appearing in and scoring the Burt Lancaster/Tony Curtis film *The Sweet Smell of Success*, the quintet featured a cellist named Fred Katz who, in addition to being a truly spectacular jazz musician, went on to write the music for Ken Nordine's acclaimed *Word Jazz* albums, the music for the Oscar-winning cartoon "Gerald McBoing Boing," and music for the Roger Corman cult classic *Little Shop of Horrors*. At the time I wrote this story, Fred Katz was my anthropology professor at Cal State Fullerton.

—⟋⟍—

Most people assume I am mute without asking. I never tell them otherwise. If anyone does ask, I simply hand them one of the "mute cards" I had printed up for just such a reason and which I always carry with me. "Peace!" the cards say. "Smile. I am a Deaf Mute."

Most people also assume I am a derelict. I dress in old, filthy, raggedy clothes, I seldom bathe, and I never cut my hair or trim my beard. I have noticed, over a period of years, that people do not ordinarily talk to derelicts, and I became one for that reason.

I have done everything possible to minimize my human contacts and to keep people from speaking to me or addressing me in any way.

I have not uttered a single intelligible word since 1960.

I know that, for all intents and purposes, I *am* a mute, but I have never been able or willing to make it official. I have refrained from saying the words. I should have proclaimed, "I am mute," years ago. But that would be permanent. It would be irreversible.

I guess I've been afraid.

To be honest, there is very little of which I am not afraid. I have spent half of my life being afraid. For nearly a decade, I was afraid to write anything down. I would neither speak nor write. What if, I thought, it happened with writing as well as speaking?

But those years, those ten long years of almost total isolation, were sheer and utter hell. I did not realize how important communication was to me until it was denied. And after a decade of such isolation, I literally could not take it anymore. It was driving me mad. So one night, my blood running high with adrenaline and bottled courage, I decided to take the chance. I locked the door of my motel room, shut the curtains, sat down in front of the desk, and wrote on a blank sheet of paper: "I am black."

My hand did not change color as I finished the last arm

of the *k*. Neither did my other hand. I rushed to the mirror: neither had my face. God, the joy, the sheer exquisite rapture with which that simple sentence filled me! I danced around the room like a madman. I wrote all night.

I still write prolifically to this day and have actually had several fiction pieces published in assorted literary magazines under various pseudonyms. I have six unpublished novels sitting in my desk drawer.

But I am not a snob. I write anything and to anyone. Once a day, I make it a point to write to a business and complain about one of their products. You'd be surprised at the responses I get. I've received free movie passes, free hamburger coupons, several rebate checks, and a huge amount of apologetic letters.

And of course I have several pen pals. They are the closest thing I have to friends. My best friend, Phil, is a convict in San Quentin. He murdered his brother-in-law and was sentenced to life imprisonment. I would never want to meet the man on the street, but I have found through his letters that he can be a deeply sensitive individual. Out of all my pen pals, he best understands what it is like to be isolated, alienated, alone. I also write to a middle-aged woman named Joan, in France; a young single girl named Nikol, in Belgium; and a small boy named Rufus, in Washington, D.C.

I have not told any of them the truth.

But how can I? I do not really know what "the truth" is myself.

The first experience occurred when I was twelve. At least, that's the first instance I remember. We were playing, my cousin Jobe and I, in the unplowed and untended field in back of my grandmother's farm. We had just finished a furious game of freeze-ball tag and were running like crazy through what seemed like acres of grass, racing to the barn. The grass was tall, almost above my head, and I had to keep straining my neck and jumping up to see where I was going.

I did not see the rock I tripped over.

I must have blacked out for a few seconds, because I found myself lying on the ground, staring at an endless forest of grass stalks. I stood up, stunned and hurt, and started walking toward the barn where I knew Jobe was waiting, a self-satisfied winner's smile on his face.

I must have hit my head harder than I thought, because I kept walking and walking, and still did not reach the clearing and the barn. Instead, the grass kept getting thicker and taller, and soon I was lost in it. I did not even know in which direction I was traveling.

With the bump on my head still throbbing and with my heart starting to pound at the prospect of being lost in the grass, I decided to call for help. "Jobe!" I cried loudly, cupping my hands to my mouth to amplify the sound. "I'm lost!"

I heard Jobe's older, mocking laughter from an indeterminate direction.

"I mean it!" I called. "Help!"

Jobe giggled now. "Yeah," he called back, "the barn's a tough one to find."

By now I was ready to burst into tears. "*Mom!*"

"She can't hear you," Jobe said. He paused. "I'll come and get you, but you'll have to pay the price."

"I'll pay!" I cried.

"All right. Say, 'I'm a yellow belly, and I give up in womanly defeat.' "

I was desperate and, with only a moment's hesitation, I cast my pride away and shouted out the words. "I'm a yellow belly, and I give up in womanly defeat!"

A minute later, I heard Jobe crashing through the weeds. He came through the wall of grass to my right. "Come on," he said, laughing. I followed him to the barn.

That night, as I undressed for my bath, I discovered that the skin on my stomach, instead of being its normal peach pink, had somehow turned a dark and rather bright yellow. I was baffled; I didn't know what had happened. Perhaps, I thought, I had accidentally touched some type of chemical dye. But the yellow color would not come off—even after a full ten minutes of hard scrubbing.

I did not tell my parents about this, however, and a few days later the color simply faded away.

I had no other experiences for almost ten years.

I was a history major in college. Midterms were over and, after nearly a full two weeks of nonstop studying, I decided to accompany some newfound friends and some recently acquired acquaintances to a club in Long Beach to hear the Chico Hamilton Quintet, the current musical sensation among the college crowd. I sat there in my shades, rep tie in place, smoking my skinny pipe and listening intently in the fashion of the day.

After the set, one of the others at our table, a student named Glen whom I barely knew, took a long, cool drag on his cigarette and looked up at the departing musicians. "Crap," he pronounced.

I could not believe what I'd just heard. "You're joking," I said.

He shook his head. "Highly overrated. The music was banal at best."

I was outraged! I could not believe we had heard the same group. "You know nothing about music," I said to him. "I refuse to discuss it with you."

Glen smiled a little. "And I suppose you're a music expert?" he asked, addressing his cigarette.

"I'm a music major," I lied.

And I was a music major.

As simple as that.

My whole life shifted as I spoke those words. I remembered the myriad music courses I had taken and passed; I recalled names, faces, and even particular expressions of piano teachers I had studied under. I knew details about people I had not even known existed minutes before. I knew what the band had just played, and how and why.

I looked around at my companions. Doug, Don, and Justin, the three people at the table I knew best, were glaring at Glen. "That's right," they concurred. "He's a music major."

They were serious.

I did not know what was going on. I retained a full memory of my "previous life," yet I knew that it was no longer true. Perhaps it never had been. And I knew that whereas a few minutes ago I could have recited the names of all the battles of the Revolutionary War and the outcome of each but could not have played the piano to save my life, now the opposite was true.

I slept fitfully that night. I woke up still a music major.

I decided to check my school transcripts to find out exactly what was going on. I went to the Office of Admissions and Records, got my files from the clerk, and took them over to a booth to study. I opened the folder and looked at the first page. The words typed there stunned me. I was officially enrolled as a music major with an emphasis in piano composition. I had never taken more than an introductory history course.

This can't be happening, I thought. But I knew it was,

and something in the back of my mind made me push on. I looked up; the records clerk had turned her head for a moment. "I am a history major," I said to the transcripts in front of me.

The music classes were gone.

And then I knew.

Of course, the first feeling was one of power. Incredible, uncontrollable, unlimited power. I could be anything. Anyone. And I could change at will.

But that disappeared almost immediately and was replaced by the more penetrating feeling of fear. Could I control this power? If so, how? If not, why not? Would it eventually fade? Or would it get stronger? Did this power or curse or miracle change only me, or did it change my immediate surroundings, or did it change the entire world in which I lived? Could I alter history? What exactly were the implications, ramifications, and all the other -cations of this? A million thoughts voiced themselves simultaneously in my mind.

A test, I thought. *I need to test this out. I need to make sure this isn't some type of elaborate hoax or psychological mind game being played on me.*

First, I tried thinking of a command. *I am a giraffe,* I told myself.

Nothing happened.

Well, that proved something. To effect a change, the statement had to be said aloud. I was about to speak the phrase when I stopped myself. If I said, "I am a giraffe," and actually became one, it was quite possible that I would permanently remain that way. A giraffe cannot speak. I would not be able to say, "I am a human being," and change myself back.

The fear hit again; stronger, more potent. I began to

sweat. I would have be very careful about this. I would have to think before I spoke. If I did not consider all the possibilities and potential side effects of each statement I made from now on, I could permanently alter my life. And not just for the better.

So instead of testing out my newfound proclivity then and there, I returned my transcripts to the clerk, mumbled a simple "Thank you," and hurriedly returned to my room. Once inside, I closed and locked the door and pulled all the curtains. I left all the lights on. I wanted to see this.

I had a full-length mirror on the back of my closet door. Being something of a clotheshorse, I had always considered such a mirror a necessity and would never have been without one. Now it really was a necessity. I opened the closet door, took off all my clothes, and stood before the mirror. "I am fat," I said.

The change was not visible. That is to say, it did not occur in time. I was thin, then I was fat. I did not bloat up or suddenly gain weight or anything of the sort. In fact, I did not physically change. I did not change at all. Rather, reality changed. One second, I weighed my typical 145 pounds. That was a fact. The next second, the facts changed. I weighed nearly 300 pounds. This too was a fact.

And it altered the world.

I retained a full memory of my "real life," but I also had a new and completely different life—my fat life. And the world corresponded to it. I knew that I had always had a bit of a weight problem, and that, after my girlfriend died from leukemia, eating had become a compulsion, a neurosis, a serious problem. I had tried several diets since then, but nothing worked. Eating was a need. And I loved pistachio ice cream.

I looked in the mirror at my triple chins and my overflowing gut. I looked like nothing so much as a big ball of white dough. "I am thin," I said.

The world changed back. I was not fat. I had never had a girlfriend with leukemia. I hated pistachio ice cream.

This was a different reality.

That was as far as my "tests" or "experiments" went. I quit then and there. I did not understand this power; I did not know how to use it; I did not want to cope with it. And I was determined not to employ it for any reason. I vowed never to utter another sentence which contained the word *I*.

But it is amazing how people adapt; how human beings have this sort of innate ability to adjust themselves to change, no matter how radical. People living next to chemical dump sites soon stop noticing the stench; people living on the beach soon cease to hear the endless crashing of the waves.

All this is rationalization. For I got used to the power rather quickly, though I kept my vow and abstained from its usage. The power became an accepted part of me. It became comfortable.

And it happened.

One day, having failed miserably on a final in one of my more important classes, sitting in my room, feeling depressed and sorry for myself, I thought, *Why not? Why not use the power? Why not use it to get something I want out of life?*

I planned my speech carefully. I did not want to screw this up. Finally, I had worked out what seemed a perfect statement for my purposes and was ready to say it. Once again, I stood before the mirror. "I graduated from Harvard with a Ph.D. in political science, and I am now a presidential consultant," I said.

And it was all true. The knowledge of my previous life as a financially and academically struggling history major at the University of Southern California during Eisenhower's administration was still there, but it was a memory of the past. I was a different person now—establishing myself as one of the more brilliant minds in the popular Stevenson White House.

There was no transition period. I knew my job and was good at it. Everyone knew and accepted me. The transformation had gone perfectly.

The power was an annoyance in my everyday life, however. I would greet people with the customary, "I'm glad to see you," and would suddenly find myself overjoyed that they had stopped by. Or I would say to people, "I'm sorry you have to go," and, by the time they had finally departed, I would be near tears. On particularly frustrating days, I would mutter to myself, "I'm sick of this job," then, feeling the effects immediately, I would have to blurt out, "I love this job, it makes me feel good!"

But I could function. The power caused me no major problems.

Until June 5.

A particularly nasty and involved crisis had come up involving both Germany and the Soviet Union, and we were at an emergency cabinet meeting in the president's office, arguing over our course of action. The secretary of defense had suggested that we "bluff" our way out of the possible confrontation with a first-strike threat. "Hell, they're already afraid of us," he said. "They knew we've dropped the bomb once, and they know we're not afraid to do it again."

A surprising number of cabinet members agreed with him.

"No," I argued. "A diplomatic solution is needed in this instance. Military threats would only aggravate the situation."

The secretary smiled condescendingly. "Look," he said,

"your theories may be fine in college classes, they may work in textbooks, but they don't work in real life. I've been around these matters for the past twenty-six years, most of my life, and I think I know something about them. You've been here a little over a year. I hardly think you're in a position to decide these things."

I was furious. "I may not have been here as long as you have, but I do possess something which you seem to lack—common sense. Do you honestly think threats of a nuclear war are going to put an end to this crisis? Of course they won't. I know that and you know that. Furthermore, I believe that such actions would lead to a full-scale military confrontation. And none of us want that. We have to talk this out peacefully."

The arguments soon wound down and the president, looking tired and a little strained, thanked us for our contributions and went off to make his decision.

I was in my office when word came that the Soviets had launched an all-out nuclear attack. "Please file into the fallout shelter," a voice said through the speaker above my door. "Do not panic. Please file into the fallout shelter. This is not a test."

The realization hit me immediately. "I believe," I had said. "I know." The fate of the secretary's plan, the country, and, possibly, the entire world had been in my hands, and I had not known it. I had botched it horribly. The attack was a direct result of my statements.

I panicked. I was not sure that I could think fast enough to stop the impending death and destruction, and prevent the holocaust. But I knew that I had to save myself. That much was instinctive. "I'm a history major at USC trying to get financial aid from the Eisenhower administration," I screamed.

And I was on a couch in the financial aid office. A woman

was staring at me, as if waiting for the answer to a question. I was sweating like a pig and shaking as if palsied. I am not even sure I was coherent as I ran out the door and to my room.

But it was not my room. The same Expressionistic prints were on the walls and the same furniture was arranged in the same way, but the room was different. I was in room 212 instead of room 215.

This was not quite the same reality I'd started from.

Thus I learned that my statements could have delayed actions and unforeseen consequences. If I did not study in detail all the possible meanings of all my words and/or did not phrase my sentences carefully, things could change beyond all reason. And once again, I grew afraid. Only this time the fear was deeper. This time it did not go away.

I made the decision. I would speak no more. I could not afford to gamble with the lives of other people, nor could I bear the responsibility of changing reality or even particular circumstances. Even the most innocent comments, devoid of all malevolent intent or meaning, could, I realized, wreak havoc I could not envision. I could not take the chance of speaking ever again.

I had to leave school. That was my first move. It was impossible to live in a college environment without uttering a word, and I knew that the temptation would be too great for me. My friends would talk to me, teachers would ask me questions, acquaintances would stop and engage me in casual conversation. I had to leave.

I quickly gathered all my belongings together and packed what I needed. I took all my money. I left.

Once on the street, however, I realized that I had no idea of what to do next. I did not even know where to start. *Time,* I thought. *I need time to think, time to sort things out, time to formulate at least some semblance of a plan.* I felt in my pockets and counted out all the money. One hundred dollars. That would buy me some time.

I did it all without saying a word. It's amazing, really, how well one can function without even the slightest form of verbal communication. I rented a small shack on the beach for a week and bought enough groceries to last me for that time without saying so much as a "yes" or a "no" to anyone. I got by with noncommittal grunts, quizzical looks, nods, and various gestures.

And then I was ready.

I had already decided never to utter another word again. Now, I knew, I must enforce that vow. I had to wean myself from the world of people. I had to cut off all ties with humanity. I had to isolate myself from everything—go cold turkey, as it were. And I had to do it in a week. In seven days, I had to reject and unlearn a lifetime of thought patterns, habits, and behavior. I had to de-acculturate myself.

It was hard at first. With the absence of human contact, I found myself wanting to think out loud. I felt, like the heroes in radio dramas, compelled to talk to myself.

But I overcame that compulsion. Soon, the urge disappeared altogether. I spent my days walking along the empty beach, occasionally swimming and reading good books. I grew used to my solitude.

Nights, however, were a different matter.

The first night, I decided to turn in early. I drank a cup of espresso, marked my place in the book I was reading, and settled down in the double bed.

I awoke in what had once been a shopping mall, now abandoned and inhabited by poor people, most of whom were wandering down the once-carpeted aisles of stores trying to hawk pieces of scrap metal they'd scavenged. A woman walked up to me and held out a rusted gear. "Want to buy it?" she whined pitifully. "Only a dollar."

I was completely baffled, trapped in that dazed and foggy netherworld between sleep and wakefulness. I did not know what was going on. I looked down at my body and got another rude shock. I was female.

Then it came to me. I remembered my warm comfortable bed in my rented beach shack. "I am back in my cabin on the beach," I blurted out. "I am the same person I was when I went to sleep last night."

And I was.

I must have been talking in my sleep. It was the only plausible explanation. No one had ever mentioned it to me—not my parents, my brother, not any of my friends or roommates—and perhaps it wasn't even audible, but apparently I was a sleeptalker. That was a problem. I could control my waking actions and my conscious thoughts, but sleep, dreams, and my subconscious were beyond my reach.

The sleeptalking continued, and I was never sure whether I'd wake up in my own bed, wake up on some alien planet, or even if I would wake up at all. Sometimes, I would awaken in the middle of the night only to find myself in some surrealistic nightmare, in a world with no recognizable features and with the bizarre juxtaposition of unrelated objects so characteristic of dreamscapes. Once, I remember, I awoke in a Wild West fort on a huge bed of ostrich feathers nearly twenty feet high. I was surrounded by soldiers. To my right, a storm was brewing over a barren plain. To my left, bright and shining, stood an ultra-modern supermarket.

Although I never broke my vow of silence during the day, I constantly talked in my sleep, and then again when I awoke—in order to return to the "real world."

Eventually, the problem did go away. Whether I willed

myself to stop talking in my sleep or whether it disappeared of its own accord I don't know. All I know is that it took a long, long time.

I refuse to let myself think about the possible reverberating effects my nighttime mumblings may have had.

When the week was up, I left my rented cabin. I traveled. At first, I wanted to get as far away from people and civilization as I could. So I headed north, to the wilds of Canada and then on to Alaska, doing odd jobs here and there for my room and board, pretending to be mute. But I'm a city person. And I found that I missed the throngs of people and the hustle and bustle of city life. I wanted to be near the crowds, even if I could not be part of them. And, truth be told, it's just as easy to remain isolated and alone in crowded cities as it is in deserted countrysides. Cities are so impersonal and cold, and the people in them so alienated from each other, that I fit right in. I mean, *I* notice my lack of communication; I have to live with it, it is an unending constant in my life and it is torture to me. But to everyone else, I'm just another person. No one notices that I don't speak.

But this is all beside the point. This is all background information. This is all a preface to what I want to say.

I have given it a lot of thought. Over twenty years of thought. And I have decided to use the power one last time. I do this not out of selfishness or greed. I do this not for myself at all. And I do not enter into this rashly or without reason. I do this after careful consideration and deliberation, and with a definite goal in mind. I do this purposefully and with a clear conscience.

For over these past decades, I have come to realize the full implications of this ability. I understand the tremendous, almost supreme and absolute power which I wield in my fallible and mortal body. It is a terrible thing to live with day in and day out, a terrible burden and responsibility. I cannot and should not be entrusted with such capabilities. Nor should any person.

I do not know if there are others with this power. Perhaps, even as I write, whole realities are coming and going, shifting and changing all around me. But no more. I intend to put a stop to it. I intend to make sure that no human being shall ever have to live through the hell which I have experienced.

Tonight I will speak. And the power will cease to exist.

I have thought this through, as I've said, for many years, and I believe I have honed down, defined, and clarified my statement to such an exact degree that it will have no effect other than the one which I intend. I have even written it down, to make sure I make no mistakes.

Of course, it is impossible to know exactly what all the consequences of my words may be. The laws of nature and science may crack and break; the world itself may change utterly. But I am willing to take that risk. I *must* take that risk.

In the process I, too, along with my power and along with any other individuals who have this ability, will cease to exist. It is for the best. My senile ravings, once I grow old, will now never be able to affect anyone; the cries of my death will not cause chaos. Instead, I will simply de-exist. I will probably never have existed at all. The people I once knew will not retain even a faint memory of me.

This, then, is my record, my proof. I have written down the events as they have transpired and have attempted to explain, somewhat, the full implications of my power. If I am successful in what I intend, the power will disappear forever and will never trouble humankind again. If I am not successful . . . who knows? I can only try. And I am willing to chance it.

Wish me luck.

The Washingtonians

During the Gulf War, I was amazed at the public's mass acceptance of the government's view of events. Something like 120,000 Iraqis were killed, not all of them soldiers or Husseins-in-training, many of them ordinary men, women, and children who happened to be living in the same geographical area in which we were dropping bombs. But the news was controlled, information filtered through official government press conferences, and on TV we saw no bodies, no blood. So people believed what they were told. I got to thinking about what it would be like if all our history was like that, if what we learned in school was simply the party line, not the actual truth. "The Washingtonians" grew from there.

—᙮᙮—

I will Skin your Children and Eat Them.
Upon Finishing, I will Fashion Utensils of Their Bones.

"It's authentic," Davis admitted. "It was written by George Washington." He flipped off the light and, with gloved fingers, removed the parchment manuscript from underneath the magnifier. He shook his head. "Where did you get this?

I've never come across anything like it in all my years in the business."

Mike shook his head. "I told you. It was in a trunk of my great-grandmother's stuff that we found hidden in her barn."

"May I ask what you intend to do with it?"

"Well, if it was authentic, we were thinking we'd donate it to the Smithsonian or something. Or sell it to the Smithsonian, if we could. What's the appraisal value of something like this?"

Davis spread his hands in an expansive gesture. "It's invaluable."

"A ballpark figure."

He leaned forward, across the counter. "I'm not sure you realize what you have here, Mr. Franks. With this one sheet of paper, you can entirely rewrite the history of our country." He paused, letting his words sink in. "History is myth, Mr. Franks. It's not just a collection of names and dates and facts. It's a belief system that ultimately tells more about the people buying into it than it does about the historical participants. What do we retain from our school lessons about George Washington? About Abraham Lincoln? Impressions. Washington was the father of our country. Lincoln freed the slaves. We are who we are as a nation because of what we believe they were. This letter will shatter that belief system and will forever change the image we have of Washington and perhaps all our Founding Fathers. That's a huge responsibility, and I think you should think about it."

"Think about it?"

"Decide if you want to make this knowledge known."

Mike stared at him. "Cover it up? Why? If it's true, then people should know."

"People don't want truth. They want image."

"Yeah, right. How much do I owe you?"

"The appraisal fee is fifty dollars." Davis started to write out a receipt, then paused, looked up. "I know a collector," he said. "He's had feelers out for something of this nature for a very long time. Would you mind if I gave him a ring? He's very discreet, very powerful, and, I have reason to believe, very generous."

"No thanks."

"I'd call him for you, set up all the—"

"Not interested," Mike said.

"Very well." Davis returned to the receipt. He finished writing, tore the perforated edge of the paper, and handed Mike a copy. "But if I may, Mr. Franks, I'd like to suggest you do something."

"What's that?" Mike asked as he took the receipt.

"Sleep on it."

He thought about Washington's letter all the way home. It was lying on the passenger seat beside him, in a protective plastic sleeve that Davis had given him, and he could see it in his peripheral vision, dully reflecting the sun each time he turned north. It felt strange owning something so valuable. He had never had anything this rare in his car before, and it carried with it a lot of responsibility. It made him nervous. He probably should've had it insured before taking it anywhere. What if the car crashed? What if the parchment burned? His hands on the wheel were sweaty.

But that wasn't why his hands were sweaty. That wasn't really why he was nervous. No. That was part of it, but the real reason was the note itself.

I will Skin your Children and Eat Them.

The fact that the words had been written by a real person and not a character in a novel would have automatically made him uneasy. But the fact that they had been written by

George Washington . . . Well, that was just too hard to take. There was something creepy about that, something that made a ripple of gooseflesh crawl up the back of his neck each time he looked at the plastic-wrapped brown parchment. He should have felt excited, proud, but instead he felt dirty, oily. He suddenly wished he'd never seen the note.

Ahead of him on a billboard above a liquor store, a caricature of George Washington—green, the way he appeared on the dollar bill—was winking at him, promoting the high T-bill rate at the Bank of New York.

He looked away from the sign, turned down Lincoln Avenue toward home.

Mike paced up and down the length of the kitchen. "He implied that rather than give it to the Smithsonian or something, I should sell it to a private collector who would keep it a secret."

Pam looked up from the dishes, shook her head. "That's crazy."

"That's what I said."

"Well, don't get too stressed out over it—"

"I'm not getting stressed out."

"Will you let me finish my sentence? I was just going to say, there are a lot of other document appraisers, a lot of museum curators, a lot of university professors. There are a lot of people you can take this to who will know what to do with it."

He nodded, touched her arm. "You're right. I'm sorry. I'm just . . . I don't know. This whole thing has me a little freaked."

"Me too. This afternoon I was helping Amy with her homework. They're studying Johnny Appleseed and George Washington and the cherry tree."

"Two myths."

"There's a picture of Washington in her book. . . ." She shivered, dipped her hands back into the soap suds. "You ought to look at it. It'll give you the willies."

He smiled at her. "I could give you my willy."

"Later."

"Really creepy, huh?"

"Check it out for yourself."

"I will. You need me in here?"

"No."

He patted the seat of her jeans, gave her a quick kiss on the cheek. "I'll be out front then."

"All right. I'll be through here in a minute. Go over Amy's math homework, too. Double-check."

"Okay." He walked into the living room. Amy was lying on the floor watching a rerun of *Everybody Loves Raymond.* Her schoolbook and homework were on the coffee table. He sat down on the couch and was about to pick up the book, when he saw the cover: mountains and clouds and a clipper ship and the Statue of Liberty and the Liberty Bell. The cover was drawn simply, in bright grade school colors, but there was something about the smile on the Statue of Liberty's face that made him realize he did not want to open up the book to see the picture of George Washington.

A commercial came on, and Amy turned around to look at him. "Are you going to check my homework?" she asked.

He nodded. "Yes," he said.

"Do it quick, then. I'm watching TV."

He smiled at her. "Yes, boss."

The pounding woke them up.

It must have been going on for some time, because Amy was standing in the doorway of their bedroom clutching her

teddy bear, though she'd supposedly given up the teddy bear
two years ago.

Pam gave him a look that let him know how frightened
she was, that told him to go out to the living room and find
out who the hell was beating on their front door at this time
of night, then she was no longer Wife but Mom, and she was
out of bed and striding purposefully toward their daughter,
telling her in a calm, reasonable, adult voice to go back to
bed, that there was nothing the matter.

Mike quickly reached down for the jeans he'd abandoned
on the floor next to the bed and put them on. The pounding
continued unabated, and he felt more than a little frightened
himself. But he was Husband and Dad and this was one of
those things Husbands and Dads had to do, and he strode
quickly out to the living room with a walk and an attitude
that made him seem much braver than he actually felt.

He slowed down as he walked across the dark living
room toward the entryway. Out here, the pounding seemed
much louder and much . . . scarier. There was a strength and
will behind the pounding that had not translated across the
rooms to the rear of the house and he found himself thinking absurdly that whatever was knocking on the door was
not human. It was a stupid thought, an irrational thought, but
he stopped at the edge of the entryway nevertheless. The
door was solid, there was no window in it, not even a peep-
hole, and he did not want to just open it without knowing
who—

    what

—was on the other side.

He moved quickly over to the front window. He didn't
want to pull the drapes open and draw attention to himself,
but he wanted to get a peek at the pounder. There was a
small slit where the two halves of the drapes met in the mid-

dle of the window, and he bent over to peer through the opening.

Outside on the porch, facing the door, were four men wearing white powdered wigs and satin colonial garb.

He thought for a second that he was dreaming. The surrealistic irrationality of this seemed more nightmarish than real. But he saw one of the men pound loudly on the door with his bunched fist, and from the back of the house he heard the muffled sound of Pam's voice as she comforted Amy, and he knew that this was really happening.

He should open the door, he knew. He should confront these people. But something about that bunched fist and the look of angry determination on the pounder's face made him hesitate. He was frightened, he realized. More frightened than he had been before he'd peeked through the curtains, when he'd still half thought there might be a monster outside.

I will Skin your Children and Eat Them.

These weirdos were connected somehow to Washington's note. He knew that instinctively. And that was what scared him.

He heard Pam hurrying across the living room toward him, obviously alarmed by the fact that the pounding had not yet stopped. She moved quickly next to him. "Who is it?" she whispered.

He shook his head. "I don't know."

He peeked again through the split in the curtains, studying the strangers more carefully. She pressed her face next to his. He heard her gasp, felt her pull away. "Jesus," she whispered. There was fear in her voice. "Look at their teeth."

Their teeth? He focused his attention on the men's

mouths. Pam was right. There was something strange about their teeth. He squinted, looked closer.

Their teeth were uniformly yellow.

Their teeth were false.

George Washington had false teeth.

He backed away from the window. "Call the police," he told Pam. "Now."

"We want the letter!" The voice was strong, filled with an anger and hatred he had not expected. The pounding stopped. "We know you have it, Franks! Give it to us and we will not harm you!"

Mike looked again through the parted curtains. All four of the men were facing the window, staring at him. In the porchlight their skin looked pale, almost corpselike, their eyes brightly fanatic. The man who had been pounding on the door pointed at him. Rage twisted the features of his face. "Give us the letter!"

He wanted to move away, to hide, but Mike forced himself to hold his ground. He was not sure if the men could actually see him through that small slit, but he assumed they could. "I called the police!" he bluffed. "They'll be here any minute!"

The pounder was about to say something but at that second, fate stepped in and there was the sound of a siren coming from somewhere to the east. The men looked confusedly at each other, spoke quietly and quickly between themselves, then began hurrying off the porch. On their arms, Mike saw round silk patches with stylized insignias.

A hatchet and a cherry tree.

"We will be back for you!" one of the men said. "You can't escape!"

"Mom!" Amy called from her bedroom.

"Go get her," Mike said.

"*You* call the police then."

He nodded as she moved off, but even as he headed toward the phone, he knew with a strange fatalistic certainty that the police would not be able to track down these people, that when these people came back—and they *would* come back—the police would not be able to protect him and his family.

He heard a car engine roar to life, heard tires squealing on the street.

He picked up the phone and dialed 911.

He left Pam and Amy home alone the next morning, told them not to answer the door or the telephone and to call the police if they saw any strangers hanging around the neighborhood. He had formulated a plan during the long sleepless hours between the cops' departure and dawn, and he drove to New York University, asking a fresh-faced clerk in administration where the history department was located. Following the kid's directions across campus, he read the posted signs until he found the correct building.

The secretary of the history department informed him that Dr. Hartkinson had his office hours from eight to ten-thirty and was available to speak with him, and he followed her down the hallway to the professor's office.

Hartkinson stood upon introduction and shook his hand. He was an elderly man in his mid- to late sixties, with the short stature, spectacles, and whiskers of a Disney movie college professor. "Have a seat," the old man said, clearing a stack of papers from an old straight-backed chair. He thanked the secretary, who retreated down the hall, then moved back behind his oversized desk and sat down himself. "What can I do for you?"

Mike cleared his throat nervously. "I don't really know

how to bring this up. It may sound kind of stupid to you, but last night my wife and I were . . . well, we were sleeping, and we were woken up by this pounding on our front door. I went out to investigate, and there were these four men on my porch, calling out my name and threatening me. They were wearing powdered wigs and what looked like Revolutionary War clothes—"

The old man's eyes widened. "Washingtonians!"

"Washingtonians?"

"Shh!" The professor quickly stood and closed his office door. His relaxed, easygoing manner no longer seemed so relaxed and easygoing. There was a tenseness in his movements, an urgency in his walk. He immediately sat back down, took the phone off the hook, and pulled closed his lone window. He leaned conspiratorially across the desk, and when he spoke his voice was low and frightened. "You're lucky you came to me," he said. "They have spies everywhere."

"What?"

"Dr. Gluck and Dr. Cannon, in our history department here, are Washingtonians. Most of the other professors are sympathizers. It's pure luck you talked to me first. What do you have?"

"What?"

"Come on now. They wouldn't have come after you unless you had something they wanted. What is it? A letter?"

Mike nodded dumbly.

"I thought so. What did this letter say?"

Mike reached into his coat pocket and pulled out the piece of parchment.

The professor took the note out of the plastic. He nodded when he'd finished reading. "The truth. That's what's in this letter."

Mike nodded.

"George Washington was a cannibal. He was a fiend and a murderer and a child eater. But he was also chosen to be the father of our country, and that image is more important than the actuality."

"Someone else told me that."

"He was right." The professor shifted in his seat. "Let me tell you something about historians. Historians, for the most part, are not interested in truth. They are not interested in learning facts and teaching people what really happened. They want to perpetuate the lies they are sworn to defend. It's an exclusive club, the people who know why our wars were really fought, what really happened behind the closed doors of our world's leaders, and most of them want to keep it that way. There are a few of us altruists, people like myself who got into this business to learn and share our learning. But the majority of historians are PR people for the past." He thought for a moment. "Benjamin Franklin did not exist. Did you know that? He never lived. He was a composite character created for mass consumption. It was felt by the historians that a character was needed who would embody America's scientific curiosity, boldness of vision, and farsighted determination, who would inspire people to reach for greatness in intellectual endeavors. So they came up with Franklin, an avuncular American Renaissance man. Americans wanted to believe in Franklin, wanted to believe that his qualities were their qualities, and they bought into the concept lock, stock, and barrel, even falling for that absurd kite story.

"It was the same with Washington. Americans wanted him to be the father of our country, needed him to be the father of our country, and they were only too happy to believe what we historians told them."

Mike stared at Hartkinson, then looked away toward the rows of history books on the professor's shelves. These were the men who had really determined our country's course, he realized. The historians. They had altered the past and affected the future. It was not the great men who shaped the world, it was the men who *told* of the great men who shaped the world.

"You've stumbled upon something here," Hartkinson said. "And that's why they're after you. That note's like a leak from Nixon's White House, and the President's going to do everything in his power to make damn sure it goes no further than you. Like I said, the history biz isn't anything like it appears on the outside. It's a weird world in here, weird and secretive. And the Washingtonians . . ." He shook his head, "They're the fringe of the fringe. And they are a very dangerous group indeed."

"They all had wooden teeth, the ones who came to my house—"

"Ivory, not wood. That's one of those little pieces of trivia they're very adamant about getting out to the public. The original core group of Washingtonians screwed up on that one, and subsequent generations have felt that the impression that was created made Washington out to be a weak buffoon. They've had a hard time erasing that 'wooden teeth' image, though."

"Is that how you can spot them? Their teeth?"

"No. They wear modern dentures when they're not in uniform. They're like the Klan in that respect."

"Only in that respect?"

The professor met his eyes. "No."

"What . . ." He cleared his throat. "What will they try to do to me?"

"Kill you. And eat you."

Mike stood. "Jesus fucking Christ. I'm going to the police with this. I'm not going to let them terrorize my family—"

"Now just hold your horses there. That's what they'll *try* to do to you. If you listen to me, and if you do exactly what I say, they won't succeed." He looked at Mike, tried unsuccessfully to smile. "I'm going to help you. But you'll have to tell me a few things first. Do you have any children? Any daughters?"

"Yes. Amy."

"This is kind of awkward. Is she . . . a virgin?"

"She's ten years old!"

The professor frowned. "That's not good."

"Why isn't it good?"

"Have you see the insignia they wear on their arms?"

"The hatchet and the cherry tree?"

"Yes."

"What about it?"

"That was Professor Summerlin's contribution. The Washingtonians have always interpreted the cherry tree story as a cannibal allegory, a metaphoric retelling of Washington's discovery of the joys of killing people and eating their flesh. To take it a step further, Washington's fondness for the meat of virgins is well documented, and that's what made Professor Summerlin think of the patch. He simply updated the symbol to include the modern colloquial definition of 'cherry.' "

Mike understood what Hartkinson meant, and he felt sick to his stomach.

"They all like virgin meat," the professor said.

"I'm going to the police. Thanks for your help and all, but I don't think you can—"

The door to the office was suddenly thrown open, and

there they stood: four men and one woman dressed in Revolutionary garb. Mike saw yellowish teeth in smiling mouths.

"You should have known better, Julius," the tallest man said, pushing his way into the room.

"Run!" Hartkinson yelled.

Mike tried to, making a full-bore, straight-ahead dash toward the door, but he was stopped by the line of unmoving Washingtonians. He'd thought he'd be able to break through, to knock a few of them over and take off down the hall, but evidently they had expected that and were prepared.

Two of the men grabbed Mike and held him.

"My wife'll call the police if I'm not back in time."

"Who cares?" the tall man said.

"They'll publish it!" Mike yelled in desperation. "I gave orders for them to publish the letter if anything happened to me! If I was even *late!*"

The woman looked at him calmly. "No, you didn't."

"Yes, I did. My wife'll—"

"We have your wife," she said.

A stab of terror flashed through him.

She smiled at him, nodding. "And your daughter."

He was not sure where they were taking him, but wherever it was, it was far. Although he was struggling as they hustled him out of the building and into their van, no one tried to help him or tried to stop them. A few onlookers smiled indulgently, as though they were witnessing the rehearsal of a play or a staged publicity stunt, but that was the extent of the attention they received.

If only they hadn't been wearing those damn costumes,

Mike thought. His abduction wouldn't have looked so comical if they'd been dressed in terrorist attire.

He was thrown into the rear of the van, the door was slammed shut, and a few seconds later the engine roared to life and they were off.

They drove for hours. There were no windows in the back of the van, and he could not tell in which direction they were traveling, but after a series of initial stops and starts and turns, the route straightened out, the speed became constant, and he assumed they were moving along a highway.

When the van finally stopped and the back door was opened and he was dragged out, it was in the country, in a wooded, meadowed area that was unfamiliar to him. Through the trees he saw a building, a white, green-trimmed colonial structure that he almost but not quite recognized. The Washingtonians led him away from the building to a small shed. The shed door was opened, and he saw a dark tunnel and a series of steps leading down. Two of the Washingtonians went before him, the other three remained behind him, and in a group they descended the stairway.

Mt. Vernon, Mike suddenly realized. The building was Mt. Vernon, George Washington's home.

The steps ended at a tunnel, which wound back in the direction of the building and ended in a large warehouse-sized basement that looked as if it had been converted into a museum of the Inquisition. They were underneath Mt. Vernon, he assumed, in what must have been Washington's secret lair.

"Where's Pam?" he demanded. "Where's Amy?"

"You'll see them," the woman said.

The tall man walked over to a cabinet, pointed at the dull ivory objects inside. "These are spoons carved entirely from the femurs of the First Continental Congress." He gestured toward an expensively framed painting hanging above the cabinet. The painting, obviously done by one of early America's finer artists, depicted a blood-spattered George Washington, flanked by two naked and equally blood-spattered women, devouring a screaming man. "Washington commissioned this while he was president."

The man seemed eager to show off the room's possessions, and Mike wondered if he could use that somehow to get an edge, to aid in an escape attempt. He was still being held tightly by two of the Washingtonians, and though he had not tried breaking out of their grip since entering the basement, he knew he would not be able to do so.

The tall man continued to stare reverently at the painting. "He acquired the taste during the winter when he and his men were starving and without supplies or reinforcements. The army began to eat its dead, and Washington found that he liked the taste. During the long days, he carved eating utensils and small good luck fetishes from the bones of the devoured men. Even after supplies began arriving, he continued to kill a man a day for his meals."

"He began to realize that with the army in his control, he was in a position to call the shots," the woman explained from behind him. "He could create a country of cannibals. A nation celebrating and dedicated to the eating of human flesh!"

Mike turned his head, looked at her. "He didn't do it, though, did he?" He shook his head. "You people are so full of crap."

"You won't think so when we eat your daughter's kidneys."

Anger coursed through him and Mike tried to jerk out of his captors' grasps. The men's grips tightened, and he soon gave up, slumping back in defeat.

The tall man ran a hand lovingly over the top of a strange tablelike contraption in the middle of the room. "This is where John Hancock was flayed alive," he said. "His blood annointed this wood. His screams sang in these chambers."

"You're full of shit."

"Am I?" He looked dreamily around the room. "Jefferson gave his life for us, you know. Sacrificed himself right here, allowed Washingtonians to rip him apart with their teeth. Franklin donated his body to us after death—"

"There was no Benjamin Franklin."

The man smiled, showing overly white teeth. "So you know."

"Shouldn't you be wearing your wooden choppers?"

The man punched him in the stomach, and Mike doubled over, pain flaring in his abdomen, his lungs suddenly unable to draw in enough breath.

"You are not a guest," the man said. "You are a prisoner. Our prisoner. For now." He smiled. "Later you may be supper."

Mike closed his eyes, tried not to vomit. When he could again breathe normally, he looked up at the man. "Why this James Bond shit? You going to give me your whole fucking history before you kill me? You going to explain all of your toys to me and hope I admire them? Fuck you! Eat me, you sick assholes!"

The woman grinned. "Don't worry. We will."

A door opened at the opposite end of the room, and Pam and Amy were herded in by three new Washingtonians. His daughter and wife looked white and frightened. Amy was crying, and she cried even harder when she saw him. "Daddy!" she screamed.

"Lunch," the tall man said. "Start up the barbecue."

The Washingtonians laughed.

The woman turned to Mike. "Give us the letter," she said.

"And you'll let me go? Yeah. Right."

Where was the letter? he wondered. Hartkinson had had it last. Had he destroyed it or ditched it somewhere, like a junkie flushing drugs down the toilet after the arrival of the cops?

And where was Hartkinson? Why hadn't they kidnapped him, too?

He was about to ask just that very question when there was the sound of scuffling from the door through which Pam and Amy had entered. All of the Washingtonians turned to face that direction.

And there was Hartkinson.

He was dressed in a red British Revolutionary War uniform, and behind him stood a group of other redcoats clutching bayonets. A confused and frightened youth, who looked like a tour guide, peered into the room from behind them.

"Unhand those civilians!" Hartkinson demanded in an affected British accent.

He and his friends looked comical in their shabby mismatched British uniforms, but they also looked heroic, and Mike's adrenaline started pumping as they burst through the doorway. There were a lot of them, he saw, fifteen or twenty, and they outnumbered the Washingtonians more than two to one.

Two of the Washingtonians drew knives and ran toward Pam and Amy.

"No!" Mike yelled.

Musket balls cut the men down in midstride.

Mike took a chance and tried his escape tactic again. Either the men holding him were distracted or their grip had simply weakened after all this time, but he successfully jerked out of their hands, broke away, and turned and kicked one of the men hard in the groin. The other man moved quickly out of his way, but Mike didn't care. He ran across the room, past arcane torture devices, to Pam and Amy.

"Attack!" someone yelled.

The fight began.

It was mercifully short. Mike heard gunfire, heard ricochets, heard screams, saw frenzied movement, but he kept his head low and knew nothing of the specifics of what was happening. All he knew was that by the time he reached Pam and Amy they were free. He stood up from his crouch, looked around the room, and saw instantly that most of the Washingtonians were dead or captured. The tall man was lying on the floor with a dark crimson stain spreading across his powder blue uniform, and that made Mike feel good. Served the bastard right.

Both Pam and Amy were hugging each other and crying, and he hugged them too and found that he was crying as well. He felt a light tap on his shoulder and instinctively whirled around, fists clenched, but it was only Hartkinson.

Mike stared at him for a moment, blinked. "Thank you," he said, and he began crying anew, tears of relief. "Thank you."

The professor nodded, smiled. There were flecks of blood in his white Disney beard. "Leave," he said. "You don't want to see what comes next."

"But—"

His voice was gentle. "The Washingtonians aren't the only ones with . . . different traditions."

"You're not cannibals, too?"

"No, but . . ." He shook his head. "You'd better go."

Mike looked at Pam and Amy, and nodded.

From inside his red coat, Hartkinson withdrew a piece of parchment wrapped in plastic.

The letter.

"Take it to the Smithsonian. Tell the world." His voice was low and filled with reverence. "It's *history.*"

"Are you going to be okay here?"

"We've done this before." He gestured toward the tour guide, who was still standing in the corner. "He'll show you the way out." He shook his head, smiling ruefully. "The history biz is not like it appears from the outside."

"I guess not." Mike put his arm around Pam, who in turn pulled Amy toward the door. The tour guide, white-faced, started slowly up the steps.

"Don't look back," Hartkinson advised.

Mike waved his acquiesence and began walking up the stairs, clutching Washington's letter. Behind them, he heard screams—cries of terror, cries of pain—and though he didn't want to, though he knew he shouldn't, he smiled as he led his family out of the basement and into Washington's home above.

Life with Father

I wrote "Life with Father" and "The Pond" for an eco-logical horror anthology titled *The Earth Strikes Back.* Both were rejected. Judging by the title of the book, I figured that most if not all of the stories would deal with the negative effects of pollution, overpopulation, deforestation, etc.

So I thought I'd do something a little different.

My wife is a hard-core recycler. Cans, bottles, newspapers, grocery bags—she saves them all. Even on trips, she brings along plastic bags in which to col-lect our soda cans.

I exaggerated her compulsion for this story.

Anything can be taken to extremes.

—⁓—

Shari has never seen a working toilet. She will—she goes to nursery school next year and I know they have toilets there—but right now she's only seen our toilets. Or what used to be our toilets before Father turned them into station-ary storage containers for soybean chicken.

I don't know why I thought of that. I guess it's because Shari's squatting now over the biodegradable waste recepta-cle that Father makes us pee in. There are two receptacles for our waste. The blue one for urine. The red one for excrement.

I don't know how Shari'll do in school. She's slow, I think. Father's never said anything about it, but I know that he's noticed, too. Shari doesn't catch on to things the way she's supposed to, the way I did. She was three before she could even figure out the difference between the red and blue receptacles. She was four before she said her first word.

Sometimes I want to tell Father that maybe his seed shouldn't be recycled, that there's something wrong with it. Look at Shari, I want to say, look at The Pets. But I love Shari, and I even love The Pets in a way, and I don't want to hurt any of their feelings.

I don't want to get Father mad, either.

So I say nothing.

My period ended a few days ago, and I know I was supposed to wash out my maxi pads in this week's bathwater and then use the water on the outside plants and hang the maxi pads out to dry, but the thought of my blood makes me sick, and I just haven't been able to do it.

I've been saving the maxi pads beneath my mattress, and tomorrow I'm going to stuff them in my underwear and take them to school. I will throw them away in the girl's bathroom, just like everyone else.

I feel wicked and nasty.

I hope Father doesn't find out.

But I know he will when he takes Inventory.

I try to tell Father that we can donate my old clothes to Goodwill or the Salvation Army, that they will recycle my clothes and give them to other people. I hint that I can buy pants and blouses that have been worn by others at those same thrift stores and that this will contribute to the recycling process *and* allow me to have some new clothes, but he will not hear of it. The clothes we have are the clothes we will always have, he tells me, and only after death will they be passed on to someone else.

So he cuts up the material, takes out old stitches, and refashions the cloth into new blouses and pants.

I attend school dressed as a clown, laughed at by my classmates.

When I come home, I feed The Pets. They are kept in an enclosure in the center of the back yard, the low fence surrounding their habitat made from refashioned cans and cardboard. I feed them the crumbs and leftovers from yesterday's meal, mixed in with the compost of our own waste. I think this is wrong, but Father says that our bodies are not as efficient as they should be and that both our solid and liquid waste contain unused nutrients that can be fully utilized by The Pets.

I stand outside their enclosure and I watch them eat and I watch them play. When I am sure that Father is not around, I pick them up and hold them. Their bodies are cold, their skin slimy, their wings rough. I gave them names at one time, and sometimes I can still call out those names, but I'm ashamed to admit that I no longer know to whom they belong. Like everyone else, I can't tell The Pets apart.

I do not know why Father keeps The Pets and why he insists that they be fed, and that frightens me. Father never does anything without a reason or a purpose.

Every so often, when I'm standing there feeding them, I think to myself that their habitat looks like a pen.

* * *

Sometimes I try to tell the kids in my class the horrors of recycling, but I can never seem to find the words to describe what I mean, and they always tell me that they enjoy accompanying their parents to the recycling center on Saturday and dropping off their cans, bottles, and newspapers.

Cans, bottles, and newspapers.

Once, during ecology week, I told my teacher that anything can be carried too far, even recycling. She tried to explain to me that recycling is important, that it will help us preserve the planet for future generations. I said that instead of recycling everything, maybe it would be better if we used things that didn't *have* to be recycled. She said that I didn't understand the concept of environmentalism but that at the end of the week, after I had completed my worksheet and seen all the videotapes, she was certain that I would.

That night I went home and urinated into the blue bucket and defecated into the red.

It is Thursday again, and I know what that means.

I sit quietly on the couch, tearing the sections of today's newspaper into the strips that we will wash and screen and turn into my homework paper. I say nothing as Father enters the living room, but out of the corner of my eye I can see his dark bulk blocking the light from the kitchen.

He walks toward me.

"I feel The Need," he says.

My stomach knots up and I can't hardly breathe, but I force myself to smile because I know that if he can't have me he'll start in on Shari. His seed can't really be recycled (although he tried it once with frozen jars and the microwave, using his semen first as a skin lotion and then as a toothpaste), but he does not want it to go to waste, so when he feels The Need he makes sure that he finds a receptacle where it might do some good. In his mind, impregnating me is better than letting his seed go unused.

That's how we got The Pets.

I take down my pants and panties and bend over the back of the couch, and I try not to cry as he positions himself behind me and shoves it in.

"Oh God," I say, recycling the words he taught me. "You're so good!"

And he moans.

It has been four days since Shari last spoke and I am worried. Father is not worried, but he is unhappy with me. He felt The Need yesterday, and I let him have me, but I could not pretend that I enjoyed it, the way I usually do. He got angry at me because my unhappiness meant that his emotion was not recycled. He does not want anything to go unrecycled. He feels that, in sex, the pleasure that he feels should be transmitted to me. I am supposed to be happy after he takes me and to utilize that transmitted pleasure, to stay happy for at least a day afterward (although usually I'm miserable and sore and feel dirty), and to do something nice for Shari. Shari is supposed to recycle that pleasure again and do something nice for one of The Pets.

But I don't feel happy, and I can't fake it this time.

I tell Shari to lock her door when she goes to bed.

When I come home from school, Shari is crying and strapped to a chair at the dinner table and Father is in the kitchen preparing our meal. I know something is not right, but I say nothing and I wash my hands in last week's dishwater and sit down at the table next to my sister. Already I can smell the food. It is meat of some sort, and I hope

Father has not decided to recycle a cat or dog that's passed away.

No matter what type of animal it is, I know that I will have to clean and carve the bones afterward and make them into forks and knives and toothpicks.

I try not to look at Shari, but I notice that her crying has not stopped or slowed even a little bit and that worries me.

Father comes in with our meal, carrying it on the single large plate that we share in order not to waste water, and it is some kind of casserole. He is grinning, and I know that grin: he is proud of himself. I take a close look at the ingredients of the casserole, at the meat. The piece I poke with my fork is strangely white and rubbery. I turn it over and see on its underside a darkened piece of skin.

Slimy, lizard skin.

I throw down my fork and glare at him and Shari is crying even harder.

"You killed one of The Pets!" I scream.

He nods enthusiastically. "In the future, it may be possible for us to be entirely self-sufficient. We may never have to go outside the family for a source of food. We can create our own meat, nurturing it with our own waste. We'll be the prototype of the family of the future." He grins, gesturing toward the casserole. "Try it. It's good." He picks up a fork, spears a chunk of meat, and puts it in his mouth, chewing, swallowing, smiling. "Tasty and nutritious."

I stare at the food and I realize that it has come from my body and will be going back into my body and will come out of my body again, and I suddenly feel sick. I start to gag, and I run out of the room.

"The yellow container!" Father calls. "Yellow is for vomit!"

I can hear Shari crying louder, the legs of her chair making a clacking noise as she rocks back and forth and tries to get away.

As I throw up into the yellow bucket, I wonder if our dinner is one of The Pets that I had named.

Father is rougher now. He seems crueler than before, and I wonder if it is because I disobeyed him.

I would run away if it wasn't for Shari.

In school we are learning about taking responsibility for our own actions and how we should clean up our own messes without Mommy or Daddy telling us to do so.

It is hard for me not to laugh.

Father says that I have caused him a lot of pain and emotional distress, and he beats me as he prepares to mount me from behind. My pants and panties are down and I am bent over the couch as he pulls out chunks of my hair and slaps my back and buttocks with the hard side of his hand. He is making Shari watch and she starts to cry as he shoves it in and begins thrusting.

I scream for him to stop it, that it hurts, not even pretending to enjoy it this time, but that seems to satisfy him and I know that he thinks he is recycling his negative emotions by imparting them to me.

When he is finished, he hits my face until I am bloody and then leaves the room.

Shari approaches me after he is gone. She stares at me with wide eyes and white face, frightened by what she has seen, and I try to smile at her but it hurts too much.

"Father hurted you," she says. She frowns, thinking for a moment, and she hunkers down next to me. "Is he a vampire?" she whispers.

"Yes," I say. "He's a vampire." I don't know why I'm

saying this, I don't know what thought process made Shari even think of it, but it sounds good to me.

Her eyes get even bigger. "Then we better kill him," she says.

Kill him.

I smile at her and I force myself to sit up. "Yes," I say, nodding at her, wiping the blood from my nose and mouth. "We better kill him."

I make a stake from a recycled piece of broken broom handle that I find in the tool cupboard next to the wash-bucket. Father has been saving that piece of broom handle for some time now, knowing that it has an untapped usage but not knowing what that usage is.

I have found a use for it, and I feel good as I stand next to The Pets' habitat and sharpen the end of the stick.

We kill him while he is sleeping. Shari asks why he sleeps at night if he is a vampire, but I tell her that he is doing it to fool us and she believes me.

Because I am stronger, I hold the pillow over his face while Shari drives the stake through his heart. There is more blood than I expected. A lot more. It spurts everywhere as he screams and his arms and legs thrash wildly around. Both Shari and I are covered with it, but we've both seen blood before, and I think to myself that it's not as bad as seeing my own.

I continue holding the pillow until he is still, until he has stopped moving, until the blood has stopped pumping.

He is smaller in death, and he suddenly looks harmless to me. I remember all of the good things he's done and all of the fun we've had together and I think maybe we made a mistake.

Shari blinks slowly, staring at the stake. "He really was a vampire, wasn't he?"

I nod.

"What we do now?"

I tell her to take our clothes and the sheets and the pillow-cases and wash them in the plant water. We strip and roll up the linens. Naked, I drag Father's body into the processing portion of the garage.

I place the biodegradable bags next to the butcher block, and as I take the knife from the drawer, I plan out where and what I'm going to cut, what I'm going to do with his skin, his blood, his hair. I try to think of the best way to utilize his bones.

Old habits die hard.

Bob

There don't seem to be many traveling salesmen anymore. The Avon Lady and the Fuller Brush Man belong to an older generation, a different time. But a couple of years ago, a traveling salesman actually came to my door. Only I didn't *know* he was a salesman. He was delivering an order for a customer on the next street over and had accidentally gone to the wrong house. *I* thought he was giving me free stuff. It took several minutes to straighten out the mix-up, and by the time I finally closed the door, I had the idea for "Bob."

—⚬—

"I'm *so* glad we found you at home!"

The aggressively overweight woman standing on his doorstep shifted a small black purse from her right hand to her left and fixed Brandon with an exuberant smile. He was still holding on to the half-opened door, but she grabbed his free hand and shook it. "I'm Ida Kimball."

"I'm sorry—" he started to say.

"These are all friends of Libby's." Ida motioned toward the group of women behind her. They smiled at him encouragingly.

Adjusting the small matronly hat on her head, Ida leaned

forward, lowered her voice. "May I use your rest room?" she asked.

He was about to direct her to the Shell station over on Lincoln, but he saw the look of almost desperate pleading in her eyes. "Uh . . . sure." Brandon opened the door wider, stepped awkwardly aside.

Ida fixed him with another blinding smile as she pushed past him. "Thank you *so* much."

"Make yourselves at home, girls!" she called out to the women behind her. "I'm sure Bob won't mind. I'll be back in a jiffy!"

Bob?

"My name's Brandon," he said, but Ida was already striding through the living room, headed for the hallway. "First door on the left!" he told her. She waved a wiggling-fingered hand in acknowledgment.

"There's been some mistake," he said to the other women filing past him.

A thin older lady smiled, nodded. "Of course," she said.

"I don't know who you think I am—"

"It's okay. We're all good friends of Libby's."

"I don't *know* Libby."

"Of course not," the old lady said.

He counted them as they walked past him into his living room. There were six of them altogether, seven including Ida. He stood there numbly, feeling strangely disassociated from what was happening. It was as though he was watching what was going on, viewing it from a distance as he would a movie or an event happening to someone else.

He didn't want to close the door, wanted to make it clear that there had been some mistake and that after Ida finished going to the bathroom they would have to leave, but it was hot outside, humid, and he didn't want to let flies in, so he closed the door and walked into the living room.

Two women, the older lady with whom he'd spoken and a mousy-looking woman with pinkish cat glasses, were snooping around his bookcase, trying to read the titles on the shelves. The others had all sat down on either the couch or the love seat and were quietly, politely, patiently waiting.

There was a roar of water and a rattle of pipes from underneath the house as the toilet flushed, and a few seconds later, Ida emerged into the living room.

She didn't wash her hands, he thought, and for some reason that made him suddenly much more eager to get her out of his house.

"Well, Bob—" Ida began.

"My name's not Bob," he interrupted. "It's Brandon."

"Why, of course it is. But the reason we dropped by today is because of Libby—"

"I don't know Libby."

"Of course you don't. But Libby is—how shall we say it?—going through some tough times. She hasn't exactly been herself, as you might imagine, and, well, we just wanted to meet you first. You know how it is. We just wanted to make sure she was doing the right thing, that she wasn't making a big mistake." She looked around the room, blinked, brightened. "I'm sorry! I forgot to introduce everybody! Where are my manners?"

"That's okay. I think—"

"Girls!" Ida said. "Best faces forward!"

The women straightened and smiled, facing him, acting in unison as though they were in some suburban version of the military and Ida their commanding officer.

"This is Shirley," Ida said, motioning toward the mousy woman with cat glasses still standing next to the bookcase.

"Pleased to meet you," Shirley said, offering an awkward curtsy.

"That's Francine next to her."

The older lady smiled, nodded, and put back the book she'd been examining.

"Alicia and Barbara," Ida said, nodding to the two non-descript women on the love seat. "Elaine and Natalie." The women seated on the couch stared at him, unsmiling.

"I guess that's everyone."

They remained staring at him, apparently waiting for him to speak, and he quickly sorted through a variety of responses in his mind: *Thank you for coming, but I think it's time you go. I enjoyed meeting you, but I'm really busy today. I have a dental appointment and I have to get going. Who are you? Get the hell out of my house.*

But, of course, it was Ida who began talking first. She laid a dry powdery hand on his. "Now, Bob, we don't want to intrude. I know you're probably a very busy man and have a lot of preparations to make, so we'll only take up a few seconds of your time."

He looked from Ida to the other women. They reminded him, for some reason, of his mother and her friends, though he was not quite sure why. There were no outward similarities, and his mother certainly wasn't as pushy as Ida, but something about the dynamic rang a bell.

Ida was smiling. "As I said, we're Libby's friends, so, naturally, we're concerned about her."

"I—"

"—don't know Libby," she finished for him. "I know how these things work."

"How *what* things work?"

"Libby's told us everything." She mimed locking her lips

and throwing away the key. "Don't worry. We won't tell a soul."

He was getting not only frustrated but angry. The intrusion was bad enough, but these constant references to a relationship he was supposed to have with this Libby were really starting to irritate him.

Ida leaned toward him confidingly. "It wasn't always this way, you know. When she and Edward first got married, they were the happiest couple in the world. Libby *adored* Edward. He really was her dream husband. She probably told you they honeymooned in Paris. After that, after they returned, they were still blissfully happy, and it was only as time wore on that they began to . . . you know."

"What?"

"Drift apart, get on each others' nerves, whatever you want to call it. That was when he started mistreating her."

Shirley shook her head. "I've told her a million times she should leave him, get a divorce. It's not as if they have kids." She looked around the room. "I think we've all told her that." Corroborating nods. "But she just couldn't see it. She was always making excuses for him, pretending like it was her fault, saying that if she hadn't screwed up and made chicken for Sunday dinner instead of turkey, or forgotten to fold his underwear properly, nothing would have happened."

Brandon couldn't help himself. "What did he do to her? Did he beat her?"

"You mean she hasn't told you?" Ida clucked disapprovingly. "She should have at least mentioned why she wanted you."

Shirley leaned forward. "I guess you don't like to know too many of the details about it, huh?"

Elaine seemed outraged. "You mean you don't even ask

questions? You just do it for the money? It doesn't matter to you *why* someone would—" She grimaced distastefully. "—*need* your services?"

Ida shushed them. "We're not here to judge you," she told him. "We're here to support Libby."

"I told you—"

"Yes, we know. This is all becoming very tiresome."

"Then maybe you'd better leave."

"Don't get me wrong," Ida said quickly. "I have nothing but the utmost respect for you. We all do. And I don't think any of us intended to suggest otherwise."

Elaine remained silent.

"She needs you. Libby. She really does."

The other women were nodding.

"And we're on her side completely. We totally understand. We're just concerned, that's all."

"Edward's a monster," Barbara said.

Next to her, Alicia nodded. "You can't believe what he does to that poor woman, how much she's had to put up with, and for so long."

Ida agreed. "Oh, he's horrible to her. He makes her do . . . nasty things . . . rude things." She waved her hankied hand at him. "You know what I mean."

He wasn't sure he did, but there were images in his mind of which he was sure these ladies would not approve.

"He'd be better off dead," Ida said matter-of-factly.

He suddenly realized what they'd been getting at, what they thought he did, and his mouth went dry. He looked around the room, at each of them in turn. All eyes were focused on him, the gazes of the women flat, unreadable.

He stood up, shaking his head. "No," he said. And, not knowing what else to say, he repeated it. "No."

" 'No' what?" Shirley asked.

He glanced over at the older lady, saw only open curiosity on her face.

"It's my fault," Ida said quickly. "I'm the one who wanted to come over and . . . check you out. Not that I don't trust Libby's judgment, mind you, but . . . well, that's just the kind of person I am."

"He's a monster," Barbara repeated. "I saw the burn marks on her arms one time, when she was wearing a blouse with real floppy sleeves. She thought I didn't see, but I saw."

"I saw them on her legs," Natalie confided in a whisper. "In the changing room at Mervyn's."

Elaine took a deep breath. "We took my kids to the pool last summer and I saw a bloodstain on the back of her bathing suit bottom. She was *bleeding* back there. She was wearing purple, and I guess she thought it was dark enough, but I could see the stain. It was leaking through."

"He *is* a monster," Ida said.

"Maybe she should just divorce him," Brandon offered.

Shirley shook her head. "No, she won't do that."

"And it's gone far beyond that stage," Elaine said.

Ida nodded. "She knows what she has to do. She's known it for a while, but she just hasn't wanted to admit it to herself."

"Remember the blood in her kitchen, when we went over there that time?" Barbara looked around at her friends. "How it was still dripping down her legs and we pretended like we couldn't see it, and she kept wiping up the bloody footprints but every time she'd walk to the sink to rinse out her washcloth she'd make even more?"

"We remember," Elaine said softly.

Ida closed her eyes, nodded, then opened them again. "Like I said, she's known what she has to do for a while now. She just hasn't known how to go about it. She realized, of course, that she couldn't do it herself. She wouldn't know how, for one thing. And of course she would immediately be put under a microscope. So it had to be someone else, someone new, someone entirely unconnected to her, who couldn't be traced back and who could be counted on to keep quiet." She smiled. "I don't know how Libby came up with you, Bob, but I must say I think she made the right choice."

Brandon sat down, not sure of what to say.

"I heard her say that next time he's going to cut it out of her." Shirley's voice was hushed.

"Next time he's going to kill her," Barbara said.

"Torture her, then kill her," Elaine corrected.

They were all nodding.

"There was a lot of blood in that kitchen." Natalie closed her eyes. "Way too much blood."

"Well, the real reason we came today," Ida said, once again taking control, "is because we couldn't let Libby pay for this herself. She needs all the money she can get, especially afterward, and since we're her friends . . . well, we just didn't think it was right. So we're going to pay for your services, Bob." She glanced at the other women. "Could you leave Bob and me alone for a minute? I'll meet you back out at the van."

The other women stood, said goodbye, and waved, and he nodded as they passed by him and walked out of the living room and through the entryway.

"I didn't want to say anything in front of the girls, because they don't know how much a service like this costs, and some of them are barely making ends meet as it is. So I collected fifty dollars apiece from them and let them think that was enough to cover it. I made up the rest."

She withdrew from her purse a folded check. He unfolded it and looked at the amount.

Fifty thousand dollars.

He tried to press it back into her hand.

"What's the matter? Not enough?" She looked at him. "Sixty? Seventy-five? A hundred? Name the amount." She reached into her purse.

"No," he said. "It's . . . it's too much."

She placed a cold hand on his. "It's worth it."

"I can't—"

"She'll never be right internally, not after what he did. I mean, last time he put her in the hospital. She was in intensive care for two days. I'm afraid that next time he'll do more than that."

"Ida—"

"Bob . . ."

He looked into Ida's eyes, and he had the feeling that she'd known all along he wasn't who they'd kept insisting he was. He looked back at the check.

"I . . . I seem to have misplaced her address," he said.

"That's all right." Ida reached into her purse, withdrew a folded piece of paper on which she'd already written Libby's name and address.

He cleared his throat. "And when was it she wanted me to . . . do it? I seem to have forgotten that as well."

"Tomorrow night. After eleven."

He nodded, found a pen, wrote it down on the paper.

She stood, closing the clasp on her purse, and he followed her silently out of the living room. In the entryway, she turned to face him. She stared at him meaningfully. "Thank you, Bob."

He nodded. "You're welcome," he said.

She smiled at him, then turned and waved to her friends as she walked down the front walkway toward the blue minivan parked on the street.

He closed the door behind her.

Bumblebee

This was one of my first attempts to write for a
"theme" anthology. Generally speaking, I don't like to
write stories following specific guidelines. I find it
difficult to work within constraints, and invariably the
stories turn out to be stilted and inferior. "Bumblebee"
came quickly, however, and turned out pretty well.

Bumblebee, by the way, is a real place, a ghost
town off Black Canyon Highway between Phoenix
and Prescott. When I was a kid, the buildings still had
furniture, but it's been looted over the years and has
become something of a tourist spot. There's even a
sign for it on the highway. I restored it to its former
ghost town glory and moved it to the southwest corner
of the state for the purposes of this story.

—⁂—

Trinidad was still alive when I found him. Barely. Julio had
called and told me that he'd seen the redneck's pickup
heading through the desert north of Cave Creek, hell-bent
for leather on the old dirt road that led to Bloody Basin,
and while Julio wasn't exactly the world's most reliable
songbird, I believed him this time, and I decided to follow
up on it.

I found Trinidad lying facedown in a low drainage ditch. He was easy to spot. The ditch ran right next to the road, and the coyote's red flannel shirt stood out like a beacon against the pale desert sand. I jumped out of the Jeep without bothering to turn off the ignition and slid down the side of the ditch. The redneck hadn't made much of an effort to either cover his tracks or hide the body, which made me think he hadn't intended to kill the coyote, only scare him, but Trinidad was still badly hurt. His face was a swollen demonstration of various bruise types, blood leaked from his nose, mouth, and both ears, and it was clear from the awkward angles at which he held his arms and legs that there'd been a lot of bones broken.

I knelt down next to the coyote. His eyes were closed, and he did not open them even when I called his name. I touched my hand to his bloody cheek, and he moaned, trying to pull away. "You okay?" I asked.

"Bumblebee," he whispered, eyes still closed.

He was obviously far gone, delirious, and I cursed myself for not having fixed the CB in the Jeep. It was a ten-minute drive back to Cave Creek, and nearly an hour's drive back to the nearest hospital in Scottsdale. Phoenix Memorial had a chopper and theoretically could fly over and pick him up, but there was no way to get ahold of them.

I was afraid to move Trinidad, but more afraid to leave him, so I quickly ran up the side of the ditch, opened the Jeep's back gate, spread out a blanket, and slid back down to where the coyote lay. Trinidad was heavier than I thought—it's never as easy to carry a man in real life as it seems to be in the movies—but adrenaline strength let me lift him up the incline. Carefully, I placed him down on the blankets, my arms soaked with the warm wetness of his blood. I closed the gate. "Don't worry," I told him. "I'll get you home safely."

He moaned in agony. "Bumblebee," he repeated.

By the time we reached Cave Creek he was dead.

The sun rose precisely at five forty-five. By six thirty, the temperature was already well into the nineties. The television weatherman on the morning news told me while I was drinking my wake-up coffee that it was going to be "another gorgeous day," and I flipped him off. To him it might be "another gorgeous day," but to those of us with no air conditioners in our cars, who had to work outside of climate-controlled offices, it was going to be another sentence in hell.

I finished my coffee and quickly scanned the newspaper to see if Trinidad's death had made the back pages or the obituary column. Nothing. Nada. Zip. I wasn't surprised. Print space in Arizona newspapers was generally reserved for those with Anglo ancestry. Even Latinos who had crossed over into mainstream success got short shrift, and the passing of people like Trinidad, who were successful only in the immigrant underground, weren't acknowledged at all.

Some days I was ashamed to be white.

Last night, I'd told everything I knew to the police. They dutifully took it down, but the case against the redneck was weak at best, the evidence based solely on hearsay accounts by notoriously unreliable witnesses, and I knew the investigation into Trinidad's death would get the "Phoenix Special"—a two-day open file with no accompanying legwork, and an UNSOLVED stamp on top of the folder. The situation might have been different if Trinidad had been white, if he'd been respectable, but then again it might not. Heat seemed to make a lot of people lazy, especially cops.

Bumblebee.

I'd been puzzling over that all night, unsure if it was supposed to mean something or if it was merely a word dragged from the depths of Trinidad's dying, hallucinating brain. I was going to assume that it was meaningful, that the coyote was trying to tell me something. I owed him at least that much. Besides, death lent weight to mysteriously muttered phrases whether they deserved it or not.

I finished my coffee, finished my paper.

Just before eight, I called up Hog Santucci, a friend of mine who worked downtown in Records, and ran the name by him. It didn't seem to ring any bells, but then it had been a shot in the dark anyway. Even if Trinidad had been trying to tell me something, I still didn't know whether "Bumblebee" was the name of a man, the code word for a booked passage, or the identification of an item or process known only to him.

I figured I'd check with Julio next, see if he knew what the name meant, see if he knew any more about Trinidad's rendezvous with the redneck at the same time.

The redneck.

That son of a bitch was really starting to get to me. Usually, when I take a case or get involved in an investigation, it's easy for me to keep my distance, to maintain my professionalism. I don't make moral judgments, I simply do what I am hired to do, and I only take a job if its parameters are well within the boundaries of legality. This Raymond Chandler crap about straddling the line, or those Bogart and Mitchum movies where the detective always falls for a pretty face and battles for her honor with the villain, that's all bullshit. Pure fiction. But the redneck really was like one of those movie villains, and I hated the son of a bitch. Especially since I couldn't seem to get a single scrap of evidence on him.

What made it even worse was that the redneck seemed to be almost a folk hero to some of the pin-striped pinheads who passed for human in the downtown offices of the INS. It was well known in certain circles that he'd had a hand in the fire that had destroyed one of the big Sanctuary safe houses down in Casa Grande, and that he'd had something to do with those fourteen illegals who'd roasted to death in that abandoned semi outside of Tucson. But while the feds and the locals were making a big show out of fighting it out over jurisdictional rights, both were making only token efforts to dredge up evidence. As they saw it, the redneck was doing their work for them, in his own crudely violent fashion. As a criminal, he was not subject to the same restrictions they were, and in a warped and twisted way they seemed to admire his racist ingenuity.

Strangely enough, I'd been hired by Father Lopez, a priest involved in the Sanctuary movement, to look into the matter. Tired of dealing with the intransigence of the blue uniforms, the gray suits, and the red tape, afraid for the safety of the dozen or so Salvadoran refugees he was hiding in the basement of his church, he'd asked me to see if I could dig up anything on the redneck which could put him away for good. Father Lopez had been threatened more than once, and he knew it was only a matter of time before those threats were carried through.

So far, I'd come up snake eyes, but I was getting close and the redneck knew it. That's why he'd roughed up Trinidad. And that's why the deal had gone wrong. I don't think he'd intended to kill the coyote, but he had. He'd panicked, gone too far, and now the noose was starting to tighten. It was only a matter of time before he slipped up, made a mistake, and I pulled that sucker taut. The law might not be willing to work to bring down the redneck, but they couldn't and wouldn't turn him out if he was dropped, case closed, into their fat blue laps.

Julio was gone when I stopped by his apartment, and his old lady didn't seem to know where he'd gone to. Or at least wasn't willing to inform a cowboy-booted gringo of his whereabouts, so I decided to drop by and see Father Lopez.

At the church it was pandemonium. Father Lopez had made the mistake of telling his guests that Trinidad was walking with God, hoping they'd help him pray for the coyote, but the result had been to panic the refugees. Trinidad had brought most of them over, was their sole symbol of strength and stability in this country, and his killing frightened them badly. They naturally thought that his murder was the result of a death squad bent on tracking them down. When I arrived, Father Lopez was trying to explain that the coyote had been killed by an American, an American acting on his own and not in the employ of their government, but it was clear even to me that few if any of them were buying it. They seemed to want to leave the church now, strike out on their own, and take their chances scattered on the street.

"Father," I said. "I need to talk to you for a minute."

"Hold on." He spoke rapidly in Spanish to the agitated people in the basement, trying to assuage their fears.

My Spanish was nowhere near fluent, but I moved next to the priest, motioned for him to be quiet, and gave the refugees my own version of the story. Since I was white and obviously American, my words carried a little more weight than those of the priest, though they were spoken haltingly. I guess to them I represented some sort of authority.

Father Lopez looked at me gratefully, then expanded on what I'd said, speaking quickly and reassuringly. It seemed to work. I went back upstairs to wait.

After the situation had settled down and Father Lopez

had emerged from the basement, I spoke to the priest alone. We were in his office off the vestibule, and I was seated in a low comfortable chair. I leaned forward. "Does the name Bumblebee mean anything to you?" I asked.

He had been casually reclining in his chair, and suddenly he sat up very straight. His face was pale. "Who told you about Bumblebee?"

"Trinidad," I said. "Although he didn't really tell me. It was the last thing he said before he died."

The priest crossed himself. "No," he said.

"Yes." I stood up. I put my hands in my back pockets and began pacing. "Look," I said. "If there's something I should know, you'd better tell me. When I work for a client, I expect that client to be straight with me, to lay all of his cards on the table. I don't care if you are a priest, I expect you to tell me everything. I'm on your side. And I can't look out for your interests if I don't have all the facts."

Father Lopez seemed to have regained his composure. He nodded slowly. "All right," he said.

"Good." I sat down again. "So what exactly is Bumblebee?"

"It's a town. An old ghost town in the Sonora desert past Tucson. I'm surprised you haven't heard of it. There was a big battle there in the late 1800s between United States troops and a small group of Mexican renegades. The renegades weren't affiliated with the Mexican government, but they were basically fighting the same fight. Only the men at Bumblebee didn't lose their battle, though Mexico eventually lost the war. Seventeen untrained fighters successfully held off and killed over a hundred American troops. The Americans just kept coming, and they just kept getting killed. Finally they gave up, decided to avoid the town and fight elsewhere. I guess they wrote it off as a loss. When the fighting was over and the boundaries were redrawn, however, Bumblebee became part of Arizona. Politics destroyed what war couldn't."

"That's a nice story," I said. "But what does it have to do with Trinidad?"

"I don't know," the priest told me, meeting my gaze.

He was lying. I knew he was lying, and he knew I knew he was lying. I sat unmoving. Father Lopez was neither a stupid nor a cowardly man, and he wouldn't have played albino and crossed himself if there hadn't been something heavy on his mind. Bumblebee and whatever that implied had scared the holy shit out of him, but I knew if I pressed him any further he was going to Pismo up on me, so I decided to drop back. I felt I had enough to work with.

It was time to take a trip.

Bookbinder Baker lived in the desert outside Tonopah amidst the bones and bodies of the cars he'd bought and scavenged over the past forty years. Traded Torinos, abandoned Audis, and roadkilled Ramblers lay bleached and rusted, sinking into the sand surrounding his three-room shack. His property covered nearly twenty acres of the most godawful terrain known to man. Tonopah itself was a town in name only, an all-night gas station and burger stand halfway between Phoenix and the California border which catered almost exclusively to long-distance truckers, and Baker's place was some fifteen miles down a dirt road beyond that, flat in the middle of the sagebrush-infested flatlands. He liked it there, though. Always had.

Baker didn't appear to be around when I arrived, didn't answer either my honks or my call, but I knew he'd be back eventually, and I went inside to make myself at home. As always, his front door was open, screen unlocked, and I simply walked into his living room and sat down on the sagging couch. He'd put a few new hubcaps up on the wall since the last time I'd seen him, and I examined those while I waited.

At one time in the dim and distant past, Baker'd been a teacher of some sort, a historian. He still knew more about the history of the Southwest, major and minute, than anyone I'd ever met. One whole wall of his bedroom was lined with books and magazines on various historical subjects. It was just that now his job and his hobby had been switched. Instead of being a teacher who tinkered with cars on the weekend, he owned an auto yard and studied history on the side, although where he got customers for his auto salvaging service I never could figure out.

I heard the sputtering cough of Baker's engine about five minutes later, and I walked outside to meet him. The tow truck pulled up, empty, in front of the shack. "Hey!" he said. "Long time no care!"

I held up my middle finger, and he laughed.

After the pleasantries, after he'd broken out the beer, we got down to business. I asked him if he'd ever heard of a town called Bumblebee. I repeated Father Lopez's story.

He chuckled. "Hell yes, I remember Bumblebee. That's not its real name, though. That's the American name, given 'cause that's where we got stung. The Spanish name is longer. It means 'magic sands,' or something like that." He took a swig of his beer. "Yeah, I been down there many times, taking pictures, checking the place out. It's kind of like our Alamo, you know? Only it never got as much publicity because there weren't nobody famous died there, and because, well, I guess Texans are just better at talking themselves up than we are."

"But why do you think the priest was so scared?"

"Well, Bumblebee was some type of, I don't know, not

sacred land exactly, but something like that. I wish I had it documented so I could look it up, but it's not anything that's been written about. I just know that the area was supposed to have some sort of significance for the Mexicans, was supposed to have some sort of magic powers. In the treaty, you know, the original boundaries of our state were different. Mexico wanted to keep Bumblebee, give us Nogales. But we wanted a nice square border, and of course they were in no position to argue." He chuckled. "The legend is that it was the magic which let the Mexicans hold off the troops, that even though they got shot they didn't die."

I looked at him, and I suddenly felt cold.

They didn't die?

"Like I said, I been there before," Baker said. "And I'm not saying I believe all that hocus pocus. But I sure as hell don't disbelieve it either."

When I got back to Phoenix it was nearly dark, and I decided to go straight home.

The police were waiting for me when I arrived.

Lieutenant Armstrong was leaning against the hood of a patrol car, and he stood straight as I got out of the Jeep. He had a wad of chaw in his mouth, and he spit at the ground before me as I walked toward him.

"How long've you been here?" I asked.

"Not long. Five, ten minutes." He smiled at me with his mouth, but his piggy eyes remained hard.

"What do you want me for?"

"Want you to take a little ride." He nodded his head, and a uniformed officer opened the car door. He spit.

I stepped over the brown spot on the sidewalk and got into the backseat.

*　　*　　*

I stood at the edge of the county cemetery and looked where Armstrong pointed. Ten or fifteen graves scattered throughout the cemetery had been dug up, caskets and all, leaving only holes and piles of dirt. One of the graves, he had told me in the car, was that of Trinidad.

They waste no time burying "indigents" in Arizona.

"You know anything about this?" the lieutenant asked.

I shook my head.

"Come on, they're your people."

"My people?"

He spit. "You know. Chili eaters. Mesikens. Gonzalez and all them other boys. I know you know what's going on."

"I don't," I said. "I really don't."

Armstrong looked at me. I saw the hate in his eyes. "You want to play it that way?"

"I'm not playing."

He poked me in the chest with a strong fat finger. "You know what you are? You're a traitor. You're . . ." He trailed off, glared at me, unable to think of the word. "What's white on the outside, brown on the inside? The opposite of a co-conut?"

"I don't know," I told him. "But I know that you're round on the outside, brown on the inside."

"What?"

"You're an asshole."

He hit me then, and I went down. The punch had not been that hard, but I was unprepared for it, and it went straight to the stomach. I tried to breathe, tried to gulp air, but my lungs seemed to have atrophied.

Armstrong stared at me, watched me clutching my gut on the ground. His face was impassive, but inside I knew he was smiling. "You can walk home," he said, turning away.

After I stood, after I caught my breath, after I called him a crooked sack of rancid racist pigshit, I did walk home.

The lieutenant spit at me as, halfway down the block, his car drove past.

I woke up the next morning sweating. The fan had crapped out on me sometime during the night, depriving my bedroom of what little air circulation I could afford, and the sheet I'd used to cover myself was sticking to my soaked skin. I was still tired, but not tired enough to remain in bed and brave the heat. I got up and walked to the bathroom to take a cool shower.

Father Lopez's murder was the top story on the morning's newscast.

I stood in the kitchen, still dripping from the shower, the empty coffeepot in my hand, staring dumbly into the living room at the TV. The scene was live. A blond female reporter was standing in the midst of a group of people in front of the church, while in the background, clearly framed by the cameraman, Father Lopez's body lay facedown on the wide front stairs. Even on television, I could see dark blood trickling down the steps in tiny waterfalls.

I heard the name Lopez, the words *murdered* and *Sanctuary movement*, but I was not listening to the reporter. I was already moving, throwing the metal coffeepot into the sink, grabbing my keys, and running out the door.

White-uniformed flunkies from the coroner's office were loading the priest's bagged body into the back of an ambulance when I arrived. Armstrong and another officer were talking closely in hushed tones to a police photographer. The television news crew was packing up and readying to go.

I hadn't known Father Lopez well enough to really feel

sad, that deep emotion reserved for people whose loss will affect the rest of our lives, but I felt hurt, disgusted, and deeply angry. I strode up to Armstrong. "What happened?" I asked.

He looked at me, said nothing, turned away, and continued his conversation with the photographer.

"Who did it?" I demanded.

The lieutenant did not even glance in my direction. "Drive-by," he said.

I started up the church steps. I knew the refugees were long gone, had probably fled at the first sound of gunfire, but I wanted to see for myself.

"Get out of there!" Armstrong said. He was looking at me now. His voice was as loud and ugly as his expression. His pointing finger punctuated each word. "This is a crime scene, and you are not allowed on it. I want no evidence disturbed."

I could have fought him on that, should have fought him—I was a licensed detective whose client had just been murdered—but I didn't feel up to it. Besides, I knew there was probably nothing I could find that the police hadn't already noted. I scanned the crowd, looking for familiar faces. I saw Julio and walked up to him.

The songbird looked sick to me, but when I got closer I saw that it was anger which had distorted his features. Anger mixed with a trace of fear. I stepped up to him. "What happened?" I asked.

He looked up at me, and for a second it was as though he didn't know who I was, then his vision focused. He saw me, recognized me. "It was the redneck," he said.

I nodded. I'd guessed as much.

Julio glanced around, to make sure others in the crowd weren't listening to our conversation. "We got him," he said.

"What?"

He stepped closer to me, until his mouth was next to my ear. I could smell his stale breath. "He's in a safe house."

"What are you talking about? The redneck?"

Julio nodded. "They caught him at a stoplight, called in reinforcements, surrounded him."

"And you didn't—?"

"No cops," he said, answering my unfinished question.

"You know I can't—"

"We're taking him to Bumblebee."

I stood there, staring at him, my next words, my next thought, stuck in my throat. Bumblebee. I didn't know why the songbird was telling me this. I didn't know how he knew about my knowledge of Bumblebee. I suddenly felt cold, chilled, though the morning sun was fiery.

"I'll pick you up," he said. "Tonight."

I wasn't sure I wanted to be picked up. I wasn't sure I was willing to keep this from the police. I wasn't sure about anything.

But then I thought of Trinidad, thought of Father Lopez, thought of those illegals in the semi, thought of the refugees.

"Okay," I agreed.

Julio nodded, and was gone, losing himself in the crowd. I saw Armstrong staring at me, and I turned away.

The songbird didn't show up at my apartment until after eight, almost dark. He pulled next to the curb, honked, and I stepped up to the open passenger window. Julio grinned. There was something about that grin which I didn't like. "Going stag," he said, motioning his head toward the backseat. "Got some extra baggage."

I peered through the back window.

Father Lopez was lying across the rear cushion in his body bag.

"Time's wasting," Julio said, chuckling. "You follow me."

I don't know why I didn't argue, why I didn't say anything, why I didn't ask anything, but I didn't. I simply nodded dumbly, went down to the carport, got in the Jeep, and followed Julio's car down the street toward the freeway. I don't remember what I felt, what I was thinking.

The trip was long. There were a lot of cars on the highway at first, but the farther we drove from the valley, the less crowded the road became, until soon Julio's Chevy taillights were the only ones before me on the road.

It was nearly midnight and we were well past Tucson when I saw Julio pull off the highway onto an unmarked dirt road. For the first time in a long while, I thought of Father Lopez's body lying across the backseat of the car. I thought of the redneck.

We got him.

The words seemed so much more sinister in the darkened moonlit desert. I realized I had no idea what was going on, what had been planned by Julio and his friends, whoever they were. I could have turned back then; I thought about it, but I did not. I had gone too far already. I had to see this through.

The road twisted and turned, snaking down unseen ravines, crossing dry washes and gulches, until my sense of direction was thoroughly confused.

And then we were there.

Bumblebee was not as big as I'd thought it would be, and did not look nearly so much like a fort. I'd imagined something like the Alamo, I suppose because of Baker's story, but the sight that greeted me was far different. Twin rows of parallel buildings ran along both sides of the dirt road, ending at what looked like a church at the far end. The buildings were old, abandoned, like those of any ghost town, but they were primarily adobe. Although there were a few dilapidated wooden structures—a one-room barbershop with a painted pole faded in front of it, a saloon with a long porch and collapsed roof—most of the buildings were a pale, weathered extract of hardened mortared desert sand.

It was then that I noticed that the town wasn't empty. In front of the church at the far end, I saw a large crowd of people, maybe sixty or seventy of them. Looking around, I saw the shadows of their vehicles blending with the surrounding saguaro and cottonwood.

Julio got out of his car.

Father Lopez emerged from the backseat.

I can't say I was surprised. It was something I'd been half expecting ever since Julio had told me this morning that they were taking the redneck to Bumblebee. But I was frightened. Far more frightened than I would have expected. I had dealt with death before, had seen more than my share of bodies, and no amount of blood or gore had ever really bothered me. But the unnaturalness of this, seeing the priest's body lurch out of the back of the car, peeling off the open plastic body bag, scared me. It seemed wrong to me, evil.

I got out of my own car. The town was dark, there were no lights, but the moon was bright enough to see by. Father Lopez walked slowly, awkwardly, like Frankenstein, but his steps grew quicker, stronger, more assured, as he followed Julio down the empty dirt street toward the church. The songbird seemed to have forgotten me, or else he had more important things on his mind than guest etiquette, so I invited myself to pursue the two of them, instinct overriding fear.

We moved down the dirt street. The buildings to my left and right loomed in my peripheral vision like hulking creatures, but I concentrated on the creature before me, the re-animated corpse of Father Lopez.

Magic powers.

Baker had said that he'd felt something here, something supernatural. Maybe it was my imagination, but I seemed to feel something, too. A kind of tingling in the air, a vibration which spread upward through the soles of my shoes as I walked and which grew stronger as I approached the crowd in front of the church. This close, I could see that most of the gathered people were women, Mexican women dressed in traditional funereal peasant garb, black dresses, and lacy mantillas.

With them, held by two or three women at a time, were dead men, men who had obviously died violently. Dead men whose eyes were blinking, limbs were moving, mouths were working. I saw bloodless bullet holes, cleaned knife wounds in pasty flesh.

They all turned to look at us as we approached. I saw similarities in the features of the dead and the living. They were related.

Now Julio acknowledged my presence. As Father Lopez continued on and two older women moved forward to take the dead priest's arms, the songbird backed up and turned to me. "Don't say anything," he warned. "No matter what happens, just watch."

"But—"

"It's up to the women," he said. "They have the faith. They make the rules."

I may not be the smartest guy in the world, but I know

when to shut my trap and go with the flow. And standing in a ghost town in the middle of the desert at midnight, surrounded by walking dead guys and their wives and mothers and daughters, I figured this was one of those times.

Led by the women, the crowd moved into the doorless church.

I followed.

Inside, the building was lit by a double row of candles which lined indented shelves along both side walls. The trappings of Catholicism which I'd expected to see were absent. Indeed, aside from the candles, the church was devoid of any sort of adornment or religious decoration. The crumbling mud walls were bare. There were no pews. I looked toward the front of the elongated room. On the raised dais, where a pulpit would ordinarily be, the redneck stood naked, tied to a post.

I wish I could say that I felt justice was being served, that in some mysteriously primitive way the natural order of things was being put to right, but, God help me, I felt sorry for the redneck. He was crying, tears of terror rolling down his blubbery face, urine drying on his legs. I knew he was crying only for himself, was sorry for his actions only because of the circumstances surrounding his capture, but I suddenly wished that I had told everything to that fat bastard Armstrong and that the redneck was sitting safely in a cell in South Phoenix. He deserved to be punished, but he did not deserve this.

No one deserved this.

But a wish and a nickel will get you a piece of gum. The redneck was not in jail in South Phoenix. He was tied to a porch at the front of this empty church.

And the dead men and their women advanced on him.

The redneck screamed, a high girlish sound which should

have been gratifying but somehow was not. At the front of the room the living and the dead separated, women filing to the left, dead men moving to the right. As I watched, the women fell to their knees and began praying. The sound of their mumbling filled the room. I was chilled, but I was sweating. I stood unmoving next to Julio.

The women sang a hymn, a minor key hymn I did not recognize in a dialect of Spanish which was unfamiliar to me.

In single file, as if part of a ritual, they left the church through a side door in back of the dais.

As one, the dead men stood.

The church was silent now save for the pitiful whimpering of the bound murderer and the amplified beating of my terrified heart. One of the dead men stood apart from the crowd, stepped out of the line, moved forward. I recognized the familiar profile of Trinidad. The blood on the coyote's head had been cleaned off, but his skin was gray, his body anorexically thin. He moved easily, normally, as though still alive, and stepped up to the redneck.

He unfastened the ropes tying the murderer's hands and feet to the post.

Another dead man moved forward, handed Trinidad a pistol, and the coyote put the gun into the redneck's hand.

There was not even a pause. "Die fuckers!" The redneck began shooting the second his fingers touched the trigger, arms twitching in panicked terror, laughing hysterically. Bullets hit the walls, slammed into the dead men. But the reanimated corpses did not fall. The pistol ran out of bullets almost immediately, and the redneck jumped off the dais, trying to escape, using the gun like a blackjack and beating on the heads of the men he had killed. They did not die again, however, and the murderer found himself unable to penetrate the corpses' defensive line.

I heard a scream, the bullwhip sound of a bone cracking. I heard the wet, sickening sound of flesh being ripped.

The dead men were tearing their killer apart.

I left the building. The sight was too much for me; I could not watch. Julio, and two other men I did not know who were standing at the rear of the church, remained watching, not flinching.

I caught my breath outside. I could still hear the screams, but the other, more gruesome and personal sounds of death were mercifully inaudible. The warm night air felt fresh and good after the dank closeness inside the church.

The women waited in front of the building with me. We did not speak. There was nothing to say.

Julio and the two other men emerged ten minutes later. Ten minutes after that, the dead men filed silently out. I had no desire to peek inside the church and see what was left of the redneck.

Julio stepped next to me. The songbird seemed happier than he had earlier, less tense, more confident. "It is done," he said. "We can go."

I looked at him. "That's it?"

He grinned. "What more did you want?"

I turned toward the dead men, now reunited with their loved ones. Women were hugging their departed husbands, kissing their late lovers, taking the corpses into their arms. I saw Trinidad, saw Father Lopez. The priest looked at me, nodded. A young woman I did not know grasped his hand, held it tightly.

I turned away.

What would happen now? I wondered. Where would they go? What would they do? The redneck's victims were still alive, even after their murderer's death, so they had not been resurrected merely for revenge. Would they wander off into the desert, eventually die? Or would they live here—no, exist here—in Bumblebee, set up some sort of dead community, pretend nothing had happened, as though they had not kicked the bucket, as though they were still alive?

I was going to ask Julio, see if he could tell me, but I suddenly realized that I didn't really want to know.

"Let's go," the songbird said. The other two men were already walking back toward the cars. "This part is for the women."

I didn't know what he meant. I didn't ask.

I followed Julio down the empty dirt street. I would talk this over later with Baker. We would sit around his shack, down some beers, and I would tell him what went down. We would get drunker, he would explain to me what this all meant, why the women ran this show, what parallels there were with the past; we would talk it all out, and everything wouldn't seem so goddamn scary, so evil and fucking horrifying as it did right now. Distance would soften this. Time would turn this into history.

I hoped.

I prayed.

I got into my car, started the ignition, looked out the window. I saw the women take the hands of their husbands, lovers, sons, lead them across the street away from the church. Through a crack between the two adobe buildings between which they were walking, I thought I could see a monstrous pile of dried manzanita and sagebrush.

I started my car, passed Julio without waving, and drove back the way I had come.

I turned on the radio. I could get nothing but a Mexican

station, but I didn't care. I just wanted to hear voices. Living voices. I floored the gas pedal.

It was a half hour later when I reached the highway. I looked once in my rearview mirror, and in the middle of the vast black expanse behind me, in the approximate spot where Bumblebee was located, I thought I saw the low glow of a faraway fire.

I turned onto the pavement. I didn't want to think about it. I turned up the radio.

The next glow I saw was the light from Phoenix as I approached the city perpendicular to the dawn.

Lethe Dreams

"Lethe Dreams" was my first major sale. My fiction had been published for years in small press magazines (most notably in David Silva's groundbreaking *The Horror Show*, which published the early work of so many current writers), but I'd never made it to the big time: *The Twilight Zone*. I kept trying, though, and finally, in 1987, "Lethe Dreams" was accepted for *Twilight Zone*'s digest-sized sister publication *Night Cry*. It was a turning point in my career.

According to Greek mythology, Lethe is the river of forgetfulness in the underworld. I came up with the title of this piece first and then built the story around it.

—ᴍ—

"Babies need their sleep," Cindy said. "Whoever heard of letting an infant stay up as late as her parents?" But that meant she was awake and crying only two hours after they'd gone to bed themselves, Marc argued. That meant they had to get up and feed her and comfort her and then try to fall back asleep before getting up again for her early morning feeding. "Why don't we put her to bed the same time we go to bed ourselves?" he asked. "That way she wouldn't wake up until four or five in the morning. It's a hell of a lot easier to get up at five than one."

"She is a baby," Cindy said slowly, shaking her head at him as if he were either too dense or too myopic to see her point. "Babies need their sleep."

"So do adults. Don't you ever get tired of waking up in the middle of the night to feed her? Every night?"

"That's one of the responsibilities of being a parent," she replied, lips tight. "Try, for once, to think of someone other than yourself."

"Look, she sleeps all day anyway. What does it matter whether she sleeps during the night or during the day? What harm can it do to move her schedule up a few hours?"

Cindy turned away from him. "I don't even want to discuss it anymore." She walked into the kitchen and he heard her banging around in the cupboards, loudly letting him know that she was preparing the baby's formula.

Marc slunk back into his chair, gently massaging his temples with the thumb and forefinger of his right hand. His headache had come back, amplified beyond all reasonable measure. The Tylenols he'd taken less than a half hour ago had already worn off. Either they were getting weaker, his headaches were getting stronger, or he was becoming immune to the medicine's effect.

"It's your turn, but I'll take care of her tonight," Cindy called from the kitchen. "How's that?"

He did not even bother to answer.

Jesus, the head . . .

He was sure the headaches were connected somehow to the unnatural hours he'd been keeping for the past two months. His body simply wasn't used to having its rest interrupted each night. His mind, too, was having a difficult time adjusting. For the past week the baby's cries had broken his dreams off in midstream, leaving his waking mind with the vestigal images of a strangely askew reality. He never remembered these dreams in the morning, but in the half-awake feeding interim they played hell with his sensibilities.

Squinting, in the vain hope that it would help relieve his pain, he stood up and walked slowly into the kitchen. He crept past Cindy, stirring the Similac in a pot on the stove, and took the bottle of Tylenol from its place in the round condiment holder in the spice cupboard. He popped off the red childproof cap with the ease of an expert and shoved two of the acidic pills into his mouth, swallowing them without the aid of water.

"You have another headache?" All traces of argument had vanished from Cindy's voice; her tone was gentle and concerned.

He waved her away as though it were nothing, even as the blood pounded agonizingly in his temples. "I'm all right."

She stopped stirring the Similac and turned off the stove burner, placing the formula-filled pot on another, colder, section of the stove. She took his arm. "Come on. Let's go to bed."

"Let's?"

"You know what I mean." She led him firmly down the hall to the bedroom. "You have to make an appointment. This has gone far enough. You've gone through half a bottle of aspirin in one week."

"Tylenol," he said.

"Whatever." She let go of his arm and pointed to the quilt-covered brass bed. "Lie down."

He grinned. "Now you're talking."

Her expression remained serious. "I mean it. You have to go to the doctor and find out what this is."

"I know what it is."

She was shaking her head before he even finished the sentence. "I'm tired of hearing that. Just go to the doctor. Be practical for once."

He let it drop. She fussed around the room for a few moments more, regurgitating her mother's sickbed advice, and went back out to the kitchen to finish preparing the formula. He sat up against the headboard after she'd gone. The headache was better already. The Tylenol worked fast.

He stared at the wall opposite the bed, at the cluster of Impressionist prints Cindy had mounted and framed last winter in a frenzy of decorating madness. She had (or they had, under her direction) also repainted the living room, converting the sterile white-white to a warmer off-white, and had drilled holes into the ceilings of each room in order to accommodate her new menagerie of hanging plants. The entire house had virtually been transformed over the space of a single weekend.

He heard Cindy's quick step clicking down the hardwood floor of the hall from the kitchen to the nursery, where Anne was busily crawling around her playpen, waiting for her dinner. Or her first dinner, to be more precise. There were two more to come.

Marc smiled. Babies were a pain. They cut into sleep time and recreation time. But they were worth it. He closed his eyes for a second . . .

. . . and opened them in blackness. Cindy was sleeping soundly beside him, her bare back pressed against his chest. She had taken his clothes off somehow, while he was asleep, and they were carefully folded over the back of an antique chair. His headache was gone, but his brain was not still. The demon phantasms of a particularly vivid nightmare were imprinted onto the backs of his pupils. He saw them wildly reeling around the room even as he noted the firm substance of reality about him. There was a woman, not unlike Cindy but with torn ragged hair and misshapen grinning teeth, who was somehow, in some way, trying to kill a low-slung scuttling monster.

The images frightened him, made him afraid to get out of bed, made him want to fall back asleep, made him *unable* to fall back asleep. He could see them, or feel them, sneaking around the edges of the room, hiding in shadows just out of range of his peripheral vision. He wanted to wake Cindy up, to have her comfort his nightmare fears the way his sister used to, but something held him back. Instead, he reached over and ran his fingers through the thin part in her silken brown hair, the part which remained perfectly straight and untouched even through the dishevelment of sleep. She stirred under his touch, her back snuggling even closer against him, and he ran his hand down the soft flesh of her thin arm.

Déjà vu.

He pulled his arm back quickly; so quickly that Cindy shifted from her side to her stomach, uttering some incomprehensible moan, before settling back down into deep sleep. He lay there staring at her. The feeling had been so strong, so powerful, so instantaneous, that he had experienced a moment of panic, of intuitive fear. He had done this before. He had lain there on this night, in this position, and had stroked her bare arm in exactly the same way. A certain amount of déjà vu was inevitable in a married relationship, he knew. There are only a finite number of things two people can do within the limited space of a bed. But this had been different. This had been . . . frightening.

But why? What had—?

He had dreamed it.

The answer came immediately and incontrovertibly. He

could feel the beginnings of a headache stirring in the back of his skull. He closed his eyes, thought of nothing, thought of blackness, thought of emptiness. He tried to fall asleep.

He knew he would remember none of this in the morning.

Marc awoke with the alarm clock. But the clock did not say six thirty; it said eight o'clock. Cindy was standing over him smiling, a glass of orange juice in one hand and a half-eaten slice of toast in the other. "I decided to let you sleep in," she said. "How's your head?"

He shook it, to test for pain. There was none. "Fine," he said.

She sat down next to him on the bed. "She was so good last night, you never would've believed it was her. Didn't cry or anything. I fed her her food and she went instantly to sleep. Just like a little angel."

Marc smiled. "Figures. Now that it's my turn, she'll probably be up all night screaming."

Cindy laughed. "Probably." She leaned over to kiss him; her lips tasted faintly of orange juice and peanut butter. "You going to work today?"

"Hell no." He leaned back on the pillow, stretching. "It's another 'staff development' day. Last thing I need is to put up with that crap."

"Good. We'll go on a picnic then. Me, you, and Anne. Our first family outing."

"We've been to the doctor. We've been to the store."

"Those aren't family outings."

"What are they?"

She socked him playfully on the arm. "Just get dressed."

They spent the day at the zoo, and although his headache came back around noon, Marc didn't say anything. He kept smiling, ignored it, and in another hour it had almost completely disappeared. There was one bad moment in the reptile house—a momentary flashback to a nonexistent dreamtime that caused the peach fuzz hairs on the back of his neck to bristle—but it passed as soon as they moved on to the next exhibit.

They got back in time for Anne's midafternoon feeding. The baby had slept through three-fourths of the zoo trip, had slept in the car on the way there and on the way back, and she fell asleep again almost immediately after her bottle. Cindy put her into the crib in their bedroom, and they made love on the living room floor, with the drapes open, the way they used to.

After dinner, Marc announced that he was going to go to bed. Cindy asked if he was still sick, if his headache had come back, but he smiled and said no, he just wanted to get enough rest to go to work tomorrow. He did not mention that he wanted to get in at least four or five hours of sleep before waking up to take care of the baby. He did not mention Anne's sleeping schedule at all. He did not want to jeopardize the peace they had made.

Cindy said she would stay up a while longer; there was an old James Bond movie she wanted to see, one of the Connery Bonds. She would wake him when it was time to feed the baby.

He walked down the hall to the bedroom, left his clothes in a discarded pile on the floor, and crawled into bed. He could hear Anne's thin breathing from the crib at the foot of the bed, whistling low beneath the rhythmic babble from Cindy's TV. He switched off the lamp on the walnut nightstand next to his head and closed his eyes, letting the baby's breath and the TV's talking lull him to sleep.

The dream was strange. Something to do with a small dark closeted room and a wide expanse of unbroken plain.

The room was filled with furtive shadows, its blackness broken periodically by flashing red and blue lights. The plain was completely devoid of all life, and its sandy floor was alternately yellow and white. The two were connected somehow, intertwined with the movements and actions of a terrifyingly evil clown.

Cindy woke him up, as promised, in time for the baby's feeding. Feeling her hands roughly shake him awake, he rolled onto his side and looked at her with half-shut eyes. "You're up already," he said. "You feed her."

Her voice was as sleepy as his. "I'm not up. And it's your turn."

"But you woke *me* up."

"And the alarm woke me up. It's an even trade."

His sleep-numbed brain could not grasp the logic, but he got out of bed anyway, slipping into his robe and lurching down the hallway to the kitchen. Once there, he took a baby bottle from the purifier, a nipple from the drawer, and heated the formula over the stove. The simple act of movement, the sheer effort of standing for several minutes on his feet while he stirred the Similac on the stove, caused him to wake up somewhat. And he was conscious, if not fully alert, as he made his way back down the hall to the bedroom.

Cindy, of course, was fast asleep by the time he returned, and he left the bedroom lights off so as not to disturb her. She had moved the crib from the foot of the bed to a spot right next to her, and he walked around to her side of the bed, holding the warm bottle tightly. He placed the bottle on top of the nightstand and reached into the crib for Anne. He hugged his daughter to him.

The slatted shafts of moonlight which fell through the partially open curtains illuminated the baby's face, and Marc saw the red mouth painted garishly onto her cheesecloth head. One of her eyes was missing, but the other eye—a sewed-on black button—stared knowingly into his. The baby's rag-stuffed arms hung limply at her sides, and her cotton doll legs swung loosely in the air.

Marc held the baby lovingly in his arms. He picked up the bottle from the nightstand and pressed it to her painted lips. The formula dripped down her face, some of it falling onto the floor, the rest being absorbed by the material of her body. When the bottle was empty, he put it aside and rocked the baby slowly in his arms, humming.

"Honey?"

He looked over toward the bed. Cindy was sitting up, smiling, holding her arms out to him. "Let me have her," she said gently.

Marc handed the baby to his wife. She expertly held the small rag doll to her shoulder. Only a single slice of moonlight reached the bed, but it cut across the baby's cheesecloth face, and Marc saw the corners of her red gash mouth creep slowly upward. "Look," he said. "Anne's smiling."

Cindy nodded. "She's happy," she said.

And the baby's legs slowly started to kick.

Paperwork

It has always seemed to me that small towns on the so-called blue highways, those dying communities on old state routes that were bypassed when the interstates were built, have more than their share of windblown trash. Even in towns that are virtually deserted, there are always newspapers and notebook paper and candy wrappers and receipts caught on barbed wire fences, bunched against curbs, plastered on the lower edges of abandoned buildings.

Where do all these papers come from?

And what if their presence isn't as innocent as we travelers think it is?

—m—

Wind buffeted the car as they drove through the desert. Josh could feel it as he held tightly to the steering wheel, though it was not visible in the unmoving branches of the desert plants. There were no other cars on the highway, and he was not sure whether he should pull over and wait out the wind or try to continue on. He was not good at this automotive kind of crap and he usually relied on others around him to determine his behavior in these situations. The car swerved a little to the left as an especially obnoxious gust of wind pushed against the Blazer, and his grip tightened on the wheel. He didn't want to end up overturned on the side of the road—particularly not on this desolate stretch of highway—but he didn't want to stop either. They were late as it was and wouldn't get to Tucson until well after the hotel's check-in time.

As if reading his thoughts, Lydia turned down the cassette player and turned toward him. "Shouldn't we pull over?" she asked. "That wind's kind of strong out there."

He shook his head. "It's not that bad."

They drove for a few moments in silence. There had been a lot of silence on the trip; not relaxed, comfortable silence but tense, awkward silence. Josh had wanted many times to talk to Lydia, to really talk, to recapture that close camaraderie they had once shared, but he had not known how to do it, had not known what to say. He felt that same need to communicate now, but once again his desires and words did not match. "We have to get gas at the next town," he said lamely. "We're almost out."

Lydia said nothing but turned up the cassette player again, as if in answer, and stared out the side window away from him.

Fifteen minutes later they reached a town. The tiny green and white sign read: Clark. Population 1298. Founded 1943.

Like most of the small desert communities they'd passed through since leaving California, Clark was dirty and run-down, little more than a collection of cafes, gas stations, and storefronts stretching along the sides of the highway, with a few shabby homes and trailers behind them to give the town depth.

Josh pulled into the first gas station he saw, a Texaco. The station looked abandoned. Where the paint on the building wasn't peeling, there were large spots of blackened soot or rot. The windows of the office were so covered with dust and grime that it was impossible to see inside, and small dunes of paper trash had collected on the windward side of the old pumps, but the prices on the swinging metal sign were current, and the open garage door indicated that the station was still in operation.

There were no full- or self-service islands, just two lone pumps, and Josh drove across the length of rubber cable which activated the station's bell, pulling to a stop in front of the unleaded pump.

The wind was blowing strong. Josh looked toward the building. The man who emerged from the office peered first around the edge of the opaque window before stepping nervously outside. He was wearing an old Texaco uniform, with pocket patches that carried the promises of two slogans ago, and he wiped his hands compulsively on a greasy red rag. His face was thin and dark, topped by a gray crew cut, and though his features were unreadable from a distance, as he drew closer Josh could see that the man was terrified.

Such naked fear triggered some sympathetic reaction, within Josh, and his first instinct was to take off and get the hell out of there. The man would not be frightened for no reason; there was probably a gunman in the office holding hostages, or a bomb planted near one of the pumps. But Josh knew that his reaction was stupid, and he got out of the car and stretched, bending his knees and raising his arms after the long drive, before moving forward. He nodded politely at the attendant. "Hi."

The man said nothing, but his eyes shifted back and forth across the length of the highway, on constant surveillance. He grabbed the nozzle of the pump before Josh could reach it, and with trembling hands lifted the catch.

"I'll get that," Josh said.

"No, I'll get it." The man's voice was old and cracked, whispery with age, and there was a tremor in it.

Josh unscrewed the gas cap, and the attendant inserted the nozzle.

"Get out of here fast," the old man whispered. "While you can. While they let you."

Josh frowned. He glanced instinctively back at Lydia in the front seat. "What?"

The attendant's eyes widened as he looked over Josh's shoulder. "Here comes one now!"

Josh turned to look but saw only the empty street, dust, and gum wrappers blowing across the sidewalk, propelled by the wind. He turned back. A stray scrap of Kleenex blew against the attendant's leg, the wadded piece of white tissue clinging to his sock, and the man suddenly leaped backward, screaming. The nozzle dropped from his hand, falling to the cement, and a trickle of gas spilled out before stopping.

The Kleenex was dislodged from the man's foot as he leaped about, and it went skittering along the ground toward the open garage door, but the attendant did not stop screaming. He continued to jump up and down in a panic dance, arms flailing wildly, scuffed workboots scraping hard against the ground.

Josh backed up slowly until he was at the door of the car, and he quickly got in, locking the door.

"Let's get out of here," Lydia said. She was staring out the window at the gas station attendant, her face pale.

Josh nodded, putting the key in the ignition. The attendant pounded on the window. "I'll send you the money we owe!" Josh yelled through the closed glass.

"The papers!" the man screamed.

Josh turned the key in the ignition, pumped the gas pedal, and the engine caught. The attendant was still pounding crazily on the window, and Josh pulled away slowly, afraid of running over the old man's feet. The attendant did not follow them across the asphalt as he'd expected, however. Instead, he ran immediately back toward the office, where he slammed shut the door.

Josh looked over at Lydia. "What the hell was that all about?"

"Let's just get out of here."

He nodded. "It's a Texaco station. I'll write to Texaco, tell them what happened, send them the money. It's only a buck or so. We'll find another gas station."

They headed slowly down the highway through town, past a closed movie theater, past an empty store. The wind, which until now had been constant, suddenly increased in power, and the heavy cloud of dust which accompanied it obscured the road like brown fog. They could hear the tiny static scratching of dirt granules on the glass of the windshield. Josh turned on the headlights and dropped his speed from thirty to twenty and then to ten. "I hope it's not going to scratch up the paint job," he said.

They were moving against the wind, and he could feel the Blazer strain against the pressure. The buildings were dark shapes silhouetted against the dim sun. As they moved closer to the edge of town, the dust cloud abated a little, though the wind continued to blow strong. A sheet of newspaper flew up against the windshield, flattening in front of Josh's face. He could not see at all, and he braked to a halt, hoping to dislodge the paper, but it remained plastered on the glass. He opened the door, got out and pulled it off, crumpling it up and letting it fly.

It was then that he noticed the bodies on the ground.

There were four of them, and they lay facedown on the sidewalk as if they had simply fallen there while walking down the street. The three bodies closest to him were entirely unmoving, trash and light debris piled up by the wind in drifts against their sides and shoes, but the body farthest away—that of a young woman—seemed to be trying to get up. Josh took a quick step forward.

"No!" Lydia yelled at him from the car.

He looked back at his wife. Her face was bleached and terrified, her eyes wild with fear.

"Let's call the police!"

He shook his head. "She's alive!"

"Let's get out of here!"

He waved away her protestations and quickly moved forward toward the struggling woman. But she was not struggling. She was not moving at all. The head he had seen trying to raise itself was merely the fluttering of a paper sack that had caught on the woman's hair. The arms attempting to push the body upward were junk food wrappers which had blown against her side and were gyrating in the breeze.

Josh stopped. In a strange objective instant, he saw the entire situation as though it was happening to someone else— the abandoned town, the crazy man at the gas station, the bodies on the sidewalk—and it suddenly scared the hell out of him. He backed up slowly, then turned around, hurrying.

Lydia jumped out of the Blazer, screaming, hitting at her legs. His heart leaped in his chest as he rushed forward. "What is it?" he demanded. "What happened?" But he had already seen the pieces of lipstick-stamped tissue clinging to her legs. Her peeked around the open door, looking into the car. The empty McDonald's bags on the floor were moving and writhing, making whispery crackling sounds. A bent paper straw thrust its way insinuatingly upward through the mess on the floor.

He slammed the door. "We have to get out of here." He

pulled the tissue from Lydia's legs and felt the thin paper twist sickeningly in his hands. He threw the tissues to the wind, which carried them away, then wiped his hands on his pants, grimacing. "Come on." He grabbed Lydia's hand, leading her down the street. She was still crying, and he could feel her muscles trembling beneath his fingers.

They ran across the asphalt.

And stopped.

A line of paper was inching toward them, moving against the wind, toothpick wrappers riding atop lunch sacks, crumpled envelopes and discarded Xerox sheets creeping in tandem along the ground. Josh swiveled around. Behind them, pages from magazines, spent teabags, cigarette butts, price tags, and grocery sacks rolled with the wind. Above them, in the sky, fluttering Kimwipes and paper towels swooped low over their heads then looped upward to make another dive. His pulse raced.

"In here!" He pulled Lydia to the other side of the street, across the sidewalk, and into a convenience store. Or what was left of a convenience store. For all of the racks and shelves had been tipped over, thrown into the narrow aisles. Rotting food lay on the floor, smashed preserves and spilled soft drinks hardened into glue on the white tile. The store was dark, the only light coming through the front glass wall, but it was quiet, free from a maddening howl of the wind outside, and for that they both were grateful.

Josh looked at his wife. She was no longer crying. There was an expression of resolve on her face, a look of determination in her eyes, and he felt closer to her than he had in a long time. Both of them moved forward spontaneously and hugged each other. Josh kissed her hair, tasting dust and hairspray but not caring. She nuzzled his shoulder.

Then they pulled silently away, and Josh grabbed a

nearby display, pushing it against the door. He shoved another small fixture against the door, pressing it hard against the glass. The makeshift barricade would not hold forever, but it would buy them a little time, allow them to think. This was crazy and unbelievable, but they would be able to get out of it if they used their wits.

"Think!" he said. "We need to think! What can we—"

Fire.

"Fire!" he cried. "We can burn them! They're just paper."

Lydia nodded enthusiastically. "We can kill them. It'll work. I'll look for matches. You check by the counter for lighters."

"See if you can find any charcoal or lighter fluid."

She moved toward the back of the small store, stepping over and through the mess, and he hopped the front counter, rummaging through the pile of impulse items on the floor. He noticed that there were no paper products behind the counter.

He was digging through a pile of overturned keychains when, from the back of the store, Lydia screamed; a shrill, hysterical cry so unlike any sound Josh had ever heard her make that it took his burdened brain a second to make the connection. Then he was off and running, vaulting over the front counter and dashing down the nearest aisle to the rear of the building.

She was standing before the row of wall refrigerators which lined the back of the store, mouth open, no sound coming out. He followed her gaze. Behind the glass doors of the refrigerators which had formerly housed beer and milk and soft drinks were the dead naked bodies of eight or nine people, crammed together like sardines. They were facing outward, eyes wide and staring. Toilet paper was wrapped tightly around each of their mouths and wrists and ankles, making them look like hostages.

He instantly grabbed her around the waist, turning her around, away from the sight. He clenched his hands into fists, letting his fingernails dig into his palms, concentrating on the pain in order to clear his mind of fear as he stared through the frosted glass at the bodies. There was terror in each of the dead eyes looking back at him, terror and an even more horrifying fatalism, as if, at the last moment, all of the victims had realized the inevitability of their deaths.

He pressed closer, and it was then that he noticed the cuts. Paper cuts—some long and straight, others short and curved—crisscrossed the chests, legs, and faces of the naked men and women. There was no blood, and the cuts could only be seen at certain angles, but the patterns they formed looked too regular to be random, too precise to be anything but deliberate.

The cuts looked like writing.

Josh put his hands firmly on Lydia's pliant shoulders and led her up the aisle toward the front of the store, away from the refrigerators, looking back as he did so, afraid of seeing a stray movement out of the corner of his eye. But the bodies remained still, the toilet paper wrapped around them unmoving.

"Stay here," he said, leaving Lydia by the front counter. He dashed quickly up and down the chaotic aisles until he found a book of matches and, buried under the sacks of charcoal, a tin of lighter fluid. He ran back to the front of the store. Papers, he saw, were conglomerating against the window and door, fluttering in the wind.

And fluttering against the wind.

He opened the red plastic childproof cap of the lighter fluid. He wasn't exactly sure how he was going to do this, but he was damned if he was going to let the papers get either him or Lydia. He glanced over at her. She seemed to have recovered somewhat and was not dazed with shock as he'd feared she'd be. She seemed cognizant, aware of what was happening, and he thought that she was a hell of a lot stronger than he would have given her credit for.

He pulled away one of the fixtures he'd used to blockade the door. "We're getting out of here," he said. "Think you can make it?"

She nodded suddenly.

He pulled away the shelves. Just in time, he noticed. There was a line of used and dirty Q-tips coming into the store from under the door, sliding silently along the floor, swab to swab, like a giant worm.

Here was a chance to try out his weaponry. He took out a match, struck it, then sprayed lighter fluid on the Q-tips and tossed the match. The tiny swabs went up in flame, twisting into charred blackness. There was agony in their death movements but no sound, and the unnatural sight sent a cascade of goose bumps down his arms. He took a deep breath. "Let's go."

He pulled open the door and leaped back, expecting a flood of paper to come flying into the store, but there was nothing, only wind and dust, and he realized that the papers must have seen his fire demonstration. He looked at Lydia. "Can you hold the lighter fluid?"

"Yes," she said.

He handed her the container, took out a match, and grabbed her hand. They walked outside. Around them, above them, papers fluttered and flew in the strong wind, but there was an empty circle surrounding them, and the circle remained the same size as they moved across the street toward the car. The newspapers which covered the Blazer fled as they approached, and they both got in the driver's side, quickly shutting the door. The McDonald's mess on the floor had disappeared.

He reached for the keys in the ignition, but they were not there. He checked on the floor, patted his pockets, looked over at Lydia. "Do you have the keys?"

She shook her head. "You didn't take them with you?"

"I left them here. Shit!" He slammed his hand against the steering wheel, causing the horn to blat loudly. They both jumped.

Outside, the papers were swirling closer, junk food wrappers inching forward along the ground toward them, ripped posters creeping alongside.

"Let's get back to the gas station," Lydia said.

Josh nodded. "I think they need another demonstration to make sure they leave us alone, though. Get out my side."

They got out of the car, and he doused the front seat with lighter fluid.

"What are you doing?" Lydia demanded. "That's our car! We need it! We'll never get out of here without it!"

"We'll get out." He lit a match and threw it onto the front seat. The cloth seat covers went up in a whoosh of flame, and the papers on the street, obviously agitated, whirled in incoherent frenzy, widening the circle around them.

Josh grabbed his wife's hand again, and they started back toward the gas station. Dust blew into their eyes, stinging. They were halfway there when he saw a car coming along the highway toward them. "A car!" he said excitedly. He moved quickly to the center line and waved his arms back and forth in the classic distress signal.

The car came closer.

"Help!" he yelled. "Help!"

The car sped by, honking its horn.

"Asshole!" Josh yelled in frustration, holding up his middle finger. "Goddamn son of a bitch—"

Lydia put a restraining hand on his arm. "Come on, let's go to the gas station. Maybe that old man can help us."

"He can't even help himself. If he could, he wouldn't still be here."

"There will be other cars. This is a major highway. Someone's bound to stop."

"If we create a disaster," Josh said, nodding. He smiled grimly. "Let's go."

The gas station was empty. They searched the office, the garage, the men's and women's bathrooms, but there was no sign of the attendant. It was now nearly five, and though neither of them said anything, they both realized that it would soon be dark. Although the highway itself was clear save for a few stray pieces of windblown trash, the desert surrounding the gas station was covered with papers and was growing more crowded by the minute.

"What are we going to do?" Lydia asked.

Josh unhooked the hose from one of the gas pumps. "Start a fire."

"What if—?"

"Don't worry," he said.

He pressed down on the handle of the nozzle and poured gas all over the dirt and cement surrounding the two pumps. He stopped pumping and handed her the matchbox, saving a handful of matches for himself. "Go up to the road and tell me when you see a car coming. If anything starts moving toward you, use the lighter fluid and torch it."

She started to say something but saw the look of almost fanatic determination on his face and decided against it. She moved slowly across the pavement toward the highway.

Josh continued to pump gas onto the ground, soaking the

entire area around the pumps. The hose was not very long, but he moved as close to the building itself as he could and watered the cement with it. The papers surrounding the gas station swirled crazily, frenetically.

"A car!" Lydia shouted. "A car!"

Josh dropped the hose, ran toward the edge of his gas pool, and struck a match on the pavement.

It caught, then sputtered out in the wind.

"A car!" Lydia screamed.

He struck another match, dropping it, and the ground exploded in a rush of fire, singeing his face. He ran toward Lydia, feeling the heat against his back, and the second he reached the edge of the highway, there was a thunderous explosion as the pumps blew. The ground shook once, and a moment later pieces of metal fell from the sky. A small hot chunk landed next to Josh's foot and another near Lydia, but none of the fragments touched them.

"Come on!" Josh ran into the highway. The car was not coming from the north but from the south, and he stood in the middle of the northbound lane, waving his arms, frantically pointing toward the burning gas station.

The car pulled to a stop a yard or so in front of them. A middle-aged man with graying black hair and a mustache stuck his head out the window. "What happened?"

"Explosion!" Josh said as he and Lydia ran forward. "We need to get help!"

"Hop in fast," the man ordered. "My wife's going to have a baby, and we don't have time to waste."

They got into the backseat of the car. Looking out the window as the car took off, Josh saw angry papers swarming over the spot where they had stood. Others flew around the spiraling smoke which billowed up from the fire.

He hoped the whole damn town burned down.

Josh reached for Lydia's hand, held it, smiled. But she was frowning, looking forward. In the front seat, the man and his wife were silent. The man was concentrating on the road. His wife, next to him, was bundled beneath a heavy blanket, though the temperature in the un-air-conditioned car was so warm it was almost stifling. "You're going to have a baby?" Lydia asked.

"Yes, she is."

"Where's the hospital?"

"Phoenix."

"But isn't Tucson closer?"

The man didn't answer.

Lydia scooted forward on the seat. "Mrs.—" she began.

"She's asleep." The man's voice was sharp, too sharp, and Lydia moved back, chastened.

Josh's heart gave a warning leap in his chest. Sitting next to the window, directly behind the passenger seat, he had a perfect view of the space between the wife's seat and the door, and he craned forward to get a better look. His muscles tensed as he saw the sleeve hanging off the edge of the seat beneath the blanket, saw the fingers of gum wrappers, the packed tissue paper palm.

But he said nothing, only held Lydia's hand tighter.

"Hope we make it in time," the driver said.

"Yeah," Josh agreed. He looked at Lydia, his mouth dry.

The car sped through the desert toward Phoenix.

The Idol

As teenagers, every time we watched *Rebel Without a Cause*, my brother would invariably suggest that we look for James Dean's lug wrench. We lived in Southern California, so we knew that the scene in which Dean goes on a field trip, has an altercation with one of his classmates, and throws a lug wrench over the side of a wall into some bushes was filmed at Griffith Park Observatory. It must still be there, my brother always argued. The people who made the movie didn't hike down the hillside and go rummaging through the bushes for it after they filmed that scene. What did lug wrenches cost back then? A buck?

He can't have been the only one to come up with this plan, I thought. A lot of people must have thought the same thing over the years.

But what kind of people were they?

—⚏—

"There! Did you see it?" Matt stopped the VCR and rewound the tape for a second. "Watch carefully."

James Dean, cooler than cool in his red jacket, backed away from the group of young toughs. "I don't want any trouble," he said. Realizing that the tire iron in his hand could be construed as a weapon, he cocked his arm and hurled it over the cliff.

Matt pressed the Pause/Freeze button on the remote and the image stopped in midframe. Dean and the gang stared, unmoving, at the long piece of metal suspended in the clear blue sky. Matt hit the Frame Advance button and the tire iron, very slowly, began to fall. He stopped the image just before the camera shifted to another angle.

"See. Right there. Right in those bushes."

I shook my head. "This is stupid."

"No, it's not. Hell, if we can find it, we'll make a fortune. Do you know how much shit like that goes for?"

Matt had taped *Rebel Without a Cause* the night before and was now trying to convince me that we should dig through the bushes down the hill from the Griffith Park Observatory, looking for the lug wrench Dean threw in the film.

"Okay," he said. "Think about it logically. How many people know that that scene was filmed at Griffith Park? Only Southern Californians, right?"

"That narrows it down to two or three million."

"Yeah, but how many of them do you think ever tried this?"

"Lots."

"You're crazy."

"Look, after he died, fans scoured the country trying to find any scrap of memorabilia they could. They were selling napkins he'd touched."

"You really think people went scrambling through the bushes trying to find that piece of metal?"

"Yes, I do."

"Well, I don't. I think it's still there, rusting into the ground."

"Fine. Go look for it. No one's stopping you."

"You know I don't like to drive into Hollywood by my-self." He turned off the VCR. "All you have to do is give me moral support. Just go with me. I'll do all the work. And if I find it, we'll go fifty-fifty."

"No deal."

"Come on."

"Are you deaf or just dumb? The answer is no."

He smiled, suddenly thinking of something. "We could invite the girls. You know, make a day of it: check out the observatory, have a little picnic . . ."

It sounded good, I had to admit. Steph had been after me for the past few weeks to take her someplace new and ex-citing and creative instead of doing the same old dinner-and-a-movie routine, and this might fit the bill.

"All right," I agreed. "But I'm not helping you dig. And if you get arrested for vandalism or something, I don't know you."

Matt grinned. "What a pal."

He left the room to call Julie, and I picked up the remote and changed the channel to MTV.

He returned a few moments later. "She can't go. Her grandpa's coming out from St. Louis this weekend and she has to be there."

"Well—" I began.

"You promised." He knelt before the couch in a pose of mock supplication. "I won't bother you. You won't even no-tice I'm there. I'll just look through the bushes by myself and you two can do whatever your little hearts desire. All you have to do is drive me there and back."

I laughed. "You're really serious about this, aren't you?"

"It's a great idea. Even if someone has thought of this be-fore—which I doubt—I don't think they spent an entire day searching through the bushes to follow up on it."

"You may be right," I told him.

I called Stephanie from his apartment, but she said she couldn't make it either. Finals were coming up and she had some serious studying to do. She'd lost too much reading time already on account of me.

"That's fine," Matt said. "It'll be me and you."

"I'm just driving," I told him. "I'm not going to waste my time following you through the bushes."

"I know," he said.

We stood in the small parking lot just below the observatory, looking over the low stone wall, in the same spot Dean had stood some forty years before. Matt was carefully studying a map he had drawn, trying to figure out exactly where the tire iron had landed. He walked three paces back from the wall and pretended to throw something over the edge. His eyes followed an arc, focusing finally on a copse of high bushes halfway down the hill. He pointed. "That's it. That's where it is."

I nodded.

"Remember that spot. Remember the landmarks next to those plants. We're going to have to recognize it from the bottom."

I nodded again. "Sure."

He laughed, a half-parody of a greedy cackle. "We're gonna be rich."

"Yeah. Right."

He made a note on his map. "Come on. Let's go."

We walked back up to the main parking lot in front of the observatory and drove down the winding road which led to the park below. We paid the dollar toll, splitting it, and pulled into a spot next to the playground.

Matt looked up the side of the hill, then down at his map.

"The way I figure it, we go straight from here, turn left maybe thirty yards in, and keep going up until we hit the big palm tree."

"Right."

We got out of the car, unloaded our shovels from the trunk, looked around to make sure no one was watching us, and hurried into the brush.

I really had intended not to help him, but I'd had to change my tune. What was I going to do? Sit in the car all day while he went traipsing off into the woods?

Besides, it might be fun.

And we might actually find something.

He kept talking as we climbed, and I must admit, his excitement was catching. He was so sure of himself, so confident in his calculations, and I found myself thinking that, yeah, maybe we were the first people ever to search for this thing.

"I'm sure the movie people didn't collect it afterward," he said, hopping a small sticker bush. "You think they'd waste their time digging through acres of brush looking for a cheap, crummy little piece of metal?"

He had a point.

We climbed for over an hour. In the car, we'd made it to the top of the hill in five or ten minutes. But walking . . . that was another story. I'd read somewhere that Griffith Park covered several square miles, and I could easily believe it.

By the time we reached Matt's palm tree, we were both exhausted.

We stopped and sat under the tree for a moment. "Why the hell didn't we bring a canteen?" I asked. "How could we be so fucking stupid?"

Matt was consulting his map. "Only a little farther. Maybe another fifteen or twenty minutes. A half hour at the most."

I groaned. "A half hour?"

He stood, brushing dead leaves off the seat of his pants. "Let's go. The sooner we get there, the sooner we'll be finished."

"What if it's not even the right place?"

"It's the right place. I went over that videotape twenty times."

I forced myself to stand. "All right. Move out."

It figured. The area where Matt thought the tire iron had landed was surrounded by thick, nearly impenetrable bushes, many of then covered with thorns. We jumped over some, slid under others, and a few we just waded through. My shirt and pants now had holes ripped in them.

"You owe me," I said, as we traversed a particularly difficult stretch of ground. I stepped over a monstrous science fiction–looking beetle. "You owe me big time."

He laughed. "I hear you." He grabbed a low tree branch above his head and swung over several entangled manzanita bushes. I followed suit.

"Shit!"

I heard his cry before I landed. I miscalculated, fell on my side, then stood, brushing off dirt.

We were in a small clearing, surrounded on all sides by a natural wall of vegetation. In the middle of the clearing stood a makeshift wooden shed.

And on the shed wall, carefully painted in white block letters was a single word:

GIANT

"They found it. The fuckers found it." Matt dropped his shovel. He looked as though he had just been punched in the gut. "I thought for sure we'd be the first ones here."

I didn't want to rub it in, but I *had* told him so. "I warned you," I said.

He stood in silence, unmoving.

I looked over at the shed, at the white-lettered word—GIANT—and though it was hot out and I was sweating, I felt suddenly cold. There was something about the small crude structure, about its very existence, that seemed creepy, that made me want to jump back over the wall of bushes and head straight down the hill to the car. The fanatic interest and posthumous adulation that surrounded people like James Dean and Marilyn Monroe and Elvis had always disturbed me, had always made me feel slightly uncomfortable, and the shed before me increased that feeling tenfold. This was not part of a museum or a collection, this was some sort of . . . shrine.

And the fact that it was obviously homemade, that it was in the middle of nowhere, hidden in an impossible-to-get-to location, intensified my concern.

I did not want to meet up with the fanatic who had put this together.

Matt still stood silently, staring at the shed.

I feigned a bravery I did not feel. "Let's check it out," I said. "Let's see what's in there."

"Okay." He nodded tiredly. "Might as well."

We walked across the short grass covering the clearing and stepped through the open doorway. After the morning brightness outside, it took our eyes a moment to adjust to the darkness.

Matt's eyes made the transition first. "Jesus . . ." he breathed.

Hundreds, maybe thousands, of photographs were pasted onto the walls of the shed. The pictures were of women, some young, some middle-aged, some old.

All of them were naked.

They were in various poses, and at the bottom of each photo was a signature.

But that was not all.

In the center of the room, embedded in a large square chunk of stone, was the tire iron. The tire iron Dean had thrown. The bottom half of the tool, with its curved chisel end, was sunk deep into the rock. The top half, with its rounded wrench end, stuck straight up. The metal was immaculately polished and showed not a hint of rust.

Obviously someone had been taking care of it.

The chill I'd felt outside returned, magnified.

"Jesus," Matt whispered again. He walked into the center of the room and gingerly fingered the tire iron. "What the hell is this?"

I tried to keep my voice light. "It's what you've been hunting for all morning."

"I know that, dickmeat. I mean, what's *this*?" He gestured around the room.

I shook my head. I had no answer.

He climbed on top of the stone slab and straddled the tire iron. Using both hands, he attempted to pull it out. His face turned red with the effort, the veins on his neck and arms bulged, but the tool would not move.

"You know what this reminds me of?" I asked.

"What?"

" 'The Sword in the Stone.' You know how all those knights tried for years to pull the sword out of the stone but no one could? And then Arthur pulled it out and became king of England?"

"Yeah."

"Maybe if you pull this out, you'll be the next James Dean."

"If I pull it out, we'll both be rich." He strained again, trying to loosen the unmoving piece of metal. He reached down for his shovel and started chipping at the base of the tool.

I watched him for a moment, then let my gaze wander back over the photos on the wall.

The nude photos.

I turned. Before me, level with my eyes, was a photograph of a gorgeous redhead lying on a bed, spread-eagled. Her breasts were small but the nipples were gigantic. Her pubic hair proved that the red hair on her head was natural. The name scrawled across the bottom of the picture was Kim something.

The photograph next to that was taken from behind. A large bald vagina and a small pink anus were clearly visible between the two spread cheeks of the woman's buttocks. Not as visible was her face, blurred in the background and looking out from between her legs. Her name was Debbie.

Next to that was a picture of—

Julie.

I stared at the photo for a moment, unable to believe what I was seeing, unwilling to believe what I was seeing. Julie, Matt's girlfriend, was standing, her arms at her sides, her legs spread apart, smiling at the camera.

I looked away. The pose wasn't that intimate or that graphic. All I could see were her overdeveloped breasts and the thick triangle of dark brown pubic hair between her legs. But I did not like looking at my friend's girlfriend naked. It seemed obscene somehow, my viewing of the photo an invasion of their privacy.

Matt was still trying to pull the lug wrench out of the stone.

I debated with myself whether I should tell him. On the

one hand, he was my friend, my best friend, and I didn't want to see him hurt. On the other hand, this was something he should know about, something he would want to know about, no matter how unpleasant it was, and if I were really his friend I would tell him.

I cleared my throat. "Matt?"

"What?" He did not even bother to look up.

"There's something here you gotta see."

"What is it?"

I took a deep breath. "Julie."

He stopped yanking on the tire iron and jumped off the stone. All the color had drained out of his face. "What are you . . . ? You're not serious."

I pointed at the photo.

He stared at the picture, then looked at the surrounding snapshots. He took a deep breath, then reached out and grabbed the photo of Julie, ripping it off the wall. Beneath her photo was another, older picture of a nude girl with a 1960s beehive hairdo.

"Fuck," he said quietly. He began tearing Julie's photo into tiny pieces, letting the pieces fall onto the dirt. There were tears in his eyes. "Fuck," he repeated.

I knew what he was feeling, but I tried to smooth it over. "Maybe she—"

He turned on me. "Maybe she what? How can you explain this, huh? What possible rational explanation could there be?"

I shook my head. There was nothing I could say.

A tear rolled down his cheek. "Fuck," he said, and the word caught in his throat.

I felt even worse now. I'd never seen Matt cry before, and somehow the sight of that was more disturbing, more intrusive, than having seen Julie naked. I felt as though I should reassure him, touch his shoulder, clap a hand on his back . . . something. But I had never done that before and did not know how to go about it, so I stepped out of the shed, leaving him alone with his pain. If I couldn't give him comfort, I could at least give him privacy.

I thought about Stephanie, and for the first time since we'd started going together, I was glad that she was a hardcore Christian. Her straitlaced morality had frustrated and irritated me in the past, and more than once we had almost broken up because of her unbudging commitment to virginity, but for once I was glad that she did not believe in premarital sex. I might not be getting any, I might be forced to relieve my sexual tension through masturbation, but at least I knew that Steph's picture was not on that wall.

Why was Julie's?

I had no idea. Maybe an ex-boyfriend had posted it there. Maybe—

"It's right through here!"

I jerked my head toward the bushes.

"God, I've been waiting for this since I was ten!"

Two voices, female, coming this way.

There was a sinking feeling in the pit of my stomach. I hurried back into the little building. "Matt!" I hissed. "Someone's coming!"

"What?"

"Two women are coming this way."

He grabbed the shovels from the center of the room and smiled. There was something in that smile that put me on edge. "You mean we're going to catch them in the act?"

I waved him into silence. "We've got to hide!" I whispered.

"Why?"

I didn't know, but I felt it, sensed it, was certain of it. I glanced quickly around the room. In the far corner was a small stack of boxes and packing crates.

"Come on!" I whispered. I led the way over to the boxes, climbed into one, and was grateful to see Matt follow suit.

The voices were close now, just outside the door.

"Do you have your picture?"

"Of course."

We ducked.

I heard them enter the shed. Their voices were silent now, but their shuffling feet were loud. It sounded like there were a lot more than two of them.

I peeked over the rim of the box, my curiosity getting the better of me. There *were* more than two of them. The number was closer to fifteen or twenty. There were the two girls I'd heard talking, both of whom were around sixteen or seventeen, and a bunch of other girls in their late teens. They were accompanied by four or five women in their mid-thirties.

I quickly ducked back down before anyone spotted me.

There were whisperings and shuffling noises, and a few nervous coughs and throat-clearings. One of the middle-aged women spoke up. "You know what to do?"

"My mother explained everything to me," one of the teenagers replied.

"You are a virgin?"

"Yes."

"Good. When you are through, you may place your photo next to that of your mother."

Her mother?

Jesus.

The room grew quiet. Too quiet. I could hear Matt's deep breathing in the box next to mine, and my own breathing sounded impossibly amplified. I was terrified that we would be found out, though I could not say why the prospect of discovery frightened me so badly.

There was the sound of a belt being unfastened, the sound of a zipper. Something dropped onto the dirt, something soft, and it was followed by a low rustling noise. Someone walked into the middle of the shed.

Then there was silence again.

All of a sudden I heard a sharp gasp. A small moan of pain and an exhalation of air. Another gasp.

I had to know what was going on. Once again, I hazarded a peek over the rim of my box.

And immediately crouched back down.

One of the young girls, the prettiest one, was lowering herself onto the tire iron. She was squatting over the stone, completely naked, the rounded end of the lug wrench already inside her. Her face was contorted, physical pain co-existing with what looked like an underlying spiritual rapture.

The other girls and women were crouched on the ground before her, in a similar squatting position, intently watching her every move.

What the hell was going on here? I stared at the faded brown cardboard of my box, breathing deeply. Were these women part of a fanatic James Dean fan club or was this some sort of bizarre cult?

And what about Julie?

The girl gasped loudly, then moaned.

It was not a moan of pain.

The moans intensified, coming loudly and freely, the girl's breath audible in short heavy pants.

I thought of the photos on the walls, the thousands of photos. Had all of those women done this? They must have.

The girl had said that her mother told her what to do. How had the rest of them found out about it? From their mothers?

How many women knew about this shack?

All of the women in Southern California?

Goose bumps rose on my arms and neck. This was wrong, this was unnatural, and though I should have been aroused, I was frightened. I did not understand what was happening, and I did not want to understand.

Julie.

I found myself thinking of those secret societies of old, of horror movies and novels about the eternal mysteries of women and the secrets they could never share with men. I recalled—

Stephanie

—how, invariably, the men who did attempt to penetrate those mysteries were killed.

If Julie knows, Stephanie knows. They're best friends.

The thought burst into my consciousness. I had been assuming that Stephanie was not involved in all this, but maybe I was wrong. Maybe she was. Maybe her picture was here, too, somewhere. Or maybe her mother's was. Both she and her mother had been born in Los Angeles.

But she was religious. She was a Christian. And a virgin.

The girl on the stone had been a virgin, too. Apparently, it was a requirement.

Julie had probably been a virgin when she'd come here.

I crouched lower in the box.

On the stone, the girl gasped her last. I heard her jump onto the ground, and then the shed was filled with the sounds of talking and laughing as the girl was congratulated.

"How do you feel?"

"I'll never forget when it happened to me. Greatest moment of my life."

"Wasn't it wonderful?"

"Could you feel His presence?"

The girl signed her photo with great fanfare and hung it somewhere on one of the walls.

Finally, after another twenty minutes or so, everyone left.

I stayed crouched in the box for another five minutes, just to be on the safe side, then slowly, painfully, stood. I reached over and hit Matt's box. "Come on," I said. "Let's get the fuck out of here."

I glanced over at the tire iron. Even in the diffused light of the shed, it glistened wetly.

I wondered where the girl had put her picture.

Matt stepped silently out of his box. Carrying his shovels, he walked out the door. I stood for a moment alone, glancing around the room at the overlapping layers of photos. Was Stephanie's here somewhere?

Had she fucked James Dean's lug wrench?

The chill returned, and I was suddenly acutely conscious of being alone in the small building.

I hurried outside.

We walked back to the car in silence. I opened the trunk when we reached the parking lot, and Matt threw the shovels inside. We did not speak on the drive home.

I saw Steph the next day, and debated whether or not to ask her about the shed. The question of whether or not she knew of the place was torturing me; my mind had conjured up all sorts of perverse and gruesome scenes.

But in the end, I said nothing.

I decided I didn't really want to know.

A week later, I found the nude Polaroid in her dresser drawer.

She was in the bathroom, getting ready for our date, and I, as usual, was snooping. The photo was lying on top of a pile of panties, and I gingerly picked it up. I had never seen her completely naked, although only a few days before I had finally managed to get her top off in the backseat of my car, and I examined the picture carefully. She was seated, her legs in front of her, knees up, and the pink lips of her vagina were clearly visible.

She was shaved.

I heard the door to the bathroom open, and for a brief second, I considered confronting her with the photo. *Who had taken it? Had she taken it herself with a self-timing camera? Had some guy taken it? Had some girl taken it?* But, almost instinctively, I threw it back on top of her panties and hurried over to her bed, where I quickly grabbed a magazine and leaned back, pretending to read.

The door opened, and I looked up.

The dresser drawer was still open.

I'd forgotten to close it.

Steph noticed immediately. She looked at the drawer and looked at me, but I smiled, feigned innocence, pretended not to see, and she smiled back and surreptitiously closed the drawer.

She walked across the room and sat next to me on the bed. "I forgot to tell you," she said. "I'm going to have to cancel out on next Saturday."

"Why?"

"Something came up."

I threw aside the magazine. "But we've been planning to go to Disneyland for months."

She put an arm around me. "I know, but my mom and a few of her friends are having, like, a picnic, and I have to go."

My mouth was suddenly dry. I tried to lick my lips. "Where?"

"Griffith Park."

"Can I go?"

She shook her head. "I'm afraid not. It's only for us girls this time."

"I won't—"

"No." She smiled, reached over, tweaked my nose. "Jealous?"

I looked at her, looked at the closed drawer, thought for a moment, and shook my head. "No," I said slowly. "No, I guess I'm not."

"The next weekend we'll do something special. Just us."

"Like what?" I asked.

"You'll see."

"You have something planned?"

She nodded.

"Okay," I said.

We kissed.

Skin

I've always loved the roadside attractions that seemed to proliferate in the desert Southwest during the 1960s. When I was a child, my parents would stop at those that had some sort of historical significance, but the gross ones, the tacky ones, the ones that promised the things I really wanted to see were off limits. I'd obtain brochures and pamphlets for these tourist spots at the hotels where we stayed, but that was as close as I'd come to them.

I'll go there myself when I grow up, I thought.

But by the time I grew up, most of them were gone.

"Skin" is an homage to those sorts of ancillary vacation destinations. I couldn't shake my parents' influence completely, though. The house in "Skin" is historically significant. And the family in the story should *not* have stopped there.

—⁂—

The brown-and-white sign at the side of the road was small, and even though he was wearing his contacts, Ed could not read what it said. He slowed the car as they approached. "What's it say?" he asked Bobette.

"It says 'Historical Landmark. Chapman House. One Mile.'"

Ed turned toward the kids in the back. "Want to stop?"

"Okay," Pam said.

Eda shrugged noncommittally.

"We're stopping." Ed drove slowly, allowing the other cars and trucks on the road to pass him, until he saw another brown-and-white sign, identical to the first. He turned off the highway onto the narrow, barely paved road which ran in a straight line across a grassy meadow to the forest on the other side.

"Here we come!" Pam said. She unbuckled her safety belt and began bouncing up and down in her seat.

Bobette, hearing the click of the belt, looked sternly at her daughter over the headrest. "Young lady, you put that back on right now."

"I was just—"

"Right now."

Pam rebuckled her seat belt.

The road continued in an unwavering line, going through the front line of trees and into the forest before finally widening into a closed cul-de-sac in front of a small brown one-room cabin. The cabin was not log but appeared to be made of wood, with a sod roof. One open window and door faced outward.

"All right," Ed announced. "Hop out. We're here."

It had been several hours since they'd eaten lunch at a Burger King in Cheyenne, and all of their legs were cramped and tired. Pam and Eda jumped about, crunching gravel beneath their tennis shoes, while Ed stretched loudly, groaning. Bobette stood in place, exercising isometrically. They had gotten so used to the artificially cooled air in the car that they had not realized how warm it was outside. The temperature was well into the nineties, and there was no wind. Above them, the sky was blue and cloudless, and from the bushes they heard the constant buzz of cicadas.

"I hope they have a bathroom here," Bobette said.

Ed grinned. "There're plenty of bushes."

"Very funny."

"And we have empty Coke cups in the car."

She shook her head. "You're sick."

They moved across the small dirt lot toward the cabin, Ed leading the way. He stopped before another sign, this one mounted on a platform of cemented stones. " 'The Chapman House,' " he read aloud. " 'Built in 1896, the Chapman House is believed to be the oldest extant skin dwelling in Wyoming.' " He frowned. "Skin dwelling?" He walked toward the cabin, the others following. This close, he could see that the cabin was not made from wood as he'd originally assumed but was made from tanned animal hides stretched taut across a wooden frame. In places, the skin had been stretched thin, lending it a translucent quality, and he could see in the direct sunlight a network of spiderweb veins stretching across the wall.

Bobette shivered. "Gruesome."

Ed shrugged. "I suppose building supplies were scarce in those days. Who knows? Maybe they didn't have the right tools to use traditional materials."

"There's a wooden frame," she pointed out. "And there doesn't seem to be any shortage of wood or stone around here."

"Come on, let's go inside."

"I'd rather not."

"Come on."

"I'll wait here."

"Suit yourself." He turned to the girls. "You two coming?"

"Yeah!" Pam said excitedly. She and Eda followed him through the low doorway into the cabin. It was dark inside. The one door and window faced east, and while they probably let in plenty of light during the morning, they let in very little now. Across one wall ran a low bench, also made from animal hide, and in the center of the room was a low pit for fires. The floor was dirt.

They should have been excited, they should have been having fun, they should have at least been interested, but somehow all those emotions left them when they passed through the doorway. Pam and Eda's bubbly conversation died almost immediately, and his own curiosity gave way to a feeling remarkably close to dread. There was something heavy and claustrophobic about the air in the cabin, something undefinable which made all of them feel uncomfortable and ill at ease. He found himself staring at a small round patch of light-colored skin sewn into the wall near the window.

"Ed!" Bobbette called from outside. Her voice was loud, a little too loud, and there was a hint of panic in it.

Grateful for a reason to leave the cabin, he stepped back into the sunlight. The girls followed silently. They hurried over to where Bobette stood reading the rest of the sign. "What is it?"

"The cabin was made with human skin," she said. "Not animal skin. Read this."

He scanned the rest of the text. According to the sign, the Chapman House was one of a series of homes and buildings constructed from human skin in this part of Wyoming during the late 1800s. The builders of the dwellings were not known. He looked at Bobette.

She shivered. "Let's get out of here," she said.

He nodded, motioning for the girls to get into the car. Before closing his own door, he snapped a photograph of the cabin. He didn't really want the picture, but he'd been taking photos of every place they had stopped at and he took this one out of habit, for completeness.

They drove silently back to the highway. Ed tried to concentrate on his driving, but he found himself thinking of the small round patch of skin he had seen near the window of the cabin. He couldn't get it out of his mind, and he couldn't help thinking that the skin had come from the head of a child. The thought disturbed him, and he drove without speaking, speeding along the highway, passing other cars, as if trying to get as far away from the cabin as possible.

A little farther on, they saw another small brown historical landmark sign by the side of the road. Ed sped by, but not before Pam had made out the message. " 'Bone House One Mile,' " she read.

"Can we stop?" Eda asked.

"Not today," Bobette told her. "You and your sister just find something to do for a while."

Bone House, Ed thought. It didn't take much imagination to figure out the material from which that building was made.

He felt the skin prickling on the back of his neck.

The station wagon sped down the highway through the forest. It was late afternoon, and according to his calculations they would reach Singleton by five. He'd made reservations there at a Best Western, and check-in time was supposed to be at four, but he figured they'd hold the room for an extra hour. From Singleton, it was a five-hour drive to Yellowstone, where they'd made reservations at the Old Faithful Inn for four nights.

He felt tired already, worn out, and he couldn't wait until they got to the motel and his head hit the mattress. He just wanted to sleep. He just wanted this day to be over.

They drove into the outskirts of Singleton just before five. The town was tiny, a few homes scattered amongst the trees, an Exxon station, a Shell station, a restaurant, their hotel, a few stores. It was the sort of picturesque town they had been looking for when planning their itinerary—a postcard community.

But there is something a little off about the buildings, Ed thought, as he pulled into the parking lot. *Something is wrong.* And looking up at the wall of the motel he knew exactly what it was.

The buildings were made of skin and bone.

And the bricks used here and there in construction had a peculiarly red tinge.

He backed up immediately, swinging onto the highway.

"What are you doing?" Bobette demanded, grabbing on to the armrest as the car swerved in reverse. "You'll get us all killed."

"We're getting out of here."

"But we have reservations!"

He glanced at their daughters in the backseat. "Look at the buildings," he whispered quietly. "Look at what they're made out of."

Bobette peered out the window then turned back to him, her face bleached white. "This can't be happening."

A man walking down the sidewalk, wearing farmer's overalls and a plaid shirt, waved at them.

"We're getting out of here," Ed said. "I don't care if we have to drive all night."

Their vacation ended early. They went on to Yellowstone, but somehow the geysers and bears and natural beauty did not interest them as much as they'd thought it was going to a few days before, and they returned home after two days instead of four.

They took a different route back, bypassing Singleton entirely.

Usually, after a trip, it was depressing to come home. The house inevitably seemed small and confining after the great outdoors, the neighborhood dull and moribund. But this time they were glad to be back, and both the house and neighborhood seemed cheerful and welcoming. They settled in almost immediately, the temporary communal spirit which had possessed them on the trip—in the comfortable space of the car and in the unfamiliar territories through which they'd traveled—dissipating as they reached familiar ground. They returned to their normal individualized living status: Ed and Bobette holding court in the living room and kitchen, Pam and Eda in their respective bedrooms.

In the past, they'd talked about their vacations almost nonstop for several days after they had ended, Pam in particular, trying to hold on to the feelings they'd experienced, but this time no one made any mention of the trip, and Ed was glad. He dutifully turned in both rolls of film he had taken, and when he got them back a few days later he sorted through them in the car.

And there it was.

He stared at the photo. The Chapman House lay low and dark against the background of trees, the brownish skin in the picture looking almost like wood. He could see clearly the small door and smaller window and saw in his mind's eye that tiny patch of round
infant
skin.

He tore the photo into little pieces, dropping them out the

car window onto the drugstore parking lot, before heading home.

Neither of the girls had been acting much like themselves since they'd returned from the trip, but Eda was quieter than usual that night, as was Pam, and though Bobette tried to get them to talk during dinner, both refused to answer in anything except mumbled monosyllables. After eating, they both went directly to their rooms.

"I don't know what's going on with them," Bobette said, clearing the dishes. "I tried to talk to them today while you were gone but they ignored me, stared right past me as if I wasn't there. I thought maybe you could try to get them to talk. I mean, I know it wasn't the greatest vacation in the world. I know we ran into some strange scary stuff, but nothing actually happened. It's not the end of the world."

Ed nodded slowly, sitting up. "I'll talk to them."

She looked up, dishes in hand. "Thanks, I—"

But he was already out of the room and moving down the hall.

Ed stood outside Eda's closed door, listening, but heard no music, no TV, no talking, no sounds whatsoever. He shuffled across the hall to Pam's door and listened again. He heard whispering from inside the room.

Whispering and a strange whisklike sound.

He pushed open the door.

The girls were both on Pam's bed, holding steak knives they had obviously taken from the kitchen. The classified ad section of the newspaper had been spread over the bed between them, and on top of the newspaper was a partially gutted cat. He stared silently. Large portions of the animal's black-and-white fur had been scraped off, leaving the skin whitish pink. He recognized the cat as Mrs. Miller's pet Jake.

The two girls looked at him, caught, cat blood all over their hands.

He was going to scream at them, to beat them, to tell them that tomorrow the whole damn family was going to see a psychiatrist, but his voice, when it came out, was calm and even. "What are you girls doing?"

"Making a dollhouse," Eda said.

He nodded. "Clean up before you go to bed." He closed the door behind him, heard them lock it, then went out to the kitchen to tell Bobette nothing was wrong.

Two days later, he caught Pam in the garage with the Jancek's dog. This animal was bigger, and she was having trouble with the knife. Next to her, on the floor, was the dollhouse. She and Eda had taken apart their old dollhouse and had stretched over the plastic frame the still-wet skin of Mrs. Miller's cat.

"How's it going?" he asked.

She looked up, startled. Something like horror or disgust passed over her face for a second, then was gone. She returned to her work. "We're learning," she said.

"Where's Eda?"

Pam giggled. "Getting more building materials. She's kind of slow, though."

"You girls be careful."

"We will, Dad," she said.

Ed left the garage, closing the door. Something was wrong. He could feel it, but he couldn't put a finger on it. He could sense that something was not right, that he was behaving oddly, not the way he used to behave, not the way he was supposed to behave, but he did not know what was making him feel like this.

He went into the house, where Bobette was in the living room, pedaling her exercise bicycle while watching *Oprah*.

There was something so ordinary, so wonderfully pretrip about the scene that he just stood there for a moment watching her. The sight triggered something within him, and for a split second he almost remembered what had eluded him in the garage. It perched on the tip of his brain, unable to be articulated by his conscious mind, then retreated once again into the shadows, and he was left only with a strange sadness as he watched his wife exercise.

She glanced in his direction, frowned. "Something wrong?"

He was filled with sudden anger, anger that she could go on with her normal life after the trip as if nothing had happened. Was she so damned stupid and air-headed that she'd forgotten everything already? Of *course* something was wrong.

He just didn't know what it was.

"I'm going to the store," he said.

"Okay." She continued pedaling. "Pick up some milk while you're there."

He nodded absently, then stepped out the door, pulling his keys from his pocket.

He returned several hours later. It was dark and well past dinnertime. He had walked through stores, through shopping centers, knowing he wanted to buy something but not knowing what it was. Then he had seen what he was looking for and everything suddenly clicked into place.

Now he walked across the driveway holding the sack. Pam and Eda came out of the shadows to meet him, and though he had not been expecting them, he was not surprised. He took out the boxes and handed one to each child. "These are for you," he said.

He took out one for himself, dropping the sack on the ground.

They unwrapped the boxes.

Bobette was washing dishes when they came through the door. There was an angry expression on her face and a plate of cold food untouched on the table. She looked up, glaring, as she heard the noise behind her, but the lecture that had been on her lips died when she saw the carving knives in their hands. She looked from Ed to Pam to Eda. "What are you doing?" she asked. Her voice was suddenly shaky, scared.

"The house needs redecorating," he told her.

Bobette tried to back up but there was no place to go. She was flat against the sink. She was too stunned to scream as the three of them moved forward.

Ed smiled. "We're going to wallpaper the living room."

His knife went in first. Pam's and Eda's followed.

The Man in
the Passenger Seat

I was working at a job I hated, and I stopped off one morning on the way to work to get some money from my bank's ATM. I got the money, walked back to my car, and discovered that I'd forgotten to lock the doors. There was a homeless man lurking on the periphery of the parking lot, and I found myself wondering what I would have done if the man had opened the passenger door, sat down, and buckled himself in. How would I get him out of the car? And what if he kidnapped me, made me drive him somewhere?

It would be all right, I thought, as long as he didn't injure or kill me.

At least I'd get out of work for the day.

—ᘏ—

Brian was already late for work, but he knew that if he didn't deposit his paycheck this morning he'd be overdrawn. His credit rating was already hovering just above the lip of the toilet, and he couldn't afford another bounced check.

With only a quick glance at the clock on the dashboard, he pulled into the First Interstate parking lot. He grabbed a pen, a deposit slip, and his paycheck from the seat next to him and sprinted across the asphalt to the bank's instant teller machine. Behind him he heard the sound of a car door slamming, and he glanced back at his Blazer as he pulled out his ATM card.

Someone was sitting in the passenger seat of his car.

His heart lurched in his chest. For a split second he considered going through with the deposit transaction and *then* going back to his car to deal with the intruder—Kendricks was going to be climbing all over his ass for being late as it was—but he realized instantly that whoever had climbed into his vehicle might be attempting to steal it, and he pocketed his card and hurried back to the Blazer.

Why the hell hadn't he locked the car?

He pulled open the driver's door. Across from him, in the passenger seat, hands folded in his lap, was a monstrously overweight man wearing stained polyester pants and a small woman's blouse. Long black hair cascaded about the man's shoulders in greasy tangles. The car was filled with a foul, sickeningly stale smell.

Brian looked at the man. "This is my car," he said, forcing a toughness he did not feel.

"Eat my dick with brussels sprouts." The man grinned, revealing rotted, stumpy teeth.

A cold wave washed over Brian. This was not real. This was not happening. This was something from a dream or a bad movie. He stared at the man, not sure of what to say or how to respond. He noticed that the time on the dashboard clock was five after eight. He was already late, and he was getting later by the second.

"Get out of my car now!" Brian ordered. "Get out or I'll call the police!"

"Get in," the man said. "And drive."

He should run, Brian knew. He should take off and get the hell out of there, let the man steal his car, let the police and the insurance company handle it. There was nothing in the Blazer worth his life.

But the man might have a gun, might shoot him in the back as he tried to escape.

He got in the car.

The stench inside was almost overpowering. The man smelled of bad breath and broccoli, old dirt and dried sweat. Brian looked him over carefully as he slid into the seat. There was no sign of a weapon at all.

"Drive," the man said.

Brian nodded. Hell yes, he'd drive. He'd drive straight to the goddamn police station and let the cops nail this crazy bastard's ass.

He pulled onto Euclid and started to switch over to the left lane, but the man said, "Turn right."

He was not sure whether he should obey the request or not. The police station was only three blocks away, and there was still no indication that the man was carrying any sort of weapon—but there was something in the strange man's voice, a hint of danger, an aura of command, that made him afraid to disobey.

He turned right onto Jefferson.

"The freeway," the man said.

Brian felt his heart shift into overdrive, the pumping in his chest cavity accelerate. It was too late now, he realized. He'd made a huge mistake. He should have run when he had the chance. He should have sped to the police station when he had the chance. He should have . . .

He pulled onto the freeway.

Several times over the past two years, on the way to work, he had dreamed of doing this, had fantasized about hanging a left onto the freeway instead of continuing straight toward the office, about heading down the highway and just driving, continuing on to Arizona, New Mexico, states beyond. But he had never in his wildest imaginings thought that he would actually be doing so while being kidnapped, hijacked, at the behest of an obviously deranged man.

Still, even now, even under these conditions, he could not help feeling a small instinctive lift as the car sped down the on-ramp and merged with the swiftly flowing traffic. It was not freedom he felt—how could it be under the circumstances?—but more the guilty pleasure of a truant boy hearing the schoolbell ring. He had wanted to skip work and shirk his responsibilities so many times, and now he was finally doing it. He looked over at the man in the passenger seat.

The man smiled, twirling a lock of hair between his fingers. "One, two, eat my poo. Three, four, eat some more."

Brian gripped the steering wheel, stared straight ahead, and drove.

There was no traffic, or very little. They traveled east, in the opposite direction of most of the commuters, and the city gradually faded into suburbs, the suburbs into open land. After an hour or so, Brian grew brave enough to talk, and several times he made an effort to communicate with the man and ask where they were going, why this was happening, but the man either did not answer or answered in gibberish, obscene non sequiturs.

Another hour passed.

And another.

They were traveling through high desert now, flatland with scrub brush, and Brian looked at the clock on the dashboard. Ordinarily, he would be taking his break at this time, meeting Joe and David for coffee in the break room. He thought of them now. Neither, he knew, would really miss him. They would file into the break room as they always did, get their coffee from the machine, sit down at the same table at which they always sat, and when they saw that he wasn't there, they'd shrug and begin their usual conversation.

Now that he thought about it, no one at the company would miss him. Not really. They'd be temporarily inconvenienced by his absence, would curse him for not being there to perform his regular duties, but they would not miss him.

They would not care enough to call and see if he was all right.

That's what really worried him. The fact that no one would even know he'd been abducted. Someone from personnel might call his apartment—the machinery of bureaucracy would be automatically set in motion and a perfunctory effort would be made to determine why he was not at work—but there would be no reason to assume that anything bad had happened to him. No one would suspect foul play. And he was not close enough to any of his coworkers that one of them would make a legitimate effort to find out what had happened to him.

He would just disappear and be forgotten.

He glanced over at the man in the passenger seat. The man grinned, grabbed his crotch. "Here's your lunch. I call it Ralph."

Shapes sprang up from the desert. Signs. And beyond the signs, buildings. A billboard advertised "McDonald's, two miles ahead, State Street exit." Another, with the name of a hotel on it, showed a picture of a well-endowed woman in a bikini lounging by a pool.

A green sign announced that they were entering Hayes, population 15,000, elevation 3,000.

Brian looked over at his passenger. A growling *whirr* spiraled upward from the depths of the man's stomach, and he pointed toward the tall, familiar sign of a fast food restaurant just off the highway. "Eat," he said.

Brian pulled off the highway and drove into the narrow parking lot of the hamburger stand. He started to park in one of the marked spaces, but the man shook his head violently, and Brian pulled up to the microphoned menu in the drive-thru. "What are we getting?" he asked.

The man did not answer.

A voice of scratchy static sounded from the speaker. "May I take your order?"

Brian cleared his throat. "A double cheeseburger, large fries, an apple turnover, and an extra-large Coke."

He looked over at the man in the passenger seat, quizzically, but the man said nothing.

"That'll be four-fifteen at the window."

Brian pulled forward, stopping when his window was even with that of the restaurant's.

"Four—" the teenage clerk started to say.

"Gonads!" the man yelled. "Gonads large and small!" He reached over Brian and grabbed the sack of food from the shelf. Before the clerk could respond, the man had dropped to the floor and pushed down the gas pedal with his free hand. The car lurched forward, Brian trying desperately to steer as they sped out of the parking lot and into the street.

The man sat up, dumping the contents of the bag in Brian's lap. The car slowed down, and there was a squeal of brakes as the pickup truck behind them tried to avoid a collision.

"Asshole!" the pickup driver yelled as he pulled past them. He stuck out his middle finger.

The man grabbed a handful of french fries from Brian's lap. "Drive," he said.

"Look—" Brian began.

"Drive."

They pulled back onto the highway.

A half hour later they caught up with the pickup. Brian probably would not have noticed and would have passed the vehicle without incident, but, without warning, the man in the passenger seat rolled down his window, grabbed the half-empty cup of Coke from Brian's hand, and threw it outside. His aim was perfect. The cup sailed across the lane, through the open window of the pickup truck, and hit the driver square in the face. The man screamed in pain and surprise, swerving out of control. The pickup sped off the shoulder and down an embankment, colliding with a small paloverde tree.

"Asshole," the passenger said.

He chuckled, his laugh high and feminine.

Brian looked over at the man. Despite his throwing capabilities, the passenger was grossly overweight and in terrible physical condition, no match for Brian. He turned his attention back to the road. They would have to stop for gas soon—at the next town, if they weren't pulled over first—and he knew that he would be able to escape at that time. He would be able to either run away or kick the shit out of the obese bastard.

But though he wanted desperately to kick the crap out of the crazy fucker, he wasn't sure he really wanted to escape. Not yet, anyway. He didn't seem to be in any physical danger, and if he were to be perfectly honest with himself, he was almost, kind of, sort of having fun. In some perverse, almost voyeuristic way, he was enjoying this, and he knew that if he allowed the situation to remain as is, he would not have to go back to work until they were caught—and he wouldn't even be penalized, he could blame it all on his abduction.

But that was insane. He wasn't thinking right. He'd been brainwashed or something, riding with the man. Like Patty Hearst.

After only a few hours?

"Holy shit," the man said. He laughed to himself in that high-pitched voice. "Holy shit."

Brian ignored him.

The man withdrew from his pants pocket a small, lumpy, strangely irregular brown rock. "I bought it from a man in Seattle. It's the petrified feces of Christ. Holy shit." He giggled. "They found it in Lebanon."

Brian ignored him, concentrating on the road. On second thought, he wasn't having fun. This was too damn loony to be fun.

But the man was finally talking to him, speaking in coherent sentences.

"We need gas," the man said. "Let's stop at the next town."

Brian did not escape at the gas station, though he had ample opportunity. He could have leaped out of the car and run. He could have said something to the station attendant. He could have gone to the bathroom and not come back.

But he stayed in the car, paid for the gas with his credit card.

They took off.

For the next hour or so, both of them were silent, although Brian did a lot of thinking, trying to guess what was going to happen to him, trying to project a future end to this situation. Every so often, he would glance over at his passenger. He noticed that, out here, on the highway, the man did not seem so strange. Here, with the window open, he did not even smell as bad. What had seemed so bizarre, so frightening, in the parking lot of the bank, in the business-suit world of the city, seemed only slightly odd out here on the highway. They drove past burly bikers, disheveled pickup drivers, Hawaiian-shirted tourists, and Brian realized that here there was no standard garb, no norm by which deviation could be measured. Manners and mores did not apply. There were only the rules of the road, broad guidelines covering driving etiquette.

Inside the sealed worlds of individual cars, it was anything goes.

Brian did not feel comfortable with the man. Not yet. But he was getting used to him, and it was probably only a matter of time before he came to accept him.

That was truly terrifying.

Brian squinted his eyes. Ahead of them, on the side of the road, was a stalled car, a Mercedes with its hood up. Standing next to the vehicle, partially leaning against the trunk, was an attractive young lady, obviously a professional woman, a career woman, with short blond hair and a blue jacket/skirt ensemble that spoke of business.

"Pull over," the man said.

Brian slowed, stopping next to the Mercedes.

"That's okay," the woman began. "A friend of mine has already gone to find a phone to call Triple A—"

"Get in the car!" The man's voice was no longer high and feminine but low and rough, filled with authority backed by a veiled threat of violence.

Brian saw the woman's eyes dart quickly around, assessing her options. There was no place to run on the flat desert, but she was obviously trying to decide if she could make it into the Mercedes and close her windows and lock her doors in time. Or if that would even help.

He wanted to tell her to run, to get the hell away from the road, that they wouldn't leave the road to find her, that the man never got out of the car. He wanted to shift into gear and take off, leaving her there safe and unharmed.

But he remained in place and did nothing.

"Get in the car, bitch!" The violence implied in the man's voice was no longer so covert.

The woman's eyes met Brian's, as if searching there for help, but he looked embarrassedly away.

"Get—" the man started to say.

She opened the door and got into the backseat of the Blazer.

"Drive," the man said.

Brian drove.

None of them spoke for a long time. The landscape changed, became less sandy, more rocky, hilly canyons substituting for rolling dunes. Brian looked at the clock on the dashboard. He would be just getting off his afternoon break now, walking through the hallway from the break room to his desk.

"Panties," the man in the passenger seat said.

Brian turned his head.

Frightened, the woman looked from him to the now grinning man. "What?"

"Panties."

The woman licked her lips. "Okay," she said, her voice trembling. "Okay, I'll take them off. Just don't hurt me."

She reached under her skirt, arched her back, and pulled off her underwear. In the rearview mirror, Brian caught a glimpse of tanned thigh and black pubic hair. And then the panties were being handed forward, clean and white and silky.

"Stop," the man said.

Brian pulled over, stopping the car. From the pocket of his blouse, the man took out a black Magic Marker. He laid the underwear flat on his knee and began drawing on the garment, hiding his work with one greasy hand. When he was done, he rolled down his window and reached outside, to the front, grabbing the radio antenna and pulling it back. He quickly and expertly pressed the metal antenna through the white silk and let it bounce back.

The panties flew at the top of the antenna like a flag.

On them he had drawn a crude skull and crossbones.

"Now we are whole." He grinned. "Drive."

The day died slowly, putting up a struggle against the encroaching night, bleeding orange into the sky. Brian's muscles were tired, fatigued from both tension and a day's worth of driving. He stretched, yawned, squirmed in his seat, trying to keep himself awake. "I need some coffee," he said. "I—"

"Stop."

He pulled onto the sandy shoulder.

"Your turn," the man said to the woman.

She nodded, terrified. "Okay. Just don't hurt me."

The two of them traded places, the woman getting behind the wheel as Brian settled into the backseat.

"Drive."

Brian slept. He dreamed of a highway that led through nothing, a black line of asphalt that stretched endlessly through a desolate, featureless void. The voice was empty, but he was not lonely. He was alone, but he was driving, and he felt good.

When he awoke, the woman was naked.

The driver's window was open, and the woman was shivering, her teeth chattering. None of her garments appeared to be in the car save her bra, which was stretched between the door handle and the glove compartment, over the man's legs, and held two thermos cups filled with coffee. From this angle, Brian could see that her nipples were erect, and he found that strangely exciting.

It had been a long time since he'd seen a woman naked. Too long.

He looked at the woman. No doubt she thought that he and the man in the passenger seat were both criminals, were partners, fellow kidnappers. Since she had come aboard, he had not behaved like a prisoner or a captive and had not been treated like one. He had also not made an effort to let the woman know that he was on her side, that they were in the same position, although he was not quite sure why. Perhaps, on some level, he enjoyed the false perception, was proud, in some perverse way, to be associated with the man in the passenger seat.

But that couldn't be possible.

Could it?

His gaze lingered on the woman's nipples. It could. In a strange way, he was glad he'd been kidnapped. Not simply because he'd been given the chance to see a nude woman, but because an experience this extreme gave perspective to everything else. He knew now that, prior to that moment in the bank parking lot, he had not been living. He'd been simply existing. Going to work, eating, going to sleep, going to work. The motions had been comfortable, but they had not been real, not life, but an imitation of life.

This was life.

It was horrible, it was frightening, it was dangerous, it was crazy, and he did not know what was going to happen from one moment to the next, but for the first time in memory he felt truly alive. He was not comfortable, he was not merely existing. Traveling through the darkness toward an unknown destination with an insane man, he feared for his safety, he feared for his own sanity.

But he was alive.

"We killed Father first," the man in the passenger seat said. His voice was low, serious, almost inaudible, and it sounded as though he was talking to himself, as though he did not want anyone else to hear. "We amputated his limbs with the hacksaw made from Mother's bones and sold his parts for change. We killed Sister second, gutting her like a flopping fish on the chopping block . . ."

Brian was lulled by the words, by their rhythm.

Again he fell asleep.

When he awoke, both the woman and the man were standing in front of the car. It was daytime, and they were on the outskirts of a large city. Houston, perhaps, or Albuquerque. The woman was still naked, and there were frequent honks and excited whoops from men who passed by in cars.

Brian stared through the windshield. The man held, in one hand, half of the woman's now torn bra, and he dipped a finger in the attached thermos cup as she fell to her knees. He placed his coffee-wet finger on her forehead as though annointing her.

He returned to the car alone.

Brian watched the naked woman run across the highway and down the small embankment on the other side without looking back.

The man got into the passenger seat and closed his door.

"Where are we going?" Brian asked. He realized as he spoke the words that he was asking the question not as a prisoner, not as a captive, but as a fellow traveler . . . as a companion. He did not fear the answer, he was merely curious.

The man seemed to sense this, for he smiled, and there was humor in the smile. "Does it matter?"

Brian thought for a moment. "No," he said finally.
"Then drive."

Brian looked at the clock on the dashboard and realized that he didn't know what he would ordinarily be doing at this time.

The man grinned broadly, knowingly. "Drive."

Brian grinned back. "All right," he said. "All right."

He put the Blazer into gear.

They headed east.

Comes the Bad Time

"Comes the Bad Time" was inspired by a shape I thought I saw in a slice of tomato. It was not a face, as in the story. It was more like an object. A vase, perhaps. I was certain that I had seen this shape before, although I could not remember where or when, and over the next few days, I found myself not only looking for the object itself but searching for its form and outline elsewhere. "Comes the Bad Time" grew from there.

I never noticed it before, but now that I think about it, quite a few of my stories seem to involve a fear of vegetables. I'm not sure why that is.

—◦—

When I cut open the tomato and saw Elena's face, I knew it was starting again. Jenny was out in the garden, feeding her plants, and I quickly sliced the tomato into little pieces, put the pieces in a baggie, and dumped the whole thing into the garbage sack. She would find out soon enough, but I wanted to stave off the inevitable as long as possible.

On an impulse, I opened the refrigerator and took out our last two tomatoes. I sliced the first one in half and it was fine. I pushed the two pieces aside.

Both of the second halves had formed into a frighteningly accurate caricature of Elena's face.

I felt the fear rise within me. I looked down at the tomato halves and saw the unnatural convergence of red spokes and clear gelatin and seeds. Elena's features, down to her crooked smile, stared back at me, doubled. I cut the pieces into tiny bits, mashed them with the palm of my hand, and dumped them into the garbage sack as well. The bits of tomato that were clinging to the serrated edge of the knife resembled Elena's lips.

I wiped the knife with a paper towel and threw the towel away just as Jenny walked through the door, She was hot and sweaty but happy. In her hand was a small green zucchini. "Look," she said. "Our first harvest of the year."

I tried to smile, but the gesture felt forced and stilted on my face. I watched with horror as she picked the knife up from the sideboard. "Let's wait," I said, attempting to keep my voice light. "You can't eat zucchini raw anyway."

"I just want to see what it looks like."

She cut it open, and she began to scream.

When Elena walked up to our door and asked if she could sleep in the barn, we thought nothing of it. Times were different then, people more open, and we immediately recognized her as one of our own. Her hair was long and blond and stringy, her tie-dyed dress dirty. She was barefoot and alone, and she obviously had no money. It looked as though she'd been walking for days.

I looked at Jenny and she looked at me, and an unspoken understanding passed between us. We would help this girl.

My gaze returned to Elena. She seemed nervous and scared, and I thought she was probably running away from something. Her parents, perhaps. A relationship. It was hard to tell. A lot of people were running in those days.

She stood on the porch, looking around at the farm, afraid to meet our eyes. She said she was just looking for a place to crash for the night. She didn't need any food or any special treatment. She simply wanted a place to lie down and sleep. Of course we said she could stay. Instead of the barn, we told her she could have the couch in the living room, and for that she seemed grateful.

She smiled her crooked smile, and I felt good.

The dinner that evening was pleasant but average. Elena was not a brilliant conversationalist, and we had to ask all the questions. She would respond with monosyllabic answers. Though she looked older, she was only seventeen, and perhaps that was part of the reason.

We could tell that she was tired, so after dinner we set up the bedding on the couch and retired to the bedroom. We heard no sounds from the living room after the first few minutes and assumed she had fallen instantly asleep.

I was awakened hours later by the screaming. I sat immediately upright and felt Jenny do the same next to me. The screams—loud, piercing, and impossibly high-pitched— came in short staccato bursts. I ran into the living room, pulling on a robe, Jenny following.

Elena was having convulsions on the floor. She had fallen off the couch and in the process had knocked over the coffee table and everything on it. Her body was jerking crazily on the floor, her spastically twitching arms running over the broken pieces of a vase, blood flowing from the ensuing cuts. She screamed painfully with each spasm, short harsh cries of unbearable agony, and the expression on her face was one of senseless dementia.

I didn't know what to do. I stood there motionless as

Jenny rushed forward and put a pillow under the convulsing girl's head. "Call the ambulance!" Jenny yelled frantically. "Now!"

I ran for the phone and picked it up. Not knowing the number for the ambulance or police, I dialed the operator.

"Wait!" Jenny screamed.

I turned around. Elena's body was floating in the air, moving upward. She was still having convulsions, and the sight of her spastically flailing body floating above the ground, blood pouring from her wounded arms, made me feel very afraid.

Jenny was stepping back, away from Elena, not sure what to do. I grabbed her, held her tight as the girl's body lowered once again and the convulsions stopped. Her bulging eyes closed, then opened again, normal. She licked her lips and winced as her conscious mind felt the pain in her arms. "I'm okay," she said, her voice weak and cracking. "I'm all right."

"You're not all right," Jenny said firmly. "I'm calling a doctor. And you're not leaving this house until you're completely well."

She stayed with us for a month.

Until she died.

I cut up the zucchini and threw it away while Jenny sat in the living room. When I went in to see her, she was sitting straight-backed on the couch, her hands in her lap, afraid to move. "It's here again," she said.

I nodded.

"What does she want with us? What the hell does she want with us?" She burst into tears, her hands trembling fists of frustration in her lap. I rushed over to comfort her and put my arms around her. She rested her head on my shoulder.

"Maybe this is it," I said. "Maybe it'll stop now."

She looked at me, her expression furious. "You know it won't stop now!"

I said nothing, holding her, and we sat like that for a long time.

Around us, we heard noises in the house.

Elena died suddenly. She had been getting steadily better and she had had no subsequent episodes. She'd been helping Jenny around the house: doing dishes, cleaning, working in the garden. Though she was by no means talkative, she had opened up somewhat and we had gotten to know her. She was a kind, fairly intelligent girl with lots of potential. Both Jenny and I liked her a lot.

That's why her death was such a shock.

We had driven into town for groceries, and Elena had gone along. We'd picked up everything we needed and were almost home when, from the backseat, I heard a low growl. I looked in the rearview mirror and saw nothing. Out of the corner of my eye, I noticed Jenny turning around. "Elena?" she asked.

"I'm fine," the girl said. "It was nothing." Her voice seemed weak and strained, and I thought of the night she had had the fit.

And floated in the air.

We had never told the doctor about the floating. I wasn't sure why. We had not even discussed it between ourselves, and I thought Jenny was probably trying to pretend to herself that it had not really happened. I knew better, and I felt myself grow suddenly afraid.

I pulled into the long dirt driveway that led to our farm and heard the back door of the car open.

"Stop the car!" Jenny screamed.

I braked to a halt, slammed the car into park, and jumped out. Elena was lying on the dirt. Both Jenny and I ran over to where she lay. "Elena!" I said. I bent over her.

Her eyes widened crazily and that look of blank dementia passed over her features. "I'll get you, you bastard," she said, and her voice was little more than a hiss. "I'll get all of you assholes!"

Her body stiffened and was still. Jenny reached down to check for a pulse. She put a hand around Elena's forearm and shook her head at me. Her face was white with shock.

I felt confused, bewildered, but I told Jenny to take the car up to the house and call the police while I stayed with Elena. She hopped in the car and took off in a cloud of dust, tires sliding. I stared down at the girl. I half expected her to float, to break apart before my eyes, to do something strange and terrifying, but her dead form lay unmoving on the dirt.

The police came, and the coroner, and we had her body cremated. We could find no family or friends, nor could the police, and we scattered her ashes on the hill in back of the barn, where she had liked to lie and stare up at the clouds.

Jenny was right, I knew. It would not stop with the vegetables. It never did. I too was filled with a sense of dread and terror, but I did my best to conceal it. Jenny needed my support.

The first time it had happened was a few years after Elena's death. That day, we could see the wind. It was clear but visible, and it swirled in the sky following billowy paths to nowhere. We sat outside, watching the wind with amazement. The few clouds above us moved quickly, propelled by the visible wind, converging.

They formed a shape. A face. Elena's face.

I saw it but did not comment on it, my mind noting the

fact but not accepting it. The wind dissipated, died, the clouds floated on. We sat there awhile longer, then went into the house. We made dinner together, ate, read our respective books, and went into the bedroom.

The sheets and bedspread had been twisted and molded into the shape of a young woman in the throes of a convulsive fit.

We both saw this manifestation, and we both screamed. Jenny ran out of the room, panicked, and I grabbed a corner of the bedspread and pulled. The cloth sculpture fell into instant disarray.

It went on from there.

For a while, the bad time came every year. One season, we decided to leave the farm, go on vacation, get away from it. We hoped to be gone when the occurrences escalated and to come back after everything had settled back down. When Jenny saw Elena's face in the pattern of autumn leaves that had fallen from one of our trees—a relatively benign manifestation—we packed our belongings and left, before the real horrors started. We were gone for two weeks, but when we came back the occurrences continued as if we had never left.

We thought of moving the next year, had even gone so far as to look for another place. We found a smaller farm upstate, but when the realtor showed us around the property, we saw Elena's silhouette in the convergence of bushes on the hill above the house. And we knew we could never escape.

The bad time did not come for several years after that. But then it came twice one fall. It has come sporadically in the succeeding years, but it has never gone away. The last time it happened, Jenny was almost killed, and as I looked at her now I could tell that she was terrified. I felt helpless and afraid myself. I didn't know what we could do.

We ate frozen pizza that night, not daring to look down at our food, afraid of seeing unnatural patterns in the placement of the pepperoni. The noises around us grew, and we ate with the television on. Beneath Dan Rather's voice, I heard scratchings on the roof and arrhythmic knockings from the basement. Once, I thought I heard high staccato screaming from the barn. I glanced over at Jenny, but she seemed not to have noticed it and I didn't say a thing.

Neither of us took a shower after what had happened the last time.

"What does she want with us?" Jenny whispered fearfully after we had crawled into bed. "What did we ever do to her? We only tried to help her."

"I don't know," I said, my standard answer.

"What was she?" Jenny snuggled closer. "What *is* she?"

I looked at Jay Leno on the TV at the foot of our bed. I usually turned the television off after the news, but I didn't want to lie there in silence that night. I didn't want to hear the sounds. Leno asked the audience how many people had taken the NBC tour before getting in line for the show, and there was a scattering of hands. Leno suddenly fell to the floor, jerking spasmodically, his eyes rolling wildly. His twisting, flailing body began to float, and the cameraman cut to a closeup of his face. "I'll get you, you bastard," Leno said, and his voice was Jenny's dying hiss. "I'll get all of you assholes!"

"Shut it off!" Jenny screamed. "Shut the damn thing off!"

I lurched across the bed and reached over to flip off the TV. The screen went blank, but there was a faded white afterimage of Elena grinning, her crooked smile seeming to project outward from the television.

I held Jenny close, and we closed our eyes to block out the horror. I'm not sure what she was thinking. I was praying.

I was awakened the next morning by the sound of a car coming up the drive. I reached over Jenny's still sleeping form and opened the curtains. A silver BMW was pulling to a stop next to the barn. I quickly got out of bed, pulled on my jeans, and went to the door. I opened it just as the man started knocking. "Yes?" I said.

He was a youngish man, late twenties or early thirties, and he was dressed neatly and fashionably. His hair was short and stylish, and he was holding a briefcase in his hand. "I think maybe you can help me," he said. He smiled.

I said nothing, only stared, the blood pulsing in my temples, racing through my veins.

His smile was that of Elena.

I killed him with the baseball bat I kept next to the door for just such emergencies. I beat his head to a bloody pulp, and the thick redness splattered all over his neat and trendy clothes. I stepped back, satisfied, waiting to see his form wiggle into the ground the way the others had done, but his inert body lay there, dead and whole and unmoving.

I swallowed hard, the realization dawning on me. This had been a real person, not a manifestation. I felt cold then hot, and I looked again at his bloody form and vomited.

Jenny came out from the bedroom, wide-eyed and frightened. "What is it?" she asked. "What happened?" She saw the body and screamed.

I did not call the police but, forcing down my nausea, dragged the dead man to the trash furnace next to the barn, doused him with kerosine, and lit him on fire.

The smoke which billowed upward from the furnace's stack was black and smelled horrible.

I returned to the house, where Jenny was already looking through the briefcase. She looked up at me, scared, and held up several photographs of Elena. I sat down next to her, digging through the pile of pictures, There were photos of men and women I had never seen before. All of them bore a strong resemblance to Elena and the young man I had just killed.

There was a crash from the kitchen.

"Oh God," Jenny cried. "Oh God, I can't take much more of this."

Outside, through the window, I saw two forms wave at us from inside the BMW. A male and a female. My skin became a field of goose bumps, and I looked at Jenny. Her lips were pale and dry, her cheeks streaked with tears.

What were these people? I wondered.

The throw rug next to the couch moved into the air until it was upright. The corners folded in on themselves and beneath the shag Elena's face pushed outward. The lips moved silently, then began twitching in hideous convulsions.

The standing lamp next to the recliner fell to the floor, and the white shade colored red, taking on the features of the young man I had murdered.

Both the rug and the lamp smiled crooked smiles.

"What do they want?" Jenny screamed, jumping to her feet. *"What the hell do they want from us?"*

The car outside started, there were screams from the barn.

"I don't know," I said, holding her. "I don't know."

It went on from there.

Against the Pale Sand

One of my favorite movies of all time is *Eraserhead.*
It's strange, slow moving, and essentially plotless.
"Against the Pale Sand" is a story in that fine tradi-
tion.

—⁓—

She sat on the dirty porcelain toilet, staring down at the
wrinkled dress and panties which lay in a fallen heap around
her ankles. She could see a worn patch in the crotch of the
stained panties and a hem of tatters on the once bright green
dress. Wind from somewhere outside blew into the bathroom, causing small pinprick goosepimples to assault her
bare skin, and she looked up from the floor, her eyes focusing on the dilapidated boards which made up the opposite
wall. There were holes in most of the planks—knotholes—
and the edges of some of the boards had been eaten away by
termites. Many of the boards had been used before, elsewhere, in other houses, other times, and vestiges of previous
paint jobs, traces of former lives, could be seen in the thickly
whorled patterns of the wood. Very few of the boards met
properly, and there were gaps between individual planks and
between roof and wall and wall and floor. Next to the toilet,
the bathtub gurgled loudly, and a few thick globules of black

viscous liquid splattered up from the drain onto the already grimy metal.

It's not coming, she thought. *It's not going to happen.* Then she felt the familiar rush of cold from inside the toilet bowl, the welcome pull of gentle arctic air. A wet slimy finger reached upward from the stagnant water at the bottom of the bowl and caressed her sensitive skin. Other fingers followed, and she felt a mucilaginous hand lightly skim across the cheeks of her buttocks and slide slowly down the crack of her ass. She was already aroused, and she closed her eyes, relaxing her muscles, as first one cold finger then another entered her. She spread her legs a little and tried to press her body downward. Opening her eyes, she looked at the reflection of her face in the single shard of mirror remaining on the wall above the broken sink. Her mouth was open, tongue pressed involuntarily between cheek and gums, and she was sweating, though cold wind continued to blow through the cracks between the boards.

There was another black gurgle from the bathtub.

A few minutes later the hand, working on its own time, withdrew, though she was far from finished, and she heard it plop back into the still water at the bottom of the toilet. She stood, pulling up her panties and then her dress. She was wet, and she felt a maddeningly unfulfilled tingling between her legs as she pulled the cotton material tight against her crotch.

She wanted to touch herself there, the way she had as a child, but she dared not.

She opened the bathroom door and walked into the hall. A pale imitation of sunlight streamed in dust-filled pillars through holes in the roof, patchily illuminating the floor where weeds pushed up from between the tiles. She stepped across the hall and walked up the double brick steps into what used to be the living room, She ignored the cocoon and nodded curtly to the toothless old man, drooling and babbling to himself in his high chair next to the ruined chimney. Walking into the kitchen, she poured herself a cup of rusty water from the pail in the sink and stared out through the glassless window at the back yard.

"Hey! Anybody home?"

The voice, disembodied, its owner hidden behind the oversized growth of weeds on the side of the toolshed, sounded clearly in the now breezeless November air. There was a hint of panic in the voice, a trace of desperation.

"Anybody here?"

A man immaculately attired in an expensive gray business suit, holding a brown leather briefcase in front of him like a shield against the vegetation, emerged from the weeds looking lost and frail and scared. She could see by the path of the trail he had blazed that he had come through the forest. He stopped at the edge of the clearing, taking in the house, then caught sight of her, dully staring out the kitchen window.

"Boy, am I glad to see somebody," he said.

She dumped the rest of her water back into the pail and ambled over to the ripped screen door. She opened it, staring at him. She tried to speak, but all that came out was a high croaking sound. She cleared her throat, coughed, and tried again. "Hello," she said, her mouth forming the word from memory. Her voice sounded slow and awkward even to herself.

The man put his briefcase down at the edge of the porch and looked up at her, wiping sweat from his forehead with the sleeve of his jacket. "My car stalled on me over on Old Pinewood Road," he said, gesturing toward the forest. "I was wondering if you'd let me use your phone."

She cleared her throat again, coughed. "No phone," she said.

His lips formed the outline of a crude word he did not say, and he stomped his foot hard on the ground, sending up a small cloud of cold dust. "You know where there *is* a phone I could use?"

She shook her head and started to retreat back into the kitchen.

The man took a step forward. "Think I could just have a drink of water or something?" He pulled at the buttoned collar behind his tie. "It's a long way back to the road, and my throat's really parched."

She thought for a moment, then cleared her throat. "Come in," she said.

He walked up the series of warped wooden steps onto the porch, opened the screen, and stepped into the kitchen. He stopped just inside the door and stared. A three-legged table sat in the center of the room, piled high with hard bread-crusts and miniscule bones. Against the far wall was a rusted doorless refrigerator; he could see rotting vegetables lying on the appliance's backwardly slanting shelves. Through another doorway, he could see into the rest of the house. It looked gutted, abandoned, as though no one had lived there for years.

The woman dipped a tin cup into the dirty pail inside the sink, and he held up his hand. "Fresh water," he said. "I'd like some fresh water."

She did not seem to understand, and he let the matter drop, accepting the proffered cup. He was thirsty.

She watched him, her eyes following the measured bobbing of his Adam's apple as he drank. From what used to be the living room she could hear the toothless old man's babble moving upward in register, becoming a shrill whine. It was almost time for his supper and he was getting hungry. She walked over to the refrigerator and drew out an old wrinkled potato. She put it in a tin bowl and mashed it with a fork. She carried it in to the toothless old man, placing it on the shelf of his high chair. He cackled, drooling, and shoved his hands in the bowl. He licked the rotten potato from his fingers.

She turned back toward the kitchen and saw the man standing in the doorway, his empty cup dangling from his hand. "You live here?" he asked, shocked.

She nodded.

He looked to the ruined fireplace, at the toothless old man who was still shoving his hands in his mouth, babbling incoherently. He walked into the room, unbelieving, trying to take it all in. All the windows were boarded up, though not very well; light still sneaked through the cracks. The couch was slanting backward, its seats ripped, white wool stuffing billowing out through the torn material. Several broken chairs lay in a heap in the center of the room.

"Who is that?" he asked, pointing to the old man.

She gave him a puzzled expression.

"Who is that man in the high chair?"

She shrugged. She cleared her throat. "Don't know."

His eyes moved over the rest of the room. He walked toward the couch, looking around.

And he noticed the cocoon.

"What the hell is that?" He walked toward it, curious.

"*No!*" the women yelled, running past him. She stood in front of the cocoon and held her hands up to bar his way.

He stopped, suddenly apprehensive. He wasn't sure what he was doing there in the first place. His car had broken down and he'd been looking for a phone. The nearest town—no more than a store and gas station—was a good thirty miles away. He'd only come here for a drink of water. Now that he'd gotten his drink it was time for him to start heading back to the highway to see if he could flag down a ride. There was no reason for him to be looking through this house.

But the place was so damn strange. . . .

He tried to look past the woman at the cocoon. She shifted her position, blocking his view. He could see a slight bluish glow emanating from the object behind her. "I just want to look," he said. "I won't touch."

"No," she said. Her eyes bored into his, glaring.

From the back of the house someplace, from the depths of the dilapidated structure, came a strange mechanical whirring. It rose in pitch until it almost hurt his ears. He winced, looking up at the sound, staring at the bare wood wall though he couldn't see past it. "What is that?" he asked.

She looked at him, uncomprehending, and he shook his head in frustration. He walked through the doorway nearest to him and found himself in what appeared to be a hallway. Brown weeds pushed up through the crumbling floor tiles, and moonlight streamed through large holes in the roof.

Moonlight!

He looked up. Through the holes, he could see darkness and the faint imprints of stars.

That wasn't possible. He had come into the house only seconds ago, and it had been midafternoon. He looked behind him, through the doorway, but both the woman and the cocoon were gone. The old man was still in his high chair by the chimney, laughing toothlessly.

The whirring, which had risen to an all but inaudible level, began a downward spiral, dropping in tone until it disappeared. He took a few tentative steps forward, toward the source of the sound, and peeked through an open doorway off to the right. Something black and shapeless lunged quickly from the center of the room to its shadowed edge.

He turned back, shocked and scared, running through the doorway the way he'd come. The woman was now lying on the ripped and legless couch, her panties down around her ankles. Both hands were shoved up her hiked dress, working furiously. She was smiling, and her eyes were wet with tears. She was moaning something in an alien tongue.

As he scanned the room quickly, he saw the bluish glow of the now unprotected cocoon in the corner. Forgetting all about the black shape in the room off the hall, he started forward, his head craned curiously. The cocoon was lying in a makeshift sandbox, its rough translucent skin flat against the pale sand. It was glowing strangely, the blue light pulsating, and as he watched it slowly cracked open. Blue light and yellow liquid poured out of the crack in a sudden rage, and he felt some of the liquid hit his arm. It felt sticky and alive. As he stood, unmoving, the liquid coalesced into some semblance of a shape—something like a twisted tree branch. And now it was pulling him. He tried to peel the dried substance from his arm but only succeeded in getting it all over his hand. Liquid continued to pour out of the cocoon. Some of it glopped onto his shoes, dried, and began pulling as well.

The whirring noise, less mechanical this time, started again.

"No!" he cried.

A glob of liquid spurted onto his face, pulling at his skin.

"No!"

The woman looked up at the cry. She took her hands from beneath her dress and sat up on the couch, pulling on her panties. She stared dully toward the cocoon. She saw the man, now covered with the yellowish drying liquid, waving his arms, screaming. There was a sudden flash of blue-white light, and the man seemed to shrink, deflating beneath the yellow covering like a balloon.

She stood up, walking toward the cocoon. The two halves closed, locking everything in. Through the rough translucent cocoon skin she could see a hunched and twisted form struggling to break free. She knew that by tomorrow the form would be gone and the cocoon would be all right again.

In his high chair the old man cackled.

She shook her head slowly and walked into the hallway, where dust-filled pillars of sunlight fell through open holes in the roof, illuminating the weeds which grew through the tiles. She shambled into the bathroom and pulled off her dress, her nipples hardening immediately as wind from outside somewhere blew into the bathroom through the cracks and knotholes in the ancient boards. She pulled down her panties, letting them fall around her ankles, and sat on the dirty porcelain toilet.

She waited, hoping it would come.

The Pond

This is a story about lost ideals and selling out—moral shortcomings which are not limited to the boomer generation depicted here.

By the way, there really was a group called P.O.P (People Over Pollution). They used to gather each Saturday to collect and process recyclable materials. Back in the early 1970s, my friend Stephen Hillenburg and I belonged to an organization called the Youth Science Center, which would offer weekend science classes and field trips. We got to do Kirlian photography, visit mushroom farms, learn about edible plants on nature walks, tour laser laboratories—and one Saturday we worked with People Over Pollution, smashing aluminum cans with sledgehammers.

Stephen grew up to create the brilliant and wildly popular cartoon *SpongeBob SquarePants*.

—◊◊◊—

"Hey hon, what's this?"

Alex looked up from the suitcase he'd been packing. April, kneeling before the box she'd found on the top shelf of the hall closet, held up what looked like a green campaign button. "Pop?" she asked.

"Let me see that." He walked across the room and took the button from her hands. A powerful feeling of flashback familiarity, emotional remembrance, coursed through him as he looked at the button.

POP.

People Over Pollution.

It had been a long time since he'd thought of that acronym. A long time.

He knelt down next to April and peered into the box, seeing bumper stickers and posters, other buttons, pamphlets with green ecology sign logos.

"What is all this?" April asked.

"People Over Pollution. It was a group I belonged to when I was in college. We collected bottles and cans and newspapers for recycling. We picketed soap companies until they came up with biodegradable detergent. We urged people to boycott environmentally unsound products."

April smiled, tweaked his nose. "You troublemaking radical you."

He ignored her and began to dig through the box, sorting through the jumbled items.

Buried beneath the bumper stickers and buttons, he found a framed photograph: an emerald green meadow, ringed by huge darker green ponderosa pine trees. A small lake in the center of the meadow grass, its still and perfectly clear water reflecting the cotton puff clouds and deep blue sky above.

Major flashback.

He stared at the photo, reverently touched the dusty glass. He'd forgotten all about the picture. How was that possible? He'd cut it out of an *Arizona Highways* as a teenager and had framed it because he'd known instantly upon seeing it that this was where he wanted to live. The photo spoke to him on a gut emotional level that struck a chord deep within him. A chord that had never been struck before. He had never been to Arizona at that point, but he'd known from the perfection presented in that scene that this was where he wanted to settle down. He would live in the meadow in a log cabin, just he and his wife, and they would wake each morning to the sound of birdsong, to the natural light of dawn.

The girls with whom he intended to live in this paradise had changed throughout his teens—from Joan to Pam to Rachel—but the location had always remained constant.

How could he have forgotten about the photo? He'd been to Arizona countless times in the intervening years, had scouted a resort site in Tucson and another in Sedona, yet the memory of his old dream had never even suggested itself to him.

Strange.

April leaned over his shoulder, resting her head next to his. She glanced at the photo with disinterest. "What's that?"

He shook his head, smiling slightly, sadly, and placed the picture back in the box. "Nothing."

That night he dreamed of the pond.

He could not remember having had the dream before, but it was somehow familiar to him and he knew that he had experienced it in the past.

He was walking along a narrow footpath through the forest, and as he walked deeper into the woods the sky grew overcast and the bushes grew thicker and it soon seemed as though he was walking through a tunnel. He was afraid and he grew even more afraid as he moved forward. He wanted to turn back, to turn around, but he could not. His feet propelled him onward.

And then he was at the pond.

He stood at the path's end, trembling, chilled to the core

of his being as he stared at the dirty body of water before him, at the ripples of bluish white foam that floated upon the stagnant black liquid.

The trees here, the grass, the brush, all were brown and dying. There were no other people about, no animals, not even bugs on the water. The air was still and strangely heavy. Above this spot, dark clouds blotted out all sunlight.

At the far end of the pond was an old water pump.

Alex's heart beat faster. He kept his eyes averted from the rusted hunk of machinery, but he could still see out of the corner of his eye the corrosion on the old metal, the algae-covered tube snaking into the water.

More than anything else, more than the dark and twisted path, more than the horrid pond or the blighted land surrounding it, it was the pump that frightened him, its very presence causing goose bumps to ripple down the skin of his arms. There was something in the cold insistence of its position at the head of the pond, in the unnaturally biological contours of its form and the defiantly mechanical nature of its function, that terrified him. He looked up at the sky, around at the trees, then forced himself to face the water pump.

The handle of the pump began to turn slowly, the squeaking sound of its movement echoing in the still air.

And he woke up screaming.

The corporation put him up at Little America in Flagstaff. The accommodations were nice, the rooms clean and well furnished, the view beautiful. It was late May, not yet summer and not warm enough to swim, but the temperature was fair, the sky clear and cloudless, and he and April spent the better part of that first day by the pool, she reading a novel, he going over the specs.

The quiet was disturbed shortly after noon by the loud and laughing conversation of a man and a woman. Alex looked up from his papers to see a bearded, ponytailed young man opening the iron gate to the pool area. The young man was wearing torn cut-off jeans, and the blond giggling girl with him had on a skimpy string bikini. The young man saw him staring and waved. "Hey, bud! How's the water?"

The girl hit his shoulder, laughing.

Alex turned back to his papers. "Asshole," he said.

April frowned. "Shhh. They'll hear you."

"I don't care."

Yelling in tandem, the couple leaped into the pool.

"Leave them alone. They're just young. You were young once, weren't you?"

That shut him up. He had been young once. And, now that he thought about it, he had at one time looked very similar to the sixties throwback now cavorting in the pool.

He'd had a beard and ponytail when he'd marched in the Earth Day parade.

What the hell had happened to him since then?

He'd sold out.

He placed the specs on the small table next to his lounge chair, took off his glasses and laid them on top of the papers. He watched the young man grab his girlfriend's breast from behind as she squealed and swam away from him toward the deep end of the pool.

Alex leaned back, looking up into the sea blue sky. Sold out? He was a successful scout for a chain of major resorts. He hadn't sold out. He had merely taken advantage of a fortunate series of career opportunities. He told himself that he was where he wanted to be, where he should be, that he had a good life and a good job and was happy, but he was uncomfortably aware that the end result of his series of lucky breaks and career opportunities had been to provide him with a job that he would have found the height of hypocrisy in his younger, more idealistic days.

He was not the person he had been.

He found himself wondering whether, if he had been this age then, he would have supported the Vietnam War.

He had supported the war in the Persian Gulf.

He pushed those thoughts from his mind. He was just being stupid. Life was neither as simple nor as morally black and white as he had believed in his college days. That was all there was to it. He was grown up now. He was an adult. He could no longer afford the arrogant idealism of youth.

He watched the couple in the pool kiss, the lower halves of their bodies undulating in the refracted reflection of the chlorinated water, and he realized that, from their perspective, he was probably one walking cliché. A traitor to the sixties. Yet another amoral baby boomer with fatally skewed priorities.

He felt a warm hand on his shoulder, turned his head to see April staring worriedly at him from her adjacent lounge chair. "Are you okay?"

"Sure," he said nodding.

"It is because of what I said?"

"I'm fine." Annoyed, he turned away from her. He put on his glasses, picked up his spec sheets, and started reading.

He met with the realtors early the next morning, seeing them not one by one but all at the same time in one of Little America's conference rooms. He'd found from past experience that dealing with real estate salespeople en masse gave him a distinct advantage, firmly establishing him as the dominant partner in the relationship, saving him from the sort of high-pressure sales talk that realtors usually used on prospective clients and putting the salespeople in clear competition with one another.

It worked every time.

After his prepared talk and slide show, he fielded a few quick questions, then scheduled times over the next three days during which he could go with the realtors individually to look at property. This time, the corporation was looking for land outside the confines of the city. Flagstaff already had plenty of hotels and motels, and Little America itself offered resort quality accommodations. To compete in this market, they had to offer something different, and it had been decided that a state-of-the-art complex in a heavily forested area outside the city would provide just the edge that they would need.

They would also be allowed more freedom in design and latitude in construction under county rather than city building regulations.

There were more sites to scout than he'd thought, more property available in the Flagstaff area than he'd been led to believe due to a recent land swap between the Forest Service and a consortium of logging and mining companies, and he realized as he penciled in times on his calendar that he and April would probably have to skip their side trip to Oak Creek Canyon this time.

It was just as well, he supposed. Sedona and the Canyon had been awfully overcrowded and touristy the last time they'd been through.

The white Jeep bounced over the twin ruts that posed as a road through this section of forest, and Alex held on to his briefcase with one hand, the dashboard with the other. There were no seat belts or shoulder harnesses in the vehicle, and the damned real estate agent was driving like a maniac.

The realtor yelled something at him, but over the wind and the roar of the engine he could only make out every third word or so: "We're . . . southern . . . almost . . ." He assumed that they were nearing the property.

Already he had a good impression of this site. Unlike some of the others, which were either too remote—with the cost of water, sewer, and electrical hookups prohibitive—or too close to town, this location was secluded and easily accessible. A paved road over this dirt track would provide a beautiful scenic drive for tourists and guests.

They rounded a curve, and they were there.

At the meadow.

Alex blinked dumbly as the Jeep pulled to a stop, not sure if he was seeing what he thought he was seeing. They were at one end of a huge meadow bordered by giant ponderosas. There was a small lake toward the opposite end, a lake so blue that it made the sky pale by comparison.

It was the meadow whose picture he'd cut out of *Arizona Highways.*

No, that was not possible.

Was it?

He glanced around. This certainly looked like the same meadow. He thought he even recognized an old lightning-struck tree on a raised section of ground near the shore of the lake.

But the odds against something like this happening were . . . astronomical. Thirty years ago, an *Arizona Highways* photographer had chanced upon this spot, taken a photo which had been published in the magazine; he himself had seen the photo, cut it out, saved it. And now he was in a position to buy the property for a resort chain? It was too bizarre, too coincidental, too . . . Twilight Zone. He had to be mistaken.

"Beautiful, isn't it?" The realtor got out of the Jeep, stretched. "This open space here, this clearing's some thirty acres, but the entire property's eighty acres, mostly that area there beyond those trees." He pointed to the line of ponderosas south of the water. "You got yourself a small ridge that overlooks the National Forest and has a view clear to Mormon Mountain."

Alex nodded. He continued to nod as the real estate agent rambled, pretending to listen as the man led him through the high grass to the water.

Should he tell the corporation to buy the meadow? His meadow? Technically, his was only a preliminary recommendation, a decision that was neither binding nor final. His choice would then be carefully scrutinized by the board. The corporation's assessors, land use experts, and design technicians would go over everything with a fine-toothed comb.

Technically.

But the way it really worked was that he scouted locations, the board rubber-stamped the go-ahead, and the corporation's legal eagles swooped down to see how they could pick apart the deals mapped out by the local realtors.

The fate of the meadow lay in his hands.

He stared at the reflection of the trees and the clouds, the green and white reproduced perfectly on the still, mirrored surface of the blue water.

He thought back to his POP years, and he realized, perhaps for the first time, that he had been a selfish environmentalist even in his most ecologically active days. There was no contradiction between his work now and his beliefs then. He had always wanted nature's beauty to remain unspoiled not for its own sake—but so that he could enjoy it.

He had never been one to hike out to remote wilderness areas and enjoy the unspoiled beauty. He had been a couch potato nature lover, driving through national parks and pretty areas of the country and admiring the scenery from his car window. He had objected to the building of homes on forest land that was visible from the highway, but had not objected to the presence of the highway itself.

He'd seen nothing at all wrong with building a home in his dream meadow, though he would have fought to the death anyone else who'd tried to build there.

Now he was on the other side of the coin.

He tried to look at the situation objectively. He told himself that at least the corporation would protect the lake and the meadow, would preserve the beauty of this spot. Someone else might simply pave it over. He might not be able to build a house here and live in the wilderness with April, but he could rent a room at the resort, and the two of them could vacation here.

Along with hundreds of other people.

He glanced over at the real estate agent. "Was this spot ever in *Arizona Highways*?" he asked.

The realtor laughed. "If it wasn't, it should've been. This is one gorgeous spot. Hell, if I had enough money I'd buy the land and build my own house here."

Alex nodded distractedly. They had reached the edge of the lake, and he crouched down, dipping his fingers in the water. The liquid felt uncomfortably warm to his touch. And slimy. Like melted Jell-O. He quickly withdrew his hand.

He stood, shaking the water from his fingers. There was a faint ringing in his ears. He looked around the meadow but found that his whole perspective had changed. The trees no longer seemed so beautiful. Rather than a miraculous example of the wonders of nature, the forest looked like a fake grove that had been inexpertly planted. The lake looked small and ill-formed, particularly in comparison with some of the pools and lagoons created for the newer resorts. The meadow, he saw now, would be perfect for either a golf course or an intra-resort park. Lighted walking paths or horse trails could be constructed through the grass and the trees. Landscaping could accentuate the meadow's natural beauty.

Accentuate natural beauty?

Something seemed wrong with that, but he could not put his finger on what it was.

"This sounds exactly like what you're looking for," the realtor said.

Alex nodded noncommittally. His gaze swept the short shoreline of the lake.

And stopped.

In the weeds on the opposite side of the water was a rusted water pump.

A chill passed through him as he stared at the pump. It was nearly identical to the one in his dream, his mind having conjured correctly even the rounded organic contours of its shape. His heart was pounding crazily, a rap rhythm instead of its usual ballad beat. He swiveled toward the realtor. The agent was staring at him and smiling. What was the expression on the man's face? Was that amusement he saw in those eyes? Was there a hint of malice in that smile?

Jesus, what the hell was wrong with him? There was nothing unusual in the real estate agent's expression. He was being paranoid.

"Should I draw up the papers?" the realtor said jokingly.

Alex forced himself to remain calm, gave the man a cool smile, did not tip his hand. "What other properties can you show me?"

*   *   *

While April was in the shower, he looked at himself in the full-length mirror on the back of the door. For the first time he realized that he was middle aged. Really realized it. His gaze shifted from his thinning hair to his expanding waist to the increasing rigidity of his previously malleable features. His age was not something of which he'd been unaware—each birthday had been a ritualized reminder of his loss of youth, each New Year's Eve a prompter of the passing of time—but he now understood emotionally what before he had comprehended only as an intellectual concept.

His best years were behind him.

He sucked in his gut, stood sideways in front of the mirror, but the effort was too much and he let it fall. That stomach was never going to go away. He would never again have the kind of body that females would look at admiringly. The women he found attractive would no longer find him attractive.

He might die of a heart attack.

That's what had brought this on. His heart had been pounding so forcefully and for so long after he'd seen the water pump that he'd honestly been afraid it would burst. It did not seem possible that his unexercised and cholesterol-choked muscle could keep up that pace for so long a time without sustaining damage.

It had, though.

He walked across the carpeted floor of the hotel room and stared out the window at the black silhouette of the San Francisco Peaks. The mountains towered over the lights of Flagstaff but were dwarfed by the vastness of the Arizona night sky. He had two more days of scouting to do, two more days of meetings and sales pitches, but he knew that he had already made his decision.

He was going to recommend that the corporation buy the meadow.

He didn't feel as bad about the decision as he thought he would, and that concerned him a little. He stared out the window at the stars, tried to imagine what it would have been like if he really had followed his dream, not allowed himself to be deterred by practicality. Would he have been with April or someone else? Would he still be living there in the meadow, by the lake, or would he have long since given up and, like most of those involved in the back-to-nature movement, joined mainstream society? Would he be where he was now anyway?

He didn't know, he wasn't sure, but he felt a vague sense of sadness and dissatisfaction as he looked into the night.

"Hon?" April called from the bathroom. "Could you bring me my panties from the suitcase?"

"Sure," he answered.

He turned away from the window and walked over to the suitcase on the floor near the bed.

He dreamed of the pond.

He walked down the narrowing, darkening path until he reached the blighted clearing, where the filthy water lay in a sickening pool. He stared at the pond and he was afraid. There were no monsters here, no evil spirits. This was not sacred Indian land that had been unthinkingly desecrated. There were no strange creatures swimming beneath the surface of the brackish liquid.

There was only the pond itself.

And the pump.

These were the things that were scary.

Against his will, he found himself moving across the dead ground to the edge of the water. He looked across the pond at the pump and the hose protruding from its side wiggled obscenely, moving upward into the air, beckoning him.

He awoke drenched in sweat.

Two days later, he faxed his preliminary report, along with the appropriate documents and estimates, to corporate headquarters, then took April out to look at the site. He drove himself this time, using the rental car, so the going was much slower.

He parked the car at the end of the tire-tracked path and said nothing as April got out of the vehicle and looked around. She nodded appreciatively as she took in the trees, the meadow, the lake. "It's pretty." she said.

He'd been expecting something more, something like his own initial reaction when he'd first seen that photo years ago, but he realized that she had never shown that sort of enthusiasm for anything.

"It is pretty," he said, but he realized as he spoke the words that they no longer held true for him. He knew, objectively, intellectually, that this was a beautiful spot, a prime location for the resort, but he no longer felt it. He remembered the slick and slimy feel of the water on his fingers, and though his hands were dry he wiped them on his pants.

The two of them walked through the high wispy grass to the edge of the lake. As before, the placid surface perfectly reflected the sky above and the scenery around. He let his gaze roam casually across the opposite shore, pretending to himself that he had no object, no aim, no purpose in his visual survey, but the movement of his eyes stopped when he spotted the water pump.

He glanced quickly at April to see if she'd noticed it. She hadn't.

He looked again toward the pump. Its metal was dark, threatening in the midst of the yellow-tan stalks of the weeds, its hose draped suggestively over the small mud bank into the water. He didn't want April to see the pump, he realized. He wanted to protect her from it, to shield her eyes from the sight of that incongruous man-made object in the middle of this natural wilderness.

Was it man-made?

What kind of thought was that?

He made a big show of looking at his watch. "We'd better get back," he said. "It's getting late. We have a lot of things to do, and I have a long day tomorrow. There are a lot of loose ends to tie up."

She nodded, understanding. They turned to go, and she took his hand. "It's nice," she said as they walked back toward the car. "You found a good one."

He nodded.

In his dream, he brought April to the pond. He said nothing, only pointed, like a modern-dress version of the Ghost of Christmas Yet to Come. She frowned. "Yeah? So it's an old polluted pond. What of it?"

Now he spoke: "But why is it polluted? How did it get that way? There are no factories here, no roads to this spot—"

"Who knows? Who cares?"

She obviously didn't feel it. To her, this was nothing more than a small dirty body of water. There was nothing sinister here, nothing malicious. But as he looked up at the blackness of the dead sky he knew that she was being deceived, that this was not the case.

He turned around and she was gone, in her place a pillar of salt.

Again, he awoke sweating, though the room's air conditioner was blowing cool air toward him. He got out of bed without disturbing April and walked into the bathroom. He did not have to take a leak, did not have to get a drink of water, did not have to do anything. He simply stood before the mirror, staring at himself. His eyes were bloodshot, his lips pale. He looked sick. He gazed into his eyes and they were unfamiliar to him; he did not know what the mind behind those eyes was thinking. He leaned forward until his nose was touching the nose behind the glass, until his eyes were an inch away from their mirrored counterparts, and suddenly he did know what that mind was thinking.

He jerked away from the mirror and almost fell backward over the toilet. He took a deep breath, licked his lips. He stood there for a moment, closed his eyes. He told himself that he was not going to do it, that he was going back to bed.

But he let himself silently out of the hotel room without waking April.

He drove to the property.

He parked farther away this time, walking the last several yards through the forest to the meadow.

The meadow.

In the moonlight, the grass looked dead, the trees old and frail and withered. But the lake, as always, appeared full and beautiful, its shiny surface gloriously reflecting the magnificent night sky.

He wasted no time but walked around the edge of the lake, his feet sinking in the mud. The opposite shore was rougher than the side with which he was familiar, the tall weeds hiding rocks and ruts, small gullies and sharp, dead branches. He stopped for a moment, crouched down, touched the water with his fingertips, but the liquid felt slimy, disgusting.

He continued walking.

He found the pump.

He stared at the oddly shaped object. It was evil, the pump. Evil not for what it did, not for what it had done, not for what it could do, but for what it was. He moved slowly forward, placed his hand on the rusted metal and felt power there, a low thrumming that vibrated against his palm, reverberated through his body. The metal was cold to his touch, but there was warmth beneath the cold, heat beneath the warmth. Part of him wanted to run away, to turn his back on the lake and the pump and get the hell out of there, but another stronger part of him enjoyed this contact with the power, reveled in the humming which vibrated against his hand.

Slowly, he reached down and pulled the lever up. The metal beneath his fingers creaked loudly in protest after the years of disuse. Yellow brackish liquid began trickling out of the pipe, growing into a stream. The liquid splashed onto the clear water of the lake and the reflection of the sky darkened, disappeared. The water near the pump began foaming, the suds blue then brown in the darkness.

He waited for a moment, then pushed the lever down again. He knelt, touched his fingers to the water. Now it felt normal to him, now it felt good.

He rose to his feet. Dimly, from the far side of the clearing, he thought he heard April call his name, but her voice was faint and indistinct and he ignored her as he began to strip. He took off his shoes, his socks, his shirt, his pants, his underwear.

He looked across the lake, but there was no sign of April. There was no one there.

The last time I went skinny-dipping, he thought, *I had a beard and a ponytail.*

"POP," he said, whispered.

Naked, he dived into the water. His mouth and nostrils were filled instantly with the taste and odor of sulfur, chemicals. He opened his eyes underwater, but he could see nothing, only blackness. His head broke the surface and he gulped air. Above, the sky was dark, the moon gone, the stars faint.

The water felt cool on his skin, good.

He took a deep breath and began to swim across the lake, taking long brisk strokes toward the dark opposite shore.

Roommates

I've known people who have roomed with strangers for financial reasons, but to me the idea of sharing an apartment with someone I don't know sounds like a prescription for hell. Although I've never had to advertise for a roommate, this is what I think it would be like.

—∿—

I should have charged Ira a cleaning deposit, Ray thought.

He looked around the empty bedroom. The fat son of a bitch had left cigarette butts, old Coke cans, crumpled paper, and other assorted trash all over the stained and dirty carpet. Bushes of fluffy dust had grown in the sharp corners of the room. The small adjoining bathroom was even worse. Used toilet paper clogged the sink and bathtub drain. The water in the toilet was black, the shower curtain covered with mold, and the entire bathroom smelled of rot and decay, dried urine and wet feces, old vomit. He'd almost puked when he'd peeked through the doorway.

I should have charged him a big *deposit.*

Ray sighed. Hell, if he'd known that Ira had been this much of a pig, he would have kicked him out months ago.

After all, it was his apartment, registered in his name. If any damage occurred, he'd be the one liable for it.

But he'd been a nice guy. He'd left Ira his privacy, had not ventured into the territory beyond the closed door of Ira's room. He'd even let the fat cow slide on the rent for two months after he'd lost his job. And how had the bastard repaid him? He'd skipped out, owing Ray nearly a thousand dollars in bills and back rent, leaving behind this putrid pigsty to be cleaned up.

Ray walked over to Ira's bathroom and shut the door, almost gagging on the smell. He had to get this place cleaned up and find another roommate within the next two weeks or he'd be out of an apartment. Rent was due on the first of the month, and there was no way he'd be able to make the payment alone.

But he was going to lay down the law for his next roommate.

And charge a hefty security deposit.

He took another look around the filthy bedroom and went into the kitchen to get a garbage sack, the broom, the mop, the vacuum cleaner.

The Lysol.

ROOMMATE WANTED

W/M, 28, non-smkr, lkng for rmmte

to shr xpenses. 555-5715.

Ray came home from work, threw his tie on the couch, and walked immediately across the living room to check his answering machine.

Nothing.

He sat down on the couch. He was starting to get worried.

The ad had been running in the paper for three days and he hadn't gotten a bite. Not even a nibble. Yesterday he'd stopped off at the university after work and put up a notice on the housing bulletin board, figuring that since it was near the beginning of the semester he'd be able to find a respectable, trustworthy college student to room with him. But no one had called from the college, either.

He could feel himself starting to panic. After the Ira disaster, he'd sat down and written out a long list of ground rules: "The Law," as he called it. It was his intention to read The Law to all prospective roommates and to get their signed agreement in case he needed it as proof should he ever have to take them to court. But for the past two days he'd found himself mentally striking items from the list, adjusting his rules, rationalizing the dropping of standards and requirements.

He sorted through the mail in his hand. There was an envelope addressed to Ira, and he opened it without hesitation. He had no idea where the pigman was or how to get ahold of him, but he probably wouldn't have forwarded the mail even if he had known. Inside the envelope was an overdue notice from Ira's bank, warning that if his car payment was not received his vehicle would be repossessed.

Ray smiled as he tossed the envelope into the trash. He hoped they'd nail that bastard's ass.

He turned on the TV and was about to start dinner— macaroni and cheese—when the phone rang. He rushed across the room and picked up the receiver before the machine answered it. "Hello?"

"Hello. I'm calling about the apartment?" It was a woman's voice, tentative and hesitant, sounding as though she was not quite sure what to expect.

Ray tried to keep his voice light, to sound as unthreatening as possible, knowing that the woman might not be entirely comfortable with the prospect of sharing an apartment with a strange man. "The room's still available."

"Room?"

"Well, room and bathroom. You'd have the master bedroom even though the rent would be split evenly."

She was silent.

"If you're worried about rooming with a man—"

"No, it's not that," she assured him.

"Well, would you like to come over and look at the place?"

"Sure. Will you be there tonight? About eight?"

"That'd be fine," Ray said. He did some quick mental calculations. If he skipped dinner, he would just have enough time to vacuum, dump the garbage, and straighten up the living room. He could grab some McDonald's after she left.

"Okay," she said. "I'll see you then."

"What's your name?"

"Lilly."

"Okay, Lilly. I'll see you at eight."

The doorbell rang at seven fifty-five, and Ray ran a hand through his hair and tucked in the back of his shirt before opening the door. "Hello," he said, smiling.

The smile froze on his face.

On the phone, Lilly's voice had been low, sensuous, seductive. In person, she was a thin, emaciated wraith, all elbow angles and pointy facial features. The plain white suit she wore accentuated the angular boniness of her frame, and both her light blue eyes and thin-lipped mouth were hard.

She carried in her hands a small, particularly unpleasant-looking monkey, a brown hairy beast with too many teeth.

"I should have told you over the phone that I was looking for a place for me and my baby," she said.

Baby? Ray frowned. Was that an affectionate term for her pet or . . . ?

"Baby?" he said aloud.

She lifted the monkey. "My daughter." Her voice, which until now had been comparatively soft, was now as cold and hard as her appearance.

"I'm sorry—" Ray began, starting to close the door.

But the woman ignored him, walking into the dining room. "I suppose we could set the altar here," she said.

"Altar?"

"For my baby. The faithful will need a place to worship her."

"Look . . . ," Ray said.

She stared at him. "You don't know who this is?" The ugly monkey grimaced at Ray. "She is the Christ child, the Second Coming. She was born to me a virgin and—"

"I'm sorry," Ray said quickly. "You'll have to go." He pressured her toward the door.

The monkey chattered angrily.

"You'll be damned to hell," the woman said, and there was nothing soft about her voice now. "You're like all the rest of them, and you will burn forever in the fiery pit, your skin will melt and your bones—"

"Get out of here now!"

"My baby damns you for eternity!" Lilly was screaming as she backed out the doorway. "Your teeth will crack open and your cock will rot and—"

He slammed the door.

She was still screaming her curses as, with trembling hands, he locked the door and retreated back into the apartment.

*   *   *

The answering machine broke the next day, and though he could tell that a message had been left, Ray had no way of hearing what it was. The recording mechanism had gone out on him and would play back only garbled static. On the off chance that it was someone who was interested in looking at the apartment, he washed and put away the breakfast dishes and threw away the newspaper that was spread out over the dining room table.

He was just straightening the magazines on the living room coffee table when there was a knock at the door. He ran a quick hand through his hair, rubbed a finger across his teeth, cleared his throat, and opened the door.

The man who stood there could not have been more than three feet high. He was wearing only a dark green bathing suit and his hairless skin was albino white. He was completely bald, and even his eyebrows had been shaved off. "Mr. Feldman?" he asked in a high squeaky voice.

Ray nodded, and the man stepped inside, looking around the apartment. "TV!" he squealed and ran quickly across the living room, plopping down on the floor in front of the television.

Ray waited a moment, but the small man remained unmoving, mesmerized by the commercial that was on.

"Do you have cable?" he asked.

"The apartment's been rented," Ray said in as an authoritarian voice he could muster. He didn't like lying, but this was just getting too damn weird.

The little man stood up and faced Ray. His lower lip was trembling and tears were forming in his eyes. His small white hands began clasping and unclasping.

"I'm sorry," Ray said, softening. "But I rented the place out yesterday—"

With a loud wail, the man streaked past Ray and out the door. By the time Ray turned around, he was gone, the hallway outside empty.

"I'm sorry," Ray called out, but there was no answer, no sound outside, and he closed the door.

He walked back into the living room and sat down tiredly on the couch. What the hell was he going to do? The month was almost over, and if things continued the way they were going, he was not going to find a roommate. There was no way he could afford another month by himself—

The front door opened.

Ray jumped to his feet. The man who stood in the doorway must have weighed four hundred pounds. He was bearded and bespectacled, wearing a faded *Star Wars* T-shirt which bunched in folds around his gut. Next to him on the stoop were two suitcases and a huge piece of sheet metal. "You saved my life," he said, picking up the suitcases by their handles and clamping the sheet metal beneath his arm. He walked into the apartment, looking around. "Nice place."

"W-What . . ."

"I saw your invitation at the university."

"That wasn't an invitation. It was an advertisement. I'm just interviewing applicants—"

"Well, you can stop interviewing. I'm here." The man put his suitcases down on the floor. He leaned the sheet metal against the wall next to the dining room table and opened one of the suitcases, taking out a hammer and some nails.

He began nailing the sheet metal to the wall.

"What the hell do you think you're doing?"

"This here's for my war game."

Ray ran across the room. "You're not putting that on my wall."

A cloud passed over the man's face, and his smile faded.

He pushed roughly past Ray and strode into the kitchen, pulling open drawers until he found the one he wanted. He picked up two carving knives, one in each hand, and advanced on Ray, the expression on his face one of furious rage. "What's all this talk of knives, boy?" He drew out the word *knives,* stretching it into several syllables.

"I—" Ray began.

One of the knives whizzed by his head as the man threw it.

"What's all this talk of knives?"

Ray ducked. "I don't know what you're—"

Another knife flew past his head, embedding itself in the wall above the couch.

"I'm calling the police!" Ray ran toward the phone.

The fat man stood there for a moment, frowned, blinked his eyes, then smiled. He picked up his hammer and began nailing the sheet metal to the wall. "I put game pieces on here," he explained. "They're attached with magnets."

Breathing heavily, angered adrenaline coursing through his veins, Ray turned toward the man, dropping the phone. "Get out!" he yelled. He pulled one of the knives from the wall and advanced on the fat man.

"What'd I do?"

"Get out!" Ray rushed forward, and the man, panicking, dropped his hammer and ran out the door. Ray picked up first one suitcase, then the other, throwing them out the door. Comic books tumbled out. And pewter fantasy figures. And game pieces.

"My board!" the man cried.

Ray picked up the sheet metal and tossed it out the door.

Fury swept over the huge man's face once again. "Knives!" he said.

Ray closed the door just as the man started to run. He

turned the lock, drew the dead bolt. There was a loud roar and a monstrous thump as the man rammed into the door, but the door miraculously held.

"I'm calling the police!" Ray said again.

But there was no answer, and he knew the man was gone.

"Hello. My name's Tiffany, and I'm calling in regard to the roommate-wanted ad in the paper." The woman's voice was lilting, almost musical, possessed of a thick southern accent.

Ray said nothing, only sighed tiredly.

"I'm getting desperate. I really need to find a place."

He took off his tie, throwing it on the couch. Cradling the receiver between his neck and shoulder, he started taking off his shoes. "Look, Miss—"

"Tiffany. Tiffany Scarlett. I'm a nurse at St. Jude's." She paused. "Look, if you haven't found a roommate yet, I'd like to come over and look at the place. I don't know what you're looking for, but I'm very quiet, and although my hours are sometimes a little weird because I work the second shift, I can assure you I would not disturb you. You probably wouldn't even notice I was there."

Ray was silent. This was sounding good. Too good. This was exactly what he wanted to hear, and he tried to read between the lines, searching for a catch.

"Just let me come over and take a peek. It's only five thirty. You haven't found a roommate yet, have you?"

"No," he admitted.

"Well then."

"Okay," he said. "Come by at seven."

"Seven it is."

"Do you know how to get here?"

"I have a map."

"See you at seven, then."

"Okay. Bye-bye."

"Bye." He hung up the phone, closed his eyes. *Please God*, he thought, *let her be normal.*

The knock came at seven sharp. He stood for a moment unmoving, then opened the door.

He immediately stepped back, gagging. The smell was familiar, that unmistakable compound odor of putrescent filth and bodily waste which had permeated Ira's living quarters. He stared at the young woman who stood before him. If she had been clean, she would have been a knockout. She possessed the thin graceful body of a model or a dancer, and her face was absolutely stunning. But she was wearing a man's coveralls stained with food and mud and God knew what, and her face and hands were brown with grime. Her hair stuck out from the sides of her head in greasy matted clumps.

In her hands she held two metal pails filled with dirt.

"This'll do nicely," she said in her thick southern accent. "This'll do fine." She stepped into the apartment and immediately dumped both pails of dirt onto the rug.

"What do you think you're doing?" Ray demanded.

"The rest of it's out in the truck," she said. She walked straight into the kitchen and began filling up one of the pails with water.

"You have to leave," Ray said flatly.

Tiffany laughed. "Oh, don't be silly." She walked back into the living room, poured the water on top of the dirt, and dropped to her knees, mixing the dirt and water into mud and spreading it over the carpet.

"That's it!" he roared. He picked her up around the waist and carried her to the door.

"But—" she sputtered.

"No more!" He threw her outside. She fell hard on her buttocks, and before she could get up, he threw her pails out after her. They bounced and clattered across the concrete.

He slammed the door, locked it.

He threw himself down on the couch, opened the paper and started looking through the classified ads.

Ray glanced down at the small square of newspaper in his hand:

GUESTROOM: *M. N/Smoker. N/Drugs. N/Parties. Clean, $350 mth. Mike. 1443 Sherwood #7.*

He looked up at the address on the side of the apartment building. This was it. 1443 Sherwood. He smiled. It was even better than he'd expected. He'd known that this address was in the nicest section of town, and he'd expected it to be well kept, but he hadn't thought it would be this nice. He walked through the wrought iron gates and looked down at the freestanding map of the complex in the entryway, finding number seven.

It was upstairs, and he walked alongside the wide banister, around the corner, until he found the right doorway. He stood there for a moment, looking down at the manicured shrubbery, at the blue swimming pool.

He knocked on the door.

The smell assaulted his nostrils the moment the door opened: the clean scent of flour and sugar. He looked past the smiling man who stood in the vestibule. The floor of the apartment was covered with wet dough, as were the walls. In the center of the room was a barbed wire pen, and in the pen a snorting, snuffing creature that looked almost like a pig.

Almost, but not quite.

"As you can see," the man said, gesturing toward the pen, "it's just my sister and me—"

"I'll take it," Ray said.

Llama

"Llama" was basically my response to astrology, numerology, and those sorts of pseudo-sciences. I wanted to show that patterns can exist, can recur, in nature, in society, and not necessarily mean anything. In the story, the protagonist's wife and unborn child died during the act of childbirth, and this man sees patterns everywhere, in everything, telling him what to do to avenge those deaths. The patterns might exist, but a lot of them are coincidence and have meaning only in the guy's head. They have no real objective meaning at all. That's how I feel about the fortune-telling arts.

When I wrote this story, there really was a llama living across the alley from my friend Dan Cannon's bookstore.

—∿—

Measuring:

The leg of the dead llama was three feet, two inches long. And everything fell into place.

Three feet, two inches was the precise length of space between the sole of my hanging father's right foot and the ground.

By the time my wife's contractions were three minutes and two seconds apart, she had only dilated 3.2 centimeters and the decision was made to perform a caesarean.

My wife was declared dead at three twenty.

The date was March 20.

I found the llama in the alley behind the bookstore. It was already dead, its cataract eyes rimmed with flies, and the retarded boy was kneeling on the rough asphalt beside it, massaging its distended stomach. The presence of the retarded boy told me that secrets lay within the measurements of the dead animal, perhaps the answers to my questions, and I quickly rushed back inside the store to find a tape measure.

In 1932, Franklin Roosevelt bought a new Ford coupe. The license plate of the coupe, which Roosevelt never drove, was 3FT2.

My father voted for Franklin Roosevelt.

I thought I saw my wife's likeness in a stain in the toilet in the men's room of an Exxon station. The stain was greenish black and on the right side of the bowl.

I breathed upon the mirror above the blackened sink, and sure enough, someone had written her name on the glass. The letters appeared—clear spots in the fog cloud of condensation—then faded.

In the trash can, partially wrapped in toilet paper, I saw what looked like a bloody fetus.

I left the llama in the alley undisturbed, did not tell the police or any city authority, and I warned the other shop owners on the block not to breathe a word about the animal to anyone.

I spent that night in the store, sleeping in the back office behind the bookshelves. Several times during the night I awakened and looked out the dusty window to where the unmoving body lay on the asphalt. It looked different in the shadows created by moonlight and streetlamp, and in the lumped silhouette I saw contours that were almost familiar to me, echoes of shapes that I knew had meant something to me in the past but which now remained stubbornly buried in my subconscious.

I knew the dead animal had truths to tell.

Weighing:

The hind end of the llama, its head and upper body still supported by the ground, weighed one hundred and ninety-six pounds.

My dead wife's niece told me that she was sixteen, but I believe she was younger.

I have a photograph of her, taken in a booth at an amusement park, that I keep on the top of my dresser, exactly 3.2 inches away from a similar photo of my wife.

The photo cost me a dollar ninety-six. I put eight quarters into the machine, and when I happened to check the coin return I found four pennies.

My father weighed a hundred and ninety-six pounds at his death. He died exactly a hundred and ninety-six years after his great-great-grandfather first set foot in America. My father's great-great-grandfather hanged himself.

A hundred and ninety-six is the sum total of my age multiplied by four—the number of legs of the llama.

*   *   *

The Exxon station where I saw my wife's likeness in a stain in the men's room toilet is located at 196 East 32nd Street.

I do not remember whose idea it was to try the pins. I believe it was hers, since she told me that she'd recently seen a news report on acupuncture that interested her.

I showed her some of the books in my store: the photographic essay on African boys disfigured by rites of passage, the illustrated study of Inquisition torture devices, the book on deformed strippers in an Appalachian sideshow.

She told me that if acupuncture needles placed on the proper nerves could deaden pain, wasn't it logical to assume that needles placed on other nerves could stimulate pleasure?

She allowed me to tie her up, spread-eagled on the bed, and I began by inserting pins in her breasts. She screamed, at first yelling at me to stop, then simply crying out in dumb animal agony. I pushed the pins all the way into her flesh until only the shiny round heads were visible, pressing them slowly through the skin and the fatty tissue of her breasts in a crisscross pattern, then concentrating them around the firmer nipples.

By the time I had moved between her legs, she had passed out and her body was covered all over with a thin shiny sheen of blood.

When the retarded boy finished massaging the llama's distended stomach, he stepped back from the animal and stood there soundlessly. He looked at me and pointed to the ground in front of him. I measured the space between the retarded boy and the llama. Five feet, six inches.

At the time my father hanged himself he was fifty-six years old.

My stillborn son weighed five pounds, six ounces.

Five times six is thirty.

My wife was thirty years old when she died.

According to the book *Nutritional Values of Exotic Dishes*, a single 56-ounce serving of cooked llama meat contains 196 calories.

This information is found on page 32.

The young man did not object when I took him in the men's room of the gas station.

He was standing at the urinal when I entered, and I stepped behind him and held the knife to his throat. I used my free hand to yank down his dress slacks, and then I pressed against him. "You want it, don't you?" I asked.

"Yes," he said.

I made him bend over the side of the lone toilet and although his buttocks were hairy and repulsed me, I made him accept me the way my wife had. All of me. He tensed, stiffened, and gasped with pain, and I felt around in front of his body to make sure he was not aroused. If he had been aroused, I would have had to kill him.

I slid fully in and nearly all the way out fifty-six times before my hot seed shot into him and with my knife pressed against his throat I made him cry out "Oh God! Oh God!" the way my wife had.

I left him with only a slight cut across the upper throat, above the Adam's apple, and I took his clothes and put them in the trunk of my car and later stuffed them with newspaper and made them into a scarecrow for my dead wife's dying garden.

I hoped the young man was a doctor.

*   *   *

I realized the importance of measurements even as a child. When my sister fell out of the tree in our yard, I measured the length of her legs and the total length of her body. Her legs were twenty inches long. Her body was four-foot-five.

My mother was twenty years old when she gave birth to my sister.

My sister died when my father was forty-five.

Requirements:

I was required to pay for the knowledge gained from my sister's measurements.

My sister had two arms and two legs.

I killed two cats and two dogs.

My wife was Jewish. Before coming to the United States, her parents lived 196 miles from the nearest concentration camp and 32 miles from the city where Adolph Hitler spent his youth.

My wife was born in 1956.

I showed Nadine a book on self-mutilation, letting her look at photographs of men who were so jaded, who so craved unique experience, that they mutilated their genitalia. She was fascinated by the subject, and she seemed particularly interested in a photo of a man's penis which had been surgically bifurcated and through which had been inserted a metal ring.

She told me that the concept of self-mutilation appealed to her. She said that she had grown tired of sex, that all three of her orifices had been penetrated so frequently, so many times in so many ways, that there were no sensations that were new to her. Everything to which she submitted was either a repeat or a variation.

I told her I would make her a new opening, a new hole, and I took her to the forest and I tied her to the cross-stakes and I used a knife to cut and carve a slit in her stomach big enough to take me.

She was still alive when I entered her, and her screams were not entirely of pain.

She kept crying, "God."

My white semen mixed with her red blood and made pink.

I wanted to kill the doctor who killed my wife, but I saw him only once after her death and it was with a large crowd and the opportunity did not arise again.

So I rented a small apartment and stocked the shelves with medical books and arranged the furniture in a manner consistent with the way I believed a doctor would arrange it.

The apartment number was 56.

I made friends with a young man who, save for the beard, resembled my wife's doctor fairly closely. I invited the young man into my apartment, smiling, then I showed him the gun and told him to strip. He did so, and I made him put on the white physician's clothes I had bought. I forced him into the bathroom, made him shave, then made him put on the surgical mask.

I had purchased a puppy from the pet store the night before, and I had killed the animal by slitting its throat, draining the blood into a glass pitcher. I splashed the blood on the young man and now the illusion was complete. He looked almost exactly like the doctor who had killed my wife.

I had written out the lines I wanted the surrogate doctor

to say while I killed him, and I'd typed them out and had them bound in plastic.

I cocked the pistol, handed the pages to the young man, told him to speak.

End Exchange:

DOCTOR: I killed your wife.

ME: You wanted her to die!

DOCTOR: She deserved to die! She was a bitch and a whore!

ME: You killed my son!

DOCTOR: I'm glad I did it! He was a son of a bitch and a son of a whore and I knew I couldn't let him be born!

ME: That means that you deserve to die.

DOCTOR: Yes. You have the right to kill me. I killed your wife and son. It is only fair.

I shot him in the groin, shot him in the mouth, shot him in the arms, shot him in the legs, left him there to die.

In the newspaper article, it said he had bled to death four hours after the bullets had entered his body.

He had been a stockbroker.

I have clipped my toenails and fingernails once each week since my wife died. I save the clippings and store them in a plastic trash bag that I keep underneath my bed.

On the tenth anniversary of her death, on what would have been our son's tenth birthday, I will weigh the bag of nail clippings and then set the bag on fire.

I will swallow ten teaspoonfuls of the ashes.

The remainder I will bury with the body of my wife.

I will use the information gained from the weighing to determine the date and manner of my death.

John F. Kennedy was assassinated on the date of my birth.

My initials are J.F.K.

Cataloguing:

My store has sixteen nonfiction books containing information about llamas. There are five fiction books in which a llama plays an important role. All of these are children's books, and three of them are Hugh Lofting's Dr. Dolittle stories.

I have killed sixteen adults since my wife's death. And five children.

Three of the children were siblings.

The llama has changed my plans.

The llama and the retarded boy.

I stare out the window of my store at the dead animal, at the retarded boy next to it, at the occasional gawkers who pass by and stop and whisper. I know that one of them, one of them over whom I have no control, will eventually notify the authorities and they will take the carcass away.

I cannot let that happen.

Or maybe I can.

For the presence of the llama in my alley indicates that I have done wrong and that a sacrifice is demanded.

But who is to be the sacrifice, the retarded boy or myself?

Neither of us knows, and we stare at each other. He outside, next to the animal, me inside, with my books. Through the dirty window he looks vague, faded, although the llama still seems clearly defined. Is this a sign?

I don't know. But I know I must make the decision quickly. I must act today. Or tonight.

I have measured the body of the llama and it is four feet, ten inches long.

Tomorrow is April 10.

Full Moon on Death Row

Some years ago, a British editor decided to put together an anthology for which authors would write stories based on titles the editor provided. The titles were all clichéd horror images, and the one assigned to me was "Full Moon on Death Row."

I knew I didn't want to feature a literal full moon or a literal death row. That would've been too easy. And too corny. As luck would have it, *Dances with Wolves* was on television, and I thought, Aha! I'll make "Full Moon" a Native American man's name. I got the idea for making "Death Row" the name of a street from the song "Sonora's Death Row," which appears on the great Robert Earl Keen Jr.'s album *West Textures*.

Unfortunately, the anthology never came to pass, the editor disappeared, and I shelved the story. This is its first appearance.

---~m~---

He saw the man in the casino.

Full Moon thought at first that he was mistaken, that it was only someone with a cowboy hat and dirty blond mustache who *looked* like the man from Death Row. But then the man turned to face him, staring from across the crowded gaming room, and smiled.

A chill passed through him. It wasn't possible, it couldn't be.

But it was.

It had been thirty-five years, and he himself had grown from a frightened boy into the middle-aged manager of the tribe's gambling enterprises, but the man with the mustache had not aged a day and looked exactly as he had all those years before, the eyes staring at him from across the noisy smoky room, the same eyes that had haunted his nightmares for the past three decades.

And the man recognized him.

That was the scary part. The cowboy knew who he was. Amidst the turmoil of the room, the people walking from slot machine to roulette wheel to card table, the man stood still, unmoving, staring.

Smiling.

Full Moon looked away. He was sweating, and his legs felt weak. He knew as surely as he knew his own name that the man had not come here to gamble or drink or meet with friends or sightsee or hang out.

He had come for him.

Full Moon looked up, glanced across the room to where the man had been standing.

He was gone.

He saw the other two playing bingo.

Like their compadre, they had not aged a day. Both the man with the patch over his eye and the fat man with the beard looked exactly as they had over three decades ago.

When they'd killed his father.

Full Moon looked around for help, caught the eye of Tom

Two-Feathers. He was breathing hard, his heart pounding, but he forced himself to smile at the customers and act as though nothing was wrong while he made his way to the side of the bingo board where Tom was standing.

"What is it?" Tom asked, frowning.

Full Moon gestured toward the left side of the third bingo table. "Do you see—?" he began.

But they were no longer there.

He met that evening with the council, calling them together in a special meeting at his house. Rosalie made sandwiches, John brought beer. The atmosphere was supposed to be informal, relaxed. But Full Moon felt anything except relaxed. He had told no one of what he had seen, had spent the better part of the afternoon wondering what he should do, whether he should ignore it, forget it, tell no one, or announce it to everyone, and he had finally decided that the best course of action would be to lay it out before the council and let them decide what, if anything, was to be done.

By the time the men of the council pulled up in front of his house in two cars and a pickup, he was already starting to wonder if he had made the right decision. Maybe he should have kept it to himself. Maybe he should have discussed it with Lone Cloud first. But it was too late to change his mind now, and he had John get the door while he told Rosalie to either go into the bedroom or stay in the kitchen.

"What?" She looked at him as if he had just asked her to strip in public.

"There's something private I have to discuss with the council."

"Private? What do you mean 'private'? There's something you can say to them that you can't say in front of me?"

"I'll tell you about it later," he promised.

"You'll tell me now."

He grabbed her shoulders, held her. "I don't want to fight in front of them. You know what they're like. And you know they don't like women to—"

"You could've told me earlier." She pulled away from him. "What's with you tonight? Why are you so secretive? What's going on?"

"I'll tell you later."

"So I should just smile and bring in the sandwiches and keep my mouth shut and leave."

"Exactly," he said.

"I was being sarcastic."

The front door opened. He heard John greeting the council members. "I know you were," he said, dropping his voice. "But please? Just this once? For me?"

She looked into his eyes, licked her lips. "It's bad, isn't it? Whatever it is, it's bad."

He nodded.

She took a deep breath.

"Please?" he asked.

She sighed, not looking at him. "Okay."

He smiled at her, gave her a quick kiss on the forehead. "I know you're going to listen in," he said. "But at least don't let them see you. Keep the kitchen door closed."

She nodded, kissed him back on the lips. "Don't worry."

He walked out of the kitchen and shook hands with Graham, Ronnie, and Small Raven before nodding to Black Hawk and offering the council leader a seat on the recliner. The old man sat down slowly and awkwardly, and the other council members waited until he was settled before sitting on the couch.

Full Moon was silent until John left the room, then came straight to the point.

"I've seen the men who killed my father," he said. "The men from Death Row."

Silence greeted his announcement.

"They were in the casino."

Black Hawk shifted uncomfortably on the chair. "Mustache, Beard, and Patch-Eye?"

"Yes."

Black Hawk and the others nodded, and Full Moon noticed immediately that none of them seemed shocked or surprised at the news. None of them seemed even skeptical.

"They looked exactly the same," he told them. "They have not grown old."

Again the members of the council nodded, as though murderers who never aged were an everyday occurrence. He looked from Graham to Ronnie to Small Raven to Black Hawk. Something was going on here. Something he didn't understand. He could feel it in the air, a subtext to the silence. He glanced toward the closed kitchen door where he knew—he *hoped*—Rosalie was listening.

He cleared his throat. "Has anyone else seen them?"

The others looked at each other, shook their heads. "It is only you," Black Hawk said. "You are the one."

"Lone Cloud's father was killed there also—"

"Have you spoken to Lone Cloud?"

"No," Full Moon admitted.

"Do not."

"Why?"

"This is a council matter. You did the right thing in coming to us." Black Hawk leaned forward. "You have told no one else?"

"No. But I'm going to tell Lone Cloud."

"You cannot. The council—"

"They killed his father, too. He has a right to know."

"What do you expect to accomplish by telling him?" Ronnie asked. "What do you think he can do?"

"It will only bring pain," Graham said.

"Well, what are *you* going to do?" Full Moon asked. "What's the council going to do about this?"

Small Raven's voice when he spoke was frightened. "You are not going to go there?"

He had not known it until that moment, but, yes, that was exactly what he was going to do. "I have to," he said.

Black Hawk nodded. "It is right," he said. "If he saw them, he saw them for a reason."

"But—" Ronnie began.

Black Hawk silenced him with a look. "It is not for us to say."

"I'm telling Lone Cloud," Full Moon said.

Black Hawk nodded. "It is yours to decide."

After the council left, Rosalie emerged from the kitchen. She was scared but supportive, and he hugged her and held her and the two of them sat down in the living room with John and told him about Death Row.

It was after midnight by the time they finished talking and Rosalie was tired and wanted to go to bed, but Full Moon was still wide awake. He told her to go on ahead, he was going to stay up for another hour or so.

He wandered outside, looked up through the cottonwoods at the night sky. There was a warm desert breeze tonight and it carried with it the soothing sounds of the Gila River, many miles away.

Many miles away.

He thought of Death Row. He had not been back to the street, or to Rojo Cuello, since his father had been killed. Neither, to his knowledge, had anyone else from the tribe. It was probably a regular city now, like Tucson or Tempe or

Casa Grande, with malls and subdivisions and cable TV, but for himself and for most members of the tribe, it was a bad place, an evil place, tainted forever by its history, its character determined by its past.

He had learned of Death Row from his father. He had been nine, maybe ten, when his father brought him to the hill overlooking the town and pointed out the street to him. It was called "Death Row," his father explained, because so many of their people had died there.

Had been murdered there.

His father had been killed on the Row, he said. As had his father before him and his father before him. "They were killed in the street like dogs. Beaten and stabbed while other people, white people, stood there laughing."

"But that's against the law."

"Don't make no difference on the Row. The law has no power there. Never has, never will."

"How old is the Row?" Full Moon asked.

A shadow passed over his father's face. "Old."

"How old?"

"It was here before the town. Rojo Cuello grew up around it."

"Is it older than—?"

"It's older than the tribe," his father said, and that shut him up. Full Moon looked down at the street, and though he'd felt nothing before, there now seemed something sinister about the false fronts on the old buildings, about the wooden sidewalks and the hitching posts. It looked like a street out of a western, the type of movie he loved best, but at the same time it looked different, set apart from that glamorized screen world in a way that he could not identify.

Older than the tribe.

That scared him, and he wondered why his father had brought him there.

"I will die on Death Row also," his father said quietly.

Full Moon could still remember the horrifying, frightening feeling that had lodged in the pit of his stomach when his father spoke those words. "Let's get out of here," he said.

"It won't happen now."

"If we don't come back, it can't happen at all."

"It don't make no difference."

"Why?" Full Moon was close to panic, as unnerved by his father's attitude of resigned fatalism as by the substance of his words. "We could move. We don't have to stay on the reservation. We could move to California."

"No matter where I move, no matter what I do, I will have to return."

"If you know what's going to happen, then you know how to change it," Full Moon said.

His father shook his head. "If you know what will happen," he said softly, "it will happen."

He had been right.

He'd been killed on the Row less than two years later.

And Full Moon had watched him die.

He stopped the next day by Lone Cloud's house. "You heard?" he asked after his friend had opened the door, invited him inside, and the two of them were seated on the couch.

Lone Cloud looked away, nodded. "I heard."

"What do you think?"

"I haven't seen anything."

"I know that. But what do you think?"

"I think they killed our fathers. I think we should blow the fuckers away."

Yes. Full Moon found himself nodding. He'd known that he had to return to Death Row, but he hadn't known why he needed to return or what he was going to do when he got there. But this sounded right. No, it *felt* right.

"What if they're . . ." His voice trailed off.

"Ghosts?" Lone Cloud finished for him.

Full Moon nodded.

"Dead or alive, we kick their asses."

Full Moon smiled. The smile grew. Then he started to laugh. He hadn't realized how tense he'd been, how tightly wound. This whole thing had frightened him more than he was willing to admit, and it felt good to laugh again.

Lone Cloud smiled back at him, but there was no humor in it.

Full Moon thought of the way the man with the mustache had smiled at him from across the casino.

His own smile faded, his laughter dying.

"We're going to kill those sons of bitches," Lone Cloud said.

Full Moon nodded. "Yes," he said.

But was that really what they should do? Was that what their fathers would have wanted? Revenge?

He didn't know.

He felt like a teenager again, unsure and indecisive. His father had not been there for his high school years, but Full Moon had always acted as though he was, behaving the way he thought his father would want him to behave, doing things that he thought would make his father proud. Somehow, though, he had always fallen short. It was not that he had not done well, it was just that he had the feeling that his father would have expected more from him.

What would his father expect him to do now?

"I think we should talk to the council," he said. "Tell them our plans."

Lone Cloud snorted. "What for? It's a free country. We don't need their permission."

"They know more than we do," Full Moon said. "Maybe they can help us."

Lone Cloud thought for a moment. He nodded. "Okay. But we'll tell them. Not ask them. Tell them."

"Deal."

He let Lone Cloud do the talking when they met with the convened council later that afternoon. His friend was typically forceful in his presentation, typically defensive in his attitude.

"No," Black Hawk said vehemently when Lone Cloud finished. "No guns. You cannot bring guns."

"Why not?"

"It is not the way."

"It's *our* way," Lone Cloud said.

Black Hawk stood with difficulty, his hand shaking as his finger pointed at the younger man. "No!"

"We're not asking you, we're telling you," Lone Cloud said.

The other council members looked nervously at each other.

"You will die!" Black Hawk said. His voice was an enraged whisper.

"Then what should we do?" Full Moon asked him.

"You are the one who saw the men. You go there—"

"They killed my father, too."

Black Hawk glared at Lone Cloud. "You did not see them."

"What do I do when I get there?" Full Moon asked.

"I do not know. Perhaps it will be revealed to you."

"What do you think?" Full Moon asked his friend as they left the meeting a few minutes later.

"We bring the guns," Lone Cloud told him.

He dreamed that night of a saloon. The type of saloon that could be found in old westerns.

Or on Death Row.

There was no liquor behind the bar of the saloon, only jars filled with organs floating in watered-down blood. Skeletons, posed as stereotypical gamblers, sat around the round oak tables.

Full Moon stood alone in the middle of the saloon. From outside, he heard the sounds of a gunfight: shouting, then shooting, then silence. A moment later, he heard boots on the wooden sidewalk outside. A tall man was silhouetted from behind by the sunlight. He walked through the swinging doors into the saloon, and as he came into the room, Full Moon saw that the man was his father.

His father tipped his hat, and the top of his head came off. Blood poured down his face in even rivulets.

"You killed me, son," he said. "You killed me."

They set off in the morning, leaving just after dawn in Lone Cloud's pickup.

Full Moon brought a .22.

Lone Cloud brought a .45 and a shotgun.

They did not speak as they drove through the desert. Lone Cloud was at the wheel, and Full Moon stared through the passenger window at the empty, overgrown parking lots and the abandoned, broken-windowed buildings that periodically fronted the highway.

He thought about the men he'd seen in the casino. What

if they weren't ghosts? he wondered. What if they were regular men, men who just happened to have aged well?

They weren't.

But did that make any difference? He didn't know. The men had killed his father, and Lone Cloud's father, and he supposed they deserved what they were going to get, but it was still a dirty business and the whole situation made him extremely uncomfortable.

Full Moon cleared his throat, turned away from the window. "I've never killed anyone before."

Lone Cloud did not take his eyes off the highway. "Neither have I. But they have."

"What will that make us if we do kill them?"

"They're not alive," Lone Cloud said. "Or, if they are, they're not human."

"Then how are we going to kill them?"

"What do you mean, how? We brought guns."

"What if guns don't work on them?"

"We'll cross that bridge when we come to it."

They drove for a moment in silence.

It is only you. You are the one.

"Why did they come to the casino?" Full Moon wondered aloud. "And how come I was the only one who saw them?"

"Doesn't matter."

"Maybe it does."

"Black Hawk doesn't know any more about this than we do."

Full Moon didn't believe it, but he nodded. "I hope you're right," he said.

Death Row.

Full Moon got out of the pickup and stood on the hill

above Rojo Cuello, looking down. The street looked exactly as he remembered it. Around the street, the city had been transformed, the empty ground between buildings paved over with parking lots, built up into condominiums, the buildings themselves torn down or made over.

But Death Row remained unchanged.

He had known that would be the case, and it frightened him. He glanced over at Lone Cloud, and the blanched look on his friend's face mirrored his own emotions perfectly.

For all of his bravado, Lone Cloud was just as scared as he was.

He scanned the street below for the spot where his father had been killed, found it almost instantly.

The past returned in a rush.

He'd been awakened by his father in the middle of the night, shaken awake, and he opened his eyes to see his father sitting on the edge of the bed. "Get dressed," his father said. "It's time to go."

"Go where?"

"Rojo Cuello. Death Row."

He cried almost all the way there, begging his father to turn back, but his father drove on through the darkness, repeating grimly that he had no choice.

Full Moon was supposed to drive the pickup back home.

His father would give his life to Death Row but not his truck.

Truth be told, Full Moon had been frightened more for himself than for his father, filled with dread and terror and the horrifying certainty that he too would be killed, but when his father parked the pickup on the hill above town, gave him the keys, told him to take off, and started walking down the path that led through the weeds and brush on the side of the hill, Full Moon drove down the Rojo Cuello highway in-

stead, his heart thumping so hard it felt as though it would burst through his rib cage as he sped down the winding road to Death Row.

He and his father reached the street at the same time.

And he saw the men take his father down.

He'd driven to the street with no plan, with only the vague notion that he would rescue his father and save his life, but his mind had been a terrified blank as he'd sped down the curving road, and though he often thought later that if he had floored the pedal and barreled down the street he might have run over the murderers, he braked to a stop at the head of Death Row.

His father emerged from between two buildings, walking slow and straight, head held high as though unafraid, and the man with the mustache came out from the lingering sunrise shadows and shoved a knife deep into his stomach.

Full Moon screamed, and the man looked down the street at him and grinned.

His father fell, clutching his midsection and rolling on the ground, and the other two appeared out of nowhere, the man with the patch laughing as he yanked down his father's pants and cut off his penis, the man with the beard screaming as he used a hatchet to hack off the top of his head.

For a brief second, Full Moon considered speeding down the street and running over all three of them, but he knew he'd hit his father's body as well, and then the three men were bending over his father and there were even more knives in their hands, the multiple blades glinting orange in the dawn sun, and he understood that if he did not get out of there then, the men would come after him, too.

He threw the truck into reverse and took off, barely able to see through his tears, looking more at the rearview mirror than through the windshield, seeing the men gleefully carving up what was left of his father, and then he smashed into a bush, nearly going off the road, before he quickly righted the vehicle and sped back up the hill, this time keeping his eyes on the pavement.

He stopped at the top of the hill and looked down, but Death Row was empty, and he quickly put the truck into gear and took off.

"I don't see anyone down there."

He glanced over at Lone Cloud, wondering how his friend's father had been killed. They had never discussed the details.

Full Moon walked toward the pickup. "It's getting late," he said. "Let's go."

They parked in the middle of the street, in front of an old livery stable at the east end of the Row. The pavement had faded into dirt some yards back, and before them the dusty road narrowed as it passed between the wooden buildings. There was something threatening about the stillness of the street, about the silence and the utter lack of life. One block over, cars and trucks were driving by office buildings and fast food restaurants, but here on Death Row it was as if the modern world did not exist.

Except for them.

Lone Cloud got out of the pickup, tucking the .45 in his belt, the shotgun cradled in his hands. Full Moon followed his friend, holding the .22, ready to shoot anything that moved.

Lone Cloud cleared his throat. The sound was loud, jarring. "Do you think they're hiding?" he asked.

Full Moon shrugged.

"You think we should look for them? Or should we wait for them to find us?"

Full Moon did not know, and he was about to shrug again, when he noticed a one-story building halfway down the street on the left side, situated between a small hotel and what looked like a sheriff's office. The building stuck out, protruding into the street, and its architectural style was radically different from that of the surrounding structures.

He took a tentative step forward, sucking in his breath. A wave of cold washed over him as he looked at the building. It was their house, their old house, the one his father had built.

The one that had burned down after his father's death.

His father's murder.

How had the house burned down? Was it arson? A fireplace accident? A leaky gas line? He couldn't remember.

Had he ever known?

His gaze was drawn to the blackness within the open doorway. He could not remember the last time he had thought of their old home, but now that he considered it, everything about the situation seemed suspect. And the fact that he could remember no details, that his mind glossed over the specifics of that time, retaining only the broad brushstrokes of occurrence, worried him.

He walked toward the house, toward the open door, his hands gripping the rifle so tightly that his palms and fingers hurt. He heard Lone Cloud following behind him.

It is only you. You are the one.

There was something about Black Hawk's words that didn't sit well with him, that made him uneasy, though he hadn't really thought about it until now. *The one?* What did that mean? Was he the one chosen to kill these creatures? Or was he the one chosen as a sacrifice to them?

Had his father been sacrificed?

Full Moon stopped walking. He had never thought of that

before, had never even considered that the tribe might be complicitous in the killings that had occurred on the Row. But it made sense. He had wondered at the time why the law had never been brought in to investigate, why there had never been any police or FBI or BIA or any sort of officials looking into the murder of his father, but when he'd asked his mother about it, she had told him to shut up, to not say anything, that there was nothing that could be done about Death Row.

He stared at the house, and he remembered how, after their home had burned down, they had been given a new one, a bigger one, one built especially for them by two of the tribe's contractors.

Given?

Since when had the tribe *given* houses away?

He turned toward Lone Cloud. "After . . ." He cleared his throat. "After what happened to your father, you moved, didn't you?"

Lone Cloud nodded. "They were tearing down our old house to build the gas station."

"And they gave you a bigger house?"

Lone Cloud nodded, puzzled. "Yes."

"Payoff," Full Moon said. "They sacrificed our fathers and paid us off."

Lone Cloud shook his head. "What the fuck are you talking about?"

"You don't see it?"

"See what?"

"Why did they let our fathers come here alone? Why didn't they get a posse together? They knew what the Row was like. They knew what happened here. Why didn't they come with our fathers? Or try to stop them?"

"What could they do?"

"Why did they let *us* come here? Why didn't they want us to bring guns?"

Lone Cloud blinked. He stared down the street. "Black Hawk," he said slowly.

Full Moon nodded.

"He was council leader when our fathers were killed."

"And he was old even then." Full Moon licked his lips. "How long do you think he's been head of the council?"

"You know the tribe's history."

"No, I don't. You tell me."

Lone Cloud thought for a moment. "I don't either," he admitted.

"How old do you think he is?" Full Moon asked.

Lone Cloud did not answer, and the only sound on the silent street was their overloud breathing.

You are the one.

Damn right, Full Moon thought. He took a deep breath. "Let's do it," he said.

They strode forward. The fear was still there, but it had been shunted aside by anger, and Full Moon was grateful for that. He walked into the black doorway of the house his father built, Lone Cloud a step behind.

Only it wasn't the house his father built.

The outside was exactly the same, down to the chipped white paint on the right upper edge of the doorframe, but there was no coat closet entryway leading into the living room. There was only a long, narrow, black-floored, black-walled, black-ceilinged hallway that stretched forward to what looked like a bloodred room.

Where someone was screaming.

His father.

Full Moon ran down the hallway, not noticing if Lone Cloud was following him, not caring. He heard only the screams, and he remembered clearly, though he had forgotten it until now, how his father had screamed when they'd killed him, how the screams had continued long past the point when his father should have been dead, how he'd heard them clearly even as he drove away in the truck.

He reached the doorway at the end of the hall.

His father stood alone in the center of the windowless room, screaming. There were no pauses for breath, only one long continuous cry. He had heard that scream before, in the soundtrack to his nightmares, a hellish variation on the original death screams he had head on the Row.

His father was skinned and scalped, and though it had been years—decades—ago that it had occurred, the blood was still flowing, still fresh. It oozed from exposed musculature, droplets forming into drops, drops into rivulets, the rivulets cascading down skinless flesh, puddling on the floor, dark crimson against the lighter rose.

"Father!" Full Moon cried.

His voice was lost amidst the screams, and the frozen muscles of his father's face did not even twitch as Full Moon yelled, the white staring eyes not budging from their focus on nothing.

Instinctively, without making a conscious decision to do so, he raised the rifle to his shoulder and shot his father in the face.

The screams died instantly as his father's head exploded, his skinned body falling in a heap. There was a jerking spasm, then a shifting and shrinking of the form on the floor as it compressed itself into a fetal position and began to melt, the now liquified substance of his father soaking into the floor.

The walls and ceiling of the room darkened almost imperceptibly, and then the room was empty, the floor dry, and it was as if his father had never been there.

Full Moon was shaking, breathing heavily, the air harsh in his throat and lungs. He turned, but Lone Cloud was not behind him, and he hurried back down the hall toward the front of the building, reloading as he ran. He saw another red room off to his right, and he stopped, grabbing the door-frame.

He watched Lone Cloud shoot his screaming father in the face.

He watched Lone Cloud's father melt into the floor.

"Come on!" Full Moon yelled.

The two of them ran outside.

Death Row was no longer silent. A hot wind was blowing, and it carried with it screams. The screams of men, women, and children, pitched at different tones and volumes, all sounding without pause. The street still appeared to be empty, but it felt as though it wasn't, and the two of them looked through the swirling sand for a sign of movement.

A black cowboy-hatted figure walked toward them through the dust from the far end of the street.

Full Moon raised his rifle. Lone Cloud took the .45 from his belt and aimed it.

"What's going to happen if we kill them?" Lone Cloud asked.

Full Moon shook his head. "I don't know."

"You think anyone's ever tried this before?"

"I don't know."

The figure walking toward them was carrying a hatchet, and as he drew closer, Full Moon could see that it was the man with the beard. The one who had cut off the top of his father's head.

Full Moon raised the .22, sighted the man, and shot him in the chest. The man's head jerked back at the same time that his chest exploded, dark liquid spewing out from behind, and though he hadn't heard the report, Full Moon knew that Lone Cloud had shot the man as well.

"Behind you!" Lone Cloud yelled.

Full Moon swiveled as he heard the thunderous sound of Lone Cloud's gun. He saw, for a second, the man with the mustache, arm raised, a knife clutched in his fist, but then the man was gone, disappearing instantly, appearing seconds later far off to the left. Lone Cloud shot again, this time hitting the man in the arm. The man dropped the knife, and Lone Cloud shot once more, hitting the man in the gut. Mustache doubled over and fell, unmoving, onto the dirt.

The wind had died down by this time, and the temperature had dropped. Full Moon tried to reload his rifle, but his hands were shaking and he dropped a shell. He took another one from his pocket and inserted it in the chamber.

"Two down," Lone Cloud said. "One to go."

"I give up!"

They looked to their left at the sound of the voice. Patch-Eye emerged from the sheriff's office, arms raised in surrender. He began walking toward them, and there was something about the lack of hesitation in his movements, his obvious lack of fear, that made Full Moon uneasy.

Full Moon raised his rifle. "Stop right there!" he ordered.

The man continued walking.

Lone Cloud gripped his .45, straightened his arm.

"Wait," Full Moon said. "Don't shoot him. Let's hear what he has to say."

"Halt!" Lone Cloud yelled.

Patch-Eye moved toward them, arms still raised. This close, Full Moon could see that his skin was not all skin. Most of it was, but it was so old that it was cracked and split, and the fissures were filled with what looked like painted hair. It was as though the form they were looking at was a mask, a hastily repaired costume that hid the real creature within.

"I don't think he's human," Full Moon said.

"We killed the other two, we can kill him. Whatever he is, he can die."

Lone Cloud had not even finished the sentence when the knife sliced open his upper arm. He screamed, dropping the gun.

Patch-Eye stood unmoving, arms still raised.

Full Moon jumped back, startled. His grip on the rifle tightened, and he glanced quickly to the left and the right. Who had thrown the knife? Beard and Mustache were still lying on the ground. And Patch-Eye had had his arms up the entire time.

Or had he?

Full Moon had been half looking at Lone Cloud as he spoke. Could Patch-Eye have moved that fast, throwing the knife and then immediately putting his hands back up in the air?

"Why are you trying to kill us?" Full Moon asked.

Patch-Eye looked at him, smiling. "Why are you trying to kill *us*?"

"Why did you come looking for me?"

"Why did you come looking for *me*?"

"You killed my father."

"And you killed my friends."

"You killed my father's father. And his father." Full Moon swung the rifle over. "And now I'm going to kill you."

"This isn't part of the deal," Patch-Eye said.

"What deal?"

"This wasn't in the bargain."

Before Full Moon could ask another question, the man's face exploded in a spray of red.

Lone Cloud dropped the shotgun and fell to his knees. He rolled over on his left side, clutching his wounded right arm and closing his eyes. "Got the fucker," he said.

The wind was now completely gone. Full Moon looked from one body to another, then glanced down the street. Behind the windows of the buildings, he saw faces. The faces of the dead. Some were faces he knew, others were familiar but not immediately recognizable, related to faces he knew. One by one, they disappeared, winking out of existence like lights that had been switched off. The faces were still troubled as they stared at him, still frightened or in pain, as though their owners did not realize what had happened, but in the instant before they winked out of existence, an expression of gratitude passed over each.

Full Moon bent down next to Lone Cloud, and as he helped his friend stand and saw the dirt of Death Row blur and shift in his sight, he realized that he was crying.

He left Lone Cloud at the hospital in Rojo Cuello.

He'd planned to stay, to wait around until his friend's arm was patched up, but that was going to take several hours, and because it was a knife wound, the hospital was required to inform the police, and there would probably be several more hours of questioning.

Lone Cloud told him to leave, to drop him off and go.

To return and confront Black Hawk.

There was an ambulance in front of the casino when he arrived back at the reservation. Inside, a huge crowd had gathered around one of the blackjack tables, and Full Moon pushed his way through the gawkers until he reached the front.

"Jesus," he breathed.

John and Tom Two-Feathers moved next to him, and he turned toward them. "What is it?" he asked.

John licked his lips. "Black Hawk," he said.

Full Moon looked down again at the floor. All that was left of the council leader was a brown spiderlike thing that walked lamely around in a closed circle, hissing and spitting at those who looked upon it. The two paramedics, who had obviously arrived some time ago, stood with their stretcher, unsure of what to do.

This wasn't in the bargain.

Full Moon climbed onto the top of the blackjack table, raising his arms for silence. He glanced around the casino, making sure everyone could see him, and he told them what had happened. He told them of his father and his father's father and all of the other tribe members who had been killed on Death Row over the years, their deaths blamed on either outlaws or cowboys, whites or Mexicans. He told them what he had seen, what he had heard, what he had learned, and there was silence in the casino.

The thing that had been Black Hawk screamed, a high, piercing, almost birdlike sound, and Full Moon jumped off the table.

"This is for my father," he said.

He lifted his leg, brought his boot down hard on the creature's body. There was a loud crack and a lower squelching sound, and the hairy brown legs protruding from beneath his boot jerked once and then were still. Red blood spread outward in uneven rivulets, slowly pushing a gum wrapper and cigarette butt across the cement floor.

"What was he?" someone asked, and everyone looked around, searching the faces of the older people, who shook their heads, confused.

"Traitor!" White Dog yelled, and spit on the dead body of the Black Hawk thing.

The other council members, gathered behind the paramedics, were backing up, frightened by the mood of the room.

"Kill them, too!" someone yelled. A woman.

Jimmy Big Hands and White Dog grabbed Ronnie, the nearest council member.

"Let him go," Full Moon said quietly.

"What?"

"Let him go. Let them all go."

"But they knew!" White Dog yelled.

"They knew, but they are still here. They are not like him. They are like us."

He didn't like using words like *us* and *them*. It made him uncomfortable, and he thought of the whites on the Row who had stood and watched and laughed as his grandfather had been murdered in the street. But, like it or not, it was true, and once again he held up his hands. "It's over!" he announced. "Death Row is dead. It's over."

He looked around the room at the members of the tribe, the eyes, old and young, that were trained on him, and suddenly he felt like crying. Other people were crying already. Older people mostly. People who remembered. He saw the faces of the men and women he'd grown up with, his friends and family. He scanned the crowd for Rosalie but didn't see her.

"She's at home," John said, touching his elbow.

He nodded, and the crowd parted before him as he started to walk. The people were silent as he headed toward the door, and he walked out of the casino, outside, and into the sunlight.

He looked up at the sky, the sun, the clouds, breathing deeply, the tears beginning to flow.

His father, he knew, would have been proud.

The Show

In high school, a student in my class claimed to have seen a snuff film. No one thought he really had, but he traded on that story for our entire senior year. I didn't believe him either, but the idea haunted me, and when I was in college I decided to write a story about a teenage boy who watches a snuff movie. I had just seen Stephen Sondheim's *Sweeney Todd* on TV, and it occurred to me that maybe snuff films were not murders staged specifically for the camera but were, like *Sweeney Todd*, filmed plays, events produced for live audiences that also happened to be recorded. I liked the idea of the boy going to a snuff "show," and wrote this story.

—ɷ—

My parents were fighting again in the front of the house, my dad calling my mom a stupid boring bitch, my mom calling my dad a cheap insensitive bastard. I closed the door to my room and cranked up my stereo, hoping it would drown out the screaming, but their words ran as an angry undertone to my music, the meanings clear even if the words weren't. I lay on the bed, reading a *Rolling Stone*, forcing my mind to concentrate on something else.

When the phone rang, I answered it immediately. I half hoped it would be for one of my parents, which would at least provide a momentary break in the battle, but it was only Jimmy. "Hey," I said. "How's it going?"

"Parents fighting again?"

"What else?"

He cleared his throat. "How'd you like to do something different tonight? I mean really different?"

"What?"

"I can't tell you."

"Knock off the crap."

"Look, do you want to do something tonight, or do you want to sit there alone and listen to them fight?"

He had a point. "Okay," I said. "What's the plan?"

"You just meet me at my house in fifteen minutes. I'll drive. We have to be there by eight." He laughed. "You're gonna love this. It's gonna blow you away."

My curiosity was stimulated and he knew it. "What is it?"

"You'll see. And make sure you bring some bucks. It cost twenty dollars last night, but the guy who took me said it's sometimes more." He laughed again. "See you."

I hung up the phone and slipped on my shoes. I pulled a shirt from the pile next to my bed, grabbed the pickup keys from the dresser, and carefully opened my bedroom door. They were still arguing, their screaming now more furious, their words more overwrought. They were in the living room, and I crept down the hall into the kitchen and snuck out the side door.

Outside it was still hot. The dry desert heat had not dissipated with nightfall, and Phoenix was not blessed with a breeze. Above me, the sky was clear and I could see billions of stars. There was no moon.

I pulled up in front of Jimmy's house five minutes later. He was already outside, sitting on the hood of his Jeep, waiting. He walked toward me as I hopped out of the pickup, his boots clicking loudly on the asphalt driveway, and there was something in his expression I didn't like. "All right," I said. "What're we doing?"

"We're going to a snuff show," he said.

I stared at him, not sure I was hearing right. "What did you say?"

"I didn't want to tell you until we were there, but then I thought it would be better to prepare you for it."

"A snuff movie? One of those movies that show someone actually getting killed?"

"Not a movie," Jimmy said. "I didn't say snuff movie. I said snuff show. This is a live show."

My mouth felt suddenly dry. "You're bullshitting me."

"I'm serious. I saw it. I was there last night."

"It has to be fake," I said. "It can't be real."

"It's real."

"I know a guy who saw one of those movies, and he said it was real cheap and amateurish. He said you could tell it was fake. I mean, if legitimate movies have a tough time showing realistic deaths, these guys with no budgets at all must be really bad at it."

"It's not a movie," Jimmy said. "And it's real."

I looked at the expression on his face, and there was no horror or revulsion in it. There was only an open interest and what appeared to be a look of excited anticipation. Jimmy was not stupid, and I realized that if he thought the show was real, it probably was real. I thought suddenly how little I really knew my best friend.

"Come on," he said, motioning toward his Jeep. "It's getting late. Let's go."

I shook my head. "I don't think I want to go."

"Yes, you do," he said. "Come on."

And I followed him to the Jeep.

We drove in silence. I looked out at the empty streets of Phoenix as we drove toward the outskirts of the city. I really didn't want to see this. But I remembered the time when Jimmy and I were both eight and we had seen an even younger boy hit by a brakeless Buick. The car had slammed into the boy's tricycle, and the kid had been carried halfway down the street, his head smashed into the vehicle's grille. I had thrown up then, as had Jimmy, and I had had nightmares for months. But in school, on my papers, I had drawn endless variations of the accident, and I realized that I was both attracted to and repelled by the incident.

Despite my conscious objections, I had a similar perverse interest in seeing the snuff show.

I was repulsed by the very thought of it, but I wanted to see it.

The buildings of the city became more run down and spaced farther apart. The fast food franchises were replaced by neon-lit massage parlors and bars. We traveled through one stretch of road which was still desert, though it was technically within the city limits.

Jimmy pulled into a crowded parking lot in front of a low pink building. A string of white Christmas lights hung in an inverted arc over the warped wooden door, and a faded mural on the side of the building had a picture of an eight-ball and a pool cue. The building was flanked on both sides by vacant lots in which tumbleweeds and cacti grew in abundance. Jimmy looked at me. "You have your wallet?"

"In my front pocket," I said. "I'm taking no chances."

We got out of the Jeep and walked across the gravel parking lot to the door of the building. Jimmy pulled open the door and walked in.

A table was situated right next to the entrance. On the table was a metal cashbox and two stacks of papers, each weighted down with chunks of rock. A fat, bearded man who looked like Charlie Daniels nodded at us from behind the table. "Thirty-five," he said.

Jimmy pulled two twenties from his pocket, and the man gave him a five. "Sign the release," the man said.

I paid my money, then looked over the form the man gave me. It was a pseudo-legal document which stated that I knew exactly what was occurring there tonight and that I was directly involved in the actions. I didn't know if such a document would hold up in court, but I understood that the people in charge were trying to intimidate the viewers from talking about what they'd seen. I signed on the line at the bottom.

The man glanced over the form. "Address and driver's license," he said, handing it back to me.

I felt suddenly afraid, intimidated myself, but I filled out the information anyway. I followed Jimmy down a short, dark hallway.

We went into a large, crowded room. In the center of the room, a woman was tied naked to a chair. Her mouth was gagged, but her eyes looked wildly around, as if searching for some means of escape. There were large bruises and welts on her white skin. Standing around the woman in a rough semicircle, quiet and shuffling, were thirty or forty people, mostly men, some women. Next to the chair, on a table, was a pistol, two knives, a screwdriver, a hammer, a hacksaw, and a length of wire.

Jimmy and I stood silently with the rest of the crowd. I felt suddenly sick to my stomach. I could see from the bound woman's frantic eyes that she was scared to death. She was about to be killed. And all of the people standing impassively around her had paid money to watch her die.

I stared at my shoes, looked around the unfurnished room, counted the cracks in the plaster ceiling—anything to keep from looking into the haunted eyes of the doomed woman. Once I glanced toward her, and I saw her squirming crazily, trying to release herself from her bonds, but the ropes were tight and the gag was securely in place. I looked quickly away.

Finally, a man came in and began setting up a videotape camera. He brought with him two sets of lights, which he placed at right angles to the woman. The room, which had been warm, grew even warmer with the lights, and the still air was heavy with human sweat. I was not sure I'd be able to stay for this.

And then the cameraman took off the woman's gag and she started screaming. Her voice was high, raw, filled with utter terror, and her screams came in short staccato bursts. The cameraman began filming. I put my hands over my ears. The people around me watched dully, their faces unreadable.

A man wearing a woman's stocking over his head came into the room and walked up to the woman. He pawed her naked body, touching her everywhere. She struggled so hard to get away from him that the chair tipped over. He calmly righted it and continued with his exploration of her body.

The whole thing lasted little more than half an hour. The stockinged man used the hacksaw to cut off big toes and fingers. He used the wire to tie breasts. The smell of sweat in the enclosed room was soon overpowered by the stronger smell of blood and death.

The man used both knives.

She was already unconscious from the hammer blows when he shot her in the head.

I had seen it all, I had not thrown up, I had not turned away. But I felt filthy, unclean, covered with blood although none of the flying blood had touched me. The document I had signed had been right—I was part of the murder, I was responsible. And I felt as guilty as if I had been wielding the knives.

I said nothing to Jimmy on the way back, and I got into my pickup without even saying goodbye.

At home, my parents had finished fighting. My mom was sobbing in the bedroom, and my dad was drinking from a bottle and watching TV. He looked accusingly at me as I let myself in. "Where the hell have you been all night?" he demanded.

"Jimmy's," I said.

He turned back to the TV, and I walked down the hall to my bedroom.

In my dreams, the woman was naked and screaming and begging for her life. And I smashed her face with the hammer, bringing it down again and again and again.

I did not call Jimmy for two weeks.

He did not call me.

When Jimmy finally did call, his voice was worried, scared. "Did you get anything in the mail lately?" he asked straight out.

"Like what?"

"Can you come over?" he asked. "Now?"

I didn't really want to go over to Jimmy's, but something in his voice told me that I should. "I'll be right there," I said.

My parents were arguing again. Or rather, my dad was arguing. My mom was crying incoherently, obviously drunk. She had been drunk a lot this past week, and she had been less willing to engage him in battle than usual. I wasn't sure if that was a good sign or not.

I drove to Jimmy's with the windows down. It was cooler tonight, and there was no need for the air conditioner.

He was again sitting on the hood of his Jeep, just as he had on the night we'd gone to the snuff show. Merely seeing him again made me feel unclean, brought back to me the horrible depravity of that night, and my stomach started churning. I remembered that he'd said he'd gone the night before, and I wondered if he'd gone since then. I could not imagine anyone wanting to sit through that butchery more than once.

He came toward me, and I saw that he was carrying a piece of paper in his hand. "Did you get one of these?" he asked.

I took the paper from him. It was a cheaply printed flyer from the snuff show. "Thinking of Suicide?" the headline read. "If your life is not worth living, do not end it alone. Call us and we will help you put an end to your misery." Underneath this was a telephone number.

"Jesus," I said. "We're on their mailing list."

"My sister almost found this," Jimmy said. He looked at it again. "I mean, it doesn't really look that suspicious or anything, but . . ." His voice trailed off.

There was silence between us for a moment. "Have you gone back since?" I asked.

He shook his head. "You?"

"No." I looked at him. "How come you went back a second time?"

He shrugged. "I thought it might be fun."

"Fun." I got back into my pickup and took off, without even looking at Jimmy. I wondered how he slept at night. I wondered if he had nightmares.

Driving home, the streets and buildings all seemed dirty and dingy.

I spent most of the next day in Metro Center, keeping out of the heat, staying within the artificial environment of the mall. I saw no one I knew, which was just as well. I went through bookstores, record stores, clothing stores, trying to sort out the thoughts in my head.

It was after six when I finally got back home, and no one was around. I went into the kitchen to make myself a sandwich and saw the flyer on the table.

"Thinking of Suicide?"

On the floor next to the table were three crumpled sheets of stationery. I picked one up and uncrumpled it. "Dear Dan," it said in my mother's handwriting. I picked up the next ball of paper. "Dear Dan," it said. She had gotten no further on her last note. There was only my name again: "Dear Dan."

"*No!*" I screamed aloud.

I ran out to the pickup and drove over to Jimmy's. He was out of the house before I was halfway up the lawn. "What's up?" he asked, puzzled.

"Get in the truck!" I screamed. "We have to get to the show!"

He asked me no questions but immediately hopped into the cab. I peeled out, following his directions, hoping my short detour to his house would not make me too late.

It was twenty minutes before we reached the pink building. I leaped out of the pickup and dashed through the door.

"Fifteen dollars," Charlie Daniels said. "And sign the release."

I threw him the money, scrawled my signature and ran down the hall.

"Address and driver's license," he called after me.

The camera was already rolling as I burst into the room. My mother, bound and naked, was seated on the chair. Her mouth was not gagged, but she was not screaming. Her eyes looked dead. The people staring at her were silent, uncomfortable.

"*Mom!*" I cried.

And then the man started up the chainsaw.

The Mailman

When I was a little boy, my mom and dad used to take me to the county fair each summer. Once, when I was around five or six, I was walking a few steps behind them and was accosted by a dwarf who demanded, "Give me a quarter." He was pushy, insistent, and frightened me, and it was not until I had run to catch up with my parents and saw him approach another fairgoer with the same belligerent demand that I realized he was just trying to round up customers for a ring-toss game.

I used that incident as the starting point for "The Mailman."

—⚹—

If Jack had known that the mailman was a dwarf he never would have moved into the house. It was as simple as that. Yes, the neighborhood was nice. And he'd gotten a fantastic deal on the place—the owner had been transferred to New York by the company he worked for and had to sell as quickly as possible. But all that was beside the point.

The mailman was a dwarf.

Jack got the cold sweats just thinking about it. He had moved in that morning and had been innocently unpacking lawn furniture, setting up the redwood picnic table under the pine tree, when he had seen the blue postal cap bobbing just above the top of the small front fence. A kid, he thought. A kid playing games.

Then the mailman had walked through the gate and Jack had seen the man's small body and oversized head, his fat little fingers clutching a stack of letters. And he had run as fast as he could in the other direction, away from the dwarf, aware that the movers and neighbors were staring at him but not caring. The mailman dropped the letters in the mailslot of the door and moved on to the next house while Jack stood alone at the far end of the yard, facing the opposite direction, trying to suppress the panic that was welling within him.

The dwarf jumped out from somewhere and grabbed Jack's arm. "You got a quarter? Gimme a quarter!" He held out a fat tiny hand no larger than Jack's.

The young boy looked around, confused, searching for Baker, for his father, for anyone. His glance met, for a second, that of the dwarf, and he saw an adult's face at his child's level, old eyes peering cruelly into his young ones. A hard, experienced mouth was strung in a straight line across a field of five o'clock shadow. Jack looked immediately away.

"Gimme a quarter!" The dwarf pulled him across the sawdust to a booth, where he pointed to a pyramid of stacked multicolored glass ashtrays. "You'll win a prize! Gimme a quarter!"

Jack's mouth opened to call for help, but it would not open all the way and no sound came out. His eyes, confused, frantic, now darted everywhere, searching in vain for a familiar face in the carnival crowd. He put one sweaty hand into the right pocket of his short pants and held tight to the two quarters his father had given to him.

"I know you have a quarter! Give it to me!" The dwarf was starting to look angry.

Jack felt a firm strong hand grab the back of his neck, and he swung his head around.

"Come on, Jack. Let's go." His father smiled down at him—safety, reassurance, order in that smile.

Jack relaxed his grip on the coins in his pocket and looked up gratefully at his father. He grabbed his father's arm and the two of them started to walk down the midway toward the funhouse, where Baker was waiting. As he walked, he turned back to look at the dwarf.

The little man was scowling at him. "I'll get you, you little son of a bitch." His voice was a low, rough growl.

Frightened, Jack looked up. But his father, ears at a higher level, hearing different sounds, was unaware of the threat. He had not heard it. Jack gripped his father's hairy arm tighter and stared straight ahead, toward Baker, making a conscious effort not to look back. Beneath his windbreaker and T-shirt, his heart was thumping wildly. He knew the dwarf was staring at him, waiting for him to turn around again. He could feel the hot hatred of the little man's eyes on his back.

"I'll get you," the dwarf said again.

Jack sorted through the mail in his hand. The envelopes were ordinary—junk, bills, a couple of letters—but they felt tainted, looked soiled to his eyes, and when he thought of those stubby fat fingers touching them, he dropped the envelopes onto the table.

Maybe he could sell the house. Or call the post office and get the mailman transferred. He had to do something.

The fear was once again building within him, and he picked up the remote control and switched on the TV. *The Wizard of Oz* was on, a munchkin urging Dorothy to "follow the yellow-brick road!" He switched off the TV, his hands shaking. The house seemed suddenly darker, his unpacked boxes throwing strange shadows on the walls of the room. He got up and switched on all the lights on the first floor.

It would be a long time before he'd be able to fall asleep.

Jack unpacked in the morning but spent the afternoon shopping, staying far away from his house. He noticed two mailmen on the way to the mall, but they were both of normal size.

Why hadn't he checked?

How could he be so stupid?

He arrived home at five thirty, long after the mailman was supposed to have come and gone. Was *supposed* to have. For there he was in his absurd blue uniform, lurching ever so slightly to the right and to the left, not quite balanced on his stumpy legs, three houses up from his own.

Jack jumped out of the car and ran into the house, shutting and locking the door behind him, hurriedly closing the drapes. He crouched down behind the couch, out of view from any window, closing his eyes tightly, his hands balled into tense fists of fear. He heard the light footsteps on the porch, heard the metal clack of the mail slot opening and closing, heard the small feet retreat.

Safe.

He waited several minutes before standing up, until he was certain the dwarf was gone. He was sweating, and he realized his hands were shaking.

"*Gimme a quarter.*"

His experience with the dwarf at the carnival had been scary, but though he'd never forgotten the rough voice and small cruel face, it would not have been enough to terrify him so thoroughly and utterly that he now shuddered in fear when he saw a man under four feet tall. No, it was Vietnam that did that. It was the camp. For it was there that he saw the dwarf again, that he realized the little man really was after him and had not simply been making empty threats. It was there that he learned of the dwarf's power.

The guards were kind to him at first; or as kind as could be expected under the circumstances. He was fed twice a day; the food was adequate; he was allowed weekly exercise; he was not beaten. But one day the food stopped coming. And it was three more days before he was given a cupful of dirty water and a small dollop of nasty tasting gruel served on a square of old plywood. He ate hungrily, drank instantly, and promptly threw up, his starved system unable to take the sudden shock. He jumped up, pounding on the door, demanding more food, delirious and half-crazy. But the only thing he got for his trouble was a beating with wooden batons which left huge welts on his arms and legs and which he was sure had broken at least one rib.

Sometime later—it could have been hours, it could have been days—two guards he had never seen before entered his cell. "*Kwo ta?*" one of them demanded angrily.

"English," he tried to explain through cracked and swollen lips. "I only speak—"

He was clubbed on the back of the neck and fell face-down on the floor, a bolt of pain shooting through his shoulders and side.

"*Kwo ta?*" the man demanded again.

He nodded, hoping that was what they were looking for, not sure to what he was agreeing. The men nodded, satisfied, and left. Another man returned an hour or so later with a small cupful of dirty water and a few crusts of hard bread smeared with some sort of rice porridge. He ate slowly this time, drank sparingly, and kept it down.

He was taken outside the next day and, though the brightness of the sun burned his light-sensitive eyes, he was grateful to be out of the cell. Hands manacled, he was shoved
against a bamboo wall with several other silent, emaciated
prisoners. He glanced around the camp and saw a group of
obviously high-ranking officers nearby. One of the men
shuffled his feet, moving a little to the right, and, in a moment he would never forget, he saw the dwarf.

He was suddenly cold, and he felt the fear rise within
him. It couldn't be possible. It couldn't be real. But it was
possible. It was real. The dwarf was wearing a North Vietnamese army uniform. He was darker than before and had
vaguely Oriental eyes. But it was the same man. Jack felt a
sinking feeling in the pit of his stomach.

Kwo ta.

Quarter.

The Vietnamese guards had been trying to say "quarter."

The dwarf smiled at him, and he saw tiny white baby
teeth. The small man said something to another officer, and
the other officer strode over, pushing his face to within an
inch of Jack's. *"Gi meea kwo ta,"* the man said in a thick
musical accent.

And Jack began to scream.

He spent the rest of his incarceration in solitary, where he
was beaten regularly and fed occasionally, and when he was
finally released he weighed less than ninety pounds and was
albino white, with bruises and welts and running sores all
over his body. He saw several guards on his way to the
airstrip, but though he looked wildly around before stepping
onto the plane, he saw no sign of the dwarf.

But the dwarf was waiting for him when he arrived at
Vandenburg, disguised as a cheering onlooker. Jack saw the
horrible face, the oversized head on its undersized body, be-

tween the legs of another POW's family. He had in his hand a small American flag which he was waving enthusiastically. He was no longer Vietnamese—his hair was blond, his light skin red with sunburn—but it was without a doubt the same man.

Then the face faded back into the crowd as friends and families of the newly released men rushed forward onto the tarmac.

He had avoided dwarves and midgets ever since and had been pretty successful at it. Occasionally, he had seen the back of a small man in a mall or supermarket, but he had always been able to get away without being seen.

He had had no problems until now.

He picked up the mail from where it had fallen through the slot, but the envelopes felt cold to his touch, and he dropped them on the table without looking at them.

The next day he left the house before noon and did not return until after dark. He was afraid of seeing the dwarf at night, afraid the small man would come slinking up the steps in the darkness to deliver the mail, but the mail had already been delivered by the time he returned home.

He returned the next night a little earlier and saw the dwarf three houses up from his own, in the exact spot he'd seen him before, and he quickly ran inside and locked the door and closed the curtains, hiding behind the couch.

He was gone the next three afternoons, but he realized he could not be away every day. It was not practical. He only had three more weeks until he started teaching, and there was still a lot of unpacking to do, a lot of things he had to work on around the house. He could not spend each and every afternoon wandering through shopping centers far from his home in order to avoid the mailman.

So he stayed home the next day, keeping an eye out for the mailman, and by the end of the week he had settled into a routine. He would hide in the house when the mailman came by, shutting the curtains and locking the doors. Often he would turn on the stereo or turn up the television before the mailman arrived, but he would inevitably shut off all sound before the mailman actually showed up and sit quietly on the floor, not wanting the dwarf to know he was home.

And he would hear the rhythmic *tap tap tapping* of the little feet walking up the wooden porch steps, a pause as the mailman sorted through his letters, then the dreaded sound of metal against metal as those stubby fingers forced open the mail slot and pushed in the envelopes. He would be sweating by then, and he would remain unbreathing, afraid to move, until he heard the tiny feet descend the steps.

Once there was silence after the mail had been delivered, and Jack realized that though he had heard the mail slot open, he had not heard it fall shut. The dwarf was looking through the slit into the house! He could almost feel those horrid little eyes scanning the front room through the limited viewspace offered by the slot. He was about to scream when he heard the slot clack shut and heard the light footsteps retreat.

Then the inevitable happened.

As always, he waited silently behind the couch until the mailman had left and then gathered up his mail. Amidst the large white envelopes was a small blue envelope, thicker than the rest, with the seal of the postal service on the front. He knew what that envelope was—he'd gotten them many times before.

Postage due.

Heart pounding, he looked at the "AMOUNT" line, knowing already how much he owed.

Twenty-five cents.

A quarter.

And he stood there unmoving while the shadows lengthened around him and the room grew dark, and he wondered where the dwarf went after work.

The next morning Jack went to the main branch of the post office. The line was long, filled with businessmen who needed to send important packages and women who wanted to buy the latest stamps, but he waited patiently. When it was his turn, he walked up to the front counter and asked the clerk if he could talk to the postmaster. He was not as brave as he'd planned to be, and he was aware that his voice quavered slightly.

The postmaster came out, a burly man on the high side of fifty, wearing horn-rimmed glasses and a fixed placating smile. "How many I help you, sir?"

Now that he was here, Jack was not sure he could go through with it. His head hurt, and he could feel the blood pulsing in his temples. He was about to make something up, something meaningless and inconsequential, when he thought of the dwarf's cruel little face, thought of the demand on the postage due envelope. "I'm here to complain about one of your mailmen," he said.

The postmaster's eyebrows shot up in surprise. "One of our mail carriers?"

Jack nodded.

"Where do you live, sir?"

"Glenoaks. Twelve hundred Glenoaks."

The postmaster frowned. "That's Charlie's route. He's one of our best employees." He turned around. "Charlie!" he called.

Jack's hands became sweaty.

"He's right in the back there," the postmaster explained. "I'll have him come out here, and we'll get this mess straightened out."

Jack wanted to run, wanted to dash through the door the way he had come, to hop in the car and escape. But he remained rooted in place. The post office was crowded. Nothing could happen to him here. He was safe.

A man in a blue uniform rounded the corner.

A normal-sized man.

"This is Charlie," the postmaster said. "Your mail carrier."

Jack shook his head. "No, the man I'm talking about is . . . short. He's about three feet high."

"We have no one here who fits that description."

"He delivers my mail every day. He delivers my neighbors' mail."

"Where do you live?" Charlie asked.

"Twelve hundred Glenoaks."

"Impossible. I deliver there."

"I've never seen you before in my life!" Jack looked from one man to the other. He was sweating, and he smelled his own perspiration. His mouth was dry, and he tried unsuccessfully to generate some saliva. "Something weird's going on here."

"We'll help you in any way we can, sir," the postmaster said.

Jack shook his head. "Forget it," he said. He turned and strode toward the door. "Forget I even came by."

The next day he received no mail at all, though looking out the window, he saw the dwarf happily walking down the other side of the street, delivering to other homes. The next day, the same thing. Jack stayed on the porch the following afternoon, and before he knew it the little man was walking up his sidewalk, whistling, holding a fistful of letters, a cheerful look on his cruel hard face. Jack ran inside the house, locked the door, and dashed into the back bathroom. He sat down on the toilet and remained there for over an hour, until he was sure that the dwarf was gone.

Finally, he washed his face, opened the bathroom door, and walked down the hallway to the living room.

The mail slot opened, two letters fell through, and the slot closed. He heard that low, rough laugh and the quick steps of the dwarf running off the porch.

The gun felt good in his hands. It had been a long time. He had not held a pistol since Vietnam, but using firearms was like riding a bike and he had forgotten nothing. He liked the weight against his palm, liked the smooth way the trigger felt against his finger. His aim was probably not as good as it had once been—after all, he had not practiced for almost thirty years—but it would not need to be that good at the close range at which he planned to use it.

He waited behind the partially open curtains for the mailman.

And Charlie stepped up the walk.

Jack shoved the pistol in his waistband and yanked open the door. "Where is he?" he demanded. "Where's the goddamn dwarf?"

The mailman shook his head, confused. "I'm sorry, sir. I don't know what you're talking about."

"The dwarf! The little guy who usually delivers the mail!"

"I'm the mailman on—"

Jack pulled out the gun. "Where is he, goddamn it?"

"I—I d-don't know, sir." The mailman's voice was shaking with fear. He dropped the letters in his hand and they fluttered to the walk. "P-please don't shoot me."

Jack ran down the porch steps, shoving his way past the mailman, and hopped into his car. With the pistol on the seat beside him where he could easily reach it, he drove up and down the streets of the neighborhood, looking for the small man in the tiny blue postal uniform. He had been driving for nearly ten minutes and had almost given up, the lure of the pistol fading, when he saw the dwarf crossing the street a block and a half ahead. He floored the gas pedal.

And was broadsided by a pickup as he sped through the closest intersection, ignoring the stop sign.

The door crumpled in on him, a single jagged shard of metal piercing his arm. The windshield and windows shattered, harmless safety glass showering down on him, but the steering wheel was forced loose and pushed through his chest. In an instant that lasted forever, he felt his bones snap, his organs rupture, and he knew the accident was fatal. He did not scream, however. For some strange reason, he did not scream.

From far off, he heard sirens, and some part of his brain told him that Charlie the mailman had called the police on him, though he knew they would be too late to do any good. Nothing could save him now.

He moved his head, the only part of his body still mobile, and saw another man staggering dazedly toward the sidewalk.

And then the dwarf appeared. He was wearing street clothes, not a postal uniform, but he still had on a mailman's hat. There was a look of concern on his face, but it was a false expression, and Jack could sense the glee behind the mask.

"I'll call the paramedics," the dwarf said, and his voice

was not low and rough but high and breathless. He patted his pockets, and Jack suddenly knew what was coming next. He wanted to scream but could not. "Do you have a quarter for the phone?"

Jack wanted to grab the pistol but could not move his hands. He tried to twist away, but his muscles would not work.

The dwarf smiled as he dug through Jack's pockets. A moment later, he pulled away from the wreckage. He held up a silver coin, dulled by a streak of wet red blood.

Jack closed his eyes against the pain for what seemed like hours, but heard no noise. He opened his eyes.

The dwarf laughed cruelly. He put the quarter in his pocket, tipped his hat, and walked down the street, whistling happily, as the sirens drew closer.

Monteith

How well can one person really know another? It's a question that has been asked often and one that has been addressed by numerous writers over the years. This is my take on it as a child of the suburbs, someone who grew up in the 1960s, when husbands went off to work each morning and wives stayed home.

—ᠬᠬᠵ—

Monteith.

Andrew stared at the word, wondering what it meant. It was written in his wife's hand, on a piece of her personalized stationery, penned with a calligraphic neatness in what looked to be the precise center of the page. There was only the one word, and Andrew sat at the kitchen table, paper in hand, trying to decipher its meaning. Was it the name of a lover? A lawyer? A friend? A coworker? Was it a note? A reminder? A wish?

Monteith.

He had missed it totally on his first trip through the kitchen, had simply placed his briefcase on the table and hurried to the bathroom. Coming back to pick up his briefcase afterward, he'd seen the note but had not given it any thought, his brain automatically categorizing it as a telephone doodle or something equally meaningless. But the preciseness of the lettering and the deliberate positioning of the word on the page somehow caught his eye, and he found himself sitting down to examine the note.

Monteith.

He stared at the sheet of stationery. The word bothered him, disturbed him in a way he could not quite understand. He had never read it before, had never heard Barbara utter it in his presence, it set off no subconscious alarms of recognition, but those two syllables and the aura of sophisticated superiority that their union generated in his mind made him uneasy.

Monteith.

Did Barbara have a lover? Was she having an affair?

That was the big worry, and for the first time he found himself wishing that he had not gotten sick that afternoon, had not taken off early from work, had not come home while Barbara was out.

He stood up, hating himself for his suspicions but unable to make them go away, and walked across the kitchen to the telephone nook in the wall next to the door. He picked up the phone, took the address book out from underneath, and began scanning the pages. There was no "Monteith" listed under the M's, so he went through the entire alphabet, the entire book to see if Monteith was a first rather than last name, but again he had no luck.

Of course not, he reasoned. If Monteith was her lover, she would not write down his name, address, and phone number where it might be stumbled across. She'd hide it, put it someplace secret.

Her diary.

He closed the address book and stood there for a moment, unmoving. It was a big step he was contemplating.

His jealous imagination and unfounded paranoia was about to lead him into an invasion of his wife's privacy. He was about to break a trust that had existed between them for fifteen years on the basis of . . . what? Nothing. A single ambiguous word.

Monteith.

He looked back at the table, at the sheet of stationery on top of it.

Monteith.

The word gnawed at him, echoed in his head though he had not yet spoken it aloud. He was still thinking, had not really decided what to do, when his feet carried him into the living room . . . through the living room . . . into the hall . . . down the hall.

Into the bedroom.

The decision had been made, and he strode across the beige carpet and opened the single drawer of the nightstand on Barbara's side of the bed, taking out the small pink diary. He felt only a momentary twinge of conscience, then opened the book to the first page. It was blank. He turned to the next page—blank. The next—blank.

He flipped quickly through the pages, saw only blankness, only white. Then something caught his eye. He stopped, turned the pages back.

In the middle of the middle page, written in Barbara's neatest hand, was a single two-syllable word.

Monteith.

He slammed the book shut and threw it back in the drawer. He breathed deeply, filled with anger and an undefinable, unreasonable feeling that was not unlike dread.

She was having an affair.

Monteith was her lover.

He thought of confronting her with his suspicions, asking

her about Monteith, who he was, where she'd met him, but he could not, after all the discussions, after all the arguments, admit to snooping. After all he had said over the years, he could not afford even the appearance of invading her privacy. He could not admit to knowing anything. On the other hand, maybe she wanted him to learn of her indiscretion, maybe she wanted him to comment on it, maybe she was looking for his response. After all, she had left the stationery on the table where he was certain to find it. Was it not reasonable to assume that she had wanted him to see the note?

No, he had come home early, before he was supposed to. If this had been a usual day, she would have removed it by the time he returned from work, hidden it away somewhere.

Andrew's head hurt and he felt slightly nauseous. The house seemed suddenly hot, the air stifling, and he hurried from the room. He did not want to go through the kitchen again, did not want to see that note on the table, so he turned instead toward the back of the house, going through the rec room into the garage, where he stood just inside the doorway, grateful for the cool darkened air. He closed his eyes, breathed deeply, but the air he inhaled was not clean and fresh as he had expected. Instead, there was a scent of decay, a taste of something rotten. He opened his eyes, reached for the light switch, and flipped it on.

A dead woodchuck was hanging from an open beam in the far dark corner of the garage.

Andrew's heart skipped a beat, and he felt the first flutterings of fear in his breast. He wanted to go back into the house, back to the bedroom, back to the kitchen even, but, swallowing hard, he forced himself to move forward. He crossed the open empty expanse of oil-stained concrete and stopped before the far corner. This close, he could see that the woodchuck had been strangled to death by the twine which had been wrapped around its constricted throat and tied to the beam. Hundreds of tiny gnats were crawling on the animal's carcass, their black pinprick bodies and clear miniscule wings moving between the individual hairs of the woodchuck and giving it the illusion of life. The insects grouped in growing black colonies on the white clouded eyes, swarmed over the undersized teeth and lolling tongue in the open mouth.

Bile rose in Andrew's throat, but he willed himself not to vomit. He stared at the dead animal. There was something strange about the discolored lower half of the carcass, but he could not see what it was because of the angle at which it hung. Holding his breath against the stench of rot, he took another step forward.

A section of the woodchuck's underside had been shaved and an *M* carved into the translucent, pinkish white skin.

Monteith.

Was this Monteith? Gooseflesh prickled on Andrew's arms. The thought seemed plausible in some crazy, irrational way, but he could think of no logical basis for such an assumption. A woodchuck named Monteith? Why would Barbara have such an animal? And why would she kill it and mutilate it? Why would she write its name in her diary, on her stationery?

He tried to imagine Barbara tying the twine around the woodchuck's neck in the empty garage, hoisting the squirming, screaming, fighting animal into the air, but he could not do it.

How well did he really know his wife? he wondered. All these years he'd been kissing her goodbye in the morning when he left for work, kissing her hello at night when he returned, but he had never actually known what she did during the times in between. He'd always assumed she'd done housewife-type things—cooking, cleaning, shopping—but he'd never made the effort to find out the specifics of her day, to really learn what she did to occupy her time in the hours they weren't together.

He felt guilty now for this tacit trivialization of her life, for the unspoken but acted-upon assumption that his time was more important than hers. He imagined her putting on a false face for his homecoming each evening, pretending with him that she was happy, that everything was all right, while her lonely daylight hours grew more confining, more depressingly meaningless.

So meaningless that she'd turned to animal sacrifice?

He stared at the hanging insect-infested woodchuck, at the *M* carved on its underside. Something was wrong with this scenario. Something was missing. Something did not jibe.

He spit. The smell was starting to get to him, he could taste it in his mouth, feel it in his lungs, and he hurried out of the garage before he threw up, opening the big door to let in the outside air. He took a series of deep, cleansing breaths as he stood at the head of the driveway, then walked over to the hose to get a drink. He splashed the cold rubbery-tasting water onto his face, let it run over his hair. Finally, he turned off the faucet and shook his head dry.

It was then that he saw the snails.

They were on the cracked section of sidewalk next to the hose, and they were dead. He squatted down. Barbara had obviously poured salt on three snails she'd found in the garden, and she'd placed the three dissolving creatures at the points of a rough triangle on the sidewalk. Two of the shells were now completely empty and had blown over, their black openings facing sideways, the drying mucus that had once been their bodies puddled on the concrete in amoeba-like patterns, but the third snail had not yet dissolved completely and was a mass of greenish bubbles.

With a safety pin shoved through its center.

Andrew pushed the third shell with a finger, looking more closely. The pink plastic end of the safety pin stood out in sharp relief against the brown shell and green bubbling body. He stood. He'd never had any great love for snails, had even poured salt on them himself as a youngster, but he had never been so deliberately cruel as to impale one of the creatures on a pin. He could not understand why Barbara would make a special effort to torture one of them, what pleasure or purpose she could hope to gain from such an action.

And why had she placed three of them at the corners of a triangle?

Between the woodchuck and the snails, there was a sense of ritualism emerging that made Andrew extremely uncomfortable. He wished he'd never seen the stationery on the table. He wished he'd never followed up on it. Always before, he had phoned ahead prior to coming home. Even on those few occasions when he had left work ill, he had telephoned Barbara to let her know he was coming home, believing such advance notice an example of common courtesy. This time, however, he had not phoned home, and he was not sure why he hadn't.

He wished he had.

Monteith.

Maybe it wasn't the name of a lover after all. Maybe it was some sort of spell or invocation.

Now he was being crazy.

Where was Barbara? He walked out to the front of the house, looked up and down the street for a sign of her car, saw nothing. He wanted to forget what he had seen, to go inside and turn on the TV and wait for her to come home, but the knot of fear in his stomach was accompanied by a morbid and unhealthy curiosity. He had to know more, he had to know what was really going on—although he was not sure that this had any sort of reasonable explanation.

The thought occurred to him that he was hallucinating, imagining all of this. He'd left work because of severe stomach cramps and diarrhea, but perhaps he was sicker than he'd originally believed. Maybe he didn't have a touch of the flu—maybe he was in the throes of a full-fledged nervous breakdown.

No. It would be reassuring to learn that there was something wrong with himself instead of Barbara. It would relieve him to know that this insanity was in his mind, but he knew that was not the case. His mental faculties were at full power and functioning correctly. There really was a mutilated woodchuck in the garage, a triangle of tortured snails on the sidewalk, an empty diary with only one word on one page.

Monteith.

Were there other signs he had missed, other clues to Barbara's . . . instability? He thought that there probably were and that he would be able to find them if he looked hard enough. He walked around the side of the garage to the back yard. Everything looked normal, the way it always did, but he did not trust this first surface impression and he walked past the line of covered, plastic garbage cans, across the recently mowed lawn to Barbara's garden. He looked up into the branches of the lemon tree, the fig tree, and the avocado tree. He scanned the rows of radishes, the spreading squash plants. His gaze had already moved on to the winter-stacked lawn furniture behind the garage before his brain registered an incongruity in the scene just passed, a symmetrical square of white tan amidst the free-form green.

He backtracked, reversing the direction of his visual scan, and then he saw it.

In the corner of the yard, next to the fence, nearly hidden by the corn, was a small crude hut made of Popsicle sticks.

He stared at the square structure. There was a small door and a smaller window, a tiny pathway of pebbles leading across the dirt directly in front of the miniature building. The house was approximately the size of a shoebox and was poorly constructed, the globs of glue used to affix the crooked roof visible even from here.

Had this been made by one of the neighborhood kids or by Barbara? Andrew was not sure, and he walked across the grass until he stood in front of the hut. He crouched down. There were pencil markings on the front wall—lightly rendered shutters on either side of the two windows, bushes drawn next to the door.

The word *Monteith* written on a mailbox in his wife's handwriting.

Barbara had made the house.

He squinted one eye and peered through the open door.

Inside, on the dirt floor, was an empty snail shell impaled by a safety pin.

He felt again the fear, frightened more than he would have thought possible by the obsessive consistency of Barbara's irrationality. He stood, and his eye was caught by a streak of purple graffiti on the brick fence in front of him. He blinked. There, above the Popsicle-stick house, on the brick fence wall, half-hidden by the grape vines and the corn stalks, was a crude crayon drawing. The picture was simple and inexpertly drawn, the lines crooked and wavering, and he would have ascribed its origin to a child had it not been for the subject of the illustration.

Himself.

He pushed aside the grape vines and stepped back to get a better view, to gain perspective. Seen from this angle, it was obvious whom the rendering was supposed to represent. Distance flattened out the jagged veerings of the crayon which occurred at each mortared juncture of brick, lent substance to the rough hesitations of line. He was looking at his own face simplified into caricature and magnified fivefold. The receding hairline, the bushy mustache, the thin lips: these were the observations of an adult translated into the artistic language of a child.

Barbara had drawn this picture.

He noticed dirt spots on the brick where mudballs had obviously been thrown at his face.

The question nagged at him: Why? Why had she done all of this?

He dropped to his hands and knees, crawled through the garden, fueled now by his own obsession. There was more here. He knew it. And he would find it if he just kept looking.

He didn't have to look long.

He stopped crawling and stared at the cat's paw protruding from the well-worked ground beneath the largest tomato plant. The paw and its connected portion of leg were pointed straight up, deliberately positioned. Dried blackened blood had seeped into the gray fur from between the closed curled toes.

Maybe Monteith was the name of the cat, Andrew thought. *Maybe she accidentally killed a neighbor's cat and had guiltily buried the animal out here to hide the evidence.*

But that wasn't like Barbara. Not the Barbara he knew. If

she'd accidentally killed a pet, she would have immediately gone to the owner and explained exactly what had happened.

Perhaps, he thought, *she had deliberately killed the animal in order to provide nutrients for her soil, for her plants. Or as part of a ritual sacrifice to some witch's earth deity in order to ensure the health of her crop.*

He thought of the woodchuck in the garage.

He wondered if there were dead animals hanging in other garages on the street, if pets were buried in other back yards. Perhaps the neighborhood wives took turns meeting at each others' houses while their husbands were gone, performing dark and unnatural acts together. Perhaps that was where Barbara was right now.

Such are the dreams of the everyday housewife.

The tune to the old Glen Campbell song ran through his head, and he suddenly felt like laughing.

An everyday housewife who gave up the good life for me.

The laughter stopped before it reached his mouth. What if Monteith wasn't the name of an animal at all but the name of a child? What if she had killed and sacrificed a child and had buried the body under the dirt of the garden? If he dug down, below the cat's paw, would he find hands and feet, fingers and toes?

He did not want to know more, he decided. He'd already learned enough. He stood up, wiped his hands on his pants, and began walking back across the yard toward the house.

What would he do when he saw her? Confront her? Suggest that she seek help? Try to find out about her feelings, about why she was doing what she was doing?

Would she look the same to him, he wondered, or had the woodchuck and the snails and the cat and everything else permanently altered the way in which he viewed her? Would he now see insanity behind what would have been perfectly normal eyes, a madwoman beneath the calm exterior?

He didn't know.

It was partially his fault. Why the hell had he come home early? If he had just come home at the normal time, or if Barbara, damn her, had just been home, he never would have found all this. Life would have just continued on as normal.

The question was: Did his newfound knowledge automatically mean that he gave up his right to happiness with Barbara? Part of him said no. So what if she sacrificed animals? She had, in all probability, been doing that for years without his knowledge, and they'd had what he'd always considered a good life. Unless she was unhappy, unless this was all part of some twisted way she was trying to exorcise her negative feelings about their marriage, couldn't he ignore what he had learned and continue on as normal?

Monteith.

It was Monteith he couldn't live with. He could live with the animals, with the fetishes, with the graffiti. If Monteith was some god or demon she worshiped, he could live with that. But the idea that she was seeing another man behind his back, that Monteith was a lover, *that* he couldn't abide.

Perhaps she was with Monteith now, both of them naked in some sleazy motel room, Barbara screaming wildly, passionately.

But why couldn't he live with that? If she had been doing this for years and it had not affected their relationship until now, why couldn't he just pretend as though he didn't know and continue on as usual? He could do it. It was not out of the question. He would just put it out of his mind, make sure that he did not come home early anymore without first checking with Barbara.

He walked into the house through the garage, walked back to the kitchen, sat down at the table.

He stared at the piece of stationery, but did not pick it up.

Ten minutes later, he heard the sound of a key in the latch. He looked up as Barbara walked in.

Her gaze flitted from his face to the paper and quickly back again.

Was that worry he saw on her features?

"I felt sick," he said dully. "I came home early."

She smiled at him, and the smile was genuine, all trace of worry gone—if it had been there at all. She walked over to him, patted his head with one hand, picked up the stationery with the other. She gave him a quick peck on the cheek. "Other than that, how was your day?"

He looked at her, thought for a moment, forced himself to smile back. "Fine," he said slowly. "Everything was fine."

Pillow Talk

When my wife and I were dating, we used to go to this bargain theater and basically see whatever movie happened to be playing that week. One night we sat in front of two young women who were commiserating with each other about their nonexistent love lives. Just before the movie started, one of the young women said that sometimes at night she fell asleep hugging her pillow. It was an odd image, and I found myself wondering if a man would ever do such a thing.

And then I thought, what if a man did?

And what if the pillow hugged him back?

—⚉—

When my pillow first started talking to me, I ignored it. I only heard it speaking when I drifted into sleep, and I put it down to the inevitable merging of the material world and the dream world which occurs when the waking mind relinquishes its hold on consciousness.

But when I woke up one morning and felt the pillow pulsing beneath my head, I knew something was wrong.

I jumped out of bed, simultaneously throwing the pillow away from me. It landed flat on the floor next to my dresser and was perfectly still. I bent down closely to peer at it but could see nothing out of the ordinary. I touched it with my foot, prodding it, half afraid it would leap up at me and attack, but there was no movement at all. I thought, perhaps, that I had dreamed the whole thing.

Then I heard the pillow speak.

It was a soft voice, whispery and seductive, neither male nor female. At first, it might sound like the rustling of dry sheets on a quiet morning or the gentle stirring of clean linen on a clothesline. But those soft sounds formed human words, turned those words into sentences, used those sentences to express thoughts.

"I want you," the soft voice said.

I ran from the room in a blind panic, not stopping until I was outside the apartment. I was wearing nothing but my underwear, but I didn't care. I was breathing heavily, not from the exertion of running, but from fear. I did not feel, as people often do in books or movies, that I was going mad. I knew I was sane. I knew the pillow had actually spoken to me.

I shivered as I recalled the whispery sound of those words. *I want you.* I had no idea what that meant. For all I knew, the pillow planned to kill me. But I perceived no threat in the words. Instead, I sensed an undercurrent of erotic longing.

And that scared me even more.

I heard the door to the next apartment open. A little girl came out to get the newspaper. She looked at me and giggled, averting her eyes. I forced myself to gather my courage and go back into the apartment. I looked around carefully, afraid that the pillow was hiding behind a door or a couch, but it was nowhere to be seen. I crept down the hall to the bedroom. It was still lying on the floor next to my dresser. I slammed shut the bedroom door, grabbed some dirty clothes out of the hamper in the bathroom, put them on and left.

It was after twelve noon before I was brave enough to return to the apartment. Even in the harsh heat of midday, my fears did not seem stupid or childish. The pulse of that pillow beneath me, the horror of that soft voice was still very real, and I came back to my apartment with a newly charged pitchfork and a large plastic bag.

The pillow was still lying on the floor.

Had it moved?

I couldn't be sure, so I stabbed it with the pitchfork and tossed it into the bag, using a wire twist tie to seal the opening.

Inside the bag, the pillow jumped.

I fell back, shocked, though I had been preparing myself for exactly that. In a series of short leaps, the plastic sack moved across the floor. Fighting down the dread that was building within me and threatening to take over, concentrating on my anger and trying to nurture my aggressive feelings, I grabbed the squirming plastic bag and took it outside.

The second I crossed the threshold, the pillow stopped fighting me. The movement died. I did not stop to ponder the reason for this sudden good luck, I simply ran to my car, opened the trunk, and threw in the bag. I drove to the dump, still keyed up, and was gratified to see that a pile of wood and leaves was in the process of being burned. Taking the bag out of the trunk, I threw it on the fire, not daring to move until I saw the greenish black plastic sizzle and evaporate, until I saw the pillow inside blacken and wither and burn.

I had expected to feel relieved, as if a heavy burden had been lifted from my shoulders, but the anxiety I'd been experiencing stayed with me. I felt no joy after the pillow had been destroyed; I felt no freedom. My dread became less immediate, but it was still there. The pillow was gone, but it had won its war. It had done its job.

I drove home feeling frustrated.

Before going to bed, I took a spare pillow from the hall closet—the pillow guests use when they sleep on the couch. I was still nervous, tense, but the sight of the new pillow made me smile. I took off my clothes, turned down the blanket, and got into bed. The pillow felt soft and comforting, reassuring in its ordinariness. My body was dog-tired, but I'd expected to have trouble falling asleep, afraid that my overtaxed and overactive brain would keep me up all night. My mind, however, was tired as well from the day's exertions, and I fell almost instantly into a deep, dreamless slumber.

I awoke to the sound of the pillow whispering in my ear. "Take me," it said, and there was no mistaking the intent behind *that* statement.

"Take me," it whispered again.

I'd been sleeping with one hand under the pillow, which in some grotesque way could have been considered a position of perverse embrace. My mouth was open, drooling onto the pillow cover, and in the second before I leapt out of bed, I felt the cloth press upward against my mouth.

As if to kiss me.

I spent the rest of the night sleeping outside, in my clothes, on the stoop.

In the morning, I was angry. My fear had turned to fury, as fear will do after a suitable gestation period. I refused to be intimidated by whispering voices, I refused to let squares of padded cloth rule my life. I boldly went inside, closed the bedroom door, showered, shaved, and made breakfast.

After I ate, I took every piece of linen in the house and

threw it into the Dumpster outside the apartment complex. None of it fought me. None of it even moved. I would have taken the linen to the dump but I was too angry. I refused to have my life dictated by inanimate objects, and I refused to devote anymore time to this ludicrous pursuit. I threw the sheets and pillows and bedspreads into the blue metal container, then afterward, in a gesture of supreme disgust, I emptied my garbage on top of the linen.

"Eat shit," I said.

And this time I really did feel good. The dread, the tension, the nervousness left me and was replaced by a sense of optimistic finality. The horror was over.

I slept that night on a bare bed, with no pillow, no covers. And the feeling was nice.

In the morning, after breakfast, I went outside. I'd been intending to stop by, see a couple of friends, maybe catch a movie, but the sight that greeted me on the apartment stoop stopped me cold.

A trail of sheets and pillowcases, covers and comforters led from behind the building, where the Dumpster was located, to my door. On my doorstep, leaning upright, as if they'd been trying to get inside, were three pillows.

It wasn't the pillows, I realized. It was the apartment. There was a spirit in the apartment, or a demon, which animated the linen. Factory-made cloth in and of itself could not be malevolent, could not be alive. Something else was doing this.

I took only my wallet, leaving everything else, afraid even my clothes could be contaminated, and spent the morning looking for a motel. I found one close to the library, and I spent the afternoon among the stacks of books, reading everything I could about poltergeists and TK and the super-natural.

I ate alone in the coffee shop across the street from the motel, staring through the plate glass window next to my table at the black square window of my room. I thought of white sheets climbing up the cold glass, shutting in the room from the outside world, and I shivered. Maybe I would spend the night in the car.

But no. I was being paranoid. There was no way the . . . whatever it was . . . could track me there.

It was dark when I returned to my room, and even in the antiseptic light of the motel lamp, the two long pillows on the bed appeared somewhat threatening. "Better safe than sorry," I mumbled to myself. And I threw the pillows in the bathroom and closed the door.

In my dream, a gorgeous woman, the most perfect I'd ever seen, offered me her body. I hemmed and hawed, nervous, not believing that such a woman would desire me, but she pushed me onto my back and began unbuttoning my shirt. She unbuckled my pants, pulled them down, then slipped out of her own clothes, revealing a body surpassing even the high expectations generated by her beautiful face and covered figure. She lowered herself onto me, kissing me, pressing against me, moaning with passion, promising pleasure. It was the most realistic dream I'd ever had, and definitely the most arousing. I awoke on the brink of orgasm, feeling as though I was still inside her, feeling her still-thrusting her hips with me.

And I saw the pillow pushing rhythmically against my crotch.

In one instant, my glance took in the open bathroom door, the pillow pulsing between my legs and the other pillow moving up the bed toward my face. I was too confused to react spontaneously. I knew the pillows were having their way with me, but in my sleepbound mind I saw the gorgeous face and figure of my dream lover.

I came, ejaculating heavily into the pillow, which suddenly increased its movement. I threw the pillow off me, and it landed on the carpet, glinting wetly in the diffused light from the bathroom. I grabbed the other pillow and heaved it against the wall.

I was breathing heavily, both with panic and with the exertion of my sexual activity. Other than my breathing, the room was silent.

I could hear the pillow perfectly.

"Good," it whispered, its seductive voice sounding sated. "So good."

Sickened, appalled by what had just transpired, feeling both guilty and victimized, I put on my pants and dashed out of the room to my car. I locked the doors and sat unmoving in the dark, listening to my own breathing and the sound of my heart, trying to stop my hands from shaking.

Good.

So good.

The clock in my car said it was twelve thirty. I was tired, but I could not sleep. I stayed there, unmoving, wide awake, until dawn. At a little past three, a square white shape inched its way up the side of the motel room window. Moonlight glinted off my semen, and I felt like vomiting.

I wanted to kill the pillow.

But how can you kill a piece of cloth filled with stuffing?

My vacation was almost over, and I realized that I'd have to return to work in three days. Where would I live? How could I live, knowing that whenever I tried to sleep, my pillows would try to attack me?

Have sex with me.

Kill me.

Rape me.

I knew, deep down, that the pillows meant to do me no physical harm. But what they did want to do was so terrifying, so perversely alien, that I could not think about it. I could not handle it. So I stared at the window and tried to figure out my next move. The rational ideas I discarded almost immediately. Rationality was not a legitimate defense against the irrational. What was next? An exorcist? Spiritualist? Faith healer?

When dawn arrived and the coffee shop opened up across the street, I went in for some breakfast. I ordered hash browns and eggs with orange juice. I stared at my plate after the waitress brought it, and I could think of no way to escape from this horror. No matter where I went, no matter what I did, this would continue. I knew that, even if I slept alone on a hard park bench, some article of cloth would find me and attack me.

Rape me.

I took a bite of my egg and used the napkin to wipe my mouth.

"Thank you," the cloth whispered.

I dropped the white napkin and stared at it. It looked for all the world like a miniature pillow. As I stared, I noticed that one of the creases looked almost like a smile. A smile of unbridled lust. I felt no shock, though. I felt no terror. I was too jaded for that. I'd gone through too much.

I looked down at the napkin, then across the street at the motel. In the bright light of early morning, I could clearly see the white squares against the motel room glass. But they no longer seemed like they were waiting to pounce. They no longer seemed malevolent.

They seemed forlorn.

Like they were waiting for me to come home.

I picked up the napkin. It was soft and silken. "Kiss me," it whispered. "Touch me." I looked across the street at the motel room window, and I found myself becoming aroused.

What was it they did to help people get over their fears? Made them face those fears? Made them confront their problems? I knew there was no way I could escape from the pillows. I would have to meet them head on.

The waitress brought my check, which I paid. I waited until she left the room before standing so she wouldn't see my erection.

I walked back across the street and stood for a moment in front of the window. The two pillows were pressed against the glass. The one which had taken advantage of me the night before looked soiled, dirty, and disgusting, covered with a crust of dried semen. But the other pillow, long and white, soft and supple, looked clean and fresh and innocent. Inviting.

I licked my dry lips, thought for a moment, and took the key out of my pocket.

I went into the room and closed the door behind me.

Maya's Mother

I wrote the story "Bumblebee" for Richard Chizmar's anthology *Cold Blood*. A horror story set in contemporary Phoenix with a noirish detective for a protagonist, it was written quickly. I cashed my check when payment arrived, shelved the book when I got it, and promptly forgot about the piece.

But readers didn't.

I don't think *Cold Blood* sold particularly well, but more than any other story I've written, "Bumblebee" has inspired fans to write and ask for a sequel. I finally wrote one many years later for the paperback magazine *Palace Corbie*. It was titled "The Piano Player Has No Fingers" (*all* of the stories in that issue were titled "The Piano Player Has No Fingers"; the gimmick for the issue was that all contributors would write a story using that as the title). I thought that would be the end of it, but still the requests kept coming.

So for those of you who asked, here's another one.

—⚏—

It was hot as I drove through the desert to the Big Man's. The place was out past Pinnacle Peak and at one time had probably been the only house out there, but now the city was creeping in, and there were only a few miles of open space between the last subdivision and the dirt road that led to the Big Man's compound.

I turned onto the unmarked drive, slowing down, peering through my dusty windshield. The Big Man had made no effort to landscape his property, but there was a lot more out here than just cacti and rocks. Doll parts were hanging on the barbed wire fence: arm and leg, torso and head. Mesquite crosses stood sentry by the cattle guard. A blood-drenched scarecrow with a coyote skull on its shoulders faced the road, arms raised.

I hadn't expected him to be so spooked—or at least not so superstitious—and I was starting to get a little creeped out myself as I ventured farther into the desert and away from civilization. He wouldn't say over the phone why he wanted to hire me, had said only that he had a case he wanted handled, but the few details he'd given me were enough to pique my interest.

His house was on a small rise, surrounded by saguaros, and was one of those Frank Lloyd Wrightish structures that had bloomed out here in the late fifties/early sixties when the Master himself had set up his architectural school north of Scottsdale. It was, I had to admit, damned impressive. Low, geometric, all rock and windows, it blended perfectly with the environment and bespoke an optimism for the future that had died long before they'd built the square shoe-box that was my dingy Phoenix apartment complex.

One of the Big Man's men was out front to greet me, and he ushered me inside after allowing me to park my dirty shitmobile next to a veritable fleet of gleaming Mercedes Benzes. The interior of the house was just as impressive as the outside. Lots of light. Potted palms. Hardwood floors and matching furniture. I was led to an extra-wide doorway and ushered into a sunken living room approximately five times the size of my entire apartment. "He's here," the flunky said by way of an introduction.

And I finally got to meet the Big Man.

I'd heard of him, of course. Who in Phoenix hadn't? But I'd never met him, seen him, or even spoken to him. I looked at the man before me, underwhelmed. I'd been expecting someone more impressive. Sydney Greenstreet, maybe. Orson Welles. Instead, this Richard Dreyfuss lookalike stood up from the couch, shook my hand, and introduced himself as Vincent Pressman.

Time was when I wouldn't have even returned the man's phone call. I worked strictly for the good guys, followed all of the guidelines necessary to maintain my investigator's license, dealt only with the law-abiding who had been screwed or were in some type of jam. I still try to keep it that way whenever possible, but there are gray areas now, and while I try to rationalize my behavior, I sometimes sit alone at night and think about what I do and realize that perhaps I'm not as pure and honest as I like to think I am.

Which is a long way of saying that I now take cases that interest me. There are only so many lost dogs and missing teenagers and two-timing spouses that a man can handle.

And the Big Man's case interested me.

As I said, he didn't tell me much, but the hints had been tantalizing. Water turned to blood. A shadow that followed him from room to room, building to building. Obscene calls received on a disconnected phone. He claimed he didn't know who was behind all this, but I had the feeling he did, and I figured I could act as an intermediary between the two, bring them together and settle things out of court, as it were, without any bloodshed.

At least that was my plan.

I sat down as directed on a white love seat, facing the Big Man across a glass coffee table. He cleared his throat. "I've heard you're into this stuff, this supernatural shit."

I shrugged.

"I've had this place bugged and debugged, scanned by every electronic device known to man, and no one's been able to come up with an explanation for what's happening here."

"But you don't think your house is haunted."

He glared at me with cold steely eyes and, Richard Dreyfuss lookalike or not, I saw for the first time a hint of what made Vincent Pressman the most feared underworld figure in the Southwest. "I told you, someone's after me."

I nodded, acting calmer than I felt. "And I asked you who it was."

He sighed, then motioned for everyone else to leave the room. He stared at me, his eyes never leaving my own, and I held the gaze though it was beginning to make me feel uncomfortable. He did not speak until we heard the door click shut. Then he leaned back on the couch, glanced once toward the door, and started talking.

"I had this maid working for me. Guatemalan bitch. She looked like a goddamn man, but her daughter was one fine piece of poon. Maya, her name was. Skinny little thing. Big tits. Always coming on to me. I don't usually like 'em young—I'm not a pedophile, you understand—but this babe got to me. She was sixteen or so, and she was always lounging around in her bikini, going to the fridge for midnight snacks in panties and a T-shirt. You know the drill.

"Anyway, bitch mama gives me this warning, dares to tell me that I'd better stay away from her little girl. I see the daughter later, and she's got this bruise on her cheek, like she's been hit, beaten. I call mama in, give *her* a warning, tell her if she ever touches one hair on that girl's head I'll have her cut up and fed to the coyotes." He smiled. "Just trying to put a scare into her, you understand."

I nodded.

"So the girl comes back later, thanks me. One thing leads to another, I take her into my room and . . . I fucked her." The Big Man's voice dropped. "The thing is, after I came, after I finished, I opened my eyes, and she was . . . she wasn't there. She was a rag doll. A full-sized rag doll." He shook his head. "I don't know how it happened, how they did it, but it happened instantly." He snapped his fingers. "Like that! One second I was holding her ass, rubbing my face in her hair, the next I felt her ass turn to cloth, was rubbing my face in yarn. Scared the fuck out of me. I jumped out of bed, and that doll was smiling at me, a big old dumbass grin stitched onto her head."

He licked his lips nervously. "It didn't even look like Maya. Not really. I called on the intercom, ordered my men to make sure the girl and her mom didn't leave the house, told them to hunt them down and find them, especially the mom. When I turned back around, the bed was empty. Even the doll was gone."

He was silent for a moment.

"They were gone, too," I prodded. "Weren't they?"

He nodded. "Both of them, and it was after that that the weird shit started happening. I put the word out, told my men to find the maid, have her picked up, but, as you know, she seems to have disappeared off the face of the fucking earth."

"So you want me to find the woman."

He leaned forward. "I want you to stop this shit. I don't care how you do it, just do it. Find her if you have to, leave her out of it, I don't care. I just want this curse gone." He sat back. "Afterward, after it's over, then I'll decide how to deal with her."

I nodded. We both knew how he was going to deal with her, but that was one of those things he didn't want spelled out and I didn't want confirmed.

I thought of Bumblebee, and while the memory of that situation remained sharp, the emotions had faded, and it seemed somehow more fun in retrospect.

Well, maybe not fun.

Interesting.

Kind of the way this seemed interesting.

"How did you find me?" I asked. "Phone book?"

"I told you: I heard you handle this stuff."

"From who?"

He smiled. "I have my sources."

I didn't like that. I hadn't told anyone about Bumblebee, and the only people who knew were either dead or had fled.

"Word is that you're in tight with the wetbacks, too. I figured that can't hurt."

"You hear a lot of words."

"I wouldn't be where I am if I didn't."

I looked at him for what seemed an appropriate length of time. "All right," I said. "I'll do it. But it'll be twenty-five hundred plus expenses." That was far more than I usually charged, but I knew the Big Man could afford it.

He agreed to my terms without question, and I knew that I could have and should have asked for more. But I'd always been bad at this part of the game, and once again my stupidity had screwed me out of a big payday.

"You have a picture of this maid?" I asked. "And a name?"

He shook his head.

"Not even her name?"

"I never used her name. Didn't matter to me." He motioned toward the foyer. "Maybe Johnny or Tony knows."

The arrogance of the powerful. I'd forgotten to take that into consideration.

One of the flunkies came hurrying up. Pressman asked the maid's name but the flunky didn't know, and he hurried out, returning a few moments later, shaking his head.

The Big Man smiled. "I guess that means we forgot to pay her social security tax."

"But the girl's name is Maya?" I asked.

He nodded.

"Maya's mother, then. I'll start there."

"Do what you have to," he told me. "But I want results. I expect people to complete the jobs I hire them to do, and I don't like to be disappointed. Are we understood?"

It was one of those movie moments. He'd probably seen the same movies I had and was playing his role to the hilt, but I felt as though I'd just sold my soul to the Mob, as though I'd jumped in over my head, painted myself into a corner, and was being forced to sink or swim. It was a scary feeling.

But it was also kind of cool.

I nodded, and Pressman and I shook hands. I had to remind myself not to get too caught up in the glamour of it all. These were the bad guys, I told myself. I was only working for them on a temporary basis. I was not one of them and never wanted to be.

I drove back through the desert. There was only one person I knew who might be able to decipher this: Hector Marquez. Hector was a former fighter, a local light heavyweight who'd gotten railroaded by Armstrong and his goons a few years back for a payroll heist he'd had nothing to do with. I'd gotten him a good lawyer—Yard Stevens, an old buddy who still owed me a slew of favors—but even that had not been enough to counter the manufactured evidence and coerced witnesses Armstrong had lined up, and Yard had told me, off the record, that probably the best thing for Hector would be if he disappeared. I'd relayed the message, and ever since there'd been a warrant out for Hector's arrest.

I hadn't seen him after his disappearance, but I knew someone who knew someone who could get in touch with him, and I put the word out. I expected a long-distance phone call, expected Hector to be hiding either in Texas or California, but he was still right here in the Valley, and the woman who called on his behalf said that he wanted to meet with me personally.

We set up the meeting for midnight.

South Mountain Park.

A lot of bodies had been dumped there over the years, and though the city had been trying for decades to clean up its image, the park remained a haven for gangbangers, drunken redneck teens, and the occasional naive couple looking for a lover's lane.

In other words, not exactly a family fun spot.

The view was spectacular, though, and as I got out of my car and looked over the edge of the parking lot, I could see the lights of the Valley stretching from Peoria to Apache Junction. Phoenix looked cleaner at night. The lights cut clearly through the smog, and everything had a sweeping cinematic quality that reminded me of how it had been in the old days.

I was suddenly illuminated by headlights, and I turned around to see three silhouetted men standing in front of a parked Chevy. One of them started toward me.

It had been three years since I'd seen Hector, and he definitely looked the worse for wear. He was probably in his late twenties but he looked like a man in his early fifties, and his old smooth-faced optimism had been buried under lines and creases of disillusionment and disappointment. His fighter's body had long since softened into pudge.

"Hector," I said.

He walked up to me, hugged me. The hug lasted a beat longer than was polite, and I understood for the first time that he had really and truly missed me. I didn't know why he'd stayed away if he was still living in the Valley, but I could only assume that it was because he hadn't wanted to get me into trouble, and I felt guilty for not making an effort to keep in touch.

He pulled back, looked me over. "How goes it, man?"

"My life doesn't change."

"Solid."

"As a rock."

He laughed, and I saw that he had a new silver tooth in the front.

"I don't know if Liz told you what I'm looking for, but I'm working on a case and I need to find a Guatemalan witch used to work as a maid. Her daughter's named Maya. I thought you might be able to introduce me to someone, set me up."

Hector thought for a moment. "I don't know much about Guatemalans. But you talk to Maria Torres. She run a small bodega on Central between Southern and Baseline. In an old house by the Veteran's Thrift. Her son married to a Guatemalan girl. She can get you in."

"You couldn't've told me that over the phone?" I ribbed him. "I had to come all the way out here in the middle of the night?"

"I wanted to see you again, bro."

I smiled at him. I'm not a touchy-feely guy, but I grasped his shoulder. "I wanted to see you too, Hector. It's good to see you again."

We caught up a bit on our respective lives, but it was clear that Hector's friends were getting antsy, and when the lights flashed and the horn honked, he said he'd better get going.

"I'll call," I promised. "We'll get together somewhere. In the daytime. Away from Phoenix."

He waved.

The next morning I learned that Hector had been followed.

Armstrong was the one who called me. Gleefully, I thought. He told me they'd found Hector in a Dumpster, burned beyond recognition. His teeth had been knocked out first and his fingertips sliced off so there'd be no possibility of positive identification. The cops had been able to ID the men with him, however, and one of the women who'd come down to claim the body of her husband said that Hector had been hanging with these guys and had ridden with them last night and was in all probability the other man.

The lieutenant paused, savoring his story. "That Dumpster smelled like a fuckin' burnt tamale."

I hung up on him, feeling sick. Immediately, I picked up the phone again and dialed the Big Man's number. I was so furious that my hand hurt from gripping the receiver so tightly, and when he answered the phone himself and gave me that silky smooth "Hello," it was all I could do not to yell at him.

"You killed Hector Marquez," I said without preamble.

"Is this—?"

"You know damn well who this is, and you killed Hector Marquez."

"Sorry. I don't know anyone by that name."

"I'm off this case. You can find some other sucker to do your dirty work."

"I wouldn't do that." The Big Man's voice was low, filled with menace.

"Fuck you."

He sighed. "Look, I'm sorry. If something happened to someone you know—and I'm not saying it did or that I'm in any way involved—then it was probably a mistake. If you'd like, I could look into it for you."

"I want you to make sure it never happens again. If I'm going to continue, I need to have your word that no one is going to be murdered, no one I talk to is going to be attacked. You want to follow me, fine. But just because I'm getting information from someone doesn't mean they're involved with this. You let me handle this my own way, or I'm off. You can threaten me all you want, but those are my terms, those are my rules, that's the deal. Take it or leave it."

"I understand," he said smoothly. "A slight misunderstanding. As I said, I am in no way connected to the death of your friend, but I think I have enough clout that I can assure you nothing like it will ever happen again. You have my word, and I'm sorry for your loss." He paused. "Do you have any leads?"

"Hector was a friend."

"I said I'm sorry."

I was still furious, but I knew enough not to push it. I might be brave when I'm angry, but I'm not stupid. I took a deep breath. "Hector gave me the name of a woman who might offer me an in to the Guatemalan community. I'll ask around. See what I can find out about this Maya and her mother."

There was silence on the line, but I knew he was nodding. "Keep me informed," he said.

"Of course."

I was still furious, but I pretended I wasn't, and we ended on a false note of rapprochement. I wondered after I hung up what kind of man could treat human life so casually, could order deaths as other people ordered dinner, and I told myself that the kind of man who could do that was the kind of man who would statutorily rape the daughter of his housekeeper.

The kind of man I would take on as a client.

I didn't want to think about that, and I walked into the kitchen to make my morning wake-up coffee.

Maria Torres's bodega was closed when I arrived, so I went to a nearby McDonald's to get some coffee. There were gang members signing near the blocked bathrooms and a host of hostile faces among the silently staring people at the tables, so I paid for my order, took the covered cup, and went out to wait in my car.

I didn't have to wait long. Before the coffee was even cool enough to drink, a dark, overweight woman in a white ruffled skirt walked down the street and stopped in front of the barred door of the bodega. She sorted through a massive keyring, used one of the keys to open the door, and flipped the Closed sign in the window to Open.

I went over to talk to her.

The woman was indeed Maria Torres, and when I told her that Hector had said she could put me in touch with a Guatemalan woman who might know Maya's mother, she nodded and started telling me in broken English a long involved story about her son and how he'd met and married this Guatemalan girl over the wishes of her and her family. It was clear that she hadn't heard what had happened to Hector, and I didn't want to be the one to tell her, so I simply waited, listened, nodded, and when she finally got around to telling me her daughter-in-law's name and address, I wrote it down.

"Does she speak English?" I asked.

"Therese?" Maria smiled widely. "More better than me."

I thanked her, and to show my appreciation, I bought a trinket from her store, a little rainbow-colored "friendship bracelet" that I could either give to my niece or toss away, depending on how the mood struck me.

The Guatemalans lived in a ghetto of a ghetto in the slums of south Phoenix. It was a bad area on a good day, and there hadn't been a lot of good days since the beginning of this long, hot summer.

I found the house with no problem—a crummy plywood shack on a barren lot with no vegetation—and I got out of my car and walked up to the section of plywood that I assumed to be the door.

I should've brought a tape recorder, I thought as I knocked. But it didn't really matter, because no one was home. I walked over to the neighbors on both sides, but one of the houses was empty and the tired skinny old man in the other spoke no English. My attempts at pidgin Spanish elicited from him only a blank look.

I decided to head home, get my tape recorder, then come back and see if Therese had returned, but when I reached the front door of my apartment, the phone was ringing, and it continued to ring as I unlocked and opened the door. Someone was sure anxious to talk to me, and I hurried over, picked up the receiver.

It was the Big Man.

I recognized the voice but not the tone. Gone was the arrogant attitude, the sureness and confidence born of long-held power.

The Big Man sounded scared.

"She's hit me!" he said.

"Maya's mother?"

He was frantic. "Get over here now!"

"What happened?"

"Now!"

I drove like a bat out of hell. I did not slow down even through Paradise Valley with its hidden radar cameras, and I sped up Scottsdale Road at nearly twice the speed limit, figuring I'd have the Big Man pay off any tickets that were sent to me through the mail.

One of Pressman's flunkies was waiting for me at the door of the house, and I was quickly ushered in and taken to the bedroom, where the Big Man was seated on a chair next to the gigantic waterbed, stripped to the waist. He looked at me with frightened eyes as I entered.

I felt a sudden coldness in my gut.

His right arm had withered to half its normal size and was blackening with rot. No less than three doctors, all of them obviously very highly paid specialists, were standing around him, one of them injecting something into the arm, the other two talking low amongst themselves.

"That bitch cursed me!" he shouted, and there was both anger and fear in his voice. "I want her found! Do you understand me?"

The flunkies and I all nodded. None of us were sure who he was talking to, and it was safer at this point not to ask.

The Big Man grimaced as the needle was pulled out of

his arm. He looked at me, motioned me over, and one of the doctors stepped aside so I could get close.

"Is there any way to reverse this?" he asked through gritted teeth. "Can I get this curse taken off me somehow?"

"I don't know," I admitted.

"Well, find out!"

He screamed, and the arm shrunk another six inches before our eyes. The doctors looked at each other, obviously at a loss. They seemed nervous, and it occurred to me for the first time that though they might be tops in their field, the best and the brightest the Mayo Clinic had to offer, they were just as afraid of the Big Man's wrath as anyone else. It was a sobering thought.

I started out of the bedroom, intending to find a phone, make a few calls, and see if anyone of my acquaintance knew anything about the lifting of Guatemalan arm-shrinking spells. I turned around in the doorway, wanting to ask the Big Man something else, but he screamed again and, with a sickeningly wet *pop* his arm disappeared, its tail-end nub sucked into his shoulder, the skin closing behind it as if it had never existed.

I hurried out of the room.

No one I knew had any info or any ideas, so I figured the best idea was to once again stake out Therese's shack. I told one of the Big Man's flunkies to let him know that I'd gone to find out about the spell and Maya's mother. The flunky looked about as thrilled as I felt to be telling the Big Man anything right now, and I quickly left before he could decline and insist that I do it myself.

Luckily for me, Therese was home. Alone. I put on my most official-looking expression in order to intimidate her into talking. I told her I was working for Vincent Pressman, hoping that the name carried weight even down here, and said that he wanted to know the current whereabouts of his former maid and her daughter Maya.

Word about the situation must have already spread through the Guatemalan community because Therese blanched at Pressman's name, and quickly crossed herself when I mentioned Maya.

"You know something about this," I said.

She nodded, obviously frightened. I got the feeling she wasn't supposed to be talking to outsiders.

"What's going on?" I asked. "What's happening to Mr. Pressman?"

The woman looked furtively about. "He mess with the wrong woman. She a . . . how you call it? . . . Very powerful, uh . . ."

"Witch?" I offered helpfully

"Yes! Witch! She curse him. She will kill him but she want him to suffer first." Therese crossed herself again.

"What about her daughter, Maya?"

"Daughter dead."

"What?"

"Mother kill her. She have to. Cannot live with shame. Now she blame him for daughter's death, too. His fault she have to kill girl." She shook her head. "It bad. Very bad."

I asked about removing the curse, asked if there was anyone else who could do it, another witch perhaps, but Therese said that only the one who applied the curse could lift it. She told me the other limited options for dealing with the situation, but they were all horrible, and I asked if I could talk to someone who knew more about the black arts than she did, but she would not give me any names, not even for a pair of Andrew Jacksons.

I wanted to stop by my place, pick up a few phone numbers, some people I knew who weren't Guatemalan but might be able to tell me something about lifting curses, but Armstrong was waiting for me outside my apartment, and with typically piggish glee he told me that since I was one of the last people to see Hector alive, I was automatically a suspect in his murder. I denied everything as I desperately tried to think of who could have seen me with him, who could have ratted me out, but Armstrong motioned for me to get in the cruiser so we could go down to the station and talk.

All the way over, my stomach was tied up in knots. Not because of Hector—I was innocent, and I knew there was no way that even Armstrong could make that stick—but because I needed to talk to the Big Man. He was waiting with his one arm to hear what I'd found, but I sure as hell couldn't call from a police station, and I sat in the interrogation room as I waited for someone to talk to me, and pretended I was in no hurry to do anything.

An hour or so later, a smirking Armstrong joined me. He asked me a shitload of stupid questions, then leaned smugly back in his chair. "In my estimation, you're a flight risk," he said. "I can keep you in custody for twenty-four without cause, and I think I'm going to do that while we sort through what you said and check out your alibis."

He grinned at me. He knew I was innocent, but this was his idea of fun, and I made no comment and pretended as though I didn't care one way or the other as I was led to a holding cell.

I was awakened in the middle of the night by a cowed young sergeant who was accompanied by an intimidating man in a smartly fitted business suit, and I knew that the Big Man had tracked me down and had me sprung.

I was happy to be out, but I didn't like being this close to someone that powerful, and I vowed to be careful who I took on as clients in the future—no matter how interesting their cases might be.

A limo was waiting outside, and we drove in silence out to the desert.

It was late at night, but the Big Man was awake. He was also limping. It looked like he was wearing a diaper, but I saw the grimace of pain on his face as he sat down, and I knew something else had happened, something far worse than mere incontinence.

I was afraid to ask, but I had to know. "What happened?"

"My cock," he said, his voice barely above a mumble. "It attacked me."

"What?"

"I woke up, and it'd turned into a snake. It was biting my leg and whipping around and biting my stomach, and I could feel its poison spreading through me. So I ran into the kitchen and got a knife and I cut it off."

It took a moment for that to sink in. Pressman had cut off his own penis? I imagined Maya's mother cackling to herself as she wove that spell.

"The doctors sewed me up, but they couldn't sew it back on. It was still alive. We had to kill it." He grimaced, using his arm to grab the side of the sofa and support himself. "So what'd you find out?"

I told him the truth. "Maya's dead. Her mother killed her. Now she blames you for that, too." I motioned toward his crotch. "So this is going to go on. You're going to be tortured until you die. And then she'll own you after death. She'll be able to do whatever she wants with your soul."

"I'll kill her," he said. "I'll find that bitch and kill her."

"Won't do any good. The whammy's on, and as I understand it, killing her won't stop it. All of the Guatemalans are terrified. She's one powerful woman."

"So what are my options?"

I shrugged. "Only three that I see. One: get her to stop, convince her to lift the curse, which, considering the situation, I don't think is going to happen. Two: put up with this shit until you die and then go gently into her vindictive little hands . . ." I trailed off.

"And three?"

I looked at him. "You can take your own life. That will put an end to it. Her curse is meant to kill you . . . eventually. But if you take matters into your own hands, if you interrupt it and thwart her plans, all rights revert back to you."

I was playing it cool, playing it tough, but the truth was, I was scared shitless. Not of the Big Man, not anymore, but of what I'd gotten into here, of the powers we were dealing with. I was out of my depth, but Pressman was still putting it all on my shoulders. I was supposed to be the expert, and it was a role I neither deserved nor wanted.

He was actually considering the benefits of suicide.

"So if I eat my gun—"

"No," I said. "It has to be stabbing or hanging."

He slammed his hand down on the back of the couch. "Why?" He glared at me. "What fucking difference does that make?"

"I don't know why," I said. "But it does make a difference. I don't make the rules, I just explain them. And for some reason, those are the only two ways that are guaranteed to get you out from under the curse. A shooting *might* work, but then again, it might not. And you'll only get one chance at this, so you'd better make sure it counts."

He shook his head, lurched away from the sofa. "Fuck that. There's no way in hell I'm going to off myself because some little wetback bitch put her voodoo on me. I'll take my chances. I'm going to find her and get rid of her and we'll see if *that* works."

That's what he said on Thursday.

On Friday, his teeth fell out.

On Saturday, he began shitting rocks.

His men did find the maid, and the cops found her later, her teeth knocked out, her arm amputated, her private parts cut open, her anus stuffed with gravel. Like Hector, she was in a Dumpster, having been left there to die, and over the next few days several other Guatemalans, who I suppose had some relationship to Maya's mother, were also found murdered.

But it didn't stop for the Big Man. His travails grew worse, and by midweek, he was able to walk only with the help of serious painkillers.

I asked around, checked my other sources, even went out to see Bookbinder, but the first facts proved true, and no one knew of a way to get around the witch's handiwork.

I stayed away, stayed home, tried to stay out of it, tried not to think about it, but finally he called me in, and I went. There was almost no trace left of that hard, confident crime lord I'd met the first day. He was broken and blubbering, drunk and wasted, and he told me that he wanted to hang himself.

Only he was too weak to do it on his own.

I told him he could have some of his men help him, but he said he didn't want them to do it and they probably wouldn't anyway. He also wanted to make sure he did everything right, that nothing went wrong.

"You're the only one who knows that shit," he said, his voice slurred.

I nodded reluctantly.

He grabbed my shoulder. I think he wanted to make sure

he had my full attention, but it seemed more as though he used me to steady himself. "I don't want to suffer after death," he whispered. His eyes were feverish, intense. "And I don't want that wetback bitch to win." His voice rose. "Your daughter was the best fuck I ever had!" he shouted to the air. "I took that whore the way she liked it! I gave her what she wanted! I gave her what she wanted!"

I left him in the bedroom, went out to the garage and found a rope, and set it up, throwing it over the beam, tying the knots.

He changed his mind at the last minute. A lot of people do. It's a hard way to go, a painful, ugly way, and the second he jumped off the chair, he started to claw at the rope and flail away in the air.

I thought about helping him. Part of me wanted to help him.

But I didn't.

I let him thrash about, watching him die, until he was still. I'll probably go to hell for that, but I can't seem to muster up much remorse for it. I wish I could say that I let him die for his own sake, so Maya's mother wouldn't own his soul, but the truth was that I did it because I *wanted* him dead. I thought we'd all be better off without him.

"That's for Hector," I said softly.

I stood there for a moment more, watching him swing, and I actually did feel bad. No one deserved what had happened to the Big Man, and I was glad he'd escaped, glad he wouldn't have to suffer it anymore.

But I was also glad he was gone.

I walked out of the bedroom, down the hallway to the front of the house, where I found one of his men eating crackers in the kitchen.

"Call the cops," I said. "He's dead."

The flunky looked at me dumbly. He knew what had gone down, but it still seemed to catch him off guard. "What'll I tell them?"

I patted his cheek on my way out. "Don't worry. You'll think of something."

I walked outside and got in my car, driving as quickly as I could away from the house. The air in the vehicle was stifling, but I didn't mind, and I felt as though I'd just been released from a prison as I followed the dirt road through the desert, past the crosses and the doll parts and the skull-headed scarecrows, toward the distant white smog of Phoenix, shimmering in the heat.

Colony

When H. R. Haldeman died, I found myself thinking
about the labyrinthine nightmare that was Watergate.
Which led me to think about conspiracy theories. What
if Haldeman wasn't really dead? I thought. What if he
was only pretending to be dead but had really gone
underground?

Why, though? What would be the reason?

Years later, when Hong Kong reverted back to
China, I was reminded of Britain's war with Argentina
over the Falkland Islands (or Islas Malvinas). I had not
known until the war that Britain *had* any remaining
colonies. I'd been under the impression that the em-
pire was history. Obviously I was wrong, and I wondered if there were other far-flung properties under
British rule that I did not know about.

Somewhere down the line, those two unrelated bits
of random speculation coalesced into this story.

—⁓—

It was awkward.

He had campaigned on a cost-cutting platform, pledging
to reduce spending and staff, and now with the White House

employees all assembled before him, he wanted to remain impassive, impartial, detached.

But he could not. These were real people before him. Real people with real jobs and real bills to pay. On the campaign trail, they'd been merely a faceless statistic, a theoretical conceit. But now as Adam stared out at the faces of these workers, many of whom had been employed here for longer than he'd been alive, he felt embarrassed and ashamed. He realized, perhaps for the first time, that his decisions for the next four years would have human consequences, would take their toll on individual lives—not an earth-shattering conclusion by any means, but one which he now understood emotionally as well as intellectually.

He was not going to go back on his promises, though. As hard as it was, as painful as it might be, he was going to stick to the specifics of his campaign platform. There would be none of the waffling and indecision and half measures that had so afflicted his predecessors.

Hell, that's what he had criticized and run against in his bid for the presidency.

It was why he had been elected.

He'd been intending to announce the layoffs here and now, to do the firings en masse and get them over with, but he could not. Instead, he smiled out at his domestic staff and gave a generic "We're-All-In-This-Together, Let's-Put-Our-Petty-Differences-Aside-For-The-Good-Of-The-Country" speech. It had worked well in Dallas and Tampa, had knocked 'em dead in a longer variation at the nominating convention and after the general election, and it sufficed here in a more specific, more intimate incarnation.

He smiled and waved at the applauding workers, walked away, and turned toward Tom Simons, his chief of staff, as he headed down the hall to the Oval Office. "I want a list of all employees, their job positions, and their years of service. Also get me that cost-cutting analysis we put together."

"You got it."

"I'll speak to the groups individually, by job classification, explain the situation."

Simons nodded. "You want to do it in the Oval Office?"

"Yeah."

"I'll get right on it."

They parted halfway down the corridor and Adam continued on to the Oval Office alone. He was struck each time he entered the room by how small it was. All the rooms in the White House were smaller than he'd imagined them to be. The building had been designed and constructed a long time ago, of course, but he'd expected the rooms to be bigger than those in his Palm Springs house, and the fact that they weren't left him feeling disappointed and a little uneasy.

He walked over to his desk, sat down, swiveled his chair around to look out the window. He was filled with a strange lethargy, a desire to just sit here and do nothing. For the first time in his life, he had no real boss, no one standing over him, and if he chose to unplug his phone and spend the afternoon staring out at the lawn, he could do so.

Power.

There would be demands on his time, of course. Obligations and commitments. A lot of pressure, a lot of responsibility. But the federal government ran itself for the most part. He didn't need to micromanage everything. And if he wanted to, he could simply let it all slide.

No. He had to stop thinking that way. He had gone after this job for a reason. He had ideas. He had an agenda. And he planned to go down in history as an effective activist, as a competent administrator and visionary leader, not as the first slacker president.

Simons led in the first group of employees—butlers and maids—sometime later, and Adam stood, smiling blandly, wanting to appear friendly and personable but not wanting to instill a false sense of security. "I'm sure Mr. Simons told you why I've asked you here to the Oval Office." He nodded toward the chief of staff. "As I'm sure you're well aware, we have a fairly serious budget crisis facing us this year, and as I'm sure you're also aware, I promised the American people that I would cut government spending by a third and that I would not exempt myself from this edict. I will receive no special privileges but will sacrifice along with everyone else. This means, I'm afraid, that we will be eliminating some White House staff positions. We've looked at this from every angle, and while we've considered cutting the total number of employees by doing away with certain departments, we have decided that it is fairer to simply cut each department by a third."

A balding elderly man in a butler's uniform stepped forward. "Excuse me, sir?"

Adam held up his hand. "Don't worry. The layoffs will be by seniority—"

"There aren't going to be any layoffs, sir. You can't make any cuts in staff."

Adam smiled sympathetically. "Mr.—?"

"Crowther, sir."

"Mr. Crowther, I understand your concern, and believe me I sympathize."

"I don't think you do understand, sir. I'm sorry, but you can't fire any of us."

"Can't fire you?"

"We report directly to Buckingham Palace."

Adam looked over at Simons, who shrugged, equally confused.

"We're not under you. We work for you, but we're not employed by you. Sir."

Adam shook his head. "Hold on here."

"We report to Buckingham Palace."

He was growing annoyed. "What does Buckingham Palace have to do with anything?"

"Ahh." The butler nodded. "I understand now. Nobody told you. No one explained to you."

"Explained what?"

"You are not the head of the United States government."

"Of course I am! I'm . . . I'm the president!"

"Well, you are the president, but the presidency is a fiction, a powerless position created by the Palace. The president is a figurehead. Someone to make speeches and television appearances, to keep the masses happy."

"The president is the leader of the Free World."

"I'm afraid, sir, that that distinction belongs to the Queen of England."

Crowther was still as calm and unruffled as ever, and there was something unnerving about that. It was understandable that the butler would try to save his job or the jobs of his friends, it was even conceivable that he would lie in order to accomplish that goal, but this was so bizarre, so far out of left field, that it made no sense. If this was a lie, it was a damn creative one.

If this was a lie?

Adam looked into the butler's eyes.

Yes. If.

He licked his lips, cleared his throat, tried to project a confidence he did not really feel. "We fought and won a war of independence over two hundred years ago," he said. "The

Declaration of Independence is our seminal national document."

"Independence?" The butler laughed. "America's not independent. That was a PR stunt to placate the natives."

The rest of the hired help was nodding in agreement.

Adam felt cold. There was nothing to indicate that this was a joke, and the casual, almost nonchalant way in which the butlers and maids were reacting to the whole situation gave everything a boost of verisimilitude. He looked over at Simons for help, but his chief of staff was staring blankly back at him, obviously shaken.

Did Simons believe it?

Yes, he thought. And he did, too. He did not know why, but he knew that Crowther was telling the truth, and as he stared out at the faces of the domestic staff, he felt like the stupidest kid in class, the one who did not catch on to concepts until well after everyone else.

His entire worldview and take on history had been instantly changed by a meeting with a group of servants he'd intended to fire.

He took a deep breath. "You're saying we're . . . still a colony?"

"Quite right, sir."

"But independence is the bedrock of our national character. We pride ourselves on not only our national independence but our personal freedom. Our individuality is what makes us American."

"And we encourage that. It is why America is our most productive colony."

Colony.

It was as if all of the air had been vacuumed out of his lungs. He licked his lips, trying to drum up some saliva. He had never been so frightened in his life. Not during his first term as a senator when he'd been broke and read in the newspaper that the staff member with whom he had been having an affair was about to file a multimillion dollar sexual harassment suit against him, not when he'd been on the Armed Services committee and a right-wing wacko who had threatened his life showed up after hours at his home. He did not know why he was so scared, but he was, and the Oval Office felt suddenly hot, stifling. Five minutes ago, he had intended to keep one of his minor campaign promises to the nation and lay off some members of the White House staff. Now he was cowering before a group of servants, intimidated by their unnatural calm, by their proper British accents. He felt powerless, impotent, emasculated, but he forced himself to maintain the facade, to keep up the benevolent leader demeanor. "I'm sorry," he said. "I don't believe you."

"That's perfectly all right, sir. Nixon and Carter had a difficult time believing it as well." Crowther smiled. "Ford and Reagan accepted it instantly."

He couldn't resist. "Clinton? The Bushes?"

"They all got used to it, sir. As will you."

"So you're saying the United States is ruled by . . . ?"

"The queen."

"But the queen's a figurehead as well. Britain has a parliamentary democracy—"

The butler chuckled. "Parliamentary democracy? No such thing. Again, it keeps the peasants happy, makes them think they're somehow involved. The truth is, the prime minister's like you. A front. It's the queen who runs everything. Always has, always will."

"You're lying."

"I'm not."

"I don't accept this. I was elected by a majority of the citizens of the United States to be their leader, and I will not take orders from anyone else."

"Oh yes you will, sir. You will take your orders from the queen."

Adam faced the butler. "And I damn sure won't take any orders from a two-bit monarch with a tabloid—"

"Stop right there, sir." There was something threatening in the butler's stance now, an intimation of menace in his voice. "You will bow before the queen and you will most assuredly submit to her authority."

"And if I don't?"

"We had Kennedy shot; we can arrange something for you as well."

There was silence in the Oval Office.

He faced Crowther, trying not to let his nervousness show. "The queen ordered—?"

"The queen had nothing to do with it, sir. It was a decision by the operatives in this country, based on her own best interests. She was never told." He paused. "There are a lot of things we have not told the queen."

"Then you are disloyal."

"I beg to differ, sir. Sometimes the queen does not realize where her own interests lie. It is our responsibility to determine what is best for her and best for the motherland and carry out those actions to the best of our abilities."

The butler looked from Adam to Simons. "I'm sure you two would like to be alone for a while so you can . . . absorb all this, so we will leave you in peace." He motioned with his head and the maid nearest the door opened it. The servants began filing out. "When would you like to meet again, sir?"

"Never."

Crowther chuckled. "Very well. You will let me know."

He let himself out of the room, closing the door behind him with a flourish that could only be considered mocking.

Adam turned toward his chief of staff. "So what do you make of that?"

Simons was shaking his head, still not able to speak.

"You think it's true?"

Simons nodded. "Looks that way."

"So what do we do?"

"What *can* we do?"

"Before we can do anything, I need to know the chain of command. Are we going to be simply following orders, or are we going to be given a certain level of autonomy?"

Simons smiled wryly. "You mean, is the queen a micro-manager?"

Adam snorted. "The queen. Can you believe this shit? Did you ever, in your wildest fucking dreams, ever think that something like this could happen?"

"What amazes me is the extent of it. They've corrupted our history from its simplest to its most complex level, from grammar school civics to graduate public policy. Every single person not directly involved in this . . . travesty believes the same lie. In all my years in politics, in all my years of public life, I've never even had any suspicions that something like this could be the case."

"I was a senator for twelve years," Adam said. "How do you think I feel, knowing that all of my effort and hard work was merely irrelevant grease for the public relations machine?" He kicked the swivel chair behind his desk. "Fuck!"

"What are we going to do?" Simons asked.

"I don't know."

"What do you *want* to do?"

Adam thought for a moment, looked at him. "I want," he said quietly, "to secure our country's independence."

*   *   *

They met that night, his election team, in a Denny's coffee shop. Derek, his dirty trickster, was along to scan for bugs or other listening devices, and when he'd checked the table and the surrounding plastic plants and had set up a small black square to detect long-range microphone waves, they started talking.

"The first thing we need to do," Simons said, "is get the First Lady out of here. We need to send her on a goodwill trip to Japan or something. Get her as far away from British influence as possible. Who knows how low they'd stoop?"

Adam nodded. "Agreed."

Paul Frederickson cleared his throat. The secretary of state had been with him ever since his first senatorial campaign and, next to Simons, Adam trusted his opinion more than anyone else's.

"Go ahead, Paul."

"I think what we need to do first is discover the extent of the infiltration. This Crowther told you that all of the previous presidents had come around. Does that mean that they'd been converted, that they truly believed this was the best form of government for the United States, or does that mean that they accepted the way things were but didn't like it?"

"I would suspect the latter." Ted Fitzsimmons.

"We need to talk to them, find out how much they know. They can probably tell the players well enough to put together a scorecard we can use."

"Good idea," Adam said.

"We need to know about the various branches as well. Judiciary? Do the members of the Supreme Court know? Legislative? Any senators? We know that not all of them know, but maybe some of them do. FBI? CIA? Branches of the military? We need to be able to assess our strengths and weaknesses before we can formulate a plan of action."

They talked through the night, into the wee hours of the morning, and Adam could barely keep his eyes open by the time they left the restaurant and split up. He felt good, though. Assignments had been delegated and at least a rough idea of where they were headed had been hashed out. He no longer felt as hopeless and despairing of the situation as he had when he'd called the meeting.

He said goodbye to Simons on the sidewalk, then got into the presidential limousine. "The White House," he told the driver.

"Yes sir." The man started the car, looked at him in the rearview mirror, smiled. "God save the queen."

Adam forced himself to smile back. "God save the queen."

The military was all his.

It was the best news he'd had all week. The only hold the British had over the armed forces was the basic lie, the knowledge that each and every person in uniform believed that the United States was a sovereign nation and that they were supposed to uphold the U.S. Constitution, democracy's blueprint.

But he was still commander in chief.

It was a loophole, although not a particularly practical one. What could he do? Stage a coup and invade Britain? It would look like war. People would think him a dangerous lunatic, irrationally attacking a longtime ally, and he'd be instantly impeached. He needed to wage a backstage battle, a behind-the-scenes war. He needed to free America from Britain without letting the public know. He needed to make the myth a reality.

But how?

War at least was feasible. He was commander in chief, and the military was one thing he did legitimately control. It was messy, but as a last resort it might have to do.

There was a knock on the door of the Oval Office and Simons entered, carrying a manila folder stuffed with papers.

"What have you found out?"

The chief of staff sat down in a chair on the opposite side of the desk and leaned forward, whispering, "The Secret Service is all theirs. Technically, the FBI's under their jurisdiction as well, but we seem to have most of them. The director has assured me that as many operatives as we need are at our disposal."

"Do you believe him?"

"Do we have a choice?"

"What about—"

"The other presidents? They won't talk. I don't know if they've been bought or threatened, but we can't get word one out of them."

"I can't believe that."

"Maybe they got to them before we could." He paused. "The Bushes seemed scared."

"CIA?"

"Theirs."

Adam thought for a moment. "The director can get us operatives?"

Simons nodded.

"Crowther. The butler," he said. "I want him gotten rid of."

"Do you think that's a good idea?"

"Consider it the first shot. We'll gauge from their reaction how they'll respond to . . . other incidents."

For the first time since all this had started, Tom Simons smiled.

In the morning, his breakfast was not made, his clothes were not ready. When he returned to his bedroom, the sheets had not been changed.

"You'll pay for this," one of the maids hissed at him in the hallway.

He smiled at her, leaned forward. "You're next," he whispered, and he was gratified to see a look of fear cross her face. "Now make my fucking bed."

He continued down the hallway, feeling good. Simons had called first thing with the news: Crowther had been taken care of. Somehow, just knowing that cheered him up, made him feel better. The entire atmosphere of the White House seemed to have changed with this one bold stroke. He had been skulking around for the past two weeks, certain that the staff saw him as yet another weak puppet who had been cowed into submission, but now he walked boldly through the corridors, noting with pleasure that the domestic workers were all in fear of him.

Maybe they would be able to pull this off.

The others were waiting for him in the conference room. Derek had already swept the place for bugs and positioned his listening-device detector on the table, and twin sets of FBI agents were positioned at the doors.

"So what's our next move?" Adam asked.

Paul Frederickson looked up at him. "Nixon."

"Nixon?"

The secretary of state nodded. "I've been thinking about it for the past week. If the president is only a figurehead, then all that hype about Nixon's so-called imperial presidency has to be British disinformation. How could Nixon try to circumvent the Constitution and grab additional powers for himself when he never had the power attributed to him in the first place?"

Adam smiled. "Yes! He put up a fight. He tried to do what he was elected to do."

"And they crushed him. They must have been behind his disgrace."

"Get me whoever you can from Nixon's cabinet and staff, people who would know about this."

"Done," Frederickson said. "Haldeman's already on his way."

"Haldeman?" Adam frowned. "I thought he was dead."

"Reports of his death are greatly exaggerated. He's in hiding."

"Good," Adam said. "Now we're getting somewhere."

Simons spoke up. "Crowther said that Carter didn't buy into it either. You think—?"

"Carter wouldn't talk to us, but we could feel out some of his underlings, see what we can get."

Adam nodded. "Do it."

"Those Clinton scandals must have been played up for a reason as well. The pressure was kept on him even after he left office."

"Look into it."

There was a knock on the south door and one of the FBI agents opened it carefully. He spoke for a moment to the person outside, and then the door opened wider. Larry Herbert, Frederickson's assistant walked in.

Followed by H. R. Haldeman.

He was older but still instantly recognizable. The crew cut was back, but its severity was offset by a pair of softening bifocals. Haldeman nodded at them. "Gentlemen."

Frederickson stood, looked at his assistant. "I assume you briefed him on the way over?"

Haldeman sat down in an empty seat. "Yes, he did. And I must say that I'm very happy to have you people in the fight."

They talked about the Nixon days, about the memos from Buckingham Palace, the hotline calls from the queen, the prepared speeches that Nixon refused to give, the complicity of certain cabinet members. Crowther had been around then as well, and Haldeman was shocked to learn that Adam had had the butler eliminated.

"Just like that?" he said.

Adam felt a surge of pride. "Just like that."

Haldeman shook his head worriedly. "You don't know what you're in for. There are going to be repercussions."

"That's why you're here. So we can pick your brain. I did this intentionally, to raise the stakes."

Haldeman sighed.

"There's nothing you can give us?"

"We've been training paramilitary groups for years, planning to overthrow the British."

"The militias?"

Haldeman snorted, waved his hand dismissively. "Paranoid cranks. And those hayseeds are too stupid to be able to handle something like this. No, we put together the inner-city gangs. We founded the Crips, the Bloods, and their brethren. We'd recruited minorities for the military in Vietnam and it worked beautifully, so we decided to do the same with our revolutionary force. We couldn't let the British know what was happening, though, so we disguised them as independent organizations, rival youth groups fighting over drugs and neighborhood turf. We established them as criminals, made sure they got plenty of publicity, plenty of air-time on news programs, and now they're believed to be such an intrinsic part of contemporary American life that even if one of them breaks ranks the myth is secure."

"You think it'll work?"

"Eventually. But we've already been doing this for twenty years, and we probably won't be ready for another ten or fifteen. We don't have the numbers. Britain can recruit from Australia, Canada, all of their colonies. If we went at them right now, we wouldn't stand a chance. Besides, something like this takes planning."

"We need more immediate results."

"Sorry. I can't help you there."

They continued talking, sharing secrets, comparing strategies until midafternoon. Haldeman had to fly back to Chicago, and Adam walked with him to the limo. "Thank you for coming," he said, shaking the other man's hand.

"Anything for my country," Haldeman said.

Adam smiled. "You still think of this as your country?"

"Always."

Adam watched the limo roll down the drive and through the White House gates, and suddenly an idea occurred to him. He hurried back into the White House. Several of his advisors had suggested that the entire domestic staff be executed as a way of provoking British forces in Washington to show themselves, but after talking to Haldeman he knew that that would be a suicidal gesture. This idea, though, was a good one.

This idea might work.

He ran into Simons in the corridor. "Gather everyone together again," he said. "I have a plan."

"Hello?"

Even on the amplified speakerphone of the hotline, the queen's voice was distant, muffled.

"Greetings, Your Majesty." Adam made sure his tone was properly subservient.

"Why are you contacting us? If we wish to speak with you, *we* will initiate the dialogue."

"I'm calling to apologize, Your Majesty. As you may or may not have heard, there's been some miscommunication here at our end. Apparently, some of your subjects seem to believe that I and my people are somehow involved in the disappearance of the head of my domestic staff, Crowther."

"We have heard rumors to that effect."

He attempted to make his voice sound simultaneously obsequious toward her and condescending toward everyone else. "I would like to invite you to the White House so that we might have a face-to-face discussion on some of these matters. I am afraid I am fairly dissatisfied with some of your representatives here, and I believe you would be as well. I have nothing but the utmost respect for you and your position, and I fear that your underlings here are doing a disservice to both you and Britain."

Silence on the other end.

He held his breath, waiting.

"It has been some time since we have visited the States," the queen allowed. "And your accusations, we must admit, are somewhat alarming. We will come to visit the colonies and judge for ourselves. The proper people will be in touch."

Communication was abruptly cut off, and there was only silence on the hotline's speakerphone. Adam stared at the red phone for a moment, then a smile spread slowly across his face.

He turned toward Simons, pumped his fist in the air. "Yes!"

*   *   *

She arrived on the Concorde two days later.

All the arrangements had been made. Outside White House grounds, everything continued on as usual, but within, FBI agents had rounded up and detained all domestic staff members and all known or suspected British agents. Outside contacts and government workers who were suspicious about the sudden lack of communication were placated with the promise that the queen would be arriving to sort everything out—a fact they could double-check with Buckingham Palace.

The chairman of the Joint Chiefs of Staff had assured him that the National Guard was ready for its demonstration and that the other branches of the armed forces were available as backup.

Everything was in place.

The second the limousine carrying the queen passed onto the White House grounds, and the iron gates closed behind it, National Guard troops blocked off the street and surrounded the area. Simultaneously, the White House press secretary put out the news that a bomb threat had been made against the queen and that precautions—including the use of armed guards—were being taken.

Adam waited in the Oval Office, the document he'd had drawn up by the chief justice of the Supreme Court sitting on his desk, a pen next to it. He was nervous, hands sweaty, but he was determined to go through with the plan. He would be assassinated if they failed—he had no doubt about that—but there was a good chance that they would not fail.

He was imagining his place in history when there was a knock on the door. He stood, composed himself, cleared his throat. "Yes?" he enquired.

The door opened and a host of British dignitaries and

American cabinet members entered the room, parting to allow the queen to pass by.

The queen.

She looked just like she did on TV and in magazine photographs. Even knowing the extent of her power, even with all the knowledge of her position that he'd gained recently, he could sense no aura of exaggerated importance about her, no intimidating demeanor, none of the dictatorial trappings he would have expected. It was an illusion, though. He knew that. And he bowed extravagantly as she stopped before his desk. "Your Majesty."

She acknowledged his servility with a barely perceptible nod and sat down in the specially provided chair opposite him. "Now," she said, "tell us what you have to say."

"I'd prefer to do this alone," he said, motioning toward the gathered dignitaries.

"Anything you say to us can be said in front of them."

"I'm afraid that they might have a vested interest. May we speak in private?"

She nodded, dismissing the others with a slight wave of her hand. Everyone else, American and British, filed out of the room. The door closed behind them.

Outside the office, Adam knew, FBI agents were disarming and subduing the British, herding them downstairs with their compatriots. A trickle of sweat slid from under his left armpit, down the side of his body, hidden by his suit jacket.

"I want a guarantee that there aren't going to be any repercussions simply because I tell you the truth."

"We give you our word," she told him.

"'Our' word? What about your word? I don't mean to be disrespectful," he said, "but I'd like some assurances that you, personally, guarantee that your underlings will not seek reprisals."

She looked at him as if he was a bug she had squashed on the floor. "You have *my* word," she said.

"And that is legally binding?"

"The word of the British sovereign has been legally binding for hundreds of years. It is law."

"Very well." He stood, pushed the document and pen across the desk toward her. "I want you to sign this."

The queen blinked. "What did you say to me?"

"I want you to sign this document."

She regarded him with an expression centered somewhere between horror, disgust, and outrage. "You dare to make demands on *us*?"

He met her eyes. "Yes."

He saw hesitance, what might be the first faint stirrings of apprehension, and it made him feel good.

"What is this?" she demanded, motioning toward the document.

"A real declaration of independence. A contract ceding the United States of America to its citizens and declaring that you and your nation relinquish all rights—"

"Never!"

"Never say never."

"Pembroke!" she called loudly. "Lewis!"

There was a pause.

Silence.

"They're not coming," Adam said. "We've captured them." He walked slowly around the huge desk. "Now all we need is your signature."

"You're loony!"

"Maybe so, but you're going to sign that contract."

"I most certainly will not!" In one quick movement, she was out of her chair, across the room, and almost to the door. He lunged at her, and she stepped aside, allowing him to shoulder the wall. He felt a sharp pain in his side as she jabbed him with a bony fist.

"Goddamn it!" He reached for her arm, but she was already running away, toward the opposite side of the office, yelling for help.

He tackled the queen, and her purse flew across the Oval Office. She was small but wiry, and she squirmed out of his grasp, kicking him hard in the chest with a high-heeled shoe. She scrambled for her purse and was opening it, pulling something out, when he landed on her. He wrenched her right arm behind her back, causing her to cry out. Still holding her, he struggled to his feet and forced her over to the desk.

He held her around the neck with his left hand, while he loosened his grip on her arm with his right. "Sign it!" he ordered, forcing her hand onto the desk.

"Fuck you!" she screamed. She tried to break away, but he was stronger than she was and she received only a more tightly pinched neck in return.

"Pick up the pen!" he ordered.

"No!"

"I'll break your arm, you shriveled old bitch." He increased the pressure.

Angrily, she picked up the pen.

He held her hand to the paper. "Sign it."

She hesitated.

"Now!" he screamed.

She quickly scrawled her signature. He moved her over to the left side of the desk and compared her written name with the example of her signature Simons had provided.

It was good.

He let her go.

A surge of pride coursed through him, an expression of pure patriotism he had not felt since . . . well, ever.

The queen had run immediately to the door and was rubbing her sore wrist, begging to be released. She was crying, and he thought with satisfaction that she wasn't such a tough old broad after all.

He picked up the document, placed it in his middle desk drawer, and locked it.

The United States was officially a sovereign nation.

They were free.

He looked at the queen. She was no longer crying, and he could see no tears on her overly made-up face, but she was still frowning and rubbing her wrist, and he smiled at her, feeling good.

"God bless America," he said.

Confessions of a Corporate Man

I worked as a technical writer in the early 1990s because at the time I could not support myself writing fiction. Being a bearded, long-haired liberal arts guy, I found it a bit surreal after seven years of college to find myself sitting in an office surrounded by well-groomed business, accounting, and public administration types. Even more surreal was how seriously they took their petty little turf wars and how ridiculous were their priorities.

"Confessions of a Corporate Man" is my slightly exaggerated take on those days.

—⚍—

We sharpened pencils for the War and walked over to Accounting en masse. The Finance Director and his minions were working on spreadsheets, and unsuspecting. We had the advantage of surprise.

We screamed as one, on my cue, and when the accountants looked up, we drove the pencils through their eyes and into their brains. It was glorious. I was in charge of dispatching the director himself, and I shoved the pencil in hard, feeling it puncture membrane and spear through gelatin into flesh. The director's fat hands lashed out, trying to grab me, but then he was twitching and then he was still.

I straightened up and looked around the department. The War had been awfully short, and we had won virtually without a fight. Bodies were already quiet and cooling, blood and eye juice leaking onto graph paper and computer printouts.

We would get medals for this if we were working for any sort of fair corporation, but as it stood we would probably only get notepads to commemorate our victory.

I pulled my pencil out of the Finance Director's head and gave the high sign.

We were back at our desks before the end of Break.

Restructuring went smoothly. Personnel were reassigned, duties shifted, and control of the company was decentralized. A temporary truce was called on account of our overwhelming victory, and all hostilities were suspended. A vice president was executed—beheaded in the Staff Lounge with a paper cutter—and we successfully managed to meet the Payroll.

The acting CEO refused to hire temps or to recruit outside the organization, so we ended up making coffee during the period of Restructuring. I still felt we deserved medals, but this time we did not even get our notepads. Although the Dow took no notice of my triumph, our stock shot up five points on the Pacific Exchange, and I felt vindicated.

We sent condoms through the Vacuum Tubes, back and forth, forth and back, and the women in the Whorehouse did a thriving lunchtime business. New lubrication machines were installed in the Cafeteria.

There were more changes made. The secretaries no longer had to wear masks, and pets were once again allowed in the Steno Pool. Purchasing picked a crippled child for its mascot. Machine Services switched to a mollusk.

The next War would be catered, we said. For the next War we would have hot dogs.

We all laughed.

And then . . .

And then things changed.

A questionnaire began making the rounds of the departments. A questionnaire on official black Bereavement stationery. No one would take credit for its authorship, and word of its existence preceded by days its appearance in the Inter-Office Mail. We received the questionnaire on Thursday, along with a note to complete it and return it to Personnel by Friday morning, and we were afraid to disobey.

"If Batman were a fig," it asked, "would he still have to shave?"

"If the president was naked and straddling a bench, would his mama's stickers still have thorns?"

The mood in our department grew somber, and there was a general feeling that the questionnaire had something to do with our routing of Accounting. In an indirect way, I was blamed for its existence.

I was pantsed on the day our Xerox access was denied.

I was paddled on the day our Muzak was cut off.

A month passed. Two. Three. There was another execution—a sales executive who failed to meet his quotas—but the uneasy truce remained between departments, and the War did not resume. No battles were fought.

In June, when the Budget was submitted for the New Fiscal Year, we discovered that it contained a major capital outlay for construction of a new Warehouse near the Crematorium. If the corporation was doing well enough to finance such frivolity, why had we never received our notepads?

Morale was low enough as it was, and I decided that our efforts needed to be rewarded—even if we had to do the rewarding ourselves. With funds liberated from the Safe, we bankrolled a Friday afternoon party. I brought the drinks, Jerry the chips, Meryl supplied the music, and Feena supplied the frogs. There was nude table dancing.

It was a hot time in the old office that day, but the party was cut short by Mike from Maintenance. He'd come up to install some coax cable, and when he saw that we were enjoying ourselves on company time, his face clouded over. He stood silently and whipped Kristen hard with a length of cable. She screamed as the connector end bit into the flabby flesh of her buttocks. A drop of blood flew into my highball, and Kristen fell from the desk, clutching her backside.

I turned on Mike. "What the hell do you think you're doing?"

He pointed a dark stubby finger in my face. I could see the grease under his fingernails. "This party was not approved."

"I approved it," I told him. "I'm head of the department."

He grinned at me, but the corners of his mouth did not turn up and it looked more like a grimace. His greasy finger was still pointing at me. "We're taking you out," he said. "This is War."

It started immediately.

I'd expected some lag time, a reasonable number of days in which attempts could be made to talk, communicate, negotiate. I'd assumed, at the very least, that Maintenance would need time to draw up plans, map out a strategy, but it was clear that they must have been contemplating this for a while.

It began the morning after the party.

The bathroom was booby-trapped and Carl got caught.

I'd always allowed him a little leeway and so didn't immediately go looking for him when he did not return from lunch on time. But when an hour passed and Carl still had not shown, I became suspicious. Taking David with me, I ventured into the Hall. My eyes were drawn instantly to the crude white cross painted on the door of the men's room.

And to Carl's head posted on the cleaning cart outside.

David gasped, but I grabbed his arm and drew him forward. Carl's head was impaled on the handle of a mop. His eyes had been stapled shut, his mouth Scotch-taped, and Kleenex had been shoved into his ears.

Maintenance.

"Come on!" I quickly pulled David back into the safety of our department. I was worried but tried not to let it show. I had to maintain the illusion of confidence in order to keep up morale, but I realized that Maintenance was the only department allowed unlimited access to every room in the building, the only department whose workers remained in the building at night. Their potential power was incredible.

"What'll we do?" Meryl asked. She was scared, practically shaking.

"Stockpile the weapons," I told her. I turned to David and Feena. "Post a watch in the doorways. No one gets in or out without my okay. I don't care who they are."

They nodded and hurried to carry out my orders, grateful that there was someone to take charge, someone to tell them what to do. I wished at that moment that there was a person to whom I could turn, a person higher up on the hierarchical ladder to whom I could pass the buck, but I had gotten us into this and it was up to me to get us out.

I felt woefully unprepared for such a task. I had been able to plan and pull off the Accounting coup because I'd been dealing with the tunnel-visioned minds of task-oriented number crunchers, but going up against the freewheeling, physical men from Maintenance was quite another matter. These minds were not constrained by the limits of their job descriptions. These were people who were accustomed to working on their own, who were used to dealing with problems individually.

I shut the door, locked it, waited for five o'clock.

In the Whorehouse, the women were getting restless. The number of work orders had dropped, and the lack of trade left them with no department accounts to which they could charge expenses. The women blamed the demise of Accounting for their falling fortunes, and tremors against my department and myself moved from the ground up, echoing through the chain of command. The Break Room was declared off-limits to us, its entrance guarded by Maintenance men. We could no longer leave our desks to go to the bathroom.

This was Mike's doing.

We found John in the Burster.

Al in the Forms Decollator.

I had not thought either machine capable of performing its function on anything other than paper, but at the foot of the Burster, in a pile that would have been neat were it not for the formlessness of tissue and the liquidity of blood, was the body of John, trimmed neatly and cut into legal-sized squares.

Al's body had been divided into three layers and the parts lay separated in the metal rows designed for tripartite forms.

The rollers were covered with red blood and flecks of white tissue.

It was only the fourth day of hostilities and already we had lost two of our best men. I had not expected things to become so serious so quickly, and I knew that this miscalculation might cost us our lives.

I spent that morning's Break with Jerry and David. We were Breaking in teams now, going to the Break Room heavily armed. We sat down at a table, facing the door. All three of us knew that we had to hit back hard and fast, and at the very least make a statement with our actions, but we were uncertain as to how we should proceed. Jerry wanted to ambush a custodian, take him out. He thought we should amputate the arms, legs, and penis and send them back to Mike through the Vacuum Tubes or the Inter-Office Mail. David said we should sabotage the Coffee Machine, poison the backup Coffee Maker, and send a memo to all departments except Maintenance to inform them of what was happening.

I thought we should strike at the head, assassinate Mike, and both of them quickly agreed that that would be best.

We returned to our department, alert for snipers in the hall, but something did not seem quite right. I looked past Computer Operations and saw what looked like refracted light from around the corner of the hallway.

From the battle site.

I said nothing, simply pushed Jerry and David into our department and ordered them to close and lock the door. When the door was shut, I continued down the hall, creeping slowly across the carpet. I heard the sound of clicking calculators, the rustle of paper. I peeked my head around the corner.

Maintenance had been promoted to Accounting.

I stared at the suddenly full department in disbelief. We had brought down the entire Accounting department and had received nothing for our efforts. Maintenance booby-trapped the bathroom and two machines and had been rewarded with a promotion!

Mike, wearing the Three-Piece Suit of the Finance Director, grinned at me from his oversized desk. "See you in Chapter Eleven," he said.

I blinked.

"The company's going down."

I tried to see the CEO, to tell him that things had gotten out of hand. The War was no longer confined merely to intramural battles; a single department was now aggressively pursuing and systematically working toward the total destruction of the Corporation.

But the secretary refused to hear my petition. She drew from her desk a flowchart of the Corporation hierarchy, circled in red the position of my department, and calmly handed the paper to me.

"The CEO sees nobody," she said.

On the Dow, the news was mixed. There were rumors that changes were afoot, but the nature of those changes was clearly not known to Outsiders, and we ended the week in plus territory.

Jerry took out a custodian masquerading as an accountant, cutting off arms, legs, and genitals, tagging them as Fixed Assets and returning them to the Finance Director's office. I probably should have disciplined him for acting without my okay, but, in truth, I was grateful, and I promoted him to division supervisor.

We hung the custodian/accountant scalp above the top of our door, and though it was gone in the morning, our point had been made. Mike knew we were a department to fear.

That afternoon, miniature mines were placed under the

carpet in the hallway and electrified gates were installed outside the Accounting offices.

Figures were juggled.

Budgets were slashed.

The Corporation's profit margin plummeted, at least on paper, and though in memo after memo I tried to tell the CEO that those numbers were manufactured by Mike and not to be trusted, he chose to ignore me and instituted a waist-tightening program. Medical benefits were cut, dental benefits eliminated, and several open positions were left unfilled.

A new and virtually incomprehensible complaint process was instituted by Accounting, and immediately afterward paychecks—all paychecks, Corporation-wide—were incorrectly calculated. My paycheck was halved, and under the new guidelines I could not contest the figures for a minimum of six months.

At the bottom of my check, instead of the rubber-stamped signature of the old Finance Director, was a caricatured rainbow-colored stamp of Mike's grinning, ugly face.

I was furious, and I slammed my check down on my desk, ordered David to take a hostage. He nodded, said, "Yes sir," but wouldn't look at me, wouldn't meet my gaze.

I knew he was hiding something. "David," I said.

"Meryl's defected," he told me. "She's transferred over as a clerk."

That was it. That was the last straw. I had taken an awful lot of crap from Mike and his Maintenance accountants, but this time he had gone too far. Ceasefire or no ceasefire, it was time to take up arms.

"War!" I cried.

David stared, blinked, then the corners of his mouth

turned upward. He whooped joyfully, grabbed a sharpened pencil. "War!"

The cry was taken up by Feena, Jerry, Kristen, the others. I felt good all of a sudden, the anger and depression of a few moments before having fled in the face of this energizing purpose. *This* was what we were good at. *This* was what we were trained for. Full-fledged fighting. Not the guerilla skirmishing in which we'd been forced to participate.

I lifted my ruler. "War!"

"Huh!" they responded. "Good God, ya'll!"

We were ready.

We posted the declaration of renewed hostilities on the Employee Bulletin Board.

Mike responded in kind with a statement signed in blood.

We met in the Warehouse.

The Maintenance men had heavier weapons—hammers and screwdrivers, wire cutters and soldering guns—but we had the brains, and at close quarters our weapons—scissors and staplers, X-Acto knives and paper clips—were just as deadly.

It was a short war, and more one-sided than I would have expected. Mike planned an ambush, but the positioning of his men was obvious and uninspired, and it was easy for my people to sneak behind them and stab them with the scissors. We entered through the back, through the Loading Dock, and David took out two custodians, Jerry bringing down their heaviest hitter, the Electrician, slitting his throat with an X-Acto knife.

And then it was me and Mike.

We faced each other on the floor of the Warehouse. Representatives from other departments were in attendance, peeking from behind boxes, sitting on shelves. Mike had a hammer in one hand, pliers in the other, and he kept saying, "Fucker, fucker," growling it. He seemed stupid to me, then. Stupid and almost pathetic, and I wondered how I could have ever feared someone with such an obviously limited vocabulary.

I grinned at him. *"You're* going down," I said.

I shot him in the eye with a paper clip, quickly reloaded my rubber band, and shot his other eye. Both shots were true, and though he didn't drop the hammer or pliers, he was screaming, shielding his damaged eyes with his right arm. I had a metal ruler in my belt, and I pulled it out, moving in close. He heard me coming, swung at me, but he was blinded and running on panic, and I hit his cheek with the ruler, followed it with a flat-out smack to the nose. He dropped the pliers, swung futilely with the hammer, but he'd lost and he knew he'd lost, and to the cheers of my department I leaped upon him, tearing open his neck with my staple remover, the metal fangs ripping out chunks of his flesh as he squealed in pain and rage and fear.

And then it was over.

There was silence for a moment, then pandemonium. From behind one of the boxes rushed the CEO's secretary, and she tried to hug me, but I pushed her away. "Remember your place in the hierarchy," I told her.

We were carried back to our offices on the shoulders of Computer Operations and the dwarves.

To celebrate our victory, we performed the Ritual. I ordered a virgin from the steno pool, a high school grad who had been destined for the Whorehouse because of her poor shorthand skills, and we tied her down with rubber bands and laid her out on top of my desk. Feena rubber-cemented shut her eyes; I Wited-Out her nipples. We took turns with her.

I shrunk Mike's head and kept it on my desk as a paperweight, and when the stock market reached record levels, led by our corporation, I sent his head to the CEO through the Inter-Office Mail.

This time, we got our notepads.

Blood

Before I moved in with my wife, I lived on macaroni and cheese. I spent so much time standing in front of my stove, stirring pots of boiling macaroni, that I used to stare down into the swirling, roiling water and imagine that I could see shapes in the foam the way some people see shapes in clouds.

I decided to write a story about it.

—⬿—

Alan stood and stretched as the whistle blew and halftime began. His gaze moved downward from the television to the clock on the VCR. Twelve forty. No wonder his stomach was growling.

He walked into the kitchen, took a medium-sized glass pot from the drying rack next to the sink, filled it with water, sprinkled in some salt, placed the pot on the stove's front burner, and turned the gas to "High." Opening the cupboard, he drew out a package of macaroni and cheese. He pulled off the top of the box, took out the small foil packet of dried cheese, and dumped the macaroni into the water.

It would be several minutes before the water started to boil, he knew. Not wanting to stand there in the kitchen, he returned to the living room and switched channels on the TV until he found another game. He watched it until a commercial came on, then went to the bathroom to wash his hands. When he returned to the kitchen to check on his lunch, small bubbles were starting to rise through the clear water from the hill of macaroni at the bottom of the pot. He quickly took a spoon from the drawer and began stirring, scraping. He didn't want the macaroni to stick to the bottom. It was hell to wash, almost impossible to get off.

He shifted his weight from one foot to the other and looked down idly as he stirred. The water bubbled, a thin film of white foam seeping upward from the macaroni and whirlpooling into the center of the pot. The foam thickened, thinned, swirling about as he stirred, maintaining a roughly circular shape even as the metal spoon cut through its heart, sliced its edges.

He stared at the water, fascinated both by the amazing mechanics of boiling and by the shifting patterns of the bubbles and the film on top. The effect was kaleidoscopic, though the only colors he could see were the translucent brown of the Vision Ware, the pale wheat of the macaroni, and the pure white of the foam. He continued to look down as he stirred, imagining he could make out vague shapes in the boiling water, impressionistic outlines of elephants and birds and—

a face.

He peered closely at the contents of the pot, hardly believing what he was seeing. He blinked. The features of the face, formed by clear spaces in the white foam circle, were somehow familiar to him though he could not immediately place their antecedent. As the water bubbled, individual pieces of macaroni rising to the top, the face seemed to move, eyes peering around, mouth opening and closing as if to speak.

He stopped stirring for a second.

The face smiled up at him.

Alan stepped backward as a chill passed through him. He was suddenly aware of the dim emptiness of the kitchen, of the fact that he was alone in the apartment. Unreasonably frightened, he shut off the gas. The bubbles died down as the heat disappeared, the foam face dissipating, swirling outward in fading tendrils to reveal the cooked macaroni below.

He was cold, but he was sweating, and he used a paper towel to wipe the sides of his face. His lips were dry, and he licked them, but his mouth had no saliva to spare. From the living room, he heard the roar of a football crowd. The noise sounded muffled, far off.

He thought for some reason of his mother, of his sister. Strange. He had not thought of them in years.

He looked down at the spoon shaking in his trembling hand. This was stupid. There was nothing to be afraid of. What the hell was wrong with him? Halftime would be over soon and the game would start again. He had to hurry up and finish lunch.

He turned the gas on again and tried not to pay attention as the still hot water began almost instantly to bubble. But he could not help noticing with a shiver of fear that the foam was again beginning to swirl, again beginning to take on the features of a face: eyes, nose, mouth.

He stirred. Quickly, harshly, rapidly. But the face remained intact.

He pulled out the spoon, afraid now to touch the water even through this metal conduit, and began to back away.

He heard a noise, a low whispery sound somewhere between the quiet constant hissing of the gas flame and the percolating bubble of the boiling water. He had the distinct impression that the sound was a voice, a voice repeating a single word, but he could not make out what that word was. Summoning all of his courage, he looked into the pot.

The foam mouth closed, then opened, then closed, and seeing this movement timed with the whispering sound, he knew what word was being spoken.

"Blood," the face said. "Blood."

Blood.

What could that mean? He had spent all afternoon thinking about it. More than anything else, the word had sounded to him like a command, an order.

A request for sustenance.

But that was crazy. A random pattern formed by boiling macaroni was demanding blood? If he had read this in a story, he would have dismissed it as laughably implausible. If he had heard someone else mention it, he would have considered that person a candidate for the rubber room. But he was sitting here thinking about it, had been doing so for hours, and the scary part was that he was actually trying to logically, rationally, analyze the situation.

But that wasn't really the scary part, was it?

No, the scary part was not that he believed this was happening and that therefore his mind was going. The scary part was that his mind was *not* going, that this thing really existed. This creature, this being, this demon, this ghost, this whatever-it-was could actually be conjured up by making macaroni and cheese.

But could it be conjured up at any time, or was it only on Saturdays and only at lunchtime?

He didn't know.

That night the apartment seemed much darker than it did ordinarily. There were shadows on the sides of the couch and at the foot of the bed, echoes of darkness in the corners of the rooms.

He went to sleep early.

He left the lights on.

He dreamed of a man in a doorway with an ax.

He had the rest of the week to think about what had occurred. Afraid, he stayed away from the apartment as much as possible, leaving early for work, coming home late. He cooked no meals for himself but ate out for breakfast, lunch, and dinner: Jack in the Box, Der Weinerschnitzel, Taco Bell, McDonald's.

He'd thought the fear would abate with the coming of a new day, that as the hours passed the horror of the occurrence would dim. He thought he'd be able to find a rational explanation for what he had seen, what he had heard.

But it had not happened.

He recalled with perfect and profound clarity the contours of the bubbly foam face, the way the boiling water had made it smile. He heard in his head the whispered word.

Blood.

There was nothing he could do, he realized. He could move, get a new apartment, but what would that accomplish? The impetus for this horror might lie not in his home but in himself. He could never cook again, or at least never make macaroni and cheese, but he would always know that the face was there, waiting, unconjured, below the surface reality of his daily life.

Blood.

He had to confront it.

He had to try it again.

* * *

Everything was the same. He put in the water, put in the salt, put in the macaroni, turned on the flame, and out of the pot's swirling contents emerged a face. He was not as frightened this time, perhaps because he had been prepared for the sight, but he was nonetheless unnerved. He stared down at the white foam.

"Blood," the mouth whispered. "Blood."

Blood.

There was something hypnotic about the word, something almost . . . seductive. It was still terrifying, still horrifying, but there was also something attractive about it. As he looked at the face, saw its vague familiarity, as he listened to the whisper, heard its demand, Alan could almost understand what was wanted with the blood. In a perverse way that was not at all understood by his conscious mind, he felt that it made a kind of sense.

Outside, a dog barked. Alan looked up. The barking came closer, and through the open window he heard the sound of paws on the dirty sidewalk of his small patio. The animal continued to bark loudly, annoyingly.

Alan looked down into the swirling pot of macaroni.

"Blood," the face whispered.

Nodding to himself, Alan opened the cupboard under the sink and drew out the small hand-held hatchet he used to cut rope. He moved out of the kitchen and walked across the living room to the front door.

Apparently no one had ever done the dog harm or had in any way subverted the animal's natural trust. With virtually no coaxing at all, the innocent pet happily followed him into the apartment on the soothing-voiced promise of lunch. Alan searched through the kitchen for something resembling dog food, found a can of beef stew, and walked into the bathroom, dumping the contents of the can into the tub. The an-

imal hopped over the low porcelain side and began gratefully chowing down.

He cut off the dog's head with one chop of the hatchet.

Blood spurted wildly from the open neck and severed ar-
teries, but he caught some of it in the water glass he used for
brushing his teeth.

He hurried back to the kitchen and poured the blood
slowly into the simmering pot. The blood swirled and
whirlpooled into the center before mixing with the water
and spreading outward. The foam turned red, the mouth
smiled.

Alan stirred the macaroni. The mouth pursed, opened,
closed, and beneath the bubble and hiss he heard a new
whisper.

"Human," the face said, "blood."

Alan's heart began to pound, but he was not sure this
time if it was entirely from fear.

His palms were sweaty and, as he wiped them on his
pants, Alan told himself that he was being crazy. A dog was
one thing. But he was about to cross over the line and com-
mit a serious criminal act. A violent act. An act for which he
could spend the rest of his life in jail. It was not too late to
back out now. All he had to do was go home, throw away the
pot, never make macaroni and cheese again.

He got out of the car, smiling at the child.

He used the hatchet to cut off the boy's arm.

The kid had not even started screaming by the time he
had grabbed the arm, hopped in the car and taken off, the
child's shocked brain not yet able to process the insane information it was being fed by its senses. Alan dropped the
arm into the bucket even as he put the car into gear.

It was a clean getaway.

Back home, curtains closed, he poured water into the pot, added salt, dumped in the package of macaroni. The face appeared as the water started to boil. It looked stronger this time, more clearly defined.

The mouth smiled at him as he poured in the child's blood.

As the water turned pink, then red, as he stared at the happy, bubblefoam face, he felt the mood shift in the kitchen, a palpable, almost physical, dislocation of air and space. He shivered violently. A change came over him, a subtle shifting of his thoughts and emotions, and he seemed to realize for the first time exactly what it was that he had done. The mad savagery of his actions, the complete insanity of his deeds hit him hard and instantly, and he was filled with a sudden horror and revulsion so profound that he staggered backward and began retching into the sink. For a few blissful seconds, he heard only the harsh sounds of his own vomiting, but when he stood, wiping his mouth, he realized that the kitchen was alive with the sounds of whispering. He heard the bubbling of the water, and above that the voice of the macaroni, calling to him, whispering promises, whispering threats.

Against his will, he found himself once again leaning over the stove, looking into the pot.

"Make me," the face whispered. "Eat me."

Moving slowly, as if underwater, as if in a dream, he drained the macaroni, added butter, added milk, poured in the package of powdered cheese. The finished product was neither cheese orange nor blood red but a sickening muddy brown that looked decidedly unappetizing. Nevertheless, he dumped the contents of the pot into a bowl, brought it over to the table, and ate.

The aftertaste was salty and slightly sour, and it left his

mouth dry. But when he drank a glass of milk, the taste disappeared completely.

After lunch, he chopped the boy's arm into tiny pieces, wrapped the pieces in plastic wrap, put them in an empty milk carton, buried the milk carton deep within the garbage sack, and took the sack out to the trash can in the garage.

That night, he dreamed that he was a small child. He was sleeping in his current bed, in his current bedroom, in his current apartment, but the furniture was different and the decorations on the wall consisted of posters of decades-old rock stars. From another room he heard screams, terrible horrible heart-stopping screeches which were suddenly cut off in midsound. Part of his brain told him to break the window and jump out, run, escape, but another told him to feign sleep. Instead he did neither, and he was staring wide-eyed at the door when it burst open.

The man in the doorway held an ax.

He woke up sweating, clutching his pillow as if it were a life preserver and he a drowning man who could not swim. He sat up, got out of bed, turned on the light. In the garage, he knew, the pieces of the boy's arm were lying individually wrapped inside a milk carton in the trash.

On the stove in the kitchen was the pot. And in the cupboard six boxes of macaroni and cheese.

He did not sleep the rest of the night but remained in a chair, wide awake, staring at the wall.

The next day was Monday, and Alan called in sick, explaining to his supervisor that he had a touch of the stomach flu. In truth, he felt fine, and not even the recollection of what he had ingested had any emotional effect on his appetite.

He had two eggs, two pieces of toast, and two glasses of orange juice for breakfast.

All morning, he sat on the couch, not reading, not watching TV, just waiting for lunchtime. He thought back on last night. The man in his dream, the man with the ax, had seemed vaguely familiar to him at the time, and seemed even more so now, but he could not seem to place the figure. It would have helped had he been able to see a face rather than just a backlit silhouette, but his memory had nothing to go on other than a bodily outline that somehow reminded him of a person from his past.

At eleven o'clock, he went into the kitchen to make lunch.

The face when it appeared was less ephemeral, more concrete. There were wrinkles in the water, details in the foam, and the accompanying change that came over the kitchen was stronger, more obvious. A wall of air moved through him, past him. The light from the window dimmed, dying somehow before it reached even partway into the room. He looked down. This face was scarier, more brutal. Evil. It smiled, and he saw inside the mouth white bubble teeth. "Blood," it said.

Alan took a deep breath. "No."

"Blood."

Alan shook his head, licked his lips. "That's all. No more."

"Blood!" the face demanded.

Alan turned down the flame, watched the elements of the face disperse. Details dissolving into simplistic crudity.

"Blood!" the voice ordered, screaming.

And then it was gone.

*   *   *

The shabbily dressed man on the street corner was facing oncoming traffic, holding up a sign: I Will Work for Food. Alan drove by, shaking his head. He'd never seen such people before the Reagan years, but now they were impossible not to notice. This was the fourth man this month he'd seen holding up a similar sign. He felt sorry for such people, but he wasn't about to let one of them work at his home and he could not imagine anyone else doing so either. For all he knew, such a man would use the opportunity to scope out his house, check out his television, stereo, and other valuables, casing the joint for a future robbery. There was no way for a person such as himself to check out the credentials or references of a homeless man. No one knew who these men were—

No one knew who these men were.

Blood.

He felt the urge again, and he pulled into the parking lot of a supermarket and turned around. He did not want to, but he was compelled. It was as if another being had taken control of the rational portion of his mind and was using the thought processes there to carry out its will while the real Alan was shunted aside and left screaming. He made another U-turn in the middle of the street and slowed down next to the homeless man, smiling.

"I need some help painting my bedroom," he said smoothly. "I'll pay five bucks an hour. You interested?"

"I sure am," the man said.

"Good. Hop in the car."

Alan killed the man in the living room while he was taking off his coat. It was messy and ugly, and the blood spurted all over the tan carpet and the off-white couch, but it had to be done this way. The homeless man was bigger than he was and probably stronger, and he needed both the element of surprise and the partial incapacitation provided by the undressing in order to successfully carry out the murder.

The larger man stumbled, trying to get all the way out of his jacket and free his arms to defend himself, while Alan hacked at his neck with the hatchet.

It was a full ten minutes before he was lying still on the floor, and Alan filled up the measuring cup with his blood.

The macaroni and cheese tasted good.

He had a hard time going to sleep that night. Though his body was dog tired, his mind rebelled and refused to quiet down, keeping him awake until well after midnight.

When he finally did slip into sleep, he dreamed.

Again, it was the man in the doorway. But this time he could see the man's face, and he knew why the outline of the thick body was familiar, why the contours of the form were recognizable.

It was his father.

As always, his father walked through the door, ax in hand, blood still dripping from the dark blade. This time, however, Alan was not a child and his father not a middle-aged man. The surroundings were the same—the old posters on the wall, the aging toys—but he was his real age, and his father, walking slowly toward him, had the dried parchment skin of a corpse.

With a sibilant rustling of skin on sweater, a sharp crackle of bone, his father sat next to him on the bed. "You've done a good job, boy," he said. His voice was the same as Alan remembered, yet different—at once whisperingly alien and comfortably familiar.

Had this ever happened?

He remembered flashes of his past, pieces of an unknown puzzle which he had never before stopped to organize or analyze. Had he and his father really stumbled across the bodies as they had both told the police? Or had it happened another way?

Had it happened this way?

The pressure of his father's body seated on the side of the bed, the sight of the dark bloody ax in his lap seemed familiar, and he knew the words that his father was speaking to him. He had heard them before.

The two of them said the final words in tandem: "Let's get something to eat."

Then he was awake and sweating. His father had killed both his mother and his sister. And he had known.

He had helped.

He stumbled out of bed. The apartment was dark, but he did not bother to turn on the lights. He felt his way along the wall, past furniture, to the kitchen, where, by the light of the gas flame, he poured water into the pot and started it boiling.

He poured in the salt and macaroni.

"Yes," the face whispered. Its features looked almost three-dimensional in the darkness, lit from below by the flame. "Yes."

Alan stared dumbly.

"Blood," the face said.

Alan thought for a moment, then pulled open the utensil drawer, taking out his sharpest knife.

The face smiled. "Blood."

He did not think he could go through with it, but it turned out to be easier than expected. He drew the blade across his wrist, pressing hard, pushing deep, and the blood flowed into the pot. It looked black in the night darkness.

He realized as he grew weaker, as the pain increased, as the foam face of his father grew red and smiled, that there would be no one left to eat the macaroni and cheese.

If he had not been so weak, he would have smiled himself.

And I Am Here, Fighting with Ghosts

I've always liked this story. It was rejected by nearly every magazine on the planet before finally finding a home, so maybe my perception is skewed and it's really not very good. But it has resonance for me because it's essentially four of my dreams that I altered a bit and strung together with a loose narrative thread.

I stole the title from a line in Ibsen's play *A Doll's House*.

—⁂—

I cannot always tell anymore. It used to be easy, there was a sharp distinction between the two. But the difference has become progressively less pronounced, the distinctions blurred, since Kathy left.

I have no visitors now. They, too, left with Kathy. And if I go into town I am avoided, whispered about, the butt of nervous jokes. Now children tell horror stories about me to frighten their little brothers.

And their brothers are frightened.

And so are they.

And so are their parents.

So I leave the grounds as little as possible. When I go to the store, I load up on groceries and then stay inside my little domain until my supplies run out and I must venture forth again.

When I do make the trek into town, I notice there are names carved into the gates outside of the driveway. Obscene names. I never see the culprits, of course. And if they ever see me coming down the wooded drive toward them, I'm sure they run like mad.

They do not know that their town is on the outskirts. They do not know that my house is on the border. They do not know that I am the only thing protecting them.

The last time I went for supplies, the town was no longer the town. It was the fair. But I didn't question it; it seemed perfectly natural. And I was not disoriented. I had intended to go into Mike's Market when I came to town, but after I reached the midway I knew that the funhouse was where I was supposed to go.

I heard the funhouse before I saw it. The laughter. Outrageous, raw, uninhibited laughter. Continuous laughter. It came from a mechanical woman—a fifteen-foot Appalachian woman with dirty limbs and dirtier clothes and a horribly grinning gap-toothed mouth. She was hinged at the waist, and she robotically doubled over, up and down, up and down, with Appalachian guffaws.

The woman scared me. But I bought my ticket and rushed past her into the funhouse, into a black hole of a maze that twined and intertwined and wound around, ending in a grimy colorless room with no furniture and with windows which opened on painted scenes. The room was built on a forty-five-degree slant and the door entered in the bottom right corner. I had to fight the incline to reach the exit at the top left.

Through the fake windows I could still hear the Appalachian woman laughing.

The door at the top opened onto an alley. A real alley. And when I stepped through the door, the funhouse was gone. The door was now a wall.

The alley smelled like French food. It was narrow and dark and cobblestoned, and it retained the lingering odors of soufflés and fondue. There was a dwarf hiding in one of the doorways, staring at me. There was something else in another doorway that I was afraid to acknowledge.

The tap on my shoulder made me jump.

It was the Appalachian woman, only she was no longer mechanical but human and my height and not laughing. With one hand, she pointed down a dark stairway that opened into the ground on the side of the alley. The other hand held a rolling pin. "Turn off the light at the end of the hall," she commanded.

I stepped down the stairs and it was cold. But that was not the only reason I shivered.

I turned around, intending to climb back up.

The woman was still pointing. I could see her silhouette against the overcast sky above the alley, framed by the stairwell entrance. "Turn off the light at the end of the hall," she repeated.

I started down.

The hallway was long, extraordinarily long. And dark. Doors opened off to each side, but somehow I knew that they did not lead anywhere. At the end of the hall were two rooms, one of which was lighted, one of which was dark.

I moved forward slowly. On the side, through the other doors, I could hear whispers and shuffling. Out of the corner of my eye I saw furtive shadows, dashing, darting, following. I stared straight ahead.

I grew frightened as I drew closer to the end of the hall, my fear focusing on the lighted room. It wasn't logical, but it was real. I was supposed to turn off the light, but I was afraid of the room with the light in it. The dark room was scary only because it was dark. The lighted room was scary because something was in it.

I reached the end of the hallway and ducked quickly into the darker doorway. I was breathing rapidly, my heart pounding so loud I could hear it. Trembling, I reached around the corner into the other room and felt for the light switch. I flipped it off and—

I was in an Arizona farmhouse with a man and two children I had never seen before but who I knew to be my uncle and my cousins.

I was eight years old. I lived with them.

My uncle looked out the window of the empty farmhouse at the dry dusty expanse of desert extending unbroken in all directions. "Get us something to eat," he told Jenny, my female cousin.

She went into the furnitureless kitchen and looked through each cupboard. Nothing but dust.

"Whoever lived here didn't leave no food," she said. She waited for my uncle's reply, and when he didn't say anything she shrugged and picked up a broom leaning against the wall. She began to sweep some of the dirt out of the house.

We slept that night on the floor.

The next day, my uncle was up before dawn, riding the tractor, attempting to till that dry useless soil, attempting to grow us some food. Jenny was hanging curtains, determined to make the house livable.

So Lane and I went out to play. We walked around, explored, talked, threw dirt clods, decided to build a clubhouse. He ran off and got us two trowels, and we started digging. Both of us wanted a basement in our clubhouse.

After nearly an hour of digging in the hot Arizona sun, our tools struck wood. We dug faster and deeper and harder and found that the wood was part of a trap door. I turned to my cousin. "I wonder what's under it."

"Only one way to find out," he said. "Open it."

So I slid my hands up under the board and pulled up. A cold chill ran through me as I saw the stairway descending into the ground. The stairway that led to a hall. I turned around and my cousin was no longer my cousin but a grinning, gap-toothed Appalachian woman. "Turn off the light at the end of the hall," she said.

I stood in front of Mike's Market, disoriented. I did not know where I was. What happened to the hallway? I wondered. Where was the woman? It took me a minute or so to adjust. Then I realized that *this* was reality; the fair, the alley, the hallway, and the farm were not.

And I began to be afraid. For before this, the occurrences always seemed like dreams. Even when they started happening in the daytime, they were clearly illusions juxtaposed onto a real world. But now the illusions were becoming ordinary, the surrealism real.

I was losing the battle.

If only Kathy were here. Two of us could hold the tide; two of us could dam the flood. We might even be able to have some semblance of a normal life.

Now, however, I was alone.

And they were getting stronger.

*   *   *

Last night it was the spider.

It had been a long day with no occurrences. At least, no *malicious* occurrences. I'd spent the day clearing a path through the woods to the pond. The old path had become overgrown with weeds through disuse and inattentiveness. Although the day was cool and even somewhat overcast, the work was hard. And by the time I was ready to quit, I was hot, tired, and sweating like a pig.

I deserved the bath.

I decided to use the third floor bathroom, the small one with just a toilet, tub, and sink in a space the size of a closet. The water felt soothing and good, so I leaned back and relaxed, getting comfortable. I fell asleep in the tub.

When I awoke, something was wrong. The bathwater was still warm by this time but not warm enough to stop goose bumps from popping up on my arm. Scared for no particular reason, I hurried to unstop the drain, then arose from the tub and grabbed a towel to dry myself.

It was then that I noticed the spider. Black and big as an apple, with bright blue eyes and a row of blue button teeth, it was hanging from its thread in the middle of the bathroom. I don't know how I could have missed it.

It started moving toward me; slowly, evenly, still suspended from its thread, as though the entire spiderline were on some sort of track in the ceiling. I flattened against the wall, nude and trembling. The spider kept coming.

Desperate, I jumped over the rim of the tub, hitting my knee on the edge, and rolled along the floor underneath the hanging creature. I climbed onto my throbbing knee and tried to unlatch the bathroom door, which I had stupidly locked.

But I wasn't quick enough. The spider and its thread were coming back toward me now, faster, gaining speed.

Once again, I rolled under it, and I jumped back in the tub just as the last little trickle of water swirled down the drain. I was getting claustrophobic. The bathroom seemed smaller by the second. The toilet's in the wrong place, I thought disjointedly. The sink took up too much room. I found that there was no place for me to move except along the narrow path the spider was guarding.

Maybe I could make it to the door this time. The pain in my knee almost unbearable now, I climbed on the rim of the tub, hit the side wall, and slid by the hanging horror, its large hairy body half an inch from my own.

I reached the door and turned around at the same time. No chance. There was no time. The spider was heading straight for my face, moving fast and grinning.

And then it was gone.

It had been another one of their tricks. I slumped to the floor, sweat pouring from every inch of my body though the temperature was barely above freezing. I should have known from the beginning, the way Kathy and I had always known, but I had not figured it out until the whole thing was over. I'd accepted it as reality all the way through.

I was losing the battle.

This morning I awoke early. I'd decided to spend the day just cooking. It would relax me. It would allow me to think of a way to combat this encroaching madness. I rolled out of bed and put on my robe. My eyes were still half closed, and I rubbed them so I could see clearly.

It was then that I noticed the room.

It was not my bedroom at all but a bowling alley. I was seated next to an old couple who were looking at me quizzically, as though they expected me to say something. "I'm sorry," I found myself mumbling. "I didn't catch that."

The old man stood up from his plywood folding chair and grabbed a large black bowling ball. "I said, 'Do you want to go first?'" he repeated. He stepped up to a lane. "Never mind. I'll go." He rolled the ball down the lane and it grew larger as it moved away from him. My eyes followed the ball to the pins, but there were no pins. Instead, a group of people stood in a pin formation, unmoving, as the ball rolled ever larger toward them.

One of them was Kathy.

"Oh my God!" I cried. Luckily, the old man was not a very good bowler and the ball slid into the gutter, missing Kathy completely.

"Not good, Hubert," said the old lady two seats down from me.

I could not believe this. I jumped out of my chair and ran down the lane. I grabbed Kathy in my arms. "Watch this!" Hubert announced. He rolled the ball again, and I stood there, a human bowling pin unable to move, holding my Kathy as the ball rolled ever closer. I felt the wind as the now monstrous object passed us.

Hubert was talking to his wife and getting ready to bowl again, so I threw Kathy over my shoulder (she was light) and ran up the lane, past the old couple and through the door. Outside the bowling alley, my house was a maze of cheaply paneled rooms with red carpeting and bare bulbs hanging from low ceilings. Each room had several doors and each door led into another room which, in turn, led to other rooms.

I just ran. With Kathy over my shoulder, I ran. Behind us, I could hear the sound of bowling pins being knocked over. Loudly.

Only they weren't really bowling pins.

The rooms we ran through now had furniture. In one was a low couch, in another a bed. More beds became noticeable, and in one room we ran through, a man and woman were sitting together on a waterbed.

It became apparent that we were running through the back regions of some monstrous bordello.

Then the cheaply paneled rooms ended and we were in my room, in my house. Kathy and I.

I had her back.

She was still in some type of trance, but her eyes were beginning to move, and I thought I saw her left pinky wiggle. Quickly, I carried her into the bathroom and placed her gently in the tub. I turned on the cold water and splashed it over her face in order to jar her awake. But the water was like acid to her, and she stared to melt into the liquid.

And she was gone.

From somewhere, I heard laughter.

That was the last straw. I could take anything but this . . . desecration of my life with Kathy. And suddenly I didn't care what happened. I just wanted to save myself, to preserve my sanity, to get the hell out of there.

Without even stopping to put on real clothes, still in my robe, I ran out of the house and into the garage, where the car waited. I grabbed the key from its hook on the pressboard wall, got in the car, and slammed the door. The car was a little difficult to start since it had not been used after Kathy left, but eventually it kicked in.

And I was off.

I drove straight through the town without even looking. The people must have thought I was mad. It had been so long since I'd driven that I was not very familiar with the

area, I did not know where many of the roads led. But that
didn't make any difference. I just drove. And drove fast.

The car stopped around noon in a strange city. With
smoke pouring from under the hood, I pulled into a gas station. A mechanic dressed in greasy jeans and an oil-stained
T-shirt came out of the garage and popped open the hood. I
got out of the car to join him.

"Your radiator's leaking," he said simply.

"Can you fix it?" I asked.

He closed the hood and looked at me, pulling a rag out of
his pocket to wipe his hands. "I can either patch it for you or
replace the radiator. I have a lot of parts in the back."

"Which one's cheaper?" I asked.

"Patching. It won't last forever, but it should be good for
a couple of months at least."

"Fine," I said. "Patch it."

He said it would take a couple of hours. Since I had an
afternoon to kill, I started walking down the main street of
the town. It wasn't very big. I browsed through the one
tourist shop, looked through a bookstore, sat down and had
a cup of coffee in the grimy coffee shop, and still had more
than an hour until the mechanic said he'd be done.

I decided to check out the town's department store.

I was looking through the greeting cards, wondering
whether I should warn Kathy that I was coming or just drop
by uninvited, when a gunshot rang out. I turned toward the
entrance and saw what looked like a gang of terrorists moving, commando-like, into the department store and spreading out. I hit the ground.

A burst of machine gun fire destroyed the lights and the
store was plunged into semidarkness. One woman screamed
and was shot. "Stay where you are, don't move, and you'll
be all right!" the leader of the terrorists announced. He

strode up to the checkout counter nearest me, and I could see that he had a ski mask pulled over his head. Like the rest of the group, he was dressed all in black. He picked up a telephone, punched in a number, and spoke into the mouthpiece. "Don't move," he warned again, and his voice echoed from speakers throughout the store.

I felt a hand on my shoulder. I turned around, expecting to be shot, and saw instead a man in a three-piece suit lying on the floor next to me. The name tag on his jacket said: MR. BOWLES, MANAGER. "Come on," he whispered to me. "We have to get upstairs. It's our only hope."

There was suddenly a lot of shooting and commotion in the shoe department, and the terrorist leader left our counter to investigate.

"Now!" the manager whispered.

Crawling on our hands and knees, the two of us reached the escalator. Like the lights, it was shut off. We crawled up the serrated metal steps, keeping our heads below the rails. We reached the second floor and—

We were on the ledge of a cliff, overlooking the beach. Below us, our people were playing happily in the sun and sand, frolicking in the water. We were watching them. "They don't care if they ever leave the beach," the manager said disgustedly. "Look at them. They really don't care."

And they didn't. Although the small strip of sand was surrounded on three sides by the large cliff on whose ledge we were standing, and on the other side by the ocean, the people did not feel trapped in the least. They were just happy to be alive.

"Well, we can't just sit around and play," the manager said. "We've got to get out of here."

The prospect frightened me. I had never been away from

the beach, and even climbing this high up on the cliff had been a major departure for me.

But I knew he was right.

We started up.

The cliff was mostly sand and several thousand feet high. We had to be very careful how we climbed. One slip and we'd fall to our deaths. Several times, in fact, one of us made a wrong move and slid down a couple of feet in the sand before again finding purchase.

It was dark when we reached the top.

We crawled the last few feet over the edge and found ourselves in the parking lot of a huge mansion. All of the lights were on in the gigantic house, and we could smell the scent of a multitude of gourmet foods wafting toward us.

We hid next to a bush. "It's the boss's house," I whispered.

"Yeah," the manager whispered back. "Which one of us is going to ask?"

"You," I told him. "I'm afraid."

"Okay." The manager glanced around to make sure no one had seen us, then ran across the driveway toward the door. Lights and bells went on in the trees around us and a burst of gunfire mowed down the manager. I was suddenly grabbed around my neck and—

I was sitting in my car. In my garage.

I had never left.

I could never leave.

To be honest, I do not know how long I've been here in the house. I don't know why Kathy and I moved here to begin with, and I cannot recall how all this started. I do not even know how many days or weeks or months or years or decades ago Kathy left me. For now I just exist. Every day is like every other and I cannot tell them apart. My routine is established and I seldom vary from it.

It was different when Kathy was here. We performed our duties, of course, but we also got on with our lives. We had friends. And we had each other, corny and trite as that may sound.

But they grew stronger even then. Our nights, more and more, were taken up with this . . . combat. Our dreams became less our own. Our time together became more difficult.

Finally Kathy had to leave. She too realized what our position was, where this house was located, what it would mean if we left, but in the end she didn't care. The responsibility was too much for her.

I could not leave, however.

So here I am—isolated, partly by choice, partly by circumstance, in this house. Alone. And here I stay, trying to figure out what to do next, trying to stay on top of what is real and what isn't. There is no one to help me, and with these latest developments I don't know how much longer I can make it by myself.

I need Kathy.

But Kathy is gone.

And I am here, fighting with ghosts.

The Baby

It was the late 1980s, and I was driving with some friends through a dilapidated industrial section of Los Angeles on the way to a concert, when I looked out the window and saw three dirty young boys kneeling before a cardboard box in an empty lot. They were clearly looking at something in the box, and I thought: *a dead baby*. I don't know why that thought occurred to me, but the next day I sat down and wrote this story.

—ɯ—

"You go in first."

"No, you."

"No, you."

Steve, always the bravest, stuck his head through the open doorway and peered into the dark interior of the abandoned warehouse. "Hello-o-o-o!" he called, hoping for an echo. His voice died flatly, as though it had been absorbed by the blackness, by the walls. Someone—Bill or Jimmy or Seun—pushed him from behind, and he almost lost his balance and fell through the door into the building, but he waved his arms to maintain his equilibrium and jumped quickly back out to the safety of the open air. He whirled on them, his face seething with the heat of his anger, ready to beat the hell out of whoever had done it, but all three of them looked at him innocently. He stared back at them for a moment, then laughed. "Wimps," he said.

Jimmy turned toward Steve. Nervously flipping the switch of his flashlight off and on, he asked, "Are we really going in?"

Steve looked at him scornfully. "Of course," he said. But he was far from sure himself. Back home, sitting on the cement driveway, surrounded by houses filled with grownups, the idea had sounded good. They would bring lights and ropes and Bill's metal detector and explore the old abandoned warehouse. None of them had the guts to go near the warehouse by themselves—not even in the daytime. But together they would be able to explore the old building to their hearts' content, to plumb its unplumbed depths and bring forth what treasures they could find.

Now, however, standing in front of the multistory structure, looking into the darkened doorway, the idea did not sound nearly so good or nearly so feasible. Theoretically, they should be braver in a group than they were individually. There was safety in numbers. But it turned out that they were just as scared together as apart. Steve looked up toward the top of the building, where the bare concrete wall was blackened by soot, where flames had once leaped up through the night stillness toward the moon, and he silently hoped that one of them would chicken out. Maybe Seun, the youngest of them, would start crying and want to go home.

But all three of them stared silently at him, waiting for him to make the decision.

"Let's go," he said, turning on his flashlight.

They walked slowly, softly, cautiously, through the open doorway of the warehouse, Steve leading, Jimmy and Bill following, Seun bringing up the rear. Gravel and charred rubble crunched beneath their feet.

"I don't want to be last!" Seun said suddenly. "I want to be in the middle!"

"Jimmy! Trade!" Steve hissed. He didn't want any of them to talk, but if they did talk he wanted them to whisper. He wasn't quite sure why.

"Why me?" Jimmy hissed back.

" 'Cause I said so!" Steve told him.

Jimmy and Seun switched places, and all of them moved a little closer together.

They walked farther into the darkness. Soon the doorway was little more than a patch of square white light behind them, no longer offering any illumination. The gravel crunched beneath their feet as they walked, and their flashlights played nervously upon the walls and floor. The thin yellowish beams piercing the blackness made the surrounding dark seem that much darker.

"I don't think we're supposed to be in here," Bill whispered.

"Of course we're not," Steve whispered back. "But no one cares. The place is abandoned."

"I mean, I think the other half of it's across the border."

They all stopped. None of them had thought of that. Despite the way it looked on the maps, the border between California and Mexico was not a straight line, they all knew. Several stores and homes throughout the city straddled the boundary, and many of them had rooms which were technically in both nations.

Visions of himself falling over some stray chunk of concrete and breaking his leg in the Mexico side of the warehouse pushed themselves into Steve's consciousness. He didn't know what would happen if that occurred. Would he have to be rushed to a Mexican hospital? By a Mexican ambulance? Or would he have to crawl back across that invisible border into his own country?

"Don't worry about it," he said aloud.

They started walking again.

Although it was too dark to see the sides of the warehouse, Steve had the feeling that the walls had narrowed, that they were now walking through a room much smaller than that which they had originally entered. He shined his light to the left and right, following the contours of the floor, but his beam was not strong enough to reach a wall. He decided to change course, to find a wall and follow it instead of stumbling through this inky blackness in the center of the building. He veered off thirty degrees and the other kids followed him.

He bumped his head on a beam.

Steve screamed, and his right hand shot instantly to his forehead to check for blood. His fingers came back dry. "Jesus!" he said.

"What is it?" Seun's voice was scared.

"Nothing." Steve played his light along the wooden beam. But it was not a beam. He had reached a wall. His eyes and his flashlight had been concentrated on the floor, and he had been looking through a large hole in the bottom section of the wall. He shined his light to the left and to the right and saw several similar holes. Holes big enough for a person to crawl through. He bent down on his knees and crept closer to the nearest one, shining his light through to the next room. It looked exactly the same.

"Let's crawl through," he said, "see what's on the other side."

"No!" Seun said.

Steve knew how Seun felt, but his fear was now subservient to his spirit of adventure. They had come here to explore, and they *would* explore.

He crawled through the hole.

"Steve!" Seun yelled.

"Come on through. There're no monsters."

There was a quick moment of indistinguishable mumbling from the other side of the wall, then Jimmy poked his head through. Seun followed, scrambling, and Bill came immediately afterward. They stood up and shook themselves off, Jimmy brushing what felt like cobwebs from his hair.

"What do we do now?" Bill asked.

"Search around." Steve started walking, following the wall, keeping his left hand in constant contact with the smooth concrete.

"Are we going to be able to find our way back?" Seun asked.

"Don't worry about it," Steve said.

There was not so much rubble on the floor here, and the ground seemed much softer beneath their feet. It felt like dirt. Steve pointed his flashlight up for a second and he could see no ceiling.

They kept walking.

The four boys wandered past a series of doors. Steve turned in one of them and the rest followed. They were in a much smaller room, and the walls on both sides could be made out with their flashlights. They walked out of the room through another door and found themselves in a cavernous space with an endlessly high ceiling. Their footsteps echoed as they walked.

Steve was no longer following any kind of wall, and he swung his beam back and forth across the ground in front of him to make sure he knew what was up ahead. The light touched upon an ancient rotting box in a slimy pool of water, moved across several chunks of wood and plaster, and stopped on something small and smooth and brown.

A baby.

Steve stood in place, staring at the infant trapped in his beam, and Seun ran into his back. Jimmy and Bill, walking side by side, ran into Seun.

The baby was obviously Mexican and obviously dead. It lay scrunched and unmoving, half in and half out of a puddle of stagnant water. A trail of small ants wound around its folds of fat and entered its open, toothless mouth. Steve moved slowly forward and tentatively touched the baby's skin. It was cold and soft and spongy and gave a little at the poke of his finger. Immediately he drew back.

"What is it?" Seun asked. His voice was more hushed than usual, whether from awe or fear Steve could not tell.

"It's a baby."

"How did it get here?"

Steve shook his head. He did not know himself. Had the baby been born in the warehouse and abandoned by its mother to die in the darkness of the deserted building? Had the baby been born dead and left there? Had it been brought by illegal aliens trying to sneak into the country and left behind accidentally?

Steve walked carefully around the dead infant. It was small, and there was no hair on its body. It did not look more than a week or so old.

The beam of his flashlight touched the baby's white eyes and was reflected back.

He knelt down silently in front of the infant and stared into its face, gazing raptly at its pure innocent expression. He had never seen anything like it. The infant's dead eyes stared back, seeing nothing, seeing everything, knowing all.

Jimmy knelt down next to Steve and gazed at the Mexican baby to see what was so fascinating.

Bill, captured by the look of hope on the infant's face, so incongruous in these terrible circumstances, bent down as well.

Seun, dropping silently to his knees, completed the semicircle.

The low benches, stolen from the barbecue sets of mothers and fathers, were arranged like pews in front of the altar. Candles of various sizes and colors, also stolen, burned dimly in their makeshift holders. In front of the benches, on the altar itself, the baby sat upright in a Coca-Cola crate, staring out into the darkness. The crate had been spray painted gold.

A single beam from a flashlight perched on top of a cardboard box shone into the baby's white eyes and was reflected back.

There were more than four of them now. Nearly twenty kids, all approximately the same age, sat silently on the benches staring at the dead infant. None of them spoke. None of them ever spoke.

Steve knelt before the baby, lost in thought. He saw an ant crawl slowly up the baby's fat brown arm, and he flicked it off. The ant went flying into the darkness.

There was a rustling sound from the area off to Steve's left, and he turned to see what caused the noise. A new kid— a girl—emerged from the depths of the warehouse. Her nice blue dress was dirty and sweat rolled down her face. It was obvious that she had been stumbling around in the dark for some time, trying to find them.

Steve smiled at her. He said nothing, but she understoo

She knelt down next to him in front of the baby. Her face was filled with rapture.

A few minutes later, the girl withdrew from her small purse a dead lizard. She held it gingerly by the tail and dropped it into the round fishbowl in front of the baby. There was a split-second flash of glowing luminescence, and the lizard dissolved in the bubbling liquid inside the bowl.

Steve patted the girl's head and she smiled, proud of herself.

They sat in silence, staring at the baby.

One of the candles burned all the way down and after a few last gasps of life, a few final flickers of fire, was extinguished.

They sat in silence, staring at the baby.

One by one, the candles surrounding the benches and the altar went out. When the last one had finally flickered out of existence, the kids on the benches stood up and walked silently, in single file, into the blackness. The girl, too, stood up, moved away from Steve's side, and started back the way she'd come. Jimmy and Bill and Seun walked up to the altar where Steve still knelt. They bent down for a moment themselves, then stood up as one.

They covered the baby's crate with a black cloth.

Walking back through the labyrinthian warehouse toward the outside, Steve wondered how he could have ever been afraid of the building. Now it was more friendly than home, and even little Seun traversed the way without a light. The whole tone of the place had changed.

And all because of the baby.

As always, the bright light of the afternoon hurt their eyes as they stepped out of the warehouse. The other kids were gone, already starting home, and there was no sign of them. Steve squinted in the direct sunlight, trying to keep his eyes from watering. "What time is it?" he asked.

Bill smiled. "After lunch and before dinner."

Steve scowled at him. "Anybody have a watch?"

"It's about three," Jimmy said.

They started walking. Bill picked up a stick and threw it into the bushes. Overhead, a plane sailed through the clear blue sky a few seconds ahead of its noise, leaving a trail of jet white in the air behind it.

"He seems so alone," Seun said.

Steve looked at him. "What?"

"He seems so alone. Don't you ever feel that way? I mean, what does He do when we're not there? He's all alone."

Steve stared at Seun. He had been thinking the same thing while he had been kneeling in front of the baby. He picked up a rock and looked at it. The rock resembled a frog. He held it between his thumb and forefinger and threw it. It whizzed through the air and hit a tree. "He *is* alone," he said.

"He doesn't have to be."

"What can we do about it?" Jimmy asked.

"Follow me." Seun ran down the path through the ravine and up the hill toward his house. He looked back at Steve as he ran. "I been saving this." He led the way through the wall of oleanders into his back yard. He pulled open the secret door to the clubhouse. The clubhouse had sat there virtually unused ever since they'd found the baby. The other three followed him in.

"Look," Seun said.

In the center of the floor, in a gold Coke crate, lay a little baby girl. She was dead. At her feet, Seun had poured out a jarful of black ants he had caught, hoping they would crawl up her body, but instead they had crawled onto the floor and were busily trying to find a way out of the clubhouse.

Steve knelt down in front of the baby. "Who is she?"

"Mindy Martin."

"Mrs. Martin's daughter?"

Seun nodded.

Steve looked up at him. "How did you get her?"

Seun smiled. "That's my business."

"Was she already dead or did you . . . kill her?"

"Does it matter?"

"No. I guess not." Steve looked into the box and hesitantly put his finger forth. The girl's skin was cold and springy. He felt an instant of admiration for Seun. "How long have you had her?"

"Since yesterday. I got the box last week and painted it, but I didn't get her 'til yesterday."

Steve stood up. "Let's take her out there."

Seun looked nervous. "Think He'll like her?"

"There's only one way to find out."

Seun drew out a black cloth from his pocket and spread it over the top of the crate. All four of them picked up the baby, each taking a corner of the box. They lifted it through the secret entrance. Seun closed up the clubhouse and they started through the oleanders.

"Hey, what are you doing?" Seun's mother came out onto the back porch and stared at them. "Where are you going?"

The four boys stopped, looking first at each other, then at her. "Nothing," Seun said. "We're just playing."

"Playing what?"

"Church."

She looked surprised. "Church?"

All four of the boys nodded.

She smiled and shook her head. "Okay. But you better be back in time for dinner."

"We will," Seun said.

They carried the box through the oleanders and started walking toward the warehouse.

Coming Home Again

A friend of mine's parents divorced when he was ten. His father remarried when my friend was in high school, but my friend never liked his father's new wife. She seemed all right to me, but in his mind she was a complete witch.

The two of us lost touch, but years later I saw him again, and he was *still* complaining about his wicked stepmother. I thought, "Your father could have married someone so much worse. . . ."

—⁓—

On the plane ride over, I tried to think of what I would say. The situation was bound to be awkward. I had been trying for over a decade to get my father to go out with other women, but now that he seemed to have found someone he cared about I was torn with conflicting emotions. On the one hand, I wanted him to be happy—he was my father and I loved him. On the other hand, I had also loved my mother and I couldn't help feeling, on some gut emotional level out of reach of my rational mind, that by finding someone else he was betraying her memory.

And he might love this new woman more than he'd loved her.

I guess that was my real fear. What if he found someone he loved more than my mother? What if his emotions found not just a substitute for her but a replacement for her? A woman who would supersede my mother's place in his emotional hierarchy.

It was a babyish fear, I admit. An immature, childish worry. My mother would have been happy for him. She wouldn't have wanted him to live forever in that celibate state of self-imposed social exile that he'd been inhabiting since her death. And I, too, wanted him to be happy.

I just didn't want his happiness to come at her expense.

I glanced down again at the folded letter in my lap. "I have found someone I care for very much," he'd written in his typically formal style. "I'd like you two to meet."

I leaned my chair back and closed my eyes. I wanted to like her; I really did. I hoped I would.

The plane landed in LA two hours later. I disembarked, found my luggage, and walked across the street to the coffee shop where my father had said he'd meet me. He was standing next to the open trunk of a new Pontiac in the parking lot. He was smiling, and he looked better than he had in years. The gaunt tiredness which I thought had settled into his features for good had disappeared, and his formerly sallow skin looked tan and healthy. As always, he was dressed in a formal suit—vest, tie, the whole works. My own clothes were nice, and comfortably stylish, but next to him I felt pitifully underdressed.

"It's good to see you," he said, and held out his hand.

"You too," I said. I couldn't help smiling. He looked so good, so fit and healthy and happy. I shook his hand. Our family had never been big on physical demonstrations of affection, and the pressing of palms was about as close as we ever got to a public display of closeness.

He took one of my suitcases and loaded it into the trunk; I put the other one right next to it. "How are things with you?" he asked.

"Oh, about the same as always." I grinned. "But your life seems to have taken a turn for the better."

He laughed heartily, and I realized suddenly that it had been years since I'd heard him laugh that way. "Yes," he said. "That is true. That is very true."

He unlocked my door and I got into the car, sliding across the seat to unlock his side. "So what's her name?" I asked. "You never did tell me."

He smile cryptically. "You'll see."

"Come on," I told him.

"We'll be home in ten minutes." He put the car into reverse and looked at me. "It's good to see you again, son. I'm glad you came out to see me."

We drove over the familiar side streets toward home. It was not a ten-minute drive from the airport. It was not even a twenty-minute drive. Our home in Long Beach was a good forty-five minutes from the airport even without traffic, and we happened to be driving during rush hour. But I'd known that ahead of time, and I didn't mind. We talked a lot, got caught up on new gossip, restated old positions, and fell into our old familiar patterns.

By the time we pulled off the freeway onto Lakewood it was approaching dinnertime. I hadn't had a thing to eat save an almost inedible lunch on the plane, and I was starved. "Is she going to have dinner ready for us?" I asked.

My father shook his head. "We'll eat out."

I'd been trying to determine, through subtle questioning, whether or not his new girlfriend lived with him, and I gathered that she did. I was surprised. My father had always been ultraconservative, the most proper of men, and I could not imagine him lowering his concrete moral standards enough to live with a woman outside of wedlock.

He must really love her a lot, I thought.

The house looked the same as always. The lawn was immaculately manicured, the trim on the house recently painted. Even the hose was curled into a neat circle. "The place looks good," I said.

He smiled at me. "I try my best."

We got out of the car, leaving the luggage in the trunk for later. My father found the house key on his ring and unlocked the front door, stepping aside to let me in first.

The inside of the house was demolished.

I stared in shock. Both the couch and the loveseat were overturned in the middle of the living room, their upholstery torn and ripped, stuffing leaking out. Scattered about were the broken pieces of our old dining room chairs and fragments of the dining room table. The china cabinet and its contents were heaped in a pile in the corner of the room. The walls were bare and covered with crayon scribbles. The living room rug, the rug that had been tough enough to withstand even my Tonka attacks and my G.I. Joe invasions, was a tatter of unraveled threads. Through the doorway of the kitchen, I could see smeared piles of food and bent food containers on the broken tile.

Everything was covered with a dusty white powder.

I whirled around to see my father's reaction. He was smiling happily, as if he did not see the disaster in front of him, as if he were viewing paradise itself. "How does it feel to be home again?" he asked.

There was the sound of something shattering in the back of the house, and a second later a naked boy came bounding into the living room on all fours. He was brown with filth and he smelled horrible. His hair was matted with grime, and his too-large teeth were a moldy green. He could not have been more than ten or eleven. He hopped onto the remains of the china cabinet and grunted wildly, snorting through his nose.

"There you are, my love," I heard my father say behind me, and I felt a sickening feeling of disgusted horror in the pit of my stomach. "I want you to meet David."

With an animal-like howl, the little boy bounded toward us. My father stepped forward and pulled the youth to his feet, hugging him to himself. He kissed the dirty child full on the lips. With fast and furious fingers, the boy tried to unbuckle my father's belt and pull down his pants. My father laughingly pushed him away. "Now now," he said.

The boy turned to look at me, and I could see that he had an erection.

My father smiled proudly at me. "Son," he said, "I want you to meet your future stepmother."

The filthy boy looked up at me and grinned. I could see that his mossy teeth had been filed into tiny points. He howled crazily.

I don't know what happened next. I guess I was in shock. I don't think I really blacked out, but the next thing I remember was walking down Lakewood Boulevard toward the ocean. It was dark out, night, and I was several miles away from home, so I had obviously been walking for quite a while.

I was alone.

I didn't know what I was going to do. My father had obviously gone totally insane. I looked up into the night sky, but the lights of Long Beach were bright and I could see very few stars. I wondered what my mother would say if she could see what was happening. I could not imagine my

mother's reaction to this situation. It was totally unlike anything she had ever encountered in her life.

"Why did you have to die?" I whispered aloud.

My father would have to be put away, I realized. He
would have to be committed. What he was doing was illegal, as well, and there would probably be criminal charges
filed against him.

There would doubtless be a lot of publicity.

I thought of all the times my father had let me help him
in his garage workshop, giving me imaginary chores to
perform while he himself did the real work. He looked tall
to me then, and invincible—the model man whose respect
I so desperately craved and tried to earn. The man I wanted
to be.

And then I saw him standing there in his immaculate suit,
amongst the shambles of our living room, as a filthy wild
child tried desperately to pull down his pants.

I started to cry.

I sat down on the curb and let the tears come, giving my
emotions free reign, and soon I was sobbing uncontrollably,
sobbing not only for the loss of my mother, but also for the
loss of my father.

Ten minutes later, I walked toward home. I would not call
the police, I decided. I could not do that to my father. We
would handle this crisis on our own. It was a family matter,
and it would be settled within the family.

The outside of the house looked deceptively calm. Everything was neat and ordered, in its proper place, just as it had
always been. Inside, I knew, chaos reigned. Insanity pre-
vailed.

The front door was unlocked. I pushed it open and
walked inside. My father was just putting on his shirt. His
pants were still unbuckled. Hopping around the room,

laughing crazily, was the boy. The child looked up at me with unreadable gray eyes and suddenly ran forward on two legs, carrying something in his hands. Grinning up at me, he presented his offering.

It was a framed picture of my parents, smeared with shit.

I kicked the little bastard as hard as I could in the stomach, sending him flying. His grinning mouth contracted instantly into an open *O* of pain, and I was gratified to hear him scream.

"That's no way to treat your new mother," my father said.

I ran forward and kicked the kid again. Hard. He went down, and the heel of my shoe connected with his dirty head. Blood poured freely down his brown skin from a large cut above his scalp line.

"That's enough!" my father screamed, but it was not enough. I was not through. I pulled the kid up by his hair and punched him full in the face, feeling his nose collapse under my knuckles.

And then my father's strong hands were pulling me away. I kicked and screamed and lashed out at him, but he was stronger than I was.

I was knocked unconscious.

When I came to, I was lying in a bed, my arms and legs tied to the four posts with a thick coarse twine. My father was seated in a chair next to me, a concerned expression on his face, pressing a cold compress against my forehead. He was talking in a soothing voice—more to himself than me, I think—and I listened to him silently.

". . . more than I loved your mother, but just as much I think. I can't help myself. I was lost when your mother died, lost, and I didn't know what to do with myself. I haven't felt this way in years. I'm learning how to feel again . . ."

There was a series of inarticulate howls from the front of the house. My father's face brightened. "In here!" he called.

The boy bounded into the room, and a hideous stench assaulted my nostrils. I strained against my bonds, but the twine held tight. The child looked up at me. A crust of dried blood covered the left half of his face where my foot had connected with his head, and twin rivulets of hardened blood protruded from the pulp of his broken nose. He smiled at me and I saw again his pointed teeth, covered with greenish tartar.

My father drew the boy to him and kissed him on the lips, long and hard and lovingly.

"Father," I pleaded, almost crying. "Dad."

I could not recall ever having seen my parents kiss.

The boy moved forward, whispered something in my father's ear, and glanced furtively toward me. My father stood up and drew the compress from my forehead. "I'll see you in a while," he told me. I watched him step out of the room and close the door behind him.

The boy cavorted around the room after my father had left, grunting and snorting wildly. He squatted in the corner and relieved himself.

"Help!" I screamed as loud as I could, struggling against the twine, hoping some neighbor would hear me. "Help!"

The boy hopped onto the bed, climbing on top of me. He bent his face close to my own, and I spit at him. He let the saliva drip off the end of his nose, not moving, not wiping it off. He studied me for a moment, then said something in a foreign tongue, soft whispering words. I had never heard the words before, but they frightened me.

He stood up on his knees, and I could see his erection. He bent down to undo my pants.

"No," I cried.

He laughed and said something else in his whispering tongue. He pushed his face near my own, and I could smell his fetid breath. I gagged.

He howled loudly and unzipped my zipper.

"Untie me," I said. I did not know if he could understand me, but he seemed to understand my father. I made my voice as soothing as possible. "Please untie me."

He slipped a grimy hand under the elastic of my underwear.

"I'll be able to help you better if I can move my hands," I said, keeping my voice calm. "Untie me."

To my surprise, he moved forward and began unknotting the twine tied around the bed posts. I lay there unmoving, letting him undo first one knot, then the other. I flexed my fingers, but I did not move or say a word as he untied my feet.

Then I kicked him hard in the chest, sending him flying off the bed. I jumped up, grabbed his head, and smashed it against the wall, leaving a smear of pale blood.

"What's going on in there?" my father asked from outside the door. "Love, you all right?"

I leaped out of the window. The glass cut me, but I was protected to some extent by the heavy drapes. I would not have cared if I had been sliced to ribbons. I rolled on the grass and jumped up, my arms and head bleeding from dozens of tiny cuts. I ran across the street to Mr. Murphy's house. I did not bother to knock, but threw open the unlocked front door.

Mr. Murphy's living room was a shambles, chairs and tables tumbled over, couch torn apart.

Cavorting about amongst the broken furniture, moving on all fours, was a naked wild boy, covered with filth.

Mr. Murphy stood in the hallway, stark naked.

I ran next door to Mrs. Grant's house, but her place, too, had been torn apart by the dirty boy crawling across her ragged carpet.

I ran out of the neighborhood, out to Lakewood Boulevard, and I did not stop running until I reached a phone. My hands shaking, I fumbled through my pockets for some change. My pants were still undone. I found a quarter and dropped it in the slot.

But who was I going to call?

I stood there for a moment. The police would not believe me, I knew. They would write my story off as a crank call—particularly when they traced it to a public phone. I knew none of my father's friends outside the neighborhood. I had no friends of my own left in the LA area. No one else would believe me because I looked like hell; they'd think I was crazy.

And all my suitcases were at my father's.

Retrieving my money from the coin return slot, I walked down the street to a bus stop where I caught a bus to a motel. I took a hot shower and slept, trying to calm down.

In the morning, I called my father's number, but the line was busy. I decided to call the cops.

The police didn't believe me when I told them what had happened. They gave me a urine test to see if I was on something. I called Janice back in Chicago, but she didn't believe me either.

There was nothing for me to do but use the return ticket in my wallet to fly back home.

It has been nearly a month now since I got back. Janice now believes that *something* happened out in California, but despite the continued repetitions of my story, she is not sure just what that something was. She thinks I have had some type of breakdown, and she keeps encouraging me to seek professional help.

I have not called my father since my return, and he has not called me. The bump on my head is long gone, and the rope burns on my arms have faded, but though the physical effects of my experience have disappeared, the psychological effects have not. I dream about the boy at least once a week, and the dreams are getting ever more vivid.

They are also getting scarier.

Much scarier.

In the last dream, the boy lived with me as my wife, in place of Janice.

And when I awoke from the dream I had an erection.

The Potato

When I was a teenager, friends of my parents who lived across the street from us would periodically hire me to baby-sit their son while they went out to dinner and a movie. It was an easy gig. I'd eat their food, sit on their couch, watch TV, and get paid for it.

I also used to tell their son scary stories. One of them, inspired by the short story "Graveyard Shift" in Stephen King's *Night Shift* collection, involved a huge living potato that lived in the crawl space under our house. These tales not only scared the boy, they also scared me, and I would inevitably let him stay up far past his bedtime because I didn't want to be alone in their small creepy third-story television room.

Years later, I remembered that living potato, and I put him in a new setting and different story.

—ɯ—

The farmer stared down at the . . . thing . . . which lay at his feet. It was a potato. No doubt about that. It had been connected to an ordinary potato plant, and it had the irregular contours of a tuber. But that was where the resemblance to an ordinary potato ended. For the thing at his feet was white and gelatinous, well over three feet long. It pulsed rhythmically, and when he touched it tentatively with his shovel, it seemed to withdraw, to shrink back in upon itself.

A living potato.

It was an unnatural sight, wrong somehow, and his first thought was that he should destroy it, chop it up with his shovel, run it over with his tractor. Nature did not usually let such abominations survive, and he knew that he would be doing the right thing by destroying it. Such an aberration was obviously not meant to be. But he took no action. Instead he stared down at the potato, unable to move, hypnotized almost, watching the even ebb and flow of its pulsations, fascinated by its methodical movement. It made no noise, showed no sign of having a mind, but he could not help feeling that the thing was conscious, that it was watching him as he watched it, that, in some strange way, it even knew what he was thinking.

The farmer forced himself to look up from the hole and stared across his field. There were still several more rows to be dug, and there was feeding and watering to do, but he could not seem to rouse in himself any of his usual responsibility or sense of duty. He should be working at this moment—his time was structured very specifically, and even a slight glitch could throw off his schedule for a week—but he knew that he was not going to return to his ordinary chores for the rest of the day. They were no longer important to him. Their value had diminished, their necessity had become moot. Those things could wait.

He looked again at the potato. He had here something spectacular. This was something he could show at the fair. Like the giant steer he had seen last year, or the two-headed lamb that had been exhibited a few years back. He shook his head. He had never had anything worth showing at the fair, had not even had any vegetables or livestock worth entering in competition. Now, all of a sudden, he had an item worthy of its own booth. A genuine star attraction.

But the fair was not for another four months.

Hell, he thought. He could set up his own exhibit here. Put a little fence around the potato and charge people to look at it. Maybe he'd invite Jack Phelps, Jim Lowry, and some of his closest friends to see it first. Then they'd spread the word, and pretty soon people from miles around would be flocking to see his find.

The potato pulsed in its hole, white flesh quivering rhythmically, sending shivers of dirt falling around it. The farmer wiped a band of sweat from his forehead with a handkerchief, and he realized that he no longer felt repulsed by the sight before him.

He felt proud of it.

The farmer awoke from an unremembered dream, retaining nothing but the sense of loss he had experienced within the dream's reality. Though it was only three o'clock, halfway between midnight and dawn, he knew he would not be able to fall back asleep, and he got out of bed, slipping into his Levi's. He went into the kitchen, poured himself some stale orange juice from the refrigerator, and stood by the screen door, staring out across the field toward the spot where he'd unearthed the living potato. Moonlight shone down upon the field, creating strange shadows, giving the land a new topography. Although he could not see the potato from this vantage point, he could imagine how it looked in the moonlight, and he shivered, thinking of the cold, pulsing, gelatinous flesh.

I should have killed it, he thought. *I should have stabbed it with the shovel, chopped it into bits, gone over it with the plow.*

He finished his orange juice, placing the empty glass on the counter next to the door. He couldn't go back to sleep, and he didn't feel like watching TV, so he stared out at the field, listening to the silence. It was moments like these, when he wasn't working, wasn't eating, wasn't sleeping, when his body wasn't occupied with something else, that he felt Murial's absence the most acutely. It was always there— a dull ache that wouldn't go away—but when he was by himself like this, with nothing to do, he felt the true breadth and depth of his loneliness, felt the futility and pointlessness of his existence.

The despair building within him, he walked outside onto the porch. The wooden boards were cold and rough on his bare feet. He found himself, unthinkingly, walking down the porch steps, past the front yard, into the field. Here, the blackness of night was tempered into a bluish purple by the moon, and he had no trouble seeing where he was going.

He walked, almost instinctively, to the spot where the living potato lay in the dirt. He had, in the afternoon, gingerly moved it out of the hole with the help of Jack Phelps, and had then gathered together the materials for a box to be placed around it. The potato felt cold and slimy and greasy, and both of them washed their hands immediately afterward, scrubbing hard with Lava soap. Now the boards lay in scattered disarray in the dirt, like something that had been torn apart rather than something that had not yet been built.

He looked down at the bluish white form, pulsing slowly and evenly, and the despair he had felt, the loneliness, left him, dissipating outward in an almost physical way. He stood rooted in place, too stunned to move, wondering at the change that had instantly come over him. In the darkness of night, the potato appeared phosphorescent, and it seemed to him somehow magical. Once again, he was glad he had not destroyed his discovery, and he felt good that other people would be able to see and experience the strange phenomenon. He stood there for a while, not thinking, not doing anything, and then he went back to the house, stepping slowly and carefully over rocks and weeds this time. He knew that he would have no trouble falling asleep.

In the morning it had moved. He did not know how it had moved—it had no arms or legs or other means of locomotion—but it was now definitely closer to the house. It was also bigger. Whereas yesterday it had been on the south side of his assembled boards, it was now well to the north, and it had increased its size by half. He was not sure he would be able to lift it now, even with Jack's help.

He stared at the potato for a while, looking for some sort of trail in the dirt, some sign that the potato had moved itself, but he saw nothing.

He went into the barn to get his tools.

He had finished the box and gate for the potato, putting it in place well before seven o'clock. It was eight o'clock before the first carload of people arrived. He was in the living room, making signs to post on telephone poles around town and on the highway, when a station wagon pulled into the drive. He walked out onto the porch and squinted against the sun.

"This where y'got that monster 'tater?" a man called out. Several people laughed.

"This is it," the farmer said. "It's a buck a head to see it, though."

"A buck?" The man got out of the car. He looked vaguely familiar, but the farmer didn't know his name. "Jim Lowry said it was fifty cents."

"Nope." The farmer turned as if to go in the house.

"We'll still see it, though," the man said. "We came all this way, we might as well see what it's about."

The farmer smiled. He came off the porch, took a dollar each from the man, his brother, and three women, and led them out to the field. He should have come up with some kind of pitch, he thought, some sort of story to tell, like they did with that steer at the fair. He didn't want to just take the people's money, let them look at the potato and leave. He didn't want them to feel cheated. But he couldn't think of anything to say.

He opened the top of the box, swinging open the gate, and explained in a stilted, halting manner how he had found the potato. He might as well have saved his breath. None of the customers gave a damn about what he was saying. They didn't even pay any attention to him. They simply stared at the huge potato in awe, struck dumb by this marvel of nature. For that's how he referred to it. It was no longer an abomination, it was a marvel. A miracle. And the people treated it as such.

Two more cars pulled up soon after, and the farmer left the first group staring while he collected money from the newcomers.

After that, he stayed in the drive, collecting money as people arrived, pointing them in the right direction and allowing them to stay as long as they wanted. Customers came and went with regularity, but the spot next to the box was crowded all day, and by the time he hung a Closed sign on the gate before dark, he had over a hundred dollars in his pocket.

He went out to the field, repositioned the box, closed the gate, and retreated into the house.

It had been a profitable day.

* * *

Whispers. Low moans. Barely audible sounds of despair so forlorn that they brought upon him a deep dark depression, a loneliness so complete that he wept like a baby in his bed, staining the pillows with his tears.

He stood up after a while and wandered around the house. Every room seemed cheap and shabby, the wasted effort of a wasted life, and he fell into his chair before the TV, filled with utter hopelessness, lacking the energy to do anything but stare into the darkness.

In the morning, everything was fine. In the festive, almost carnival-like atmosphere of his exhibition, he felt rejuvenated, almost happy. Farmers who had not been out of their overalls in ten years showed up in their Sunday best, family in tow. Little Jimmy Hardsworth's lemonade stand, set up by the road at the head of the drive, was doing a thriving business, and there were more than a few repeat customers from the day before.

The strange sounds of the night before, the dark emotions, receded into the distance of memory.

He was kept busy all morning, taking money, talking to people with questions. The police came by with a town official, warning him that if this went on another day he would have to buy a business license, but he let them look at the potato and they were quiet after that. There was a lull around noon, and he left his spot near the head of the driveway and walked across the field to the small crowd gathered around the potato. Many of his crops had been trampled, he noticed. His rows had been flattened by scores of spectator feet. He'd have to take the day off tomorrow and take care of the farm before it went completely to hell.

Take the day off.

It was strange how he'd come to think of the exhibition

as his work, of his farm as merely an annoyance he had to contend with. His former devotion to duty was gone, as were his plans for the farm.

He looked down at the potato. It had changed. It was bigger than it had been before, more misshapen. Had it looked like this the last time he'd seen it? He hadn't noticed. The potato was still pulsing, and its white skin looked shiny and slimy. He remembered the way it had felt when he'd lifted it, and he unconsciously wiped his hands on his jeans.

Why was it that he felt either repulsed or exhilarated when he was around the potato?

"It's sum'in, ain't it?" the man next to him said.

The farmer nodded. "Yeah, it is."

He could not sleep that night. He lay in bed, staring up at the cracks in the ceiling, listening to the silence of the farm. It was some time before he noticed that it was not silence he was hearing—there was a strange, high-pitched keening sound riding upon the low breeze which fluttered the curtains.

He sat up in bed, back flat against the headboard. It was an unearthly sound, unlike anything he had ever heard, and he listened carefully. The noise rose and fell in even cadences, in a rhythm not unlike that of the pulsations of the potato. He turned his head to look out the window. He thought he could see a rounded object in the field, bluish white in the moonlight, and he remembered that he could not see it at all the night before.

It was getting closer.

He shivered, and he closed his eyes against the fear.

But the high-pitched whines were soothing, comforting, and they lulled him gently to sleep.

*   *   *

When he awoke, he went outside before showering or eating breakfast, and walked out to the field. Was it closer to the house? He couldn't be sure. But he remembered the keening sounds of the night before, and a field of goose-bumps popped up on his arms. The potato definitely looked more misshapen than it had before, its boundaries more ir-regular. If it was closer, he thought, so was the box he had built around it. Everything had been moved.

But that wasn't possible.

He walked back to the house, ate, showered, dressed, and went to the foot of the drive where he put up a chain be-tween the two flanking trees and hung a sign which read: Closed for the Day.

There were chores to be done, crops to be watered, ani-mals to be fed, work to be completed.

But he did none of these things. He sat alone on a small bucket next to the potato, staring at it, hypnotized by its pul-sations, as the sun rose slowly to its peak, and then dipped into the west.

Murial was lying beside him, not moving, not talking, not even touching him, but he could feel her warm body next to his and it felt right and good. He was happy, and he reached over and laid a hand on her breast. "Murial," he said. "I love you."

And then he knew it was a dream, even though he was still in it, because he had never said those words to her, not in the entire thirty-three years they had been married. It was not that he had not loved her, it was that he didn't know how to tell her. The dream faded into reality, the room around him growing dark and old, the bed growing large and cold. He was left with only a memory of that momentary happi-ness, a memory which taunted him and tortured him and made the reality of the present seem lonelier and emptier than even he had thought it could seem.

Something had happened to him recently. Depression had graduated to despair, and the tentative peace he had made with his life had all but vanished. The utter hopelessness which had been gradually pressing in on him since Murial's death had enveloped him, and he no longer had the strength to fight it.

His mind sought out the potato, though he lacked even the energy to look out the window to where it lay in the field. He thought of its strangely shifting form, its white slimy skin, its even pulsations, and he realized that just thinking of the object made him feel a little better.

What was it?

That was the question he had been asking himself ever since he'd found the potato. He wasn't stupid. He knew it wasn't a normal tuber. But neither did he believe that it was a monster or a being from outer space or some other such movie nonsense.

He didn't know what it was, but he knew that it had been affecting his life ever since he'd discovered it, and he was almost certain that it had been responsible for the emotional roller coaster he'd been riding the past few days.

He pushed aside the covers and stood up, looking out the window toward the field. Residual bad feelings fled from him, and he could almost see them flying toward the potato as if they were tangible, being absorbed by that slimy white skin. The potato offered no warmth, but it was a vacuum for the cold. He received no good feelings from it, but it seemed to absorb his negative feelings, leaving him free from depression, hopelessness, despair.

He stared out the window and thought he saw something moving out in the field, blue in the light of the moon.

* * *

The box was still in the field, but the potato was lying on the gravel in front of the house. In the open, freed from the box, freed from shoots and other encumbrances, it had an almost oval shape, and its pulsing movements were quicker, more lively.

The farmer stared at the potato, unsure of what to do. Somewhere in the back of his mind, he had been half hoping that the potato would die, that his life would return to normal. He enjoyed the celebrity, but the potato scared him.

He should have killed it the first day.

Now he knew that he would not be able to do it, no matter what happened.

"Hey!" Jack Phelps came around the side of the house from the back. "You open today? I saw some potential customers driving back and forth along the road, waiting."

The farmer nodded tiredly. "I'm open."

Jack and his wife invited him to dinner, and the farmer accepted. It had been a long time since he'd had a real meal, a meal cooked by a woman, and it sounded good. He also felt that he could use some company.

But none of the talk was about crops or weather or neighbors the way it used to be. The only thing Jack and Myra wanted to talk about was the potato. The farmer tried to steer the conversation in another direction, but he soon gave up, and they talked about the strange object. Myra called it a creature from hell, and though Jack tried to laugh it off and turn it into a joke, he did not disagree with her.

When he returned from the Phelps's it was after midnight. The farmer pulled into the dirt yard in front of the house and cut the headlights, turning off the ignition. With the lights off, the house was little more than a dark hulking shape blocking out a portion of the starlit sky. He sat un-moving, hearing nothing save the ticking of the pickup's en-gine as it cooled. He stared at the dark house for a few moments longer, then got out of the pickup and clomped up the porch steps, walking through the open door into the house.

The open door?

There was a trail of dirt on the floor, winding in a mean-dering arc through the living room into the hall, but he hardly noticed it. He was filled with an unfamiliar emotion, an almost pleasant feeling he had not experienced since Murial died. He did not bother to turn on the house lights but went into the dark bathroom, washed his face, brushed his teeth, and got into his pajamas.

The potato was waiting in his bed.

He had known it would be there, and he felt neither panic nor exhilaration. There was only a calm acceptance. In the dark, the blanketed form looked almost like Murial, and he saw two lumps protruding upward which looked remarkably like breasts.

He got into bed and pulled the other half of the blanket over himself, snuggling close to the potato. The pulsations of the object mirrored the beating of his own heart.

He put his arms around the potato. "I love you," he said.

He hugged the potato tighter, crawling on top of it, and as his arms and legs sank into the soft slimy flesh, he realized that the potato was not cold at all.

The Murmurous Haunt of Flies

I'm not a poetry fan. Never have been, never will be. But while suffering through a graduate class on the Romantic poets, the phrase "the murmurous haunt of flies" leaped out at me while we were reading John Keats's "Ode to a Nightingale." I thought it was a great line and wrote it down.

Some time later, I found myself thinking of my great-grandmother's chicken ranch in the small farming community of Ramona, California. She'd died years before, and I hadn't been there in a long time, but I remembered a little adobe banya or bathhouse on the property that used to scare me (this bathhouse pops up again in my novel *The Town*). I remembered as well that there had always been flies everywhere—because of the chickens—and I recalled seeing flypaper and No-Pest Strips that were black with bug bodies. The Keats phrase returned to me, a light went on, and I wrote this story.

"Stay away," my grandpa told me. "It is a haunted place, strange with secrets."

He had lived on the farm all his life, was born on the farm

and would die on the farm. He knew what he was talking
about. And as we sat in the old kitchen, chairs pushed up
against the now-unused icebox, we grew afraid. I suddenly
felt a wave of cold pass through me, though the temperature
in the farmhouse was well over ninety degrees, and I saw
multiple ripples of gooseflesh cascade down Jan's bare
arms. Neither of us exactly *believed* the tale, but we were ur-
banites, out of our element, and we respected the knowledge
and opinions of the locals. We knew enough to know we
knew nothing.

He struggled out of his chair and, one hand on his gimp
leg, hobbled over to the screen door. The fine mesh of the
screen was ripped in several places, from human accidents
and feline determination, and a small covey of flies was
traveling back and forth, in and out of the house. He stood
there for a minute, not speaking, then beckoned us over.
"Come here. I want to show it to you."

Jan and I put the front legs of our chairs back down on
the wooden floor and moved over to the screen. I could
smell my grandpa's medication as I stood next to him—a
sickeningly acrid odor of Vicks, vitamin B1, and rubbing al-
cohol. He looked suddenly small, shrunken somehow, as
though he had withered over the years, and I could see his
scalp through the wispy strands of hair he combed back over
his head. He was going to die, I suddenly realized. Maybe
not today, maybe not tomorrow, but soon, and for all time.

I was going to miss him.

He touched my shoulder lightly with his right hand while
his left pointed across the meadow. "It's over there," he said.
"You see the barn?"

I followed his finger. A large, square, dilapidated structure of rotting, unpainted boards arose from the tall grasses
beyond the chicken coops. I remembered playing there as a

kid, when it was all new and freshly painted; playing hide-and-go-seek with my brother and my cousins, hiding in the secret loft behind the hay-baler, endless summer afternoons of sweaty searching. This was not the barn I once knew. I nodded, smiling, though I didn't feel happy.

His finger moved across the horizon, passing from the barn to a small cluster of shacks on the hillside to the west. "See those buildings there to the right of the barn?" Again I nodded. "On the hill?" I continued nodding. "That's it."

Jan was squinting against the afternoon sun, her hand perched above her eyes like a makeshift visor. "Which one is it? I see a couple buildings there."

My grandpa was already starting back across the floor. "It doesn't matter," he said. "Just stay away from the whole area." He sat down once again in his chair at the foot of the kitchen table. A sharp flash of pain registered on his face as he bent his gimp leg to sit down.

We, too, returned to our chairs. And we talked away the rest of the afternoon.

Jan awoke screaming. She sat bolt upright in bed, the acne cream on her face and her sleep-spiked hair giving her the appearance of a shrieking harpy. I hugged her close, pulling her to my chest and murmuring reassurances. "It's okay," I said softly, stroking her hair. "It's all right."

She stopped crying after a few minutes and sat up, facing me. She tried to smile. "That was some nightmare."

I smiled back. "So I gathered. Tell me about it."

"It was about the bathhouse," she said, pulling the covers up around her chin and snuggling closer. "And I don't want you to take this wrong, but your grandfather was in it." Her eyes looked out the bedroom window as she spoke, and she gazed into the darkness toward the group of buildings on the hillside. "I was just sleeping here, in this bed, with you, when I woke up. I heard some kind of noise, and I looked on the floor, and there was your grandfather. He was crawling along the ground, looking up at me and smiling." She shivered. "I tried to wake you up, but you were dead asleep. I kept shaking you and yelling, but you wouldn't budge. Then your grandfather grabbed me by the arm and pulled me down on the floor with him. I was screaming and kicking and fighting, but he had a hold on me, and he started pulling me out of the room. 'We're going to the bathhouse,' he told me. 'We're going to take a bath.'

"Then I woke up."

"That's horrible," I said.

"I know." She laid her head against my chest, running her fingers through my curly chest hair.

We fell asleep in that position.

The day dawned early, just as I'd known it would. Sunlight was streaming through the window with full force by six o'clock. Sunrise always seemed to come earlier on the farm than in the city for some reason. That was one thing I remembered from my childhood.

Jan was still asleep when I awoke, and I crept out of bed softly so as not to disturb her.

My grandpa was already up, planted in his chair at the foot of the table, drinking a tin cup of black coffee. He looked up and smiled as I walked into the kitchen. "Day's half over, city slicker. What took you so long?" His smile widened, the new ultrawhite dentures looking oddly out of place in his otherwise old face. "Where's your wife? Still asleep?"

I nodded. "I'm letting her sleep in. She had a pretty bad nightmare last night."

"Yeah, your grandma used to have nightmares, too. Bad ones. Some nights, she'd even be afraid to go to sleep, and I'd have to stay up with her." He shook his head, staring into his coffee cup. "There were some pretty bad times there."

I poured myself a cup of coffee from the old metal pot on the stove and sat down next to him. "You ever have nightmares?"

"Me? I'm too boring to have nightmares." He laughed. "Hell, I don't think I even dream."

We sat in silence after that, listening to the many morning sounds of the farm. From far off, I heard the crowing of a rooster, endlessly repeating his obnoxious cry. Closer in, cowbells were ringing dully as four bovine animals moved slowly across the meadow to the watering pond. And of course, under it all, the ever-present hum of the flies.

"It's going to be a hot one today," my grandpa said after a while. "It feels humid already."

"Yeah," I agreed.

He added a dash of cream to his coffee, stirring it with the butt end of a fork. "What are your plans for today?"

I shrugged. "We don't have any, really. I thought maybe we'd go into town, look around a bit, then maybe go for a hike."

"Not there?" He glanced up sharply.

"No. Of course not. We'd just walk around the farm here. I think the barn's about as far as we'd care to go."

"Good." He nodded, satisfied. "For it is a haunted place, strange with secrets."

Jan walked into the room then, still rubbing the sleep from her eyes, and I blew her a kiss across the table. She smiled and blew a kiss back. I turned again to my grandpa. "You said that before. What is it? Part of a poem?"

"What?"

" 'It is a haunted place, strange with secrets.' "

His face grew pale as I spoke the words, the color draining from his cheeks, and I felt my own flesh starting to creep as I saw his fear. I was immediately sorry I'd mentioned it. But there was no way to retract the question.

He looked from me to Jan; his eyes narrowed into unreadable slits. He took a sip of coffee, and I saw that his hands were shaking badly. "Wait here a minute," he said, standing up. "I'll be right back." Holding on to his bad leg, he limped across the room and out into the hall. He returned a few minutes later with a piece of folded brown paper which he tossed at me.

I unfolded the paper and read:

> For He lives here with flies in shadow and dark
> And He is happy here, at home
> For it is a haunted place, strange with secrets

I handed the paper back to my grandpa, puzzled. "What is it?"

"I found it in your grandma's hand when she died. It's her handwriting, but I have no idea when she wrote it." He folded the paper and placed it carefully in the upper-right pocket of his overalls. "I don't think she ever wrote another poem in her life."

"Then why did she write this?"

He stared into his coffee. "I don't know."

Jan sat down at the table, pulling her chair next to mine. "How do you know she wrote it about the bathhouse?"

My grandpa looked up at her. It was a minute or so before he answered, and when he did his voice was low, almost a whisper. "Because," he said, "that's where she died."

*　　*　　*

We did indeed go into town, and we had some great hamburgers at the lone diner: a dingy little hole-in-the-wall called Mac and Marg. After, we drove back to the farm and I gave Jan a guided tour of my childhood. I showed her the now-abandoned horse stalls where we used to lick the massive blocks of salt with Big Red and Pony; I showed her the old windmill; I showed her the spot where we once built a clubhouse. I showed her everything.

We ended up at the barn.

"You really used to play here?" she asked, looking up at the decaying building. "It looks so dangerous."

I smiled. "Well, it wasn't quite so bad off in those days. In fact, it was still being used." I walked up to the huge open doorway and looked in. Light now entered the once-dark building through several holes in the roof. "Hello!" I called, hoping for an echo. My voice died flatly, barely managing to scare two swallows who flew through one of the roof holes.

Jan walked up and stood beside me, looking in. "You used to play upstairs, too?"

I nodded. "We played everywhere. We knew every inch of this place."

She shivered and turned around. "I don't like it."

I followed her back out into the sunlight. The day was hot, almost unbearably so, and though I was wearing a T-shirt, cutoffs, and a pair of sandals, I was still sweating.

Jan, ahead of me by a few paces, stopped at the edge of the tall grass and stared toward the hillside, silent, thinking. I crept up behind her and gave her a quick poke in the side. She jumped, and I laughed. "Sorry," I said. "I just couldn't help it."

She smiled thinly, and her gaze returned to the small

cluster of buildings. "It *is* scary, isn't it? Even in the day-time."

She was right. The bathhouse and the small shacks sur-rounding it dominated the scenery, though they were by no means the most prominant figures in the landscape. It was as if the whole area, the scattered farmhouses, the fields and the hills, were somehow focused in on that point. No matter where one stood in the valley, his or her eyes would be drawn inexorably to the bathhouse. There was something strange about the makeshift hut, something a little off, some-thing entirely unrelated to my grandpa's story.

"Listen," Jan said, grabbing my arm. "Do you hear that?"

I listened. "No, I don't hear—"

"Shhh!" She put up her hand to silence me.

I stood perfectly still, cocking my ear toward the bath-house, listening intently. Sure enough, a low buzzing was coming from that direction, growing louder or softer with the wafting of the hot breeze. "I hear it," I said.

"What do you think it is?"

"I don't know."

She stood still for a moment, listening. The buzzing maintained its even rhythm. "You know what it reminds me of?" she said. "That poem by Keats. The one where he talked about 'the murmurous haunt of flies.'"

The murmurous haunt of flies.

It seemed suddenly hotter, more humid, if that was pos-sible. The wind, blowing from the direction of the bath-house, felt hellishly, unnaturally heated. I put my arm around Jan and held her close. We stood like that for a few minutes.

"How far do you think that is?" she asked, gesturing to-ward the hill.

"Why?"

"I'd like to go over there. You know, just take a look."

I shook my head emphatically. I may not have fully believed my grandpa's story and his repeated warnings, but I had no desire to tempt the fates. "No way," I said. "Forget it."

"Why not? It's broad daylight. It's not even two o'clock yet. What could happen to us?"

I was sweating heavily by now, and I used my T-shirt to wipe the moisture off my face. "I don't know," I said. "I just don't want to take any chances."

She gave my hand a small squeeze and looked into my eyes. "It *is* scary, isn't it?"

That night, I had a nightmare. And it was Jan who woke me up and comforted me.

I had been walking through the tall grasses beyond the barn, the overgrown groundcover reaching above my head and causing me to lose my way. It was night, and the full moon shone brightly in a starless sky. I kept looking up as I walked, trying unsuccessfully to get my bearings by the moon, trying vainly to determine in which direction I was walking. Suddenly, I stepped through a wall of grass and found myself at the edge of a small clearing—face-to-face with the bathhouse.

The bathhouse looked smaller than I'd thought it would, and not as run-down. But that in no way diluted its evil. For it was evil. It was a forbidding and terrifying presence, almost alive, and the light of the moon played spectrally across its adobe facade, highlighting the empty darkened windows, spotlighting strange irregularities in construction. There was something definitely wrong with the building, something savage and perverse, and as I looked at the structure my muscles knotted in fear.

Then something caught my eye. I glanced over the front of the building once again and saw what I had noticed only peripherally before. I screamed. Peeking out of the blackened rectangular hole which served as a doorway were two shriveled feet wearing Jan's stockings.

I awoke in Jan's arms.

And she held me, softly, closely, her calm, sympathetic voice assuaging my fears, until again I fell asleep.

The other local farmers knew about the bathhouse as well, we learned. My grandpa had several of the neighboring ranchers over for a barbecue lunch the next day, and they discussed, in hushed whispers, the recent mutilation of several hogs. They all seemed to think the mutilations were connected with the bathhouse in some way.

"I went up there exactly once," said Old Man Crawford. "The first year we moved here. That was enough for me."

I was sitting next to Jan at the head of the table, keeping my ear on the conversation and my eye on the hamburgers. I turned toward Old Man Crawford. "What was it like?" I asked.

They stared at me then, six pairs of eyes widening as if in shock. The only sound was the sizzling of the meat dripping through the rusty grill onto the burning charcoal. No one said a word; it was as if they were waiting for me to retract my question. Jan's hand found mine and held it.

"What the hell is this? A wake?" My grandpa came out of the house carrying a tray of buns. He looked from me to the silent farmers. "Anything wrong here?"

"Nah," Old Man Crawford said, smiling and downing the last of his beer. "Everything's fine."

The mood was broken, the tension dissipated, and the

conversation returned to a normal, healthy buzz, though it now revolved around other, safer, topics.

I got up and went into the house, rummaging through the refrigerator for a Coke. Jan followed me in. "What was all that about?" she asked.

I found my Coke and closed the door. "You got me."

She shook her head, smiling slightly. "Ever get the feeling this is all a joke? Some trick they're playing on the rubes from the city?"

"You saw them," I said. "That was no joke. They were scared. Every one of those old bastards was scared. Jesus . . ." I walked over to the screen door and looked toward the hillside. "Maybe we *should* go up there and look around." An expression of terror passed over Jan's face, and I laughed. "Then again, maybe we shouldn't."

We rejoined the party and sat in silence, effectively chastened, listening to the farmers talk. After a while the talk turned, as I knew it would, back to the hog mutilations. A lot of hostile glances were thrown in my direction, but this time I said nothing. I just listened.

"Herman looked fine when I went out to see him," Old Man Crawford said, running a hand through his thinning hair. "I just thought he was asleep. Then I heard, like, a buzzing coming from where he lay. I moved in a little closer, and I saw that his stomach had been sliced clean open." He made a slicing motion with his hand and his voice dropped. "He'd been gutted, all his innards taken out, and the inside of his body was nothing but thousands of flies."

A middle-aged farmer I didn't know, wearing greasestained coveralls and a cowboy hat, nodded his head in understanding. "That's exactly what happened to my Marybeth. Flies all inside her. Even in her mouth. Just acrawling around . . ."

"The bathhouse," my grandpa said, chewing the last bite of his hamburger.

Old Man Crawford nodded wisely. "What else could it be?"

That afternoon it rained—a heavy downpour of warm summer water which fell in endless torrents from the black clouds that had risen suddenly over the hills, and which formed miniature rivers and tributaries on the sloping ground outside the farmhouse. We sat in the kitchen, the three of us, talking and watching the rain.

"Good for the crops," my grandpa said, holding his leg as he limped over to the window. "It's been a helluva dry summer."

I nodded my head in agreement, not saying anything. Jan and I had decided that we would ask him about the bathhouse that afternoon—the real story—and I was trying to figure out how to broach the subject. I watched my grandpa staring out the window, looking small and frail and old, and listened silently to the depressing sound of rainwater gushing through the metal gutter along the edge of the roof. I felt sad, all of a sudden, and I wasn't sure why. Then I realized that something had happened to the kitchen; it was different. It was no longer the warm quaint kitchen of my grandparents but the curiously empty kitchen of an unhappy old man—a stranger. The feeling hit me abruptly, inexplicably, and for some reason I felt like crying. I no longer felt like asking about the bathhouse. I didn't care. But I saw Jan staring at me quizzically from across the table, and I forced myself to speak. "Uh, Grandpa?"

He turned around. "Yeah?"

He was silhouetted against the screen, the rain in back of him, and his face was entirely in shadows. He didn't look like my grandpa. I looked across the table at Jan, and she too looked different. Older. I could see the wrinkles starting.

She motioned for me to go on.

I cleared my throat. "I'd like you to tell me a bit more about the bathhouse."

He walked forward, nodding, and as he came closer his face once again became visible. And once again he was my grandpa. "Yeah," he said. "I've been expecting this. I was wondering when you were going to ask." He sat down in his familiar chair, holding his leg. A sudden gust of wind blew the screen door open then closed. Our faces were lightly splattered with water spray. He looked from Jan to me, and his voice was low, serious. "You feel it, don't you? You know it's here."

I felt unexpectedly cold, and I shivered, instinctively massaging the gooseflesh on my bare arms. Jan, I noticed, was doing the same, hugging herself tightly. Outside, the rain abated somewhat.

"It's like a magnet," my grandpa said. "It draws you to it. You hear about it, or you see it from far off, and you start thinking about it. It takes up more and more of your thoughts. You want to go to it." He looked at Jan. "Am I right?"

She nodded.

His gaze turned to me. "You're going to have to go."

There was a finality about the words and a determination in the way he said them which scared me. "I thought you wanted us to stay away," I said. My voice sounded high, cracked, uncertain.

"Yeah," he said. "I did. But once it gets ahold of you, it never lets go." His voice became softer. "You have to go there."

I wanted to argue, to tell him off, to deny his words, but

I couldn't. I knew, deep down, that he was right. I guess I'd known from the beginning.

He looked out the door. "Go after the rain stops," he said. "It's safe after the rain."

But his eyes were troubled.

We walked across the wet ground, our shoes sometimes slipping in the mud, sometimes getting caught in it. The midsummer dust had been washed from the grasses, from the plants, from the trees, and everything appeared exceptionally, unnaturally green. Overhead, the sky was a dark, solid gray broken by occasional rifts of clear, pure blue.

We walked forward, not looking back though we knew my grandpa stood on the porch of the house, watching. I don't know how Jan felt, but I was surprised to find that I was not scared. Not scared at all. I was not even apprehensive. I felt only a strange sort of disassociation; it was as if this was happening to someone else, and I was only an observer, a disinterested third party.

We passed through the wall of grasses and emerged in the clearing, just as I had in my dream. And the clearing, the bathhouse, and the other small shacks looked exactly as they had in the dream.

I was conscious of the fact that my reactions were replaying themselves along with the scene. I knew exactly what the bathhouse would look like, yet once again I was surprised by its smallness.

Jan grabbed my hand, as if for support. "Let's go in," she said. Her voice sounded strange, echoing, as though it was coming from far away.

But the spell dissolved as soon as we stepped through the doorway. I was again myself, and, for the first time in my life, I felt fear. Real fear.

Sheer and utter terror.

The room was covered with millions of flies. Literally millions.

Perhaps billions.

They covered every available space—walls, floor, and ceiling—giving the entire inside of the room a moving, shifting, black appearance. They rippled across the floor in waves and dripped from the ceiling in grotesque liquid stalactites, all shapes, sizes, and varieties. The noise was incredible—an absurdly loud sort of buzzing or humming which had definite tones and cadences. It sounded almost like a language.

Almost, but not quite.

Before I could say anything, Jan had stepped forward into the room, her right foot sinking several inches into the sea of squirming flies. But the tiny creatures did not climb up her leg. Indeed, they seemed not to notice her at all. It was as if she had stepped into a pool of black, stagnant water. "Come on," she said.

Somehow I followed her, my leg muscles propelling me forward against the protests of my wildly screaming brain. My foot, too, sunk into the flies. They felt soft, rubbery, slippery.

We walked to the middle of the room, moving slowly, then stopped. Here, there was a clearing on the floor, a space, and we could see the vague form of an unfinished clay sculpture lying on the ground. It was maybe six feet long and three feet wide, with no definite shape or features. Then the flies rippled over it in a tide, thousands of tiny fly-legs scraping against the soft clay. The wave passed and now there was more of a shape: the sculpture was definitely that of a man. Somehow, via a greater power or some collective mind of their own, the flies were metamorphosing this clay into a human figure. Each of their actions and movements, each motion of their miniscule feet, was purposefully ordered, planned out. Each step was fraught with symbolism.

Another wave passed.

And it was my grandpa.

Down to the drooping jowls, the backwardly combed wisps of hair, and the slightly askew gimp leg.

He was stretched out on the floor, his hands grasping for something that wasn't there, his eyes rolled upward into his skull. There was a look of intense, searing pain on his face.

I knew what it meant. "No!" I screamed, running out of the bathhouse and across the clearing. I did not look to see if Jan was following me or not. At that moment, I didn't care.

Behind me, the buzzing lowered into a soft whisper. As though the flies were quietly laughing.

I flew through the tall grasses and ran past the barn. The sky now was almost clear, and the day was beginning to heat up. Steam rose from the plants as I ran past them or hopped over them. I was too late, and I knew I was too late, but I kept running anyway, ignoring the flashes of pain ripping through my chest, ignoring the ragged rebellion of my tired lungs.

I bounded up the porch steps to the kitchen and flung open the screen door.

He was lying on the floor next to his chair, dead, his body in the same position as that of the sculpture.

I sat down next to him on the floor, taking his hand in mine. His face was not the same as that of the sculpture. It did not look terrified or in pain. But neither did it look pleased. Death had not been a hideous shock or a welcome relief. He was neither miserable nor content. He was only dead. His face was yellowish, drained of color, and he looked very slight and very small, almost like a child.

I wanted to cry. I wanted to cry, but I could not. I tried looking at his face, his face that I had loved, and thinking of our last conversation together. I tried thinking of the times we'd gone fishing. I tried remembering the presents he'd bought me as a youth. But it was no good. I could not make the tears come no matter how hard I tried, no matter how much I wanted them to flow.

I just sat there staring at his lifeless body.

Jan burst through the door, her face red and sweating, out of breath. She looked at my grandpa's body on the floor and her face went from red to white. A look of fear, of horror, crossed her features. "My G-God . . ." she stammered, her hands starting to twitch. "Oh my God . . ."

I felt calm for some reason, perfectly in control, and I stood up and helped her into a chair. I got her a glass of water, which she drank with shaking hands. "Sit here," I said. "Don't move. I'll be right back."

I started to walk into the living room, then stopped as the scrap of paper caught my eye. I bent down next to my grandpa and picked it up. I thought for a minute, then crumpled up the paper without even glancing at the poem he'd written.

I went to call an ambulance.

Credits

"The Sanctuary" (originally published in *Cemetery Dance,* June 1989)

"The Woods Be Dark" (originally published in *Touch Wood: Narrow Houses,* Vol II, 1994)

"The Phonebook Man" (originally published in *Eldritch Tales* #27, 1992)

"Estoppel" (originally published in *2 AM,* Spring 1988)

"The Washingtonians" (originally published in *Cemetery Dance,* Fall 1992)

"Life With Father" (originally published in *Going Postal,* 1998)

"Bob" (unpublished)

"Bumblebee" (originally published in *Cold Blood,* 1991)

"Lethe Dreams" (originally published in *Night Cry,* Spring 1987)

"Paperwork" (originally published in *The Horror Show,* Winter 1988)

"The Idol" (originally published in *Twisted,* Summer/Fall 1991)

"Skin" (originally published in *The Horror Show,* Winter 1988)

"The Man in the Passenger Seat" (originally published in *Borderlands 3,* 1992)

"Comes the Bad Time" (originally published in *The Horror Show,* Winter 1987)

"Against the Pale Sand" (originally published in *Grue* #10, 1989)

"The Pond" (originally published in *Blue Motel: Narrow Houses,* Vol. 3, 1994)

"Roommates" (originally published in *The Silver Web* #9, 1993)

"Llama" (originally published in *Hottest Blood,* 1993)

"Full Moon on Death Row" (unpublished)

"The Show" (originally published in *The Horror Show,* Fall 1987)

"The Mailman" (originally published in *The Horror Show,* Summer 1988)

"Monteith" (originally published in *Expressions of Dread,* 1993)

"Pillow Talk" (originally published in *Eldritch Tales* #25, 1991)

"Maya's Mother" (unpublished)

"Colony" (unpublished)

"Confessions of a Corporate Man" (originally published in *The Fractal,* Spring/Summer 1996)

"Blood" (originally published in *Cemetery Dance,* Spring 1990)

"And I Am Here, Fighting with Ghosts" (originally published in *Eldritch Tales* #18, 1988)

"The Baby" (originally published in *Spwao Showcase 7: Selected Works,* 1989)

"Coming Home Again" (originally published in *New Blood* #3, 1987)

"The Potato" (originally published in *Borderlands* II, 1991)
· "The Murmurous Haunt of Flies" (originally published in *Murmurous Haunts: The Selected Works of Bentley Little,* 1997)